Other Carole Ann Gibson Mysteries

PARADISE INTERRUPTED

PENNY MICKELBURY

SIMON & SCHUSTER

NEW YORK   LONDON   TORONTO   SYDNEY   SINGAPORE

SIMON & SCHUSTER
ROCKEFELLER CENTER
1230 AVENUE OF THE AMERICAS
NEW YORK, NY 10020

SIMON & SCHUSTER AND COLOPHON ARE REGISTERED TRADEMARKS
OF SIMON & SCHUSTER, INC.

DESIGNED BY KAROLINA HARRIS

MANUFACTURED IN THE UNITED STATES OF AMERICA

1 3 5 7 9 10 8 6 4 2

LIBRARY OF CONGRESS CATALOGING-IN-PUBLICATION DATA
MICKELBURY, PENNY.
PARADISE INTERRUPTED / PENNY MICKELBURY.
P. CM.
1. GIBSON, CAROLE ANN (FICTITIOUS CHARACTER)—FICTION. 2. WOMEN PRIVATE INVESTI-
GATORS—CARIBBEAN AREA—FICTION. 3. AFRO-AMERICAN WOMEN LAWYERS—FICTION.
4. CARIBBEAN AREA—FICTION. 5. DRUG TRAFFIC—FICTION. I. TITLE.
PS3563.I3517 P37 2001
813'.54—DC21   00-058801
ISBN 0-684-85991-2

ACKNOWLEDGMENTS

Isle de Paix is a fictional place. However, the destruction caused by trafficking in illegal narcotics is all too real throughout the island nations of the Caribbean. To the people of the islands who endure, and to the authorities who persevere—keep the faith. If we're all very lucky, what you're living through will be only a temporary interruption of paradise.

Peggy . . .
curtain call.

PARADISE INTERRUPTED

As judges went, Esteban Villa de los Campos was considerably better than the worst of them, and in the same league, if, perhaps, at a lower rung, than the best of what the bench had to offer. What set him apart most strikingly from the other judges was that he was brash, fearless, and willing to intimidate and threaten—witnesses and lawyers alike—when it suited his purposes. Not many lawyers would enumerate those qualities as ones to admire in a judge; but then, Carole Ann Gibson reminded herself, she was as different from most lawyers as Steve Campos was from most judges. And the truth of the matter was that qualities such as intellectualism and scholarship and erudition more often were feigned than achieved anyway. Besides, there wasn't much call for scholarship and erudition in D.C. Superior Court, and DCSC is where Steve Campos reigned.

Carole Ann was only marginally interested in what was going on in the courtroom. She was a criminal defense attorney by profession, but earned her living as a partner in a lucrative international security consulting firm. She practiced law occasionally—to keep her hand in, as her business partner, Jake Graham, liked to phrase it—and because, only occasionally, she missed it. Her presence this day in Steve Campos's courtroom was on behalf of an accountant accused of helping the owner of a chain of high-end jewelry stores, who also happened to be a major importer of cocaine, launder millions of dollars in drug money. Her client, the accountant, hadn't known about the drugs and she was looking forward to the challenge of proving that at trial. Today was a status call that would take all of five minutes. *When* her case got called. She glanced at her watch and wondered whether she'd be on time for her one o'clock lunch meeting.

As usual, D.C. Superior Court was overburdened. Judge Campos plowed through the packed docket as rapidly as humanly—and legally—possible, with his usual blend of temerity and theatrics . . . and a display of his legendary temper: A defense attorney called him "Judge Campus." The judge whipped off his glasses and glared down at the harried lawyer. "If you can't read, mister, and if you can't speak even ghetto Spanish, then at least have enough sense to ask my clerk how to say 'Campos.' It's not nearly as tough as 'Esteban.'" The lawyer wilted like an orchid in the sun and the judge, still glaring, smacked his glasses back on his face. He'd permitted the Anglicization of his name when, as a teen, he'd grown tired of having it butchered—albeit unintentionally—by a population largely unfamiliar with non-Anglo names. The judge, a native of the Mexican barrios of East Los Angeles, had been sent to live with his college-educated, government-employed aunt in D.C. after his first gang-related arrest at the age of fifteen. That was twenty-eight years ago.

Carole Ann knew the judge's background and history because she'd tried several cases before him in the past and had seen him in action and had been both fascinated and impressed: black robe notwithstanding, Steve Campos remained a gang-banger in attitude, if not in practice. The fact that they shared a hometown had bred in Carole Ann an unspoken but proprietary regard for the prickly jurist. He'd threatened, more than once, to charge her with contempt and send her to jail, and she smiled inwardly as she recalled that she'd deserved his ire. She herself was not adverse to the employment of harassment or intimidation in the defense of her clients.

Though she had observed the exchange between Judge Campos and the linguistically deficient lawyer with an amused detachment, she was slightly surprised that there still were lawyers unfamiliar with the Campos way of doing things. He dispatched half a dozen cases with his usual mixture of impatience and sympathy for the often unprepared and overworked civil service barristers, a lack of sympathy for the career criminal, and compassion for the woman or man overwhelmed by the exigencies of life in a city like Washington, all with an overlay of easy, if ironic, humor.

Then came *District of Columbia* v. *Denis St. Almain.* She watched with heightened interest, first as Fritz Barber strode through the gate to the defense table, and then as a manacled Denis St. Almain was led into the courtroom from the almost invisible door behind the judge's bench.

He was a very small man, though nobody with common sense or eyesight would make the mistake of thinking him frail; and as he drew closer, Carole Ann found herself slightly surprised to note that he was probably in his early thirties. Most drug dealers were younger simply because few lived to become thirty-something, and Denis St. Almain was one of the most discussed drug dealers in town. As infamous as his high-priced attorney, and as regal in his bearing.

He finally reached the defense table. There was no word or other sign of acknowledgment between counsel and client. St. Almain stood erect and silent beside Fritz Barber, who towered over him.

"I have several motions, Judge," Barber began as soon as his client was beside him.

"I'm sure you do, Mr. Barber, and I'm just as sure that I don't want to hear any of them because I'm also sure that I've heard them all before. Am I correct?"

"That's not the point, Judge. The point is I have a right to make them."

"And I have a right to dismiss them, which I'm doing if they're the same ones you've been rephrasing and reintroducing for the last month and a half. I'm setting a trial date for Mr. St. Almain of—"

Barber interrupted. "I think you owe it to my client, Judge, to at least hear the reason for my bail reduction motion."

"If you interrupt me again, Mr. Barber, you'll spend the next twenty-four hours in the cell with your client. And there is no reason compelling enough for me to reduce this defendant's bail, given the government's evidence."

"*Quel dommage.* You are making a very grave error." Denis St. Almain's words were spoken loudly enough to be heard throughout the courtroom, though he had not yelled or screamed; and despite the implied threat of the words, there was an eerie lack of passion contained in them. In fact, the tone almost was sorrowful. But the words sparked the crowd. Several voices called out in anger, in English and in French, and a woman wept and moaned and cried out. St. Almain's head whipped around. His eyes, searchlights, roamed the crowd and stopped. "Be quiet, Maman. Do not beg him for mercy. You disgrace yourself and me."

"Sit down and shut up, Mr. St. Almain!" Judge Campos called out in a voice that would have been heard down the hallway had the courtroom door been open, pounding his flat hand on the table instead of wielding the gavel, and making a much more impressive sound. "And everybody related to Mr. St. Almain, sit down and shut up! And I'll say that for you in French in case you didn't understand my English. And do not get up or speak up again, any of you, because if you do, you all will spend the next twenty-four hours in jail. And that goes for you, too, Mr. Barber."

Fritz Barber popped up like toast, his face alive with wild-eyed disbelief turning quickly to anger.

"You'd better sit down, Mr. Barber, and remain seated until I give you leave to rise. This is my courtroom and I'm in charge and in here, we do it my way. Kinda like the army. But then," and he paused dramatically and looked out over the courtroom, eyes traveling from side to side, front to back, and coming to rest on defense attorney Fritz Barber, "I don't imagine anybody in here has any firsthand familiarity with the army."

The bailiff lifted his head and squared his shoulders and the movement captured judicial attention. "Duly noted, Mr. Bailiff," the judge said with a tinge of honest reverence, before returning his attention to the defense table. "I hold you responsible for your client, Mr. Barber, for his behavior, for the behavior of his entourage."

Barber was halfway up before he remembered the judge's order, and he eased back down, the veins in the backs of his hands protruding as he gripped the arms of his chair, and he lowered his head. Next to him, Denis St. Almain defiantly raised his and glared up at the judge, who returned the glare.

"All of your motions are denied, Mr. Barber. Your bond remains at two hundred and fifty thousand dollars, Mr. St. Almain, and your trial—"

"You're dead, motherfucker!"

The threat came from one of the dozen or so spectators seated behind the defense bench, and Denis St. Almain turned his head slightly to seek its source. Carole Ann was surprised by what she saw in his face: dismay and anger. She quickly shifted her glance from him to the bench.

Steve Campos stood up. He was not a large man—five-nine or -ten and wiry—but in that moment, his anger was enormous and he seemed swollen with it. His dark eyes flashed and the muscles in his jaws worked. He pointed at the spectator who had yelled the threat and at that moment, four bailiffs rushed into the courtroom from the door adjacent to the judge's bench.

"You," he thundered, still pointing at the offender, "are going to jail. It is a federal offense to threaten a sitting judge and I will be filing charges against you."

Pandemonium erupted. While two of the bailiffs subdued and handcuffed the spectator who had threatened Campos, the other two grabbed St. Almain and began moving him toward the prisoners' door. The judge's bailiff drew his gun and ran up the stairs to the bench and placed himself before Campos. Half a dozen other bailiffs and several D.C. cops rushed into the room, the bailiffs from the court officials' entrance, the cops from the public entrance. Those present who were not associated with the St. Almain case moved away from the scuffle, together, in a bunch, and clustered behind the defense railing. Carole Ann already was sitting in that front row with her client and she remained seated. And she remained calm, despite the commotion, until Denis St. Almain's final and barely audible words as he exited the courtroom: "You are making a very grave error, sir, and I hope it is a result of ignorance and not arrogance."

The words were spoken in perfect, elegant French; not the patois of the uneducated immigrant that Carole Ann would have expected, and she found herself momentarily unnerved, both by St. Almain and by her thought that whoever—whatever—he was, he was no low-life, low-level drug dealer. She watched Fritz Barber stride down the aisle toward the exit, head elevated, eyes straight ahead, seeing no one, and found herself relieved that Denis St. Almain was his problem and not her own.

Judge Campos remained standing until the courtroom was cleared and order restored. The he straightened his robe, ran his hands through his thick black and silver hair, and sat, his face as calm and collected as if there had been no disturbance; as if he either hadn't heard St. Almain's parting words, or, more likely, Carole Ann realized, hadn't understood them. He wrote furiously for several moments before closing a folder and passing it to his clerk. Then he opened another folder. "Call the next matter, Madam Clerk."

"*District of Columbia* v. *Sirhan Ramsharam,* Docket number 55732001."

Carole Ann stood, looped her purse over her shoulder, picked up her briefcase, and sauntered toward the gate of the railing, Sirhan Ramsharam close behind her. She met Assistant Corporation Counsel Edgar VanBuren at the gate and nodded as he stepped aside to allow her to precede him. She smiled at the bailiff as he opened the gate for her, and thanked him.

"Carole Ann Gibson for Mr. Ramsharam, Judge Campos," she said, dropping her belongings on the table and facing the bench. "Good morning, sir." Denis St. Almain was gone from her thoughts. Nothing but the welfare of her client occupied her mind.

A wide grin spread across Campos's bronze face, exposing a gap between his front teeth that made him appear mischievous and not in the least threatening. "What's happenin', homey?" he queried with glee. "Nice of you to grace us with your presence. Don't know why you've stayed away so long."

She laughed out loud. "It's always a pleasure to see you, Judge Campos."

"I'll bet you say that to all the judges. So, tell me the truth, Miss Gibson. You do miss the practice of criminal law, don't you?"

"I miss the opportunity for such stimulating exchange with a wit such as your own, Your Honor."

Now it was his turn to laugh. Then, a smile still lifting the corners of his mouth, he turned toward the city's lawyer, the corporation counsel who was Carole Ann's opponent in this case, a harried-looking man in his fifties, as overworked as every public servant everywhere and obviously not pleased by the exchange of cordiality bordering on familiarity between the judge and defense counsel. "And good morning to you, Mr. VanBuren. What can I do for you to-day, sir?"

"Edgar VanBuren for the government of the District of Columbia, Judge. 'Morning. Ah, Your Honor . . ." He opened and began paging through a thick sheaf of file folders.

"Don't have all day, Mr. VanBuren," Campos intoned. "How 'bout I help you out? You no doubt want to respond to that bunch of motions offered by Miss Gibson. I'm giving her way on the first three, you win on the next two, and I'm splitting the difference on the last. Mr. Ramsharam can stay out on PR, Miss Gibson, but I do take seriously the possibility that he could choose to return to his native land and therefore will revoke his passport as you requested, Mr. VanBuren. You will remain in lockup, Mr. Ramsharam, until someone brings your passport here to me." He shuffled some papers and wrote on one of them. Then, "Trial is set for six weeks from today, nine A.M. Anybody got anything to say?"

"If Your Honor please—" Carole Ann began, but was swiftly cut off before she could get any further.

"If you're about to argue with me, Miss Gibson, or object, don't. I'm not in the mood. Your client has both the means and the motivation to seek refuge on the other side of the ocean. Let's not make a criminal out of an obviously honest man whose only mistake so far seems to be his willingness to do as he's told."

She stifled both a grin and a groan, lifted her shoulders in a slight shrug, and picked up her purse. "Yes, sir, Judge. Thank you, sir. See you in six weeks."

Jake laughed with her when Carole Ann recounted the morning's events for him, and then he quieted and his eyes narrowed, and she knew he was looking back into his memory to the time when he was considered an expert witness. "I've tangled with Campos once or twice," he said in a musing tone, proving her correct. "He's a good judge. Sounds like he's smoothed out a lot of those rough edges that used to piss people off."

"You consider this morning's performance 'smooth'?"

"Hell, yeah! Six or seven years ago, if anybody had called him a motherfucker, he'd have been down off the bench into the well. You can take the boy outta the barrio, but the barrio will live forever in the boy, black robe or not."

"He looked as if only the exercise of the strongest willpower kept him out of the well this morning."

"Wish we had more judges like him. Damn court system's a mess . . ."

She held up a hand to halt his tirade before he got it fully cranked up. As close as they were as friends and business partners, the legal gulf that separated them never narrowed. Carole Ann Gibson was a criminal defense attorney and Jacob Graham was a homicide detective. No matter that she no longer practiced law daily. No matter that he no longer was a D.C. cop. No matter that they owned and operated a fast-growing security company with a West Coast office and international clients. They had spent too many years of their lives representing opposing sides of the law to easily relinquish their positions or the beliefs that buttressed those positions.

"The court system is in better shape today than it's been in years, Jake. There's been a complete overhaul of the administrative operation and there are half a dozen new judges who are having a real impact." She listed them: two former defense attorneys, two former prosecutors, and two former law school professors.

"A good lawyer doesn't always make a good judge, C.A., you know that, any more than a smart judge is always a good judge. Big damn difference between what's in the textbook and what's alive in the real world. Your problem is you've been spending too much time in courtrooms these days, and not enough time out in the real world. A good undercover job is what you need."

She snorted and, in imitation of him, muttered something that sounded a lot like cussing. "You know where you can stuff undercover, and I'm not due back in a courtroom for six weeks. Not until Mr. Ramsharam's trial."

"You're finished in Montgomery County?"

"Yes, thank the Lord, as of yesterday. I wish we'd never gotten involved in that one."

"Oh, don't start, C.A. We gotta take the bad with the good. That case was a pain in the ass, but it paid well."

She wagged a finger at him. "You've got to get your sights off that bottom line, Jake."

"So you keep telling me," he replied with a snort of his own, and he leaned back in his chair, interlocked his fingers behind his head, making wings of his elbows, and propped his feet on the desk. "But I know better than to listen to you."

She got up from the table and went to stand before the wall of windows similar to the one in her own office. She looked out at the D.C. summer. And when it was hot in Washington, one literally could see it: the heat rising from the concrete shimmered and the haze hung low in the sky. Carole Ann had lived in Washington for almost twenty years, and every summer she threatened to leave, to move to a more hospitable climate; for Washington, D.C., was the South and it behaved like the South during the summer months.

"You've heard of Denis St. Almain, haven't you?"

He groaned. "You feeling sympathy pains for the drug dealer, or jealousy because you're not his lawyer?"

She shook her head emphatically. "I wouldn't trade places with Fritz Barber for all the good beer in Louisiana. I told you, Jake, I don't miss that aspect of my former life at all. I can't help wondering, though, who this guy is."

"What's wrong with you, C.A.?" His irritation caused him to drop his feet to the floor with a loud thud and sit up straight. "What's to wonder? He's a punk and a dealer and general all-around asshole. That's who he is. And that makes him just like all the rest of 'em."

"But that's my point, Jake." She turned away from the window and toward him. "He's not like the rest of them. You should have seen him, should have heard him. That was university French he was speaking."

"Then who do *you* think he is, C.A.? Charles de Gaulle?"

She smiled slightly. "I think he's the Man." She waited for Jake to grasp her meaning, and when she saw that he did, she continued. "That's why his bail is set so high—the government wants to see who makes it, see if there's a trail to follow. It is, of course, illegal to set high bail for that purpose, but I don't think that Denis St. Almain works for or answers to any higher authority. I think he's his own network. Consider that he's never been charged with murder or assault or rape or possession or any of the other drug-related felonies. He hasn't and none of his people have."

"So what? You wanna give him the Mother Teresa medal for service to his people?" Jake snapped at her.

"OK, OK, OK," she said, hands raised in good-natured defeat and acknowledgment that despite the almost two years they'd been partners in the security and investigative firm that bore their names, he'd always be a homicide detective and she'd always be a criminal defense attorney, and they'd never share the same view of crime and the accused. "I just thought it was interesting, that's all. I'm finished and done with it," she said, slapping her palms together in an up-and-down motion, signifying the truth of her words.

"Glad to hear it," her partner intoned dryly. "Now, if you don't mind, could we discuss some of those matters a little more relevant and pertinent to *our* lives? Like our contract with Isle de Paix? Since you're so interested in things of the French persuasion."

"If you're going to hassle me about the employment agreements for the government ministers, save your breath. I plan to get to them this afternoon."

He looked at her wide-eyed and innocent-faced. "I never hassle you, C.A. Wouldn't dream of it. But Philippe Collette would and has. He's already offered the jobs and he wants those agreements. He wants them by the beginning of next week."

"And I'm sure you told him they'd be there, no problem, right, Jake? After all, we can't disappoint the president," she said dryly.

The newly elected president of that newly liberated Caribbean island had hired Gibson, Graham International to help it recover from nearly twenty years of dictatorship, during which time the tourist trade had practically evaporated due to the communist leanings of the dictator; the telephone system had been blown away by a hurricane and not replaced; the hospital had been flattened by the same hurricane, leaving only a clinic to provide health care; and the global marketplace had rendered the island's tiny industry obsolete. Carole Ann and Jake initially could not imagine why President Philippe Collette had called on them; they were security specialists and Isle de Paix didn't have anything to secure. They gradually changed their minds after visiting the island four times in as many months. They came to view Isle de Paix as a blank canvas. The government would be a new creation; the island would be reborn. And GGI would be the midwife.

As exciting a prospect as it was, it was equally daunting. There were no real role models in the Caribbean. The largest, most populated, most well known of the islands—Haiti, Jamaica, Trinidad and Tobago—were experiencing dire social and political upheaval, exacerbated by, or perhaps caused by, drug trafficking spilling out of South America. Philippe and Marie-Ange Collette had spent their exile years in Paris, Isle de Paix having been for more than a century a French possession, and knew better than to return home behaving like transplanted Francophiles. They also knew better than to attempt to create a mini-U.S.A. or to emulate any other Western nation. Whatever Isle de Paix became, it would be unique. Carole Ann and Jake had alternated between riding a wave of excitement at the prospect of being part of such a phenomenon, and being overwhelmed by the peculiarity—and the absurdity—of the situation.

Philippe Collette, privately financed by wealthy French businesspeople with extensive holdings in the islands, had staged a coup d'état and overthrown the dictator, Henri LeRoi, who had himself fled to Paris. Then, he'd held an election in which he was the sole candidate. Now Collette and his justice minister and the island's only lawyer and judge were drafting a constitution. In the meantime, Philippe hired GGI to create a governmental infrastructure. "This is the damndest thing I've ever seen," Jake muttered. "Suppose they throw his ass out after the constitution gets written? We would have done all this work for nothing!" But he continued planning with Philippe: for a new government center to be constructed deep in the island's interior and safe from hurricane winds, for a modern law enforcement operation, for a modern security system. And, at the insistence of Marie-Ange Collette, for a social service delivery system.

The two decades–long dictatorship that had earned Philippe Collette his Parisian hiatus had been benign, if not necessarily benevolent, and the country's people, never wealthy, now were poorer than ever with the drying up of tourism. But the island itself—the big hurricane notwithstanding—had remained relatively intact: what few buildings and roads there were and the farms and forests and beaches existed just as before—shabbier and more eroded and windswept, but not plundered or destroyed. "We are not, after all, Haiti," Marie-Ange Collette announced. "And Henri LeRoi was not Duvalier."

That was another head-scratcher for C.A. and Jake. Whenever either of the Collettes mentioned the former dictator, now himself a resident-in-exile of Paris, it was without the slightest rancor; it was almost as if they felt sorry for him. Henri LeRoi had ridden to power on the backs of the poor and disenfranchised, people like himself, who were not related to the "aristocracy"—the descendants of the original French conquerors and colonizers of the island—to which group the Collettes belonged. "It was a detestable situation," Philippe Collette readily admitted. He also acknowledged that the ruling class never would have relinquished its stranglehold on the island economy without the coup. "The problem, however, lay in the fact that LeRoi and his associates knew nothing of governing or of managing, so Isle de Paix has suffered from those years of neglect."

"Ah, but it could have been so much worse," Marie-Ange had whispered almost to herself. "It could have been Haiti and Henri could have been like the Duvaliers."

As Carole Ann and Jake altered their perception of the island's needs, they came to share Philippe Collette's belief that Isle de Paix should be rushed into the twenty-first century as quickly and as thoroughly as possible, practically making an enemy of his wife, who continued to advocate for construction of a new hospital. Jake originally had agreed with Marie-Ange Collette, while Carole Ann had believed that whatever money was available would be better spent on farm machinery and construction tools and supplies. She was surprised to realize that her position was rooted in the memory of her years in the Peace Corps and the work she and her colleagues had done building the infrastructure of tiny villages in West Africa. Isle de Paix reminded her of that time and place in her life, and she'd made the mistake of saying as much to Philippe Collette.

"That was then and there and this is here and now," he had admonished, and challenged her to explain how he and his government could be viewed in a favorable light if he, as president, couldn't guarantee the privacy of any communication he would have with the heads of other governments. "We have virtually no technology and no security. We barely have telephones!" he had exclaimed in anger. "You make a serious mistake to ask Isle de Paix, or any place like it, to accept your Third World designation, and therefore relegation to last-century status." A serious mistake—not to mention a patronizing one—Carole Ann and Jake realized.

* * *

"*The* man's a paying customer," Jake said, innocence still etched across his face. "Of course we can't disappoint him."

"No matter that *you* make rash promises that *I* have to keep, whether or not I get any sleep."

Before he could respond, there was a rapid knocking at the door and it opened to admit Patty Baker, the chief of the GGI technical unit affectionately known as the Subterraneans, because the computer room was in the basement of the building, and because the two dozen technicians who were the heart and soul of GGI generally conformed to every stereotypical notion of those whose favorite form of social interaction involved a computer. Patty Baker was only a superficial exception to the rule, looking not at all like a geek and very much like Bonnie Raitt. As she breezed into Jake's office, she resembled Bonnie Raitt after raiding Janis Joplin's closet. She wore lavender pedal pushers and matching high-top sneakers and a purple-and-white-striped T-shirt. To say that the colors clashed with her wild, silver-streaked red hair and green eyes was to understate dramatically.

"Hi, y'all," she drawled, West Virginia still heavy in her speech despite more than thirty years in Washington.

Carole Ann and Jake offered warm greetings. They both genuinely liked Patty and harbored enormous respect for her technical abilities. But they eyed her warily, even as they crossed the room to greet her; Patty wasn't one for small talk, and she didn't leave her subterranean lair without reason.

"Take a load off," Jake said, waving his hand at the worktable in front of the windows, where Carole Ann already had seated herself and was watching Patty, strolling toward them as breezily as if on a nature hike.

Carole Ann's lips lifted in a gesture that was more grimace than grin, and she mentally reminded herself that it was bad form to shoot the messenger; for she knew instinctively that Patty Baker, chief of the Gibson, Graham International technical division, had come to say something that she and Jake probably would rather not hear.

"I thought y'all would like to know that AID is makin' some noise about our involvement down in the Caribbean," Patty said without preamble, taking a seat and crossing her arms on the table and leaning forward to look directly at her employers.

Jake's blank look and Carole Ann's puzzled one prompted Patty to explain that, as she was making an assessment of Isle de Paix's needs and comparing them with the island's existing technology, she had placed a routine call to a friend within the Agency for International Development. "I've known Mike Wong for years, since we worked together at DOD. And even though we were on the phone, I could see him freeze up when I mentioned Isle de Paix. He wanted to know how and why we were involved, so I told him." She shrugged, and explained that she'd told him what anybody who really wanted to know could find out, since there was no secrecy involved. "He said we might want to 'reassess' our involvement. I asked him why and he said there were some 'contradictory indications.'"

"What the hell does that mean!" Jake growled, jumping to his feet and almost tipping over his chair with the suddenness of his motion. "I don't need the damn government telling me what to 'reassess'!" He spit the word out and glowered at Patty. Then he turned his gaze to Carole Ann. "Do you know what the hell this means?"

Carole Ann's expression still was puzzled, but worry was beginning to creep in. She shook her head. She couldn't imagine. Since they'd taken on Isle de Paix as a client, she had boned up on her international law, but she'd been a criminal defense attorney for more than fifteen years; she knew intimately the workings of the FBI, the DEA, ATF, the court system, and all the other agencies of government that dealt with crime and criminals. All she knew of the Agency for International Development was that it existed and that it was one source of assistance for Isle de Paix that GGI had contacted. Beyond that, she had no idea what it did and even less of an idea what might constitute a reason for that agency to involve itself in the business dealings of a private corporation. Or what it really meant when such an entity as the Agency for International Development recommended a "reassessment" of something.

"Will your friend Mike talk to me, Patty?" she asked.

"You say where and when," Patty replied, standing and heading for the door, "and he'll be there. I've already made the arrangements."

"Patty—"

"Don't ask me, C.A.," Patty said, opening the office door, " 'cause I don't know. As soon as I heard the tone of his voice, I knew this was a conversation for you and Jake. I do know that you can talk to him like he's a regular guy. Which, by the way, he is." And she was gone, as breezily as she had arrived, the door closing gently but firmly behind her.

Patty Baker had spent thirty years as a federal government secretary, beginning right out of high school. That, at least, is what she was called. In reality, she was one of the first of the government's computer programmers and analysts, and worked for several agencies, including the army and the Department of Defense. Carole Ann had come to believe that Patty had been some kind of "spook," but Patty steadfastly refused to discuss her past life, except to say, not bothering to conceal the pain, that she'd never been called anything other than "secretary," and she'd never earned more than a secretary's pay. At Jake's request, she had happily come out of retirement to establish and manage GGI's computer unit, gratified to be recognized for the first time in her life for her technical skills and abilities. At Patty's request, there were no "secretaries" employed at GGI.

"You're thinking that this Mike is some kind of spook or spy?" Jake asked.

Carole Ann shrugged and exhaled a breath. "I don't know what to think, Jake. This comes out of nowhere." She smacked the tabletop with the palm of her hand. "Dammit! For once, can we have a simple, straightforward case—"

"Stop that!" he snapped, as if she were an unruly and misbehaving child. "Don't you go manufacturing some problem that we don't have yet. You should know better by now than to pay attention to anything anybody working for the federal government says. Damn bureaucrats. Sit around all day with nothing to do but shuffle paper back and forth and invent reasons and ways to make people's lives miserable. All of 'em got their heads up their asses and they think that's what the real world looks like."

She actually was able to coax a real grin onto her face. Jake Graham, she told herself for the millionth time, was one hilarious human being. And a consistent one. In addition to never having had a sympathetic feeling for a criminal in his entire life, he had a similar response to the federal government and its agencies. "If you don't mind," she said, her grin widening, "I'll accept the first part of that advice and shelve the worry. And I'll leave you with your feelings about Big Brother."

He snorted as she headed toward the door, and mumbled something that she knew was cussing. Then he reminded her that it was Patty herself who had come up with the solution to the technology problem confronting Isle de Paix. She replayed that conversation in her mind as she returned to her own office, a brief few steps down the hall from Jake's.

They'd been in her office that day, following their first visit to the island, and were allowing their excitement for the project to spill over unchecked. Patty, too, initially was excited at the prospect of creating, from the ground up, a modern-day information and communication system for their new client. As Carole Ann and Jake continued to talk, however, the absurdity of the situation dawned on Patty: at the time of the coup that had brought Henri LeRoi to power in the early 1980s, Isle de Paix, tiny as it was, didn't even have telephone service throughout the island, and generators had supplied electricity to its most remote locations. And C.A. and Jake were talking about *computers?*

"Now all we need is a few thousand phone lines," Patty had drawled, and immediately regretted her comment when she observed the effects of the remark. Jake and Carole Ann first froze, then collapsed, deflated like balloons, their spirits flat and withered. She was formulating an apology when her face changed and her eyes widened and she expelled a hoot of laughter. "Well, damn!" she exclaimed.

"Well, what!" Jake had exclaimed in return and with undisguised exasperation.

"Satellites are cheaper anyway," she said simply. The silence in the room was deafening.

"'Well, damn' is right," Jake had said with reverence. And by the time one of the Subterraneans had explained it all to Carole Ann, who was far and away the least technically inclined or computer literate of the GGI staffers, Jake was arranging to take everyone to dinner at their favorite Chinatown restaurant.

"Well, damn," Carole Ann muttered to herself as she dropped into her desk chair and recalled that the Isle de Paix official responsible for matters technological had approached AID for help procuring the satellites that would provide the uplinks that would bring the twenty-first century to the tiny paradise. "Well, damn," she muttered again as she checked the calendar on her computer to find a time that she could meet with Mike Wong.

Carole Ann groaned, grumbled, and reached for the phone even as, through the one eye that was open, she noted the time on the bedside clock's digital display and wondered why the alarm hadn't sounded. Then, as she found her ear with the phone, she entertained two simultaneous and conflicting thoughts: she had overslept and would be late for work; and it was Sunday! Nobody who knew her would call her a few minutes after seven o'clock on a Sunday morning. Unless . . .

She sat straight up. "Hello! Who is this?"

"Wake up, C.A. All the way up," Jake ordered in an unusually quiet tone of voice, one devoid of emotion.

"What is it, Jake?" She was fully awake and alert and she swung her feet over the side of the bed and onto the floor.

"Steve Campos was murdered last night—early this morning— outside his beach house on the Eastern Shore. At about the same time Campos was getting his brains blown out, Pierre Chalfont and Eric LeGrande were being turned into mincemeat by a couple of dozen rounds from AK-47s."

"Who are Pierre Chalfont and Eric LeGrande?"

"One hundred percent of the Isle de Paix police force," Jake replied. "Constables, they still call 'em, and the poor, stupid bastards weren't even armed. Didn't think they needed to be. Hasn't been a homicide on Isle de Paix in nine years."

Carole Ann stood up and, characteristically, began to pace, even though she was entertaining not a single thought. Her brain had, like some piece of machinery, momentarily shut down. Phone still squished against her ear, she paced back and forth the length of her bedroom—a room easily large enough to accommodate pacing—until she heard Jake speak again.

"I'm sorry, Jake, I was . . . woolgathering, as my mother would say. What do we know?"

"About Campos, not much more than that, but Denis St. Almain made bail late Friday, just before the court closed for the day."

"Goddammit!" Her exclamation was completely involuntary. Then she was rendered speechless, for she knew that already every law enforcement agency in D.C., Maryland, and Virginia—and there were more than two dozen of them—would be looking for Denis St. Almain; and she understood that every drug dealer in particular, and every criminal in general, would be in jeopardy until Denis St. Almain was apprehended.

"And what about the constables . . . Chalfont and LeGrande . . . Jake, are you certain about it being assault weapons?"

She could almost see his eyes narrow and grow cold. Neither of them wanted to embrace what that portended. "As certain as I can be. Collette was practically hysterical, which, as you can imagine, must have been a sight to behold. But based on witness accounts and the condition of the bodies, I'd say there's not much doubt about it."

"This is insanity," she whispered, more to herself than to Jake.

"Yeah, it is," he responded, "and you get to be the shrink."

"What does that mean?"

"Means that Collette is demanding that we come down there and do something. Immediately. And I can't leave."

"Dammit, Jake! Don't do this to me!"

"I'm not the one doing it to you, C.A. I'll meet you at the office in an hour. And if you swing by the Jefferson and get the fish and berries, I'll stop in at the Chesapeake Bagel place and get the bread and cheese." And he hung up before she could complain, acquiesce, or cuss.

She punched the phone off but continued to stand before the balcony doors, looking out at Washington's Foggy Bottom neighborhood come slowly but certainly to Sunday morning life: already there were several cabin cruisers and speedboats on the placid Potomac, and at least a dozen joggers and bikers on the path, and small clusters of early-rising tourists strolling the monument grounds. The tour buses would begin to roll in another hour, and the museums and monuments would open soon after, and the lines would begin to form. It would be another several hours, however, before the natives began stirring and making appearances into the outside world; and because Washington was essentially a company town, and because government and politics were the company and the media its handmaiden, the news of Steve Campos's murder would be the topic of choice of the natives. And just maybe, somewhere deep within the State Department, a couple of Caribbean desk officers would discuss the murders of the two cops. And the tourists, if they learned of the events and gave any thought to them at all, no doubt would not find either worthy of interrupting their vacations.

Carole Ann called to cancel her day's appointments with a little bit of guilt and major trepidation: she could tell from Mike Wong's voice that he'd heard about the Isle de Paix assassinations, though he carefully refrained from mentioning them, and she allowed him to commit her to lunch tomorrow. As if she had a choice in the matter. And she allowed Cleo, her former assistant at the law firm, to guilt-trip her about canceling brunch twice in one month. All she could do was apologize; she couldn't even reschedule, given that any day now might find her en route to Isle de Paix.

She stood in the shower for a long time, her thoughts and feelings as wild and tangled as the untamed Isle de Paix jungle. She'd come to think of the little island as a paradise; and though she wasn't naive enough to believe that even paradise was perfect these days, she hadn't once entertained the notion that the Stateside brand of ugliness had invaded the place. And she didn't want to entertain it now.

She also didn't want to be forced into a hurry-up trip to the Caribbean to fix a problem she didn't fully understand, no matter how hysterical Philippe Collette was. She allowed herself momentary amusement at the thought of the staid, formal island president's having been hysterical. Then she wondered how possible—how likely—it was that the murder of the cops hadn't been completely unexpected. Philippe Collette wouldn't be the first client to withhold negative or damaging information in order to paint a rosy picture rather than a true one; and the true one was grim enough.

"Shit." She turned off the water and stepped out of the shower. She needed coffee. And food. She remembered that Jake expected her to stop at the Jefferson Hotel for lox and capers—fish and berries to him. "Shit," she muttered again. It was barely seven-thirty in the morning, and the day already was in the crapper. But she knew better than to wonder what else could go wrong.

The central monitoring unit at Gibson, Graham International was staffed twenty-four hours a day, seven days a week, so activity in the steel-encased basement room on a Sunday morning was not unusual. The statically charged atmosphere, however, was unusual in the extreme. Better than half of GGI's employees were retirees or refugees from one of the too-numerous-to-name local law enforcement agencies in and around Washington, and the murder of a sitting judge unnerved them, put them on edge, caused their hands to clench into fists and their jaws to lock. Cops got killed in the line of duty, not judges. Not while standing with his wife in the driveway of his away-from-work retreat looking at the moon hanging over the bay. And how doubly upsetting for the two unarmed island cops to be slaughtered.

For not the first time since partnering with Jake to establish GGI did Carole Ann feel the isolation of being not only the only noncop in the group, but, as a criminal defense attorney, usually being the only one feeling concern for the accused. In this case, for Denis St. Almain, who, she wanted to remind them all, was *not* the one who had yelled the threat to Steve Campos. But she knew that didn't matter;

not to the ex-cops who worked for her, and not to the scores of on-the-job cops scouring the countryside and the tenements of the cities looking for him.

Though the atmosphere in the control center was charged and the technicians and operatives were tense and edgy, there was no inattention to duty. A GGI operative was seated before every monitor and every keyboard, completely attentive to the needs and business of his or her clients. Half a dozen others were on telephone headsets receiving or conveying the various bits and pieces of information that defined their collective existence.

"You ready to eat? I'm hungry."

She turned to find Jake sauntering toward the door and she followed, realizing that she was at least an hour past time for her first cup of coffee. He stopped and held the door for her, and they strolled down the carpeted hallway in silence to the elevator.

"Cops really piss you off sometimes, don't we?" Jake asked as he punched the elevator button.

She cut him a sideways look. "Developing new character traits in your old age?" And when he cast her an equally sideways, questioning look she continued, "Perception, insight, concern for the feelings of others . . ."

He pointedly ignored her and focused instead on one of the Subterraneans who had emerged from her cloister and was walking in their direction, headed, no doubt, for the employee lounge. She raised a hand in a laconic greeting just as the elevator door slid open. They responded in kind and stepped inside for the short but slow ride up to the main floor and their respective offices. They were comfortable in the silence between them; both spent considerable time thinking and working through problems and conflicts and therefore not only didn't require constant verbal input, but generally preferred not having their thoughts interrupted. They were content in their silence until both had plates of food and cups of coffee and were seated on the sofa in Carole Ann's office.

"Cops don't piss me off, Jake," C.A. began in a slow, almost musing tone of voice, "as much as they—you—mystify me. I don't understand how you think, any more than you understand how lawyers think, and that, in and of itself, really is quite all right. In fact, it's better than all right; it's as it should be."

He glanced sideways at her again. "Then, what?" he asked.

"I guess I don't like feeling so outnumbered," she answered with wry matter-of-factness. "Only one of me, so many of you."

"You're not thinking that we oughta hire any more lawyers!" he exclaimed, eyes widened in only half-feigned horror, and she took the opportunity to ignore him as she stood and crossed to the credenza at the center of the room and refilled her coffee cup. Her back was to the office door and she turned quickly around when she heard Jake ask somebody what he or she wanted.

"Sorry to bother you, Mr. Graham, Miss Gibson, but there's somebody here to see you . . . ?" A young operative named Cynthia or Sylvia or Celeste—Carole Ann didn't remember—stood hesitantly in the doorway.

"There ain't nobody here to see me on a Sunday," Jake growled in typical Jake fashion.

"No, sir, Mr. Graham. She's here to see Miss Gibson."

"And there ain't nobody here to see *her* on a Sunday, either," he snapped and shot her an accusatory look.

"Who is she and what does she want?" C.A. asked with mild interest while signaling Jake to behave. "And how on earth would she know to look for me here? I never work on Sunday."

Cynthia or Sylvia or Celeste smiled. "She said you used to work all the time, Sundays included, and she was just guessing that you still did." Then the smile vanished, replaced by a slight frown. "But then she said you didn't really know her."

"What's her name?" C.A. asked.

"Hazel Copeland. She said you might not remember her but she was a juror on a case you tried."

The voice faded as Carole Ann's memory pulled up the file on Hazel Copeland. It was true that the two women had never met, not in a traditional sense; had met only in the formal and rather artificial way in which lawyers introduce themselves to jurors at the beginning of a trial: *Good morning, ladies and gentlemen of the jury. My name is Carole Ann Gibson and I am the attorney for the defendant.* When she introduced herself to the jury to which Hazel Copeland belonged, Tommy Griffin was her client and Hazel was the one juror she'd had to convince to save an innocent man from ruin. Hazel Copeland. Juror number seven.

"Bring her in," Carole Ann said quietly, and waited until she was certain the hallway was empty before she addressed Jake, knowing she'd have to work quickly to assuage his pique. "I told you about her, Jake. She's the juror from Tommy's trial, the one who . . ." She stopped herself. She was about to say, "the one who changed my life," for that, in truth, was the effect that Hazel Copeland had had on her. But she didn't speak the words.

Jake's brown face compressed itself into the face of the homicide detective he'd been for almost twenty-five years, before a bullet in the back ended his career—the bullet he'd taken investigating the murder of Carole Ann's husband. "You haven't seen this woman since Tommy's trial." It was not a question and he knew the answer, but he'd had to voice the words to give his mind something to think, for neither of them could imagine a reason for a visit from Hazel Copeland, though both would be forever grateful to her. She'd saved their lives. All of them. Carole Ann and Tommy and Jake.

Standing in the doorway, she looked almost exactly as she had for the almost six weeks of Tommy Griffin's trial: indomitable. She was a tall, erect, handsome, chocolate-brown woman with, it seemed to Carole Ann, more silver in her hair than she remembered from the trial, but possessing exactly the same unfaltering, clear gaze. C.A. stood and crossed to the door.

"Mrs. Copeland. It's good to see you again."

"Thank you for seeing me, Miss Gibson. And I'm really sorry for interrupting you on a Sunday."

Carole Ann waved away the apology and moved toward the couch, beside which Jake stood, his face a mask of calm implacability. "This is my partner, Jake Graham. This is Hazel Copeland."

"Pleasure to meet you, Miz Copeland," Jake drawled, extending his hand. Hazel Copeland towered over him and it was only the magnitude of his personality that mitigated the difference in their sizes. Jake stepped away from the couch, around the table, and gestured to the woman who now had become his guest to have a seat. "Would you like some coffee, Miz Copeland?"

He brought her the cup on a cloth napkin, and a spoon and sugar and cream. He easily slipped into the role of host, but Carole Ann knew that he always was a cop, with a cop's instincts; and something about Hazel Copeland's unexpected and highly unlikely visit on a Sunday morning raised to attention the hairs on the backs of his arms. He also knew—and Carole Ann knew that he knew—how thrown off center she was by this unprecedented visit, and how much she needed his help until she could restore her equilibrium.

"Are you still at the hotel, Mrs. Copeland?" Carole Ann asked as she seated herself in the rocking chair across the coffee table. Hazel Copeland had worked her way up from maid to head of housekeeping at one of the most exclusive hotels in the nation's capital, putting four children through college along the way. She was a proud, regal woman; not the kind of person to pay unexpected visits to near strangers on Sunday morning, when she normally would have been in church.

"I'll retire in two years. When my youngest finishes college." She spoke calmly and matter-of-factly, but tension strained her voice. Jake, who had been standing adjacent to the couch—hovering, almost—abruptly sat down next to her, and Carole Ann stilled the motion of her chair midrock, and angled slightly forward.

"Why are you here, Mrs. Copeland? Is something wrong? One of your children . . ."

"Oh, Lord, no!" the woman exclaimed, and closed her eyes momentarily, as if the thought were too much to contemplate. "I . . . it's nothing like that. No, it's . . . I've been keeping up with you, Miss Gibson, ever since that trial. Reading about you and what's happened to you. You, too, Mr. Graham. And I believe Officer Griffin works for you?" She nodded to herself, neither expecting nor needing an answer. "I'm glad he was innocent. Too many of the young ones are too guilty of too much. . . .” She faltered and her voice hitched. She reached for her cup and took several sips.

Carole Ann and Jake exchanged a quick glance before returning their gaze to their guest. They sat quietly, both having extensive practice waiting for someone—client or perp—to get ready to talk. They watched Hazel Copeland ready herself.

“One of the women who works for me at the hotel, one of the maids, is named Simone St. Almain. She’s been at the hotel for almost twenty years. She’s the linen supervisor now. . . .” She had raised her eyes to look at Carole Ann. “I see you know who she is,” Hazel said quietly.

“I know who Denis St. Almain is,” Carole Ann replied.

“So does every cop in every burg and borough on the Eastern Seaboard,” Jake snapped, fully back to himself. “What is this Simone to him and why do we care, Miz Copeland?”

“She’s his mother and the police have destroyed her home and have created so much unrest at the hotel that the general manager has insisted that I put her on a leave of absence! And that’s just not right, Miss Gibson! It’s not right, Mr. Graham! Simone is a decent, hardworking woman. Denis is a grown man who hasn’t lived with his mother in more than fifteen years.”

“But she was in court with him on Friday, wasn’t she?” Carole Ann probed.

Hazel didn’t try to conceal her surprise. “Of course,” she answered. “She’s his mother. He’s her son. And he’s accused of these horrible things.”

“Like drug dealing,” Jake offered.

“He’s never done any of those things.”

Jake slid down the couch away from Hazel, and angled himself so that he could face her directly. “How do you know?”

“I’ve known Denis since he was a young boy, a teenager. He’s no more a drug dealer than either of my boys is. And . . .” she raised her hand to halt Jake’s interference “. . . I know because I know good when I see it and I know evil when I see it.” She turned away from Jake and locked eyes with Carole Ann. “You taught me that lesson, Miss Gibson. I was ready to send Officer Griffin to jail and throw away the key. A dirty cop! The worst kind of criminal there is! But you reminded me how necessary it is to always look below the surface. I've been looking at Simone and her son for twenty years. He did not kill that judge. I know that just as I know my own sons didn't kill him."

Carole Ann Gibson and Jacob Graham had spent their entire professional careers standing on different sides of the legal bar; but one thing they shared was the knowledge of the truth when they heard it, and a good witness when they saw one. Whether or not Denis St. Almain was a judge-murdering, drug-dealing lowlife may have been open to discussion. That Hazel Copeland believed him to be innocent was not.

Carole Ann sighed and stood up and began to pace along the wall of floor-to-ceiling windows, into which the sun poured, bringing with it all the glory of a summer morning. "What do you want from us, Mrs. Copeland?"

The woman shrugged and raised her palms in an almost helpless, partially placating gesture. "I'm not sure. Simone has begged for my help and I don't know how to help her. The hotel general manager said he wants to help Simone, but he doesn't know how, either. He just knows that the police have to stop hounding Simone and disturbing the guests. I thought about you. I don't know why. I told Mr. Crawford about you—he's the general manager—and the hotel will pay you."

"To do what, Miz Copeland?" Jake pressed.

"Find him. Find Denis."

Jake jumped to his feet. "Not possible. That would put us directly in the way of a major police action." He joined Carole Ann in front of the windows and paced several steps himself, hands stuffed deeply into the pockets of his khaki slacks. "I'm sorry for your friend, Miz Copeland, but there's no way we can step into the middle of this." He looked at his partner, waiting for her to corroborate his statement.

"If the police can't find Denis, we certainly can't," she replied. "And besides, even if we could look for him—which we can't—*if* we found him, we could only turn him over to the authorities. So why not let them find him?"

Hazel put her cup down with a soft thunk, pursed her lips, and looked from one to the other of them. "The police won't find Denis because they don't know where to look."

Jake was so still he could have been frozen, and Carole Ann felt the dread rise up in her like a sickness. Yet she asked the question anyway: "And you do know where to find him? Simone told you where to find him?"

Hazel dipped her head once. "He's either in Paris, with his father, or at home. They're from a place down in the Caribbean called Isle de Paix."

3

Carole Ann closed her eyes and inhaled slowly and deeply, containing the breath in her lungs for several long seconds before releasing it completely in an audible hiss that collapsed her chest. She repeated the action several times, aware that she had not and would not find relief in the exercise and that she was past the point of expecting any. Closed eyes and rhythmic breathing would not, could not halt Jake's unrelenting tirade any more than they could or would erase the last three days. She persisted because, quite simply, she did not know what else to do. She did not, as a rule, engage in wishful thinking; she not only was much too pragmatic for that, but she rarely regretted that which already had occurred and even less frequently engaged in imaginings of what might have been. Yet here she was wishing, fervently, that the last three days had not happened or, at the very least, that the events of them had happened differently; for then Jake would not be cussing a blue streak and threatening to quit and move to North Carolina and start a catfish farm and breed manx cats.

She maintained the rhythm of her breathing but eased open her eyes to catch a glimpse of him. He was furious. He had been furious since Sunday. The veins stood out in his forehead and in the backs of his hands, which were balled into fists. She closed her eyes again, aware that under different circumstances she'd have been able to find some humor in his fantasies. She massaged her temples and opened her eyes.

"Would you please sit down and stop yelling?"

"No, goddammit, I won't!"

"Then at least find some new cuss words."

"I like these just fine, goddammit! I also just love being up to my neck in a pool of watery shit with the damn government nosing around in my affairs and my partner poised to defend and protect a judge-murdering drug dealer, all of which will likely cost me a million-dollar contract! I wish to hell I *knew* some more cuss words 'cause I'd sure as hell use 'em!"

She closed her eyes again. She had no response and had given up the search for one because deep within, she agreed with him. "What do you want me to do, Jake?"

"No, you don't, C.A. Don't put it on me. What do *I* want you to do? So now *I'm* in charge? What *I* say goes? Since when, goddammit!"

She sighed and opened her eyes again and rose to her feet. "I leave tomorrow morning for Isle de Paix with a plan of action, Jake, a plan we—you and I—devised and agreed upon. But you're cussing and complaining about everything we agreed to do, which I suppose means that we didn't really agree. So. Jake. Tell me what you want to do." She stood still, watching him, waiting for his response, girding herself for another onslaught.

"Doesn't this shit bother you, C.A.? Doesn't the whole thing strike you as . . . as . . ."

"Bizarre. How's 'bizarre,' Jake? Does that get close enough to the feeling?" She managed to produce a sound from somewhere in her throat that could have been what remained of her wry, sarcastic humor.

He nodded. " 'Bizarre' 's good, though it's understating the situation by a mile."

"So I ask you again: What do you want to do? What do you want me to do? What do you want *us* to do?"

Now he sighed and rubbed his eyes and rotated his neck. "We'll do what we can, C.A. We'll do what we've been hired to do and if you come across anything that puts one client in conflict with another, we drop Simone St. Almain. Just like we agreed."

"But you don't like it." She was pacing now, slowly, head down, hands stuffed into the pockets of her black linen slacks.

"No," he said quietly and soberly, "I don't. I wish to hell I'd never heard of Hazel Copeland and Simone and Denis St. Almain or Mike Wong and the Agency for International Development. I'd like to have our nice, neat, lucrative contract with a tiny, backwater island nation that time forgot the sole focus of our entire effort. We could find out who killed the constables, nuke their asses, install the new island police force, and collect our lucrative payment. But we're long past that. We're living in the middle of a . . . of a . . ."

". . . of a Eugène Ionesco play, only this is more absurd. This situation makes his characters and their world seem normal."

He looked at her from beneath raised eyebrows. "If you say so. But when have you had time to go to the theater?"

She laughed, a real, warm, if thin laugh, and it seemed to relax him. His shoulders dropped away from where they had been hugging his ears, and his hands unclenched, and the veins rippling his forehead smoothed out and calmed his visage. He didn't quite manage a smile but he at least no longer was snapping and snarling. And he wasn't cussing, though that could well have been because he really had exhausted his extensive lexicon of idiomatic profanity. After all, he had been at it nonstop since Sunday morning. She winced. The words "Sunday morning" caused almost physical pain. She still couldn't believe what an incredibly bizarre day it had been; what impossibly bizarre fallout it still was producing.

When she returned to her office from escorting Hazel Copeland to the front exit door, Jake had been prowling and snarling and cussing, and while their erstwhile visitor had been the verbal target of his wrath, Carole Ann personally had felt his anger. He had insisted on accompanying her the following morning to speak with Simone St. Almain. And when she'd snapped at him, he'd snapped back: "No way I'm leaving you alone with the mother of a killer. No telling what you're liable to get us into." His tone had been angry and derisive and just slightly condescending. Even though she'd understood that he had no intention of wounding her, his words had hurt. He had apologized. She had accepted his apology. And then Monday came.

Simone St. Almain was a little bird, tropical, tiny, and fluttery and brightly colored and sweet voiced. Carole Ann had been surprised at her appearance; she'd seen the woman once before, briefly, at her son's arraignment three days earlier, and though she hadn't studied her at the time, she had considered that she knew how the woman looked. She found, upon confronting Simone, that she had no recollection of her diminutive stature or of her youthful beauty; for she was a beautiful woman, in a vague and fragile kind of way, as if she could easily break and shatter. Carole Ann looked more closely and saw that, in fact, Simone already had been broken, perhaps more than once, and had been glued and pieced back together. The fragments and shards were being held together by whatever force of life and will was at her disposal. Different women used different adherents, as Carole Ann herself very well knew.

"Madam, if your son murdered a judge, it won't matter whether we find him or the cops find him. He'll have to come back here, and when he does, he'll be in for it. There's just no getting around that." Jake, while he had been quietly polite, had not disguised his feelings about their visit or about Simone St. Almain's son. He had spoken without rancor or hostility and yet Simone St. Almain had flinched as if he'd struck her. Flinched and leaned back into the cushions of the flower-print sofa in her tiny, immaculate living room.

"Denis did not do that thing, sir. He never in his life has damaged another person or thing." Her voice was light and fluttery and French-accented but she had spoken with a grave vigor. "It is a mistake and when you talk to him, he will explain it to you. He can explain how everything happened." Then she'd folded her hands in her lap, pursed her coral-painted lips, and watched them, waiting for their words.

"What do you mean, 'explain how everything happened'?" Carole

Ann had heard some unspoken thing in the woman's words but Jake was not to be diverted from his principal point.

"If you know where your son is, you should tell the police . . ." Jake began but stopped at the reaction his words of advice produced. Simone St. Almain was shaking her head back and forth almost violently, causing her head to wobble on her thin neck as if it might roll off her shoulders and away from her. He had shrugged and looked at Carole Ann: "I'm done with this," his look had telegraphed. "It's all yours."

"Mrs. Copeland told us that Denis is either in Isle de Paix or in France. Is that correct, Simone, and if so, how do you know?" Carole Ann had spoken directly, without tone or inflection, the way she questioned witnesses when she wished to convey nothing of her thoughts or reveal the extent of her knowledge. While the tone was neither conciliatory nor combative, Simone St. Almain had seemed to find some comfort in it and had relaxed. She had exhaled a tiny sigh, unclasped her hands, smoothed out her dress against her thin thighs, and glanced at Jake before replying.

"If he is not here, then he is there. He has not called or visited me, so he is no longer here. There is no other place for him. He is either here, with me, or at home."

"Did you speak with Denis on Friday night?"

Simone shook her head. "I didn't know that Denis was not in jail until the police broke down my door Sunday morning. They took apart this little house looking for him. I told them that Denis doesn't live here. He is a grown man and grown men do not—should not— live with their mothers—"

Carole Ann impatiently interrupted the soliloquy. "Did you speak with Denis on Saturday or Sunday or today, Simone? Either speak with him directly or receive a message from him?"

The woman shook her head back and forth, the thin neck wobbling.

"You said that Denis either was here or 'at home.' Which is 'home'? Paris or Isle de Paix?"

"What difference does it make?" Jake snapped at Carole Ann before turning toward Simone. "Do you know how many mamas think their little boys didn't do it? If you mamas had your way, there wouldn't be any murderers or rapists or drug dealers in jail—"

Simone jumped to her feet, her tiny body trembling with a mixture of rage and fear. "If Denis is evil then so are you, sir, for he is what you are! *Un gendarme!*"

Carole Ann and Jake stood speechless before Simone, though for different reasons. Jake was merely surprised that the diminutive woman had responded so violently. Carole Ann was stunned by her words.

"What do you mean Denis is a police officer?"

Jake jumped as if he'd been hit. "What the hell are you talking about? Who says St. Almain is a cop?"

"That's what Simone just said."

"Bullshit!"

Simone rushed from the room and returned so quickly that Carole Ann and Jake had time only to glare at each other before she bore down on them, brandishing an envelope like a sword and breathing heavily. "I didn't want to show you but you must believe me. You must help Denis!" And she thrust the envelope at Jake. His reluctance to accept the parcel irritated Carole Ann, who snatched it from him, opened it, and withdrew a handful of paper.

"Good Lord," she whispered, passing the papers to Jake.

"Dammit to hell," he exclaimed.

So distressed had he been by the sight of pay vouchers from the Drug Enforcement Administration bearing Denis St. Almain's name that Jake had refused to accompany Carole Ann to lunch with Michael Wong, and she'd been only halfheartedly grateful. She hadn't wanted him unnerving her with his picky scrutiny and constant cussing, but she had wanted backup in case another bomb was to be dropped in her lap. Which is what had happened, though the thing hadn't detonated. Yet.

"Isle de Paix is believed to be a haven for international drug traffickers, Miss Gibson," Mike Wong had said in a gentle and nonaccusatory tone, his dark eyes almost sad behind wire-rimmed glasses, "and the assassination of two unarmed constables with assault weapons would suggest there's at least some justification for that belief."

"We saw no evidence of drug trafficking on our several visits to the island, Mike," Carole Ann said in what she hoped was a reasonable tone instead of a desperate one. "And I assure you that we'd never have accepted Isle de Paix as a client if we thought for a second that what you say has any merit."

"I believe you, Miss Gibson, and I trust Patty Baker and anybody she works for. But AID can't possibly fund any projects on that island until that perception is eliminated."

She had paused for a long moment, assessing both the words he'd spoken and the intent he'd implied. AID would not act on the island's request for assistance: it would neither grant nor deny. At least not yet. "Until that perception is eliminated." And if Gibson, Graham could not successfully eliminate the perception of Isle de Paix as a haven for international drug traffickers? Mike Wong had shrugged his shoulders and grinned wryly and pushed a thick shock of silver hair out of his face and shrugged again. Then the smile had evaporated and he had concentrated on his turkey and provolone sandwich while Carole Ann's appetite had evaporated.

C.A. and Jake had spent most of the night Monday, all of Tuesday, and most of Wednesday reviewing every note and every memory of their several visits to Isle de Paix, searching for some overlooked sign that the Collettes or other island officials knew of or suspected or were themselves involved in drug trafficking.

"We walked miles of that island, C.A., and drove up and down and back and forth across it, and there wasn't any odor of drug dealing!" Jake's adamancy lasted for the time it took him to pace from one end of his office to the other. "Unless we missed it, C.A. Did we? Is that possible? Could we both have missed something so big as international drug dealing?" He sounded almost panicked.

Carole Ann shook her head but a mixture of worry and exasperation creased her face. "No, Jake, I don't think we missed anything that big. But all this makes me want to take a closer look at that jet-set enclave on the north end of the island and at that resident population of scruffy-looking divers and charter boat captains. And to press Collette a little harder about his willingness to give them such a wide berth."

"Umm-hmm," Jake said, coming to an abrupt halt. "You know, I thought his tiptoeing around that group of bluenose tight asses was just typical politician-type behavior—you know, don't mess with the rich folks; don't do anything to ruffle their feathers. But there may be something else in it."

"And I want to take a closer look at the new government ministers. I met them all, but I didn't have a real conversation with anybody but David Messinger. Who I think is a first-class jerk, by the way."

"Yeah, yeah, yeah," Jake replied dismissively, "I know what you think and it doesn't matter. He's the new minister of internal security and, starting in a couple of days, you'll be seeing a lot of him and his new police chief."

"Dammit, Jake, I haven't agreed to just drop everything and run down to Isle de Paix!"

"You don't have a choice, C.A. *We* don't have a choice. I can't go because of that installation out in Fairfax County. And we can't send anybody—one of us has to handle this. That leaves you. And I don't like it either!" He jumped to his feet and rapidly rubbed the palms of his hands together, striding up and down the room. "Hell, we don't know what's going on down there, and I sure as hell don't like the idea of you wandering around in the middle of it, especially with St. Almain on the loose."

"Oh, Jake, sit down and shut up," Carole Ann said without the slightest hint of ire or anger. He sat and they both brooded in silence for a while, thinking the same thoughts but unwilling to voice them. Carole Ann finally spoke, but on a different matter than their thoughts: "Can we really speed things up and achieve the same success? Dammit, everything was so carefully planned out!"

"Yeah, it was. And, yeah, I'm worried that pushing people and plans into place too early might cause some problems."

"Do you have any doubt that Messinger is the best person for internal security minister?"

Jake shook his head. "Not a single one," he replied forcefully and emphatically. "He was waiting for his contract, but when I told him what we were up against, he agreed to report to work a week earlier, and he's bringing his police chief with him. And Collette says the interior and finance ministers are already on the job."

"Jesus, Jake, that's dangerous."

"I know it is," he replied quietly.

"Do they understand how dangerous?"

He shrugged, got up, and began pacing again. "All we can worry about is whether Messinger can get that first group of cops down there and establish control before things get too far out of control."

"Damn, I hate the thought of that!" She smacked the desktop with the flat of her hand, making a loud, cracking sound. "All those years without cops, without the need for cops or an armed presence of any kind. And in a heartbeat, it all changes."

"It was gonna change anyway, C.A. Hell, it already had changed. That's why they hired us. And already had hired a police force, remember? Tourists need to see 'em and Isle de Paix needs tourists to climb out of that financial hole."

"Yeah, but they were going to be for show, Jake."

"The hell they were!" he snapped. "I didn't hire David Messinger to be a show horse. He's a *real* cop, and that new chief is a *real* cop, and so are all the recruits. Just like violence is real, C.A."

"Even in paradise."

He gave her a wry grin and an elaborate shrug. "Paradise interrupted," he said.

"If there are drugs there, Jake . . ."

". . . and Collette knew about it, we'll back up outta there so fast they'll think hurricane season came early. I mean that, C.A. We won't compromise on something like that."

"And what about Denis St. Almain? Suppose there are drugs on the island but he's not involved?"

Jake snorted and resumed his pacing, stopping once to look at the heat rising from the pavement of the parking lot, wavy, hazy, and vaporous. Then he strolled back toward Carole Ann, who was perched on the edge of his desk, watching and waiting.

"I don't have to tell you, C.A., how much I don't give a shit about Denis St. Almain, but that doesn't mean I'm not willing to try to locate him and hear his side of the story. After all, the DEA was paying him to do *something*." He paused and allowed the implication and his disdain for the federal drug-fighting agency to sink in. "What I do care about is Isle de Paix and our contract with them. Dammit, C.A., I don't want Collette and his wife and all those people we met down there to be scumbags. I'm sick to death of scumbags and lowlifes. I really want them to be decent people and I want us to be able to do some good for them."

She was silent for a while, largely out of respect for Jake's emotional display. She'd never before witnessed him display care and concern for someone not related to him. She knew he loathed scumbags and lowlifes and she knew he loved making money, and until this moment she'd believed that his concern for Isle de Paix was motivated purely by profit.

"That's what I want, too, Jake," she finally responded. And began clearing her desk. "But suppose we don't. Or can't."

"Then we do exactly what they hired us to do: oversee the construction of a new governmental center, supervise the installation of a security network and the establishment of law enforcement, and establish make-nice links with the U.S. government. We do those things and we get the hell out and let them do and be what they're gonna do and be."

"Just like that?"

"Just like that," Jake replied, snapping his fingers.

$Bobbing$ gently in the azure waters of the Old San Juan harbor, the sixty-foot luxury cruiser could have been a toy in a pond, so easily did it roll and sway with the waves. But then the Caribbean was a gentle sea, Carole Ann thought, hurricane season notwithstanding, and boats like this one were made to be one with the water. "It's not a boat, it's a yacht," some voice inside her head whispered, and she crossed the metal gangway and boarded the elegant craft.

"Permit me to show you to your quarters, madame." The steward who had appeared silently behind her was as polished and elegant as the yacht he served. He was extremely dark-skinned, his eyes and face so flawlessly clear that it was not possible to guess his age with any accuracy—between twenty and forty, she guessed. He was powerfully built and his white uniform seemed painted on him. He spoke with a clipped British accent that she expected had been born in Barbados and nurtured in London. He removed his hat and tucked it beneath his left arm, awaiting her response. She nodded and he bowed slightly, executed a military turn, and led her toward a stateroom that seemed to be one with the ocean, owing to the expanse of glass that constituted the exterior wall. Carole Ann was wondering whether she wanted to sleep surrounded by so much water when the steward touched a button on a panel of buttons adjacent to the door. A heavy curtain glided soundlessly across the glass, obliterating the view and plunging the room into inky darkness. He touched the button again, opening the curtain, and demonstrated that the next button opened the center glass panel to the sea air. The other buttons operated the lights, the stereo system, the television screen, summoned the maid, and rang the kitchen. He showed her the fully stocked refrigerator, bar, and pantry, and the walk-in closet, where her suitcases rested neatly on padded benches. After ascertaining that he could do no more for her, he saluted, replaced his hat, turned, and left, quietly closing the door.

Carole Ann remained motionless for a long moment, looking out at the sea but not really seeing it. She tossed her purse onto the bed and sank down into a chaise facing the gently rippling blue-green vista before her. She allowed her body to relax fully, caressed by the gentle breeze. She could, she thought, fall instantly and deeply asleep. "And be wide awake at three in the morning," the voice inside her warned, and she almost replied, "So what?" out loud; she could take a nap later if she got sleepy. She was beginning a two-and-a-half-day vacation cruise of the Caribbean. No matter that the original intent of the voyage had been to gain a nautical familiarity with the string of islands between Puerto Rico and Isle de Paix. She needed the time alone. She needed to sort out the disturbing and complex circumstances involving Isle de Paix.

She also needed to clarify in her mind what her response would be if she encountered Denis St. Almain and how far she'd go to assist him. This was a personal conflict. Jake had said—and he had meant—that he didn't give a shit about St. Almain. He was concerned only for Isle de Paix. She, on the other hand, was concerned not so much for Denis personally, but for his legal rights. If they disagreed about a contract, it was their shared beliefs that bound them: They believed in the law. Not necessarily in the way the legal profession practiced it or in the way police agencies enforced it but in what the law could represent if practiced and enforced honestly. No police agency had charged Denis St. Almain with the murder of Steve Campos; he was wanted for questioning only. Jake Graham might hate scumbags and lowlifes, but he hated injustice more, and he had allowed Carole Ann to convince him that Denis St. Almain deserved to be heard, especially if he was or had been an agent of the U.S. Drug Enforcement Administration. But he steadfastly refused to make equals of St. Almain and Isle de Paix on the scale. And she couldn't separate Denis and Hazel Copeland.

She stood and stretched. A change of clothes and a cold drink were called for. She surveyed the contents of the refrigerator and the bar and concluded that what she wanted was rum based, and that she wanted lots of it. She pressed the button that rang the kitchen and ordered a jug of planter's punch, reasoning—correctly—that it would arrive by the time she got changed. She ordered dinner from the waiter who brought the punch and settled down in the lounge before the open door to watch the sunset and to not think. She was, she decided, tired of thinking, tired of wondering and worrying. At least for today.

Carole Ann knew nothing of knots and nautical miles or of how islands came to exist in the vast stretches of ocean or of how people managed to find the islands in order to inhabit them. On the map, some of the islands they passed seemed little more than spots, and cruising past them in the magnificent morning light did little to change that impression.

She breakfasted with the ship's captain, a dapper, light-brown man with wind-weathered and lined skin named Lionel Metier, who spoke French-accented English and who readily and easily answered all her questions with scholarly detail. Though he was Haitian by birth and a veteran of the French navy, he knew Isle de Paix and its history as well as the history of most of the islands in the chain from Haiti south to Trinidad and Tobago. He spoke with sadness of the turmoil that plagued his homeland and a tinge of despair crept in when he spoke of the increasing violence visited upon these pristine, almost primitive cultures due to drug trafficking.

"Ah, *oui*, madame. It is true," he said sadly at Carole Ann's reaction, though he only partially misread her response. At the moment that he mentioned drug trafficking, she was wondering how she could delicately broach the subject with him, and he had opened the door himself. "Six times this vessel has been stopped and boarded by authorities looking for the drug dealers."

"Good Lord!" she exclaimed, genuinely shocked. "Why?"

"We were mistaken for the traffickers."

"Drug dealers travel in such luxury?"

"Oh, *certainement,* madame! The drug dealers have more money than anyone, and therefore can buy more luxury than anyone, though the craft they prefer usually are smaller and faster than this one."

"Do you own this boat, monsieur?" she asked, and was surprised by the suddenness of the grin that opened his face and reminded her of Jake when he smiled: the smile transformed the gravity of his face and made him handsome. In this moment, Lionel Metier was happily handsome. He thanked her for thinking that he, a sailor, could own a million-dollar vessel, then explained that he worked for a French company that owned cruising yachts in the Mediterranean and the Caribbean. He worked nine months of the year, the exception being the hurricane-spawning months of August, September, and October. This yacht—*Le Splendide*—was "his" craft in that he piloted it exclusively and with the same crew, and had done so for a dozen years. The yacht could be rented in its entirety by a group or individual, though usually, as was the case currently, the individual staterooms were rented by couples or individuals for cruises of various durations.

"At the moment, madame, there are three couples and yourself aboard. We will pick up two couples at St. Maarten and a family of six at Antigua. We leave you, unfortunately, at Isle de Paix, and we pick up another couple at Martinique. Then we cruise for two weeks, stopping at Bridgetown in Barbados, Port of Spain, Trinidad, and around the top of Venezuela to the Lesser Antilles. Then we come back to do it all again," he said with a smile.

As interested as she was in the life of the captain of a Caribbean luxury yacht, she needed to return him to the subject of drug trafficking, and once again, he obliged as if privy to her thoughts. "Our passengers are, almost exclusively, wealthy Europeans. They fly to the islands and then spend a week or two cruising the Caribbean. They resent the intrusion of the police. They don't like being mistaken for the criminal element."

"I can imagine," Carole Ann replied dryly, then asked quickly, "Should I be concerned about conducting my business on Isle de Paix?"

He shook his head quickly and smiled brightly. "Oh, *mais non,* madame. Isle de Paix is quite safe. No, I regret to say, Haiti is considered one of the more significant problem areas, along with the Dominican Republic and Jamaica and Trinidad. Some of the smaller islands are sometimes used as hiding places for the drugs or for the boats and, on occasion, for the traffickers themselves, but it is the larger islands that create the problems." And he proceeded to relate, in the kind of detail that marked his historical discourse, the increasing severity of the anti-drug raids in which literally hundreds of drug traffickers were arrested and tons of drugs worth many millions of dollars were confiscated. "But always it is the peons who are arrested. The man who is crazy enough to drive a boat at forty knots across the open sea at night, risking his own life and the lives of all who work on the sea at night. The man who owns the boat, he is safe at home, unseen and unknown. So the ignorant, illiterate peon spends half a lifetime slowly going mad in a rotting prison while the real drug dealer buys a faster boat and hires another peon to risk his life. It is truly a scourge on our society, madame."

Carole Ann thanked Captain Metier, in French, both for his hospitality and for the information he shared with her, and was rewarded with a wide smile, a bow, and a kiss of her hand, along with the pledge to be "eternally" at her service. She returned to her stateroom disquieted by her conversation with the captain and reluctantly opened the file on Caribbean drug trafficking that she had sworn not to read until she arrived in Isle de Paix. She read the first paragraph of the report compiled by one of the GGI researchers and closed the file. The single paragraph told the tale: "Along with the land route through Mexico, the Caribbean sea-lanes are the primary paths for the transport of illegal drugs from their South American production points into the United States." She opened the map provided by the researcher and spread it out on the table. The horseshoe-shaped loop from Miami, down through the islands of the Caribbean, across the top of Venezuela and then to the unbroken "land route" through Panama, Costa Rica, Nicaragua, Honduras, Guatemala, Mexico, and, finally, into the United States could have been designed by an outlaw. Instead, it was the result of a million-year-old seismic upheaval.

She closed the map and folded it and placed it with the report and was prepared to return them both to her briefcase when some thought or idea or urge took over. Suddenly tense and on edge, she began pacing. The stateroom was long enough for pacing but too crammed with furniture to allow for an uninterrupted flow, so she stood by the open window and stared out at the water. They were, she knew, because Captain Metier had told her, cruising the Caribbean side of the islands, close enough to see hints of green trees and white sand beaches. On the other side of the islands was the Atlantic Ocean. Pirate ships once roamed these same waters, she mused, their intentions and activities as lethal and evil as those of modern-day drug traffickers. And armies and navies chased the pirates then just as anti-drug agents and the coast guard chased the drug dealers now.

She returned to the desk and the file and the map. Lionel Metier was certain that Isle de Paix was no haven for international drug traffickers. At least two agencies of the United States government believed otherwise. It was in Carole Ann's best interest that the yacht captain be correct; and why couldn't he be believed? The islands were his business. But Isle de Paix was Carole Ann's business. She sat down at the desk and opened the research file on Caribbean drug trafficking. For not the first time in her almost twenty years of proximity to what social scientists call the criminal element, Carole Ann imagined what a different place the world would be if criminals used their cunning and intelligence to produce good instead of evil; because the skill and determination required to outwit and outrun the DEA and coast guard was formidable.

* * *

Le Splendide glided into the harbor at Ville de Paix, the capital city of Isle de Paix, as if she were glad to be home after a long journey. It was the first time Carole Ann had approached the island by sea, and the view was breathtaking. Marie-Ange Collette had told her and Jake that one of the features that attracted the wealthy, even during the dictatorship of Henri LeRoi, was the island's deep-water harbor on its Caribbean side. Until this moment, Carole Ann hadn't appreciated what that meant. Now she knew: *Le Splendide* was by no means the grandest dame in the harbor. Despite her splendor, she appeared almost tiny and shabby compared with some of the craft moored there. Was there a nautical mandate that all seagoing vessels of a certain size be white? Or was it purely aesthetics? For all of the houseboats, cabin cruisers, and yachts gleamed white in the bright sunlight and reflected their brilliance off the pale green water. And, she knew, it wouldn't be long before the cruise ships returned to Isle de Paix, now that the reign of the communist dictator, peaceful though it might have been, was over.

Cobblestone streets and walks led from the dock into the town, and Carole Ann could see that the new government had been busy since her last visit three months earlier. The government buildings, up a slight rise directly away from the sea, had all been freshly painted white and they glittered like diamonds in a raised setting: Government House in the center, the courthouse to the left, the post office and tourist board to the right. On either side of the street, flanking the governmental structures like soldiers and leading up to them from the docks, and behind them farther up the hill, were shops and stores, restaurants and banks, hotels and guest houses, all freshly painted in a variety of pastels: pale pinks and yellows and greens and corals and blues. The entire impression was of some kind of toy with a wide center and legs extending front and back on both sides.

As they entered the harbor and docked, Carole Ann read the names and registries of the other craft in the harbor, paying particular attention to the larger ones. About half of them were registered in

Isle de Paix, the others from as far away as Newport, Rhode Island, Annapolis, Maryland, and Charleston, South Carolina, and as near as Miami and Nassau. Two, she noted, were from Kingston, Jamaica, and one each from Barbados and Trinidad. Only white-clad crew were visible on the decks of any of the large craft. Could any of them belong to drug traffickers? Would a drug-running craft be parked—anchored—at the front door of the Isle de Paix government for all to see? Her wondering stopped when she looked up to see a car speeding down the hill toward the harbor, bumping up and down on the cobblestones, followed closely but more sedately by a black sedan with a discreet governmental flag on its antenna.

On each of her prior visits to the island, Carole Ann's guide had been Jacqueline LaBelle, a niece of Philippe Collette and a recent graduate of George Washington University's Graduate School of Foreign Service. Jackie drove a raggedy turquoise Volkswagen convertible; drove it at breakneck speed in defiance of her elders, who begged the young woman to behave either like the high-born that she was, or like the diplomat she was to become. Instead, Jackie behaved like a normal twenty-five-year-old, which meant she defied her elders at every opportunity. She and Carole Ann had become fast friends, owing largely to the fact that Carole Ann expressed a preference for being driven by Jackie in the ugly Beetle rather than by a liveried chauffeur in an air-conditioned Peugeot.

By the time *Le Splendide* was tied up at the dock, the steward had her luggage on a cart and followed her up the ramp to Jackie and the VW.

"*Bonjour, Carole Ann! Comment ça va?*" Jackie greeted her with hearty kisses on both cheeks, and a warm American-style hug. "I'm so glad you're back."

"I'm glad to be back, Jackie," Carole Ann said, returning the girl's greeting, "though the reason for my speedy return makes me more than a little sad."

Jackie sobered immediately. "Everyone is in a state of shock and disbelief, Carole Ann. Murder! It's unthinkable! This is not America, after all."

Carole Ann ignored the comment and watched as her luggage was loaded into the sedan, the driver of which assured her that everything would be at her residence when she arrived. Jackie either misread Carole Ann's silence or failed to notice it, for she asked whether Carole Ann wanted to see "where it happened."

"Where what happened?"

"The murders, of course! It's the favorite attraction of the locals, you know? Though I don't think the tourists understand all the fuss. They're all Americans and Europeans and have such a different view of crime." And she clambered into the VW, slammed the door, started the engine, and roared off, bumping up and down on the cobblestones so violently as to make C.A. grit her teeth. She swung onto the Coast Road and turned toward the sea. Carole Ann frowned her confusion but did not speak. The road wound down close to the harbor, then angled in so that it was directly beneath Government Square, and here it reached its end. Down here, behind Government House, where the private yachts and craft of government officials were moored. Jackie eased the VW into a nonexistent space beside a gray Peugeot that Carole Ann believed to belong to Marie-Ange Collette and cut the engine. "This is it."

"This is . . ." Carole Ann's mouth dropped open in surprise, and a shudder crawled up her spine. "They were killed here, Jackie? Isn't that Philippe's boat? Isn't that Marie-Ange's Peugeot?" She jumped out of the car and ran around it to stand in the middle of the road, her back almost against the cliff wall, the sea sparkling before her. On the ground—rutted, ragged asphalt—rusty splotches were evident. Bloodstains. She shuddered again and realized that she was perspiring heavily.

Jackie eyed her strangely. "You didn't know? He didn't tell you?"

"Didn't know what? Didn't tell me *what?*" Carole Ann paced back and forth a couple of steps. "*What*, Jackie?" she demanded.

"Perhaps I shouldn't . . ." Jackie hedged.

"You'd damn well better, and right now," Carole Ann snapped.

The young woman stiffened. "I can't, Carole Ann. It's not my place . . . if he didn't tell you, then surely I cannot."

"Then tell me this, Jackie: Were they here on the boat?"

Jackie gave a slight nod of her head and replied in a quiet voice, "He was. Uncle Philippe. The constables were on board with him. And the . . . the men with the guns tried to board and the constables stopped them."

Carole Ann's mouth went dry. She whirled around and sprinted for the VW, snatching open the door and sliding in. "I need to see him right away. Come on, Jackie! Let's go!"

"He's not here," Jackie said, starting the engine. "He's not even on the island."

"Goddammit! Is he *trying* to get himself killed? Wait! Stop! Is Marie-Ange on the boat?"

Jackie looked puzzled but she stopped the car in the middle of the road. "Why would she be on the boat?"

"Isn't that her car?" Carole Ann asked, pointing toward the Peugeot.

Jackie nodded. "But it's been here since . . . since that night. She's with Philippe on Martinique."

"All right." C.A. sighed. "You'd better get me home, Jackie. I need to call Jake and tell him . . . something."

Jackie put the car into gear and rumbled up the hill. C.A. turned around for a look at Government House, this time seeing not its historical significance or its pristine beauty, but its total inappropriateness as a seat and center of government. Any hurricane blowing up the Caribbean could veer inland and flatten it in a matter of moments. And any bush-league terrorist could park a boat down the hill and blow the entire governmental complex to smithereens and disappear before the dust settled. Not to mention the fact that anybody could walk in the front door and have practically complete access to every government official, including the president. Who, at the moment, wasn't even on the island . . . "Oh, Christ, what a mess," Carole Ann muttered to herself.

"But aren't you accustomed to it, Carole Ann?"

"Sane people don't get accustomed to murder, Jackie."

"But it seemed that way to me, when I lived in Washington. There was so much crime and people just went about their business as if it were normal. Isn't that what you do, too, Carole Ann? Isn't that what you must do?"

Carole Ann stifled a sigh of frustration and wished she could ignore the question, but she knew that it was born of a desire to understand, and therefore deserved a response. She recalled how her own husband was gunned down on the sidewalk in D.C., walking home from a business dinner, and she told the girl about Steve Campos. "I knew him and I respected him and I'll never consider murder normal. And every victim belongs to somebody, and for the sake of those people, I won't ever consider murder normal. But go on? Yes." She executed a perfect Gallic shrug. "That is exactly what we must do."

"That aspect of Washington and the States I don't miss at all. My God! It sounds like Colombia or Mexico, where even the judges aren't safe from the drug dealers."

Jackie had slowed the car, allowing Carole Ann to notice that the town's face-lift had not yet extended beyond the dock and the buildings immediately adjacent to Government Square. Most of the buildings and houses on the adjoining streets just beyond the four spokes extending from the square were still weathered and worn, though the streets themselves were clean and the grass and shrubbery were deep green and neatly pruned. Newly installed street signs and historical markers stood like proud sentries on corners and in the roundabouts.

Carole Ann let pass, again, the commentary on American violence and remarked, instead, on the obvious civic improvements, receiving an oddly dismissive shrug from Jackie, who had retreated into a stiff silence. Unperturbed, Carole Ann focused her attention on her surroundings, quickly reacquainting herself with the layout of the island and realizing that Jackie was not taking her directly to the house that would be her home for the next six weeks, for she had turned south on the Coast Road.

Ville de Paix was almost exactly in the middle of Isle de Paix, on its west coast—the Caribbean side of the island. In addition to being the seat of government and the largest town on the island, Ville de Paix shared with adjacent Ville de Mer six miles of the most spectacular white-sand beach in the Caribbean and a coral reef that attracted divers from all over the world. On most days, the two towns teemed with bare-legged, barefooted, and often bare-chested tourists of both genders, who, in season, filled the shops and bars and cafes and restaurants and hotels and guest houses. Deauville, another town, was on the island's northeast or Atlantic Ocean coast, where the luxury hotels and villas and the equally posh homes of the permanent residents perched on a steep hill overlooking the rough, rocky waters of the Atlantic, the structures as imperious and unapproachable as the sea itself, and where the tourists not only were clothed, but elegantly so.

It was the case throughout the Caribbean islands that the most exclusive resorts were constructed on the hilly Atlantic coast, safe from the marauding hurricanes that spawned in the Caribbean and churned up the sea and quite often destroyed large chunks of the islands on an annual basis. Not every island was damaged every year, and not all the damage was devastating; but damage occurred often enough and significantly enough that on those islands large enough to support dual economies, the richest enclaves—which also tended to be private enclaves inhabited by movie legends and rock stars and corporate magnates—were constructed on the Atlantic side. It also was a fact of island life that permanent residents who were legal descendants of the original colonizers and conquerors and therefore tended to be white also lived on the Atlantic side, while the "other" descendants—who tended not to be white—lived and worked on the Caribbean side. Isle de Paix was no exception.

Then, completely different from Ville de Paix and Ville de Mer and Deauville, there was the town of Petit Haiti—the congested enclave of refugees from the decades of horror that the Caribbean's first independent island nation had endured. Miami was a haven for thousands of Haitians, as were other French-speaking islands of the Caribbean, Isle de Paix included. Petit Haiti was on the far south end of the island, and inland, up a narrow, rutted road that was due to be paved early next year, Carole Ann recalled. And the sooner the better, she thought, remembering the excruciating drive up that road on her previous trip. The road out of town rose slightly, then leveled out as the smattering of weather-beaten, tin-roofed houses gave way to dense, tropical foliage. Here and there a house appeared within the underbrush, and when the road curved, the sea sparkled like a gem of rare quality. Carole Ann remembered that the island was seven or eight miles across at its widest point, and about fifteen miles long, making it one of the larger islands in the region. Yet, there existed but a single paved road into the island's interior, and it was a private road.

One of Carole Ann and Jake's first recommendations to the new president was that the government undertake the immediate construction of a road at least three miles into the island's interior, and that the road be secured and guarded at all times. Eventually, it would lead to the new executive office building and police headquarters and political and diplomatic offices. And the government's central computer system and its support satellites would be located here, safe from hurricane wind damage or the possibility of internal or external sabotage. Given recent events, construction on that road should have begun yesterday. So when Jackie slowed the car almost to a stop at a new-cut road, Carole Ann was both surprised and confused: this was not *her* road, nor was this *her* construction.

"What is this, Jackie?"

"The proposed new primary school," Jackie replied tonelessly, making a U-turn and gunning the engine before Carole Ann could comment. "And just around this next bend," Jackie added in the same flat voice, "the proposed new health clinic." She slowed the car long enough for Carole Ann to view a cleared and leveled lot fronted by an architect's drawing on a post of an L-shaped, white stucco structure with a red-tiled roof.

"When did this happen?" Carole Ann asked, working to keep her tone neutral.

"Two weeks ago," Jackie answered, and gunned the VW's little engine, preparing to take off. Carole Ann stopped her with an upraised hand and Jackie pulled the car off the road and onto the shoulder, cut the engine, and opened her door. A warm, wet sea breeze wafted in, bringing with it the distant cry of a gull and the gentle lapping of the ocean against the cliffs across the road. Carole Ann was oblivious.

Philippe Collette had never mentioned this construction and he hadn't mentioned his proximity to the two murdered constables; and though, under the circumstances, she didn't wonder why, Carole Ann did wonder what he hoped to accomplish by concealing these events.

"Something else Philippe didn't mention," Jackie said, and when Carole Ann didn't respond, she continued, "Aren't you going to ask why?"

"Yes," Carole Ann responded, "I certainly intend to ask why, but I'll ask the president."

"Hah!" Jackie snorted. "He won't tell you. Or at least he won't tell you the truth," she added, the dull, flat tone of voice replaced by something close to a sneer, which surprised Carole Ann. Jackie usually was quite respectful of her uncle, even if she did occasionally tweak his stuffiness, and Carole Ann knew that she genuinely liked him.

"Well, you obviously want to tell me the truth, Jackie, so out with it."

"This is all Marie-Ange. Her idea, her scheme," she said, the bitterness she'd been suppressing rising to the surface.

Carole Ann frowned. She knew very well how committed Marie-Ange Collette had been to the notion that Isle de Paix was in dire need of more modern health care and educational facilities; and she knew that the president's wife blamed Gibson, Graham International—blamed Carole Ann and Jake—when Philippe Collette agreed that the initial projects to be funded would be a road to the interior of the island, a new government center, satellites, and a computer system linking all the agencies of the government. Carole Ann knew that Marie-Ange had been disappointed . . . had been angry. But she also believed that she had accepted the decision to strengthen the government first, to provide some much-needed basic services to the people, like paved roads, and to schedule the big-ticket social service items for later. For the time when the tourist dollars were flowing plentifully and would fund an elementary school and a hospital.

Carole Ann peered through the VW's windscreen at the new road and at the architect's rendering of the proposed new health clinic and felt the anger rise, and with it, the words that would express that anger. But she held them tight in her throat. Jacqueline LaBelle was not the appropriate recipient of her anger. Philippe Collette was who Carole Ann wanted to excoriate, for Philippe Collette, as president of Isle de Paix and the executive who signed the contract with Gibson, Graham International, surely must be the one held responsible for so flagrant a violation of both the letter and the intent of that contract, no matter what his wife wanted. What the hell was Collette doing? Carole Ann looked over at Jackie, the tiny distance between them in the tiny vehicle compressed by the emotion they both were containing. She wanted to ask Jackie why Philippe had changed his mind. She knew that Jackie wanted her to ask. She knew also that to ask would be inappropriate. Philippe Collette was the president of Isle de Paix and their employer. She'd ask him herself what the hell was wrong with him! And if she didn't like the answer, she'd be back at her desk in Washington on Monday morning instead of at a desk down the hall from Philippe Collette in the hundred-year-old white government building overlooking the Caribbean.

5

Carole Ann and Philippe alternated blowing hot and cold with each other, and as both were masters of offensive and defensive maneuvering, their argument didn't progress very far or very quickly. The president grudgingly admitted his error in not informing his hired security specialists of his proximity to the murdered cops, but he was more angry at Jackie for having revealed the information than remorseful toward Carole Ann, which further angered her.

"Please, Philippe, don't chastise Jackie. She was concerned for you, and frightened."

"She had no right to discuss my private affairs!" he thundered.

"You don't have any private affairs!" Carole Ann thundered right back. "You're the president of a nation. Everything you do, everywhere you go, is public."

"This is not America! I'll not have my private affairs put under a microscope, and I'll not live like a prisoner, followed about by armed guards."

"And what message do you wish to leave your grieving constituency?"

He frowned, thrown off balance, his stride broken. "What do you mean?" he practically snarled at her.

"When you're assassinated on your boat or in your office or in your backyard swimming pool, wherever they catch you without your armed guards," she tossed back, matching his snarl.

"This is not America!" he thundered. "Such things do not happen here!"

"Listen to yourself, Philippe! This is Isle de Paix and you were not a hundred yards from your office when two men armed with assault weapons boarded your unguarded boat and murdered two men. Unarmed and poorly trained men who died in service to you."

"You don't know they were after me!"

"I don't care who they were after! They boarded *your* boat, which should never have been possible. That's my point, Philippe. Don't you understand that? It should never have been possible for drug dealers to board the yacht of the president."

He made a strangled sound in his throat that brought Carole Ann up short. "Drug dealers? Drug dealers! Who said . . . what makes you think . . ."

She stopped his angry, frightened sputtering with a raised hand. "Philippe, please, calm down. Perhaps I shouldn't have used that terminology. Habit, I suppose, given that assault weapons are the drug dealers' signature weapon in the States."

"There are no drug dealers on my island." He had spoken quietly but with a controlled fury. "This is not, nor will it ever be, Haiti or Jamaica or Trinidad. There are no drug dealers on Isle de Paix, Miss Gibson. Is that clear?"

"But there are assassins with assault weapons who don't mind using them to slaughter unarmed law officers, and that both concerns and frightens me, Mr. President. And it points up, in much too dramatic fashion, the need for a secure environment for you and your government. Which," she said, adjusting her tone of voice and body language, "brings me to the other matter that you conveniently forgot to mention to us."

"I already explained that," he said hotly and impatiently.

"Yes, you did," she replied coldly. "A gift you neither want nor need. In the meantime, no work is being done on the new government road. I'm sorry, Philippe, but that just is not acceptable."

"It was acceptable to me, Miss Gibson. When the wealthiest resident of the island wishes to make a gift of a school and a health clinic to its citizens, I find it acceptable. To refuse would be most ungracious, and certainly unforgivable."

"Your good manners, Mr. President, are costing you time and ultimately will cost you money, which could result in a cost to GGI. I wish you'd discussed it with us first."

"I'm not required to discuss my decisions with you." The president of Isle de Paix straightened his already ramrod-straight back, seeming to add additional height to his more-than-six-foot stature. And he looked down his nose at Carole Ann Gibson.

"You most certainly are," she snapped at him, "when your decisions affect me. And in the future, Mr. President, you will consult with GGI prior to violating the terms of our agreement or I will terminate the contract. You've already given me grounds and, believe me, I won't hesitate to do so. The only reason I haven't yet is your assurance that we can proceed as agreed with construction of the road to the interior. I am correct that I have that assurance?" Carole Ann asked, fully expecting an answer, and, instead of stretching her five-foot-nine-inch frame in imitation of her adversary, she seated herself in a damask armchair, crossed her long legs, draped her arms over the chair arms, and waited. Since she refused to look up at him, she studied the toe of her right shoe and tried not to imagine Jake's response to her deliberate antagonizing of Philippe Collette and "risking a shitload of money" in the process. For Jake had been adamant in his insistence that she "treat the man like he's some kind of French royalty," and she had been just as adamant in her refusal, and their hour-long telephone call had not produced an inch of movement in either of their positions. But Jake was in Washington and she was in Ville de Paix, seated mere feet away from the president of Isle de Paix.

"Surely you wouldn't address the president of the United States in that tone of voice, Miss Gibson."

"If he insulted me, I certainly would. As surely as I'd terminate his contract, too." She stood up in a quick, fluid motion. "I'll be leaving now, and I'll be leaving the island as soon as I can arrange transportation."

"But you said you'd remain! I don't understand!"

"I said I'd remain with your assurance, Mr. President, that construction would halt immediately on the school and the clinic and begin just as immediately on the road to the interior, and I haven't heard that assurance."

Philippe Collette sighed with exaggerated exasperation and nodded his head at her. "You have my assurance, Miss Gibson. Though it may not be possible to do so with the immediacy you suggest."

"Why not?" she asked.

He shrugged and pursed his lips. "It is not so easy to return a gift. Especially to Hubert de Villages. I must visit him personally to explain and that could require several days."

Carole Ann shook her head. "Not acceptable. Either construction begins on that road first thing tomorrow morning, as scheduled, or we abrogate our contract. Please understand, Mr. President, that many factors hinge upon the timely execution of the GGI contract with Isle de Paix, not the least of which is other GGI business. I'm committed to being here for six weeks to oversee the initial stages of the projects, and not one day longer. Additionally, I've made certain representations to other agencies and organizations that depend upon meeting the various deadlines of the contract. For example, the Agency for International Development and the World Bank will not respond positively to knowing that you decided to build a school and a clinic instead of the governmental center and tourist bureau GGI promised when we solicited their assistance." She paused and allowed the gravity of the implied threat to sink in. She saw that it did, and then allowed time for him to process it all.

She turned away from him and crossed the long room, her feet making no sound on the Persian-carpeted floor, to stand before the French doors that were open to the balcony and the view of the harbor beyond. It was the opposite scene of the one that greeted her just two days previously: the two pastel-colored rows of shops and stores projecting spokelike from the government buildings down to the harbor, where the glittering white yachts and cabin cruisers bobbed gently up and down, the craft, even at this distance, imposing and magnificent and elegant. But it was the tourists, strolling the cobblestone street, wandering in and out of the shops and cafes, relaxed and easy and aimless, that returned Carole Ann to the other end of the room to resolve the dilemma with Philippe Collette.

"You make your points excellently, Miss Gibson," he said with a tight smile, "which, of course, accounts for your presence here. I must honestly admit that I'd be disappointed in you if you behaved otherwise. Very well, then: we begin the road construction tomorrow morning." He gave her the tight smile again, though this time the humor reached his eyes, and he bowed slightly in her direction.

"I'm relieved to hear it, Mr. President. And since you're being so magnanimous, I've another request." His eyes narrowed and his shoulders tightened and he looked at her from beneath raised eyebrows, but he did not speak. "Please stay away from your boat and whatever other public places you habitually frequent until David Messinger arrives. Don't you or Marie-Ange open the door to your home; don't drive yourselves anywhere alone or allow yourselves to be alone in a public place. Keep your office door closed and locked."

"My God, Carole Ann, I'll be a virtual prisoner!" he exclaimed, hurt and anger and a bit of fear, finally, in his voice.

"Yes, sir, Mr. President, but you'll be alive, and right now, that's my raison d'être: keeping you alive."

She walked out of Government House into the square teeming with tourists. The large number of people notwithstanding, the atmosphere was calm and relaxed. It seemed that vacationers did not bring the intensity of their daily lives to the Caribbean with them. The sky was brilliantly blue and the sun reflected and shimmered off the azure sea. She walked across the square and stopped, turned, and let her gaze wander over the arches and curves of the building she'd just left. It was a lovely structure—old and graceful, a prima ballerina in the jazz age. Not that dancers ever, in any age, were anything less than magisterial, C.A. mused; but even the greatest of them, even Markova and Kirkland and Jamison, knew when it was time to stop dancing. And it was time for Government House to serve purely ceremonial functions.

She turned away from the three-storied stucco building with its double-wide marble staircases and floor-to-ceiling louvered windows and began the short walk to her house. She had to stop and close her eyes for a moment. Even though she was wearing sunglasses, staring at the pristine white building in the glaring sun was blinding. Government House shimmered on her corneas, stunningly beautiful and impossible to secure or protect. She opened her eyes and began walking, paying careful attention to the condition of the buildings she passed, remembering from her car trip with Jackie the previous day that renovation on the back side of the square had seemed sketchy . . . and it was. All of the buildings behind Government House were residential. A dozen of those, by her count, were hotels or bed-and-breakfasts or hostels. Most were well kept; two obviously were luxury accommodations; and another two just as obviously were little more than flophouses, with sagging shutters and peeling paint.

The private residences—including the one Carole Ann was calling home—were farther away, at the ends of the spokes, where the sidewalks ended and the road took hard, ninety-degree turns. The right-turn road would lead, eventually, to the Coast Road and to the enclaves and communities of permanent and semipermanent residents who lived and worked near the Caribbean. The left-turn road wound up into the hills and fed the private roads to the villas of the wealthy overlooking the Atlantic.

Carole Ann was perspiring when she reached the last house on the street and opened the gate, and she sighed with relief when she stepped into the walled-in and tree-shaded front garden. So dense was the foliage and so ancient and towering were the trees that very little sunlight or heat penetrated the leafy canopy overhead. The brick walkway was a straight line from the front gate through the garden to a second gate within an arched doorway that required a key to open and which led to the courtyard around which the house was built. She opened it, stepped inside, and received a little push when the heavy-hinged spring on the gate closed it quickly behind her. Not very impressive by Western security standards, she thought, but then, Isle de Paix wasn't Washington; nor was it Haiti or Mexico City or Bogotá or any of the places where officials habitually feared for their lives, and with good reason. Although, she thought as she followed the curved path around the interior garden toward the living quarters, had Henri LeRoi been as security-conscious as Philippe Collette, he might still be in charge here instead of in exile in Paris. Which is why GGI had designed and would implement state-of-the-art security for Philippe Collette. If he'd stop stonewalling and allow it.

The house was lovely, though extremely modest in comparison to the luxurious residences of Philippe and Marie-Ange Collette and the other island aristocracy. Henri LeRoi had not lived like a king. It was a single-story stucco structure of vaguely Moorish influence, built around a center courtyard. There were four bedrooms, three bathrooms, a library, an office, an impressively modern kitchen, a wine cellar, and, directly to the rear of the garden courtyard, a lap pool. The dictator's one indulgence, perhaps? That and walking to work, a habit Carole Ann would share.

She opened a heavy wooden door set within an arched opening— noticing immediately the unarmed security station to the left of the door—and stepped into a dark, cool, and fully furnished living room. The entire house was still furnished; the LeRoi family apparently took nothing with them but personal belongings, books, and artwork, for the library shelves were practically naked and imprints were visible on the walls where obviously pictures had hung. The house and its furnishings had, however, been kept clean and well maintained during its year-long abandonment, and it was that state of readiness, along with its proximity to Government Square, that made it an attractive base of operations for Carole Ann and GGI. That and the fact that in the former dictator's former office, there were three operational telephone lines, even if the computer, fax machine, copier, and other office essentials were absent. Perhaps the escaping Henri LeRoi concluded that his PC had more long-term value than the left-behind china and furniture.

Carole Ann quickly changed from white linen slacks and a silk T-shirt into white cotton drawstring slacks and a white cotton T-shirt, and padded barefoot through the master bedroom, down the hall past two other bedrooms, and into the office. It was modestly sized and functionally furnished: The desk was in the center of the room in front of French doors that opened onto the courtyard. Three morocco leather armchairs were grouped in a semicircle in front of the desk, and a half-dozen identical chairs surrounded a table at one end of the room. A sofa and love seat upholstered in the same emerald fabric flanked a coffee table at the other end. A mahogany worktable was positioned several feet behind the desk and though there was nothing on it, Carole Ann suspected that it once had held the computer and perhaps a fax machine and a couple of telephones, since a clear, hard plastic runner covered the floor space between the desk and the table.

She dropped into the deep leather desk chair, leaned back, propped her feet on the desk, and called Jake. "We're still employed," she said without preamble when he answered his phone, and she grinned at his "We damn well better be" response before launching into the explanation of why they very well could not have been, omitting her deliberate antagonism of the client as a possible reason, and emphasizing Collette's own complicity in what easily could have been his assassination. Jake cussed for a good while, then, when he was spent, Carole Ann told him about the school and the clinic. He didn't react at all for a moment; then, in his inimitable fashion, he termed the island president's inability or unwillingness to tell the island's oldest and richest resident that he didn't want his gift "goddamn silly," and the fact of the gift itself "even goddamn sillier." But he accepted her proffered opinion that elderly rich people tended toward impracticalities that bordered on the eccentric if not the ridiculous. They also expected, she added, to be catered to and obeyed.

He agreed that she should spend the remainder of the day memorizing the particulars of the engineering design for the two-lane road into the interior of the island, and backing up the mental work with a hands-on survey of the terrain. She assured him that she had the topographical, geological, and oceanographic maps of the area and would study them. He also agreed to speed up the arrival of the internal security minister, the police chief, and the first uniformed officers. And he warned her to follow the same self-safety and security measures she had prescribed for Philippe Collette.

"You just remember, C.A.," he said, "that an island is nothing but a little country town surrounded by water. Everybody knows everybody else's business. Everybody on that floating molehill knows who you are and why you're there. Don't forget that there was a revolution down there just a year ago, and not every Henri LeRoi supporter tucked tail and ran to France." Jake called the exiled dictator "Henry Lee-Roy" and even as she giggled at his non-French, she acknowledged the necessity of the warning behind the words. And of that implied by his next words: a GGI technology specialist would arrive that evening, he reminded her, bringing with him a computer, fax machine, copier and shredder, and the security devices to protect them from invasion.

She hung up the phone feeling much calmer and more focused, though she retained a residual sense of unease from Jake's warning. Certainly her presence on the island, and the reason for it, would be known, though by whom she couldn't begin to imagine. Nor could she imagine that her presence would be considered threatening. Unless somebody didn't want the Isle de Paix government secure and stable, didn't want its president secure and safe. Denis St. Almain flashed into her mind. Was he here now? Could he have been here Saturday night? And if he did show up, how could she find him? The island wasn't so large that he could disappear completely, but it was unfamiliar territory and, with the exception of the north coast, she had no idea where to look for him.

"Hellfire and damnation." She stood up and stretched. Maybe instead of working she'd drive around, scouting out a good jogging route. "Bullshit, C.A.," her self muttered, and she resumed her seat at the desk, picked up her briefcase and dumped out its contents, and got to work, poring over schematics and dry, technical assessments and reports, after a brief time not minding that they were technical and dry. It was information, it was knowledge, and she thrived on learning. So she wasn't surprised to realize that the hunger pangs that interrupted her concentration were due to the fact that it was after one o'clock and that she'd consumed nothing but coffee and a croissant more than five hours earlier.

The refrigerator, freezer, pantry, and cabinets of the ultramodern kitchen were stocked to overflowing, but Carole Ann by now was too hungry to take the time to cook. Besides, there were, she knew from previous visits, excellent restaurants on the island, three of them within walking distance. But even as she was remembering the places near the harbor where she and Jake had dined, she was deciding to drive along the Coast Road instead. She'd be sure to find a stretch of beach suitable for jogging, and good food at one of the smaller places that catered to the beach trade and to the locals. After all, she reasoned, she was a local and therefore in need of a hangout, a place in which to be recognized and accepted as a regular. A place in which to find, if not friends, at least people who would be comfortable talking to her and sharing island lore with her, if not island secrets.

"Dream on," she chided herself, knowing the chances of that occurring were remote. She was no more likely to fall privy to secrets here than in any town, large or small, as long as she was an outsider. But there was an up side to outsider status: locals always were curious about newcomers, and often would accidentally reveal information. So, for those curiosity seekers who didn't know who she was and what she was doing on the island, she'd happily share tidbits of information about herself in exchange for tidbits of island information. Like, did any of them know Denis St. Almain? Did any of them know any drug traffickers? Was Isle de Paix a hotbed of illegal drug activity? Or of any kind of illegal activity?

She rounded a bend in the road and found the Caribbean stretched out before her, a gently rippling, pale green silk scarf spread out endlessly against a backdrop of cloudless blue sky. She slowed and eased the car onto the verge and stopped. Certainly a view of the ocean was not a novel occurrence; she was a native of Los Angeles and had spent the formative years of her life observing the behavior of the Pacific Ocean. But this was different. As magnificent and as stirring and as awesome as her hometown ocean was, she'd never been tempted to confuse it with paradise. Here, the temptation was strong. This vista was as beautiful as anything she'd ever seen. Then she recalled the words of the GGI report prepared for her on drug trafficking in the islands: "The Caribbean sea-lanes are the primary paths for the transport of illegal drugs . . . into the United States." And she recalled her conversation with *Le Splendide* captain Lionel Metier.

"Shit," she muttered to the view, and swung the Jeep back onto the road, alternating her gaze: right, toward the beach, for a good place for running; and left, toward the roadside businesses, for a good place to eat. Her mind was busy formulating a cover story to use when introducing herself around town. She need not have expended the energy. She slowed at the sight of the first buildings that signaled her arrival in Ville de Mer: a dive shop and boat rental place that was little more than a shack with side boards that let up and down; a bar of quite modest proportions bearing the impressive name Eiffel Sud; and a string of tiny shops, obviously new and painted pastel colors in an impressive imitation of the Government Square establishments. Then two car horns sounded simultaneously and Carole Ann started, thinking perhaps that she was driving too slowly and holding up the flow of traffic. Then came the hands raised in greeting and the blast of several other car horns—greetings, too, and all directed at her.

"Damn you, Jake Graham, for *always* being right!" She smiled and tapped her car horn twice and stuck her left arm out of the car window in a wave that she hoped acknowledged all the greetings directed at her. Then she spied a long, low-slung, clapboard structure set farther back from the road than the other buildings, in better repair than the dive shop and the Eiffel Sud, though not as spiffy as the pastel-colored boutiques. There were a dozen cars parked haphazardly in front of the building, and a new neon sign above it that glowed AUX FRUITS DE MER in bright yellow, flanked by bright blue fish on either side. Without hesitation, Carole Ann swung into the lot and parked precariously near the edge of the road between an ancient, battered Citroën and a shiny new Peugeot.

She knew when she opened the door to the restaurant that the food would be wonderful. Nina Simone was on the jukebox, the place was packed, and the young waitress who passed before her just as she stepped into the room was carrying a tray of Red Stripe beer, the bottles cold with ice dripping down the sides. It was the kind of place that one would have expected to be dark and smoky but which was anything but, owing to the fact that the back of the place opened onto a patio—the back of the place *was* a patio—and the slatted front shutters were angled open so as to permit plenty of light and ocean breeze. She suddenly was so hungry that she felt faint and her eyes roamed the room—including the back patio—in search of an empty table.

"You're still alive, so that means Monsieur le Présidente est mort. What did he say about the school and the clinic?"

Carole Ann turned and found herself embraced by a laughing Jacqueline LaBelle. "Au contraire," she replied with a grin. "Monsieur le Présidente is alive and well and seeing to it that the earthmoving equipment will be in place on the North Coast Road promptly at seven o'clock in the morning to begin excavation of the new government road. Or whatever it eventually will be called."

"However did you manage that?" Jackie's amusement completely dissipated, to be replaced by shock. "Was he furious with you? Is he furious with me?"

Carole Ann shrugged and resumed her search for an empty table. "I'm too hungry to talk about it, Jackie."

"I've got a table on the patio with a sea view. Care to join me?"

"Lead the way," Carole Ann exclaimed, following the young woman through the crowded room, noticing whom she noticed and acknowledged, who noticed and acknowledged her, and by whom she herself was noticed and acknowledged. By the time they reached the umbrella-covered table and seated themselves, she was ready to concede that indeed, Isle de Paix's fifteen thousand residents *did* all know that she was on the island, but before she could decide how she felt about that, the young waitress she'd noticed earlier arrived.

"Good afternoon, madame," she said in island-accented English, throwing a familiar grin toward Jackie.

Carole Ann acknowledged the greeting with a smile. "I'm so hungry I could eat sand. Would you, as quickly as possible, bring me a Red Stripe and the fastest, easiest appetizer you have? Then I'll look at the menu."

"Red Stripe and a seviche," the waitress said with a nod of her head toward Carole Ann. "Rum and tonic and conch fritters, Jackie?"

"Yes, thanks, Helene," Jackie replied, and they watched the waitress glide off and disappear around the corner. "Surely Uncle Philippe didn't recommend that you come here," Jackie said dryly.

"No," Carole Ann replied. "I stopped in by chance. I was looking for a place to eat on this end of the island and the packed parking lot beckoned. But why would Philippe 'surely not' recommend that I come here?"

"Because," Jackie said with a wide grin, "Henri LeRoi's sisters are the owners."

Carole Ann didn't respond for a moment, due to the fact that she was cussing Jake in her mind: Right again, dammit! Not only hadn't all of Henri LeRoi's supporters tucked tail and run for France, all of his immediate family obviously hadn't felt the need or the desire to depart. "It really was a bloodless coup, wasn't it?" Carole Ann asked, genuinely curious at the way things seemed to work on the island, and contemplating the nature of the virulent hatred that existed among and between political opponents in Washington. "And obviously the LeRoi family isn't so disenchanted with the new regime that they didn't feel uncomfortable remaining here."

Jackie laughed. "It has nothing to do with politics or democracies or dictatorships. At least, not the way you mean. The LeRois and the Collettes have been rivals for almost a hundred years. Kind of like the Capulets and the Montagues . . . and like them, nobody remembers the reason for the enmity. Just that it exists and always has and probably always will."

"So," Carole Ann posed, slowly, musingly, "does that mean the LeRoi sisters would find me persona non grata in their restaurant?"

"Are you kidding? They're delighted!" Jackie chortled. "When they found out you were here instead of at Le Petit Paris or Le Champignon they danced in the kitchen—"

"Wait, wait, wait!" Carole Ann raised her hand to stop Jackie's recital. "I've been here all of three and a half minutes and I've been on the island less than seventy-two hours. How could they possibly know—"

"Ma chérie, people on the island know everything about everything," Jackie said with the same shrug and pursing of the lips that Philippe had employed earlier. "It is the way of things. I hated it growing up, and was so relieved to get to Paris and to Washington, where I could own my thoughts and feelings. Then I found that I missed knowing that I was known." She shrugged again and Carole Ann was spared having to respond by the arrival of Helene with their drinks and appetizers.

"So people know who I am and why I'm here?" she asked after several moments spent savoring the excellent marinated fish and the marvelous beer native to Jamaica.

"And where you live and the fact that, even though you live in Henri LeRoi's house, you refused to drive his car. And by nightfall they will know that you demanded and won the cessation of construction of His Excellency's—Hubert de Villages'—school and clinic."

Carole Ann sat back in her chair as a wave of discomfort washed over her. All of a sudden she felt the eyes of the room on her, knew that she'd been observed constantly since her arrival; knew that Jackie must have been alerted to her arrival since the front door was not visible from the table.

"You're part of the new government, Jackie. Part of the family of the new regime. Yet you seem scornful of it and of your uncle. Am I to assume that you take lightly your role as a liaison between the government of Isle de Paix and the other nations of the Caribbean?" Carole Ann made no attempt to conceal a growing wariness that was bordering on anger, nor did Jackie LaBelle conceal her reaction to it.

Jackie sat up straight, her smile tightened on her lips. "Au contraire, madame. I am both grateful for and humbled by the chance to serve my government in so important a capacity and at so young an age. But I am under no illusion about the nature of my employment. Philippe Collette did not wrest control of the government from Henri LeRoi. Henri LeRoi left because he realized that the island's economy was crashing and that only an infusion of external capital—read United States capital—could save it. And he further realized that as long as he ruled, the U.S. would refuse aid. So, he left, and perhaps he needed to, in order to truly restore some form of democracy to this island. And that may finally be possible because, in truth, Philippe is not quite the snobbish bastard the other island 'royalty' are. Ergo, LeRoi made a bargain with the lesser devil. But in six years, when the next elections are held, the reelection of Philippe Collette is by no means guaranteed."

"Are you suggesting that Henri LeRoi will attempt to return?"

"I'm suggesting nothing," Jackie replied calmly.

Carole Ann looked around, taking in the charm of the restaurant, the obvious comfort of the patrons, thinking that she certainly had a lot to learn about how things worked on an island, and wondering whether any of it was any of her business. After all, nothing in the GGI–Isle de Paix contract required that she understand the subtleties and internal rhythms of island life. Enjoying its beauty would be sufficient, she thought, gazing at the Caribbean to her right and the white sand of what apparently was a beach to her left. With the potential to be a jogging route? she wondered. The sight of a man walking across the sand interrupted her thoughts abruptly. Jackie looked up in surprise and followed Carole Ann's gaze.

"There are houses behind the trees and it's a shorter walk through there to the beach than along the road," Jackie offered, mistaking Carole Ann's reaction for surprise at the emergence of the man from the trees.

But that's not what surprised Carole Ann; she knew that people lived within the forest groves, and had come to understand that on the island, walking was an accepted if not preferred means of travel.

What surprised her was the fact that the man was Denis St. Almain, sans beard and dreadlocks. He was wearing a colorful print shirt and khaki slacks and sandals instead of an orange prison jumpsuit and slip-on tennis shoes—his wardrobe when last she saw him—but it definitely was Denis St. Almain and he was walking across the sand toward her.

"*There's* nothing I can do, Jake, except hope to stumble upon him by accident again, and in a setting where I could just walk over and speak to him. Jackie didn't know him and I certainly couldn't approach him or seem to take any particular notice of him. And it's not like I can look up 'St. Almain' in the phone book and start calling people, hoping that one of 'em is where he's staying while he's on the run." Carole Ann was talking to Jake on her newly secured telephone line, sipping coffee between yawns and trying to finish dressing, unable to halt the rising crest of frustration she was feeling.

A GGI technician named Harold Collins had arrived the previous evening by boat bearing gifts: a computer, monitor, printer, scanner, shredder, and a telephone with a built-in scrambling device and, as a backup, a mechanism that literally would howl if it detected evidence of an attempt to access the telephone line. Harold attached a "howler" to all three phone lines, virtually guaranteeing, he said, not that the phone lines would never be tapped, just that she'd know it if they were. The two of them were up most of the night. First, Harold set up the computer and the other equipment. Then he rearranged the furniture, placing the two desks closest to the interior wall next to one of the bedrooms, and the conference table on the other interior wall, the one adjacent to the hallway that led to the front garden. The sofas and coffee table he placed in front of the French doors with the admonition that she never discuss anything she didn't want overheard while seated there. Then he positioned debuggers at strategic locations throughout the room, and in her bedroom.

"This is giving me the creeps," she said to Jake while Harold slept in one of the guest bedrooms. "Who do you think is going to be listening to my nocturnal activities? That is, if I had any."

Jake snorted and muttered something she didn't understand and which she had a feeling she was better off not knowing. Then he reminded her of the conversation with Jacqueline LaBelle that she'd just related to him, putting his own interpretive spin on it: "The president's own family won't take long odds on him, the ex-dictator's family's in a position to poison half the island, and somebody down there isn't shy about using assault weapons, and you're wondering why you need security? C.A., listen to everything Harold tells you, then write it down, then memorize it, then do it, goddammit! Otherwise, I'll come down there myself. By the way, you've got your gun with you, don't you?"

She hung up on him. It was seven-fifteen and she was due at the construction site at eight. Fortunately there was no rush-hour traffic on the island, which meant she could take the time to have another cup of coffee and a boiled egg and a roll. What she wanted was another four hours' sleep! Despite the growing mound of corroborating evidence, she still was unwilling to embrace with any warmth the notion that there never could be too much security, especially as its installation kept her awake half the night. Perhaps heads of state and creators of secret recipes and discoverers of cures for diseases needed scramblers and howlers and shredders, but why did she? All she did was sell the stuff for a living—along with the concept that there never could be too much security.

She yawned as she acknowledged the absurdity of it all, and made a final check of her purse and briefcase. She looked balefully at the tiny cellular telephone that, at Jake's insistence, she'd become dependent upon and which now, according to Harold Collins, was useless because, even if she could get a signal, practically everyone in the Caribbean would be privy to her conversation. She took it from the briefcase and tossed it into the desk drawer. The .32 revolver in its case she dropped into the bottom of her purse and covered with her wallet, makeup kit, a small bottle of sunblock, and a baseball cap.

She straddled one of the stools at the butcher block island in the middle of the kitchen and hurriedly ate her breakfast. She left a note for Harold Collins telling him to help himself to anything he found to eat or drink and assuring him that she'd return in time to take him to the airport to make his noon flight. She tossed a mango into her purse, and, when she opened and closed the kitchen door on her way out, she was cognizant of the fact that it would be the last time she did so without arming or disarming the security pad. Activating it would be Harold's final act before leaving the island. "I do it at home, I can do it here," she told herself.

The Jeep she was driving—the one she chose because it looked like half the vehicles on the island and therefore, she reasoned, would provide a measure of anonymity—received three horn blasts and five waves before she turned off Government Street onto North Coast Road. She had refused to drive Henri LeRoi's red Peugeot to avoid just this kind of notoriety. He'd been a populist dictator who had prided himself on his proximity to the people; a man who had walked the almost-mile to work and who had driven himself around the island. Living in the man's house was one thing; driving his car quite another. Carole Ann hadn't wanted the recognition, the notoriety, the possible resentment. It hadn't mattered. She returned the horn blasts and waves and then, suddenly, wondered whether she should. Were they cordial greetings, as she assumed, or, in a less friendly vein, a statement that her presence was noted?

A short, shrill siren blast preempted further mental wanderings, and she looked in her rearview mirror to see the black Lincoln Continental limousine belonging to Philippe Collette hard on her bumper. She controlled a flash of anger and pulled over to allow the uniformed driver to pass her. As the powerful car glided by, the president raised a hand in what seemed to her definitely not a cordial greeting. Well, she thought to herself, at least he's got some protection, though the driver didn't look as if he could shoot fish in a barrel.

Both uncharitable suspicions were proved correct several minutes later when she joined them on the side of the road beside the earth-mover and the dozen or so workers who would do manually what the heavy equipment left in its wake. The chauffeur was studying his manicure and there was a definite coolness in Philippe Collette's demeanor.

"Good morning, Mr. President."

"Miss Gibson," he said with a slight nod, his eyes behind a pair of dark glasses staring straight ahead at the large yellow machine. Though he wore the guayabera and lightweight trousers not only commonplace but necessary in the heat of the islands, his bearing suggested that he was encased in the dark suit, starched shirt, vest, and tie of his business executive days.

"I assume we're waiting for the foreman?" It wasn't really a question but she posed it as such, as much to force conversation on him as to ascertain immediately whether there would, after all, be a delay; for she knew enough about construction sites to know that if the foreman were on the job, the workers wouldn't be standing around idle.

"There is a new construction manager and, yes, we're awaiting his arrival. On the ferry from Martinique."

Carole Ann allowed the remark to hang there between them, as it had been intended to do, for a few seconds before she spoke. "I suppose that means that Monsieur de Villages didn't receive with a positive attitude the news that you don't want his school and clinic, and as a manifestation of his displeasure, he has deprived you of two earthmovers and one construction foreman."

Philippe Collette snatched the sunglasses from his face and looked down his nose at her. Again. "Might I inquire as to the source of your information, Miss Gibson?"

She shrugged, the gesture not entirely successful in controlling the irritation she felt. "I'm a lawyer, Mr. President, and I've spent a career observing and calculating human behavior. And one of the most predictable of human behaviors is the power play, which very often is a result of pique. Mothers call such behavior temper tantrums and, as I recall, swat the offender on the fanny if it gets too out of control."

His lips lifted in a slow smile and he returned the dark glasses to his face. "I should have sent you to talk to His Excellency. I imagine you'd have enjoyed yourself considerably more than I did."

"Well, sir, that would have depended on whether I could have swatted him on the behind, or whether I had to kiss it."

The island president laughed, relaxed his shoulders, and nodded in the direction of a pickup truck approaching at an almost break-neck speed. "Our construction manager. I imagine you'll enjoy him as well."

The truck, relatively new and not-too-recently cleaned, skidded to a halt on the gravelly shoulder, spraying dust and rocks on those unfortunate enough to be too close to its arrival. In what seemed to be a single motion, the driver threw the gearshift into park, cut the engine, opened the door, and propelled himself outward, slamming the door. He was thin and wiry and his skin so leathery that there could be no doubt that he all but lived out of doors. His hair, long enough to appear in need of cutting, was bleached almost white. Dressed in jeans, a T-shirt, and scuffed work boots, he looked like any construction worker anywhere. He took a quick look around and aimed himself toward Carole Ann and Philippe Collette.

"Monsieur," he said with a crisp salute, ignoring Carole Ann. "*Je suis Paul Francois.*"

"Monsieur," Philippe said with a curt nod. "Thank you for responding so quickly. Permit me to introduce Madame Carole Ann Gibson, from Washington, D.C. You will be working with her on this project—"

"I don't work with women."

"Then you and your truck had better take the first boat back to Martinique, Monsieur Francois," Carole Ann snapped at him, turning away and heading toward her Jeep.

"Miss Gibson! Carole Ann!" Philippe Collette struggled to control the panic and anger in his voice.

"Sir?" She stopped and turned back toward him and found herself drained of her own anger at the look on his face and the slump of his shoulders. "Mr. President," she said almost gently, "I really don't have time to waste on pettiness. However, because I am committed to this project, I personally will hire and have on site by the end of the week a professional foreman. Of course, that puts us a full week behind schedule, but no doubt we can make up some of the time by working a Saturday here and there. In the meantime, so we don't lose this day and the crew, I'll get them started."

"Like hell you will! This is my job and I intend to do it, woman or no woman."

"If you do this job, Monsieur Francois, it *will* be woman. Is that clear?"

He squinted at her, his pale blue eyes reflecting both annoyance and acceptance, along with a hint of amusement. A tangle of crow's-feet emanated from the corners of his eyes and, because he was frowning and squinting in the bright sunlight, his forehead was an accordion of wrinkles and ridges. "Do you really think you can run this job?"

"What do you care? You won't be around to find out," she replied dryly.

"Then I guess I'd better save you from yourself," he answered with a snort, turning toward the forgotten crowd of construction workers, who had been observing the scene with obvious interest. Suddenly he whipped back around to face her. "Do you want to wait until the men can put up a shack, or do you want to have our site meeting now?" He shot the words at her.

"What works best for you, Monsieur Francois?" she fired back almost before he'd finished speaking, her rapid response catching him by surprise.

"Well, ah, if it's all the same to you, tomorrow morning would be better. After I get the shack built and the blueprints hung."

"Tomorrow morning it is, then. Eight-thirty?"

He threw her a salute and hustled over to the cluster of workers waiting for orders so they could begin earning what by island standards was a good living, and Carole Ann got busy earning hers. She reconfirmed her one o'clock meeting with Philippe, ignoring his be-mused look. Since she'd originally planned to be on site for the better part of the morning, she wasn't dressed to do anything else—like Paul Francois, she wore jeans, a T-shirt, and work boots—so she de-cided to head home. She reasoned she could spend a couple of extra hours being briefed by Harold Collins on the intricacies of the secu-rity devices he'd installed, and change for her afternoon meetings at Government House. But first:

She leaned against the Jeep, baseball cap pulled down low to shade her eyes from the brilliant sun, peeled the mango and ate it, tossing the leathery skin and, ultimately, the pit into the tangled, tropical foliage that grew right up to the roadway, then wiped her sticky hands on her jeans. Then, instead of climbing into her truck, she walked a few yards up the road, noting that it was relatively level and free of potholes. A great place to run, she thought, noting the ab-sence of traffic. She walked back toward the construction site and her truck, scrutinizing the dense growth, and she silently cursed Hubert de Villages, whoever he was, for being such a small-minded, petty bastard. They needed the two additional earthmovers that he some-how controlled. She hoped that he'd recover from his temper tantrum within a day or two; otherwise, she'd have to figure out how to get construction equipment to the island. Which, she told herself with an inward smile, would be a hell of a lot easier than finding and import-ing a construction foreman.

Jacqueline LaBelle agreed, expressing surprise that Paul Francois had backed down so easily. "I can only think that he envi-sioned you bringing in someone from the States, because surely he'd know that you wouldn't find such expertise in the vicinity." Carole Ann's final meeting of the day was with the young diplomat. She had been intrigued by Jackie's assessment of relations among the various island factions and she wanted to learn more. She also wanted to delve into the psyche of the president's wife.

Her understanding of the shift of power from Henri LeRoi to

Philippe Collette was related to the version offered by Jackie on the previous day the way kiwifruit were related to watermelons: both were green-covered fruit with black seeds but you wouldn't mistake one for the other. The version given to Carole Ann and Jake by Philippe Collette and, subsequently, by an official on the Caribbean desk at the U.S. State Department was that while LeRoi had not been a despotic ruler like the Duvaliers of Haiti or the Marcoses of the Philippines or Noriega of Panama, he had been ineffective and the people had tired of him, especially as the tourist trade evaporated, sucking island income into the vapor with it. According to that version, Collette, with the combined support of the wealthy island families and the island's commercial establishment, and with French financial support, had hired an army of mercenaries and, without the firing of a single shot, seized control of the government. Henri LeRoi was said to have departed quietly with his family. But according to Jackie's version, LeRoi all but invited Collette to return home and take over.

"Henri was liked. Philippe is respected. He is, you know, eminently qualified to be president. He's quite well educated, and for years he was a director of a French manufacturing company, in Europe and in America. But as you know, he's a bit formal and stuffy. He'd never dream of walking to work, even if he lived in town, in a regular house. Which, of course, he would never do." She hesitated, a tiny frown knitting her brows. "At least, Marie-Ange would not. I don't think Philippe really cares . . ." Her words trailed off uncertainly.

"Is she really so shallow, Jackie?" Carole Ann probed, relieved that Jackie herself had introduced Marie-Ange as a topic of conversation. "That's not the impression I had of her."

Jackie's frown deepened, and along with it, the uncertainty in her voice. "She's not really shallow. It's more that she's . . . um . . . Marie-Ange enjoys wealth and the trappings of wealth and power. But, I think, she appreciates the wealth more. She was really divided about their return here."

"Again, I was under the impression that Marie-Ange was completely supportive of Philippe."

"Of course she supports him. It's just that . . . well . . . being president of Isle de Paix isn't exactly a well-paying job. In addition, there
are so many responsibilities that Philippe has that don't involve
Marie-Ange, so much loss of a private life. She feels a bit . . . um . . .
on the outside looking in. Is that how you say it?"

Carole Ann nodded absently, her thoughts at full speed. "Everybody on this island seems to know about every event almost as soon
as it occurs, the fracas at the construction site this morning, for instance. How could Marie-Ange feel left out?"

Jackie lowered her voice conspiratorially. "That's a perfect example. Marie-Ange was really angry at Philippe because he hadn't told
her there was any difficulty with the new clinic and school. She didn't
learn until this morning of Philippe's visit to His Excellency last
night; he didn't tell her for exactly the reason that he knew how she'd
respond. So, while he was with you on the North Coast Road this
morning, someone from the de Villages camp called Marie-Ange to
complain. I don't know which was more humiliating for her: being
chastised by the aristocracy or being kept in the dark by her husband. Anyway, she was waiting for him in his office when he returned
from the site, and she was furious."

"The perils of living with the president, huh?" Carole Ann said
with a smile, remembering that, due to a dearth of living space for
single young professionals on the island, Jackie lived in a suite of
rooms in the Collette mansion.

"Marie-Ange is a complicated woman, Carole Ann, and I don't
want you to think she's shallow. Yes, she revels in her status as a
high-born, and all the things that come with that. At the same time,
though, she really and truly does concern herself with the well-being
of the people. This island desperately needs a new school and clinic,
without a doubt, and Marie-Ange sees herself as the only person willing to fight for them."

"But does she," Carole Ann asked carefully, "recognize the need to ensure the stability of the government? To protect the president and the ministers as individuals, as well as the knowledge and information they possess and generate?"

Jackie smiled a wise smile, giving a hint at why she would, with time and experience, blossom into a true diplomat. "You're asking whether she understands why it's necessary to construct a road into the interior of the island and why it's necessary to construct a new government building? Of course she does. In addition to all the other things she is, Marie-Ange is extremely intelligent. But does she like to lose? *Oh, mais non!* She likes losing less than practically anything! Except, perhaps, being poor."

"So what are you saying? That this is a game for her? A power struggle between the two of them?"

Jackie's wise smile converted to a Cheshire-cat grin and she raised her palms heavenward in a *comme ci, comme ça* gesture.

Carole Ann stood up and began to pace, caught herself, and resumed her seat across the desk from Jackie. Her thoughts, however, were not so easily corralled. She was remembering the conversation she and Jake had had with Philippe and Marie-Ange in Washington six months ago, in which Marie-Ange passionately acknowledged that the return to democracy—political and social and economic democracy—was long overdue on Isle de Paix and that her husband was the only person who possessed the requisite combination of skill and ability and desire to succeed. "It must happen," she had said in her French-accented English. "Isle de Paix's royal families must relinquish the scepter if we are to survive into the new century. There is no longer room for the old ways." And Carole Ann had believed her; had believed in the passion and commitment of her words.

"You look worried, Carole Ann," Jackie said, her face serious but humor still evident in her voice, "and there is no need for it. Marie-Ange and Philippe are partners dedicated to serving the people of Isle de Paix. Even, perhaps, to their own detriment. Do not doubt or question that even for a moment."

"But why would it be to their detriment?"

"Because," Jackie replied solemnly, "restoring democracy to Isle de

Paix and serving the people, of necessity and by definition, means no longer catering to the aristocracy. Philippe and Marie-Ange are of the aristocracy, *n'est-ce pas?* The construction of schools and clinics and the paving of roads will mean an increase in taxes, no matter how many tourists come, no matter how many gifts flow from the aristocracy."

"Aren't you part of the aristocracy yourself? Don't you belong to one of the wealthy, old families?" C.A. asked Jackie.

"*Mais oui.* My mother and Philippe are brother and sister and their grandparents on both sides are directly descended from wealthy Frenchmen who may have been slave traders and rum runners for all I know. The point is, the old ones all are dead and gone; the middle ones, like my parents, are in Paris earning lots of money; and all that's left of the past is a short supply of money and long memories of a time when inherited wealth and title mattered. Even the British have dismantled the House of Lords after almost a thousand years, which explains why I work for a living," she said with a wry grin. "This job is not my hobby."

Carole Ann walked back to her house from Government Square deep in thought. She knew that every place possessed its cultural peculiarities and she had expected to have to feel her way around the island and its mores. She had not expected to feel that her ability to perform her contractual obligations would be in jeopardy. And perhaps, she chided herself, she was overreacting. After all, Jackie believed strongly in Marie-Ange and her commitment to securing the government's stability, and Jackie knew both the island and the Collettes intimately. She was even part of the aristocracy and, theoretically, had as much at stake as the Collettes if democracy failed. And yet, Carole Ann knew, she could not blindly trust Jacqueline LaBelle or anyone else. GGI wasn't hired to trust other people or to take somebody's word for something. Which meant paying a visit to Marie-Ange as soon as possible and practical, to assess in person how much or how little commitment the president's wife had to her husband's objectives.

"Goddammit!" The alarm beeped when she pushed open the door and she jumped, her mind so full of her thoughts that for an instant she had forgotten that earlier that day, Harold Collins had activated the security system in the house. Then, she didn't recall the password that would turn the thing off. "Goddammit!" she muttered again, running toward the kitchen as her brain finally kicked in and she remembered that the codes and passwords to everything that Harold had booby-trapped were on a pad on the kitchen counter. She punched in the numbers for her brother's birthday and the alarm whimpered and silenced, the green light glowing happily at her as if she'd done something wonderful.

"Technology is my life," she mumbled as she padded down the hallway to the office. "I love technology." She dropped her purse and briefcase on the floor and plopped down into the desk chair, whirled it around, and rolled to the computer table. She wiggled the mouse and cursed again. "I don't know the damn password!" she whined as she pushed the chair back to the desk and grabbed the pad. She typed in her grandmother's maiden name and waited patiently for the computer to allow her to access the GGI–Isle de Paix contract. "The computer is my friend," she intoned.

Although she knew, because she'd drawn up the document, exactly what GGI had been contracted to do, she pulled it up onto the screen anyway and reread it, searching for any hint or suggestion that the plan of action GGI had recommended for Isle de Paix subverted the true needs of the people. After all, their response, hers and Jake's, had been based on the needs of the government as an entity, not on the needs of the people who made up the government. Yes, they had discussed—at length—the need for more and better social services on the island, and had agreed on a plan. Had that been the correct decision? And was it any of their business anyway? She could imagine Jake's response, and so she concentrated on what they were being paid to do: the construction of a new governmental center in the island's interior that would house a central computer system and security monitoring apparatus. GGI would design both systems, oversee their installation, and provide training for their use, in addition to long-term assessment and management; they would also establish and train an island police force, utilizing the most modern equipment and training procedures.

She stood and stretched, rotating tension out of her neck. It was only Tuesday. She'd been on the island for four days, and already she was feeling a strange exhaustion. She had not allowed herself to think much about why, focusing instead on the work to be done. Without the additional earthmoving equipment, the road would not be cut through and paved in the allotted forty-five days, which would mean that the foundation for the new government building would not be poured on time, before the advent of hurricane season. Six weeks . . . forty-five days until all but natives left the islands for the peak months of hurricane season. She arched her back and performed the yoga posture her mother had taught her called the Half Moon. She slowed and deepened her breathing and felt the tightness begin to release. But no matter how deeply she breathed, her mind would not empty itself of the thoughts and worries that crowded there.

She exhaled a sigh instead of a breath and returned to the desk, picking up her notepad as she sank into the chair and checking the notations there. She was enormously relieved that David Messinger would arrive sometime over the weekend so that she could lift the weight of worrying about Philippe's safety from her shoulders. Messinger was the cop; protecting people was his job, not hers. She was much more interested in learning why the interior minister hadn't been at the construction site this morning; that was *his* job, not the president's, and if he'd been there, she wouldn't have had to worry about Philippe standing out in the open, powerless along with the others against an ambush or an attack. She etched a dark, heavy line under his name and the time of their meeting tomorrow.

"Enough," she muttered and tossed the notebook back on the desk. She switched off the computer, grabbed her purse, and headed for the door, remembering to enter the security code before exiting, being reminded as she punched in the numbers of her brother's birthday that she owed him a letter. Her mother, too.

"A table for one, please, Helene," Carole Ann said, smiling at the young waitress, who met her as she hesitated at the entrance of the restaurant, scanning the room for an available table. Then, she added, "You're not Helene. I'm sorry, I thought you were."

The young woman smiled. "I'm Eliane. Helene is my sister. And my mother would be pleased if you'd join her at her table," Eliane said and turned away, plunging into the depths of the restaurant before Carole Ann could respond. So she followed, aware of being noticed every step of the way and realizing as they approached the front table who Eliane's mother must be.

"*Bonsoir,* madame. Thank you for joining me. I am Odile Laurance and I'm counting my blessings that you grace us with your presence twice in one day."

Carole Ann smiled and returned the warm handshake that was extended to her. "The pleasure is mine, Madame Laurance, though certainly you expected my return, after so magnificent a lunch. And besides, where else would I go to learn what people are saying about me?"

Odile Laurance threw back her head and laughed out loud, a full, rich, resounding noise that attracted the attention of practically everyone in the room. Those who didn't pivot in their chairs to stare were exercising the most stringent self-control. "*S'il vous plaît, asseyez-vous.* You will eat and drink as my guest tonight and I will tell you every word that has been said of you since your arrival. And there have been many!" C.A. sat and Odile dipped her head slightly, though in no particular direction, and, as if by magic, Eliane reappeared, trailed by a waiter, an older man carrying a napkin-wrapped bottle. He showed it to Odile, who nodded, and he unwrapped and opened the bottle and placed it on the table to breathe.

"My sister will join us momentarily, and I must, of course, visit with the other customers," she said, waving her hand at the room. "This is my domain; the kitchen belongs to Viviene. Enjoy the wine.

The salad will come soon, with some conch, perhaps, and I will return before too long. You will not, I trust, feel abandoned and alone."

"I feel very well cared for, madame. Please, attend to your guests and do not worry about me." Carole Ann sat back in her chair and slowly raised her head and her eyes, to give those who were observing her time to shift their own gazes. As earlier, the room was packed. From this position, the patio was not visible but she had no doubt that every table there, too, was occupied. She casually studied the diners, finding it difficult, in most cases, to discern tourist from islander: only two tables were occupied by wearers of shiny new vacation wardrobes. However, she easily could differentiate between the wealthy and those who worked for a living, and the line was not one of color.

"*S'il vous plaît*, madame." She looked up to see Eliane with a tray containing salad, the conch fritters that Jackie had seemed to enjoy so much earlier that day, and a basket of bread. She put the food on the table, poured the wine, and left Carole Ann to begin her meal. She recalled that not very long ago she'd have been sadly unhappy at the prospect of dining alone in a restaurant such as this, and she congratulated herself for having healed so many of the raw places. She could now think of Al and their life together without grieving his death. Of course she'd always miss him and she'd always love him. But she'd stopped insisting that she'd never marry again, and she'd even permitted intimacy to flower with Warren Forchette, a lawyer who lived in New Orleans. Warren, she thought, would love it here. . . .

She shook off that thought. Not the time or the place for romantic meanderings. She should be thinking of a way to ask the LeRoi sisters how they felt about the Collette government. She wanted to know if they believed that a true democracy was in the making here, or if Philippe Collette was merely a despot in savior's clothing. Or perhaps that wasn't the question to ask of women whose brother had been called a dictator? Above all, she wanted help understanding the social construction of the island. Surely Odile and Viviene were wealthy, given the popularity of

Aux Fruits de Mer, and their family had deep roots here; yet, they were not the landed gentry, so where did they fit on the social ladder? Where did they fit in the Collette government?

"You are thinking too much for the enjoyment of good food, madame."

"Nothing interferes with my enjoyment of good food, madame," Carole Ann responded, looking up in surprise at the tall, almost gaunt figure standing next to her.

"I am relieved to hear it. I am Viviene LeRoi. You are welcome here."

Carole Ann stood and extended her hand and marveled at the difference between the two sisters. While Eliane and Helene looked enough alike to be mistaken for each other, Viviene and Odile could not have been more different. Viviene's visage was not unpleasant; indeed, upon close inspection, the lines around her eyes and mouth suggested laughter rather than sourness, and her speaking voice was low and melodious. But this definitely was a no-nonsense woman, whereas one definitely got the impression that the shorter, rounder Odile would tolerate quite a bit of nonsense. "I appreciate the warm welcome, Madame LeRoi, and I promise that my appetite will demonstrate how appreciative."

She was rewarded with a gentle smile and an invitation to return "whenever your appetite or your curiosity brings you to us."

She left Carole Ann to finish her appetizer and to realize that her appetite indeed was just getting primed. The wine was crisp and properly chilled, and she was, surprisingly, totally relaxed. "Laid-back," Jake would have described how she was feeling. But it was short-lived. She snapped to attention as Denis St. Almain made his way through the dining room to the bar. He was more tanned than before, and dressed in island chic: silk shirt over silk slacks and French loafers. He slid onto a stool next to what C.A. would later describe to Jake as a smooth-looking character; too smooth by half. The kind of man that negative stereotyping would instantly label a drug dealer, at best—tall, dark, handsome even in profile, well dressed in silk and linen, expensive even from across the room.

"You know him, perhaps?" Odile had returned and was settling herself in a chair, turning it to give her a full view of the room. "It is possible," she said in answer to her own question with an offhanded shrug. "You are from Washington, D.C., and Denis lives in Washington. He has since he was a little boy. You know him," she said again, and it was not a question this time.

Carole Ann contemplated the possible answers and settled on a version of the truth. "No, I don't know him, but I know his mother."

Odile's eyebrows rose, as did her voice. "You know Simone? But I am surprised; Simone keeps so much to herself. How do you come to know her?" The question was asked in such a way that failure to answer, and answer fully, would, Carole Ann knew, terminate whatever relationship she was building with Odile Laurance.

"A friend of hers hired me to prove that Denis isn't a murderer."

Odile had leaned in close when Carole Ann dropped her voice, all but placing her ear to C.A.'s mouth to hear the words clearly. She sat back a bit now. "Who is this friend?"

Rather than show her surprise at the question, Carole Ann answered it. "Her name is Hazel Copeland and she is Simone's supervisor at the hotel where they both work. They have known each other for a long time." She wanted to ask how Odile knew of the trouble Denis was in, for her concern was focused not on Denis's predicament but on the identity of Simone's friend—though perhaps trouble for Denis was so commonplace as not to warrant surprise or concern.

Odile sat all the way back in her chair, her face closed and expressionless, her body still. She didn't move when Eliane brought Carole Ann's dinner—lobster, shrimp, and crab sautéed in butter and herbs, along with asparagus and some other greens that she couldn't identify. Odile would speak when she decided whether or not to trust her, Carole Ann reasoned; and in the meantime, she thought, she would be just as well served eating what obviously was a magnificent dinner.

But Odile didn't need a long time to compose her thoughts, and her words, when she spoke, were sharp and direct. "Does Philippe Collette know of this arrangement?"

The question came as Carole Ann was chewing, and took her completely by surprise. She shook her head in the negative.

"He must never, ever find out." Odile's face still was an impassive mask, but her voice quivered with emotion. "He must never find out, and you must tell no one else what you have told me." She'd leaned in close, resting her plump, chocolate arms on the table. Then she smiled broadly, completely throwing Carole Ann off balance until she realized that the smile was a ruse, a tactic to convey to the diners who certainly were observing the interaction between the two women that their conversation remained lighthearted. Carole Ann raised her napkin to her lips and when she lowered it a smile was there.

"Where can we talk, Odile, privately?"

Odile stood and smoothed her skirt of geometric designs in brushed silk. She poured more wine into Carole Ann's glass, then patted her gently on the shoulder. She leaned in close again. "We cannot. What you are doing is extremely dangerous and quite impossible. You cannot assist Denis while serving Philippe. It is quite impossible and places you in great danger. I am surprised that Simone would permit you to place yourself in such a position. But then, Simone has never listened to reason and has only done that which pleased her, no matter how badly others might have been affected." Odile stepped away from the table, already in conversation with another diner. But she turned back to Carole Ann. "I will happily deliver lunch or dinner to you, madame, at any time. You need only to call and request it." And she was gone, blended into the room like a thread within fabric. But she left something behind—not fear, exactly, and not anger—but it was a bitter, harsh taste on Carole Ann's palate.

Carole Ann's meetings had gone exactly as she'd imagined they would: Paul Francois was brusque but businesslike, and obviously qualified to do the job. The shack was up, the blueprints were hung, the crew was hard at work, and already there was evidence of the road that was to be. He shared her concern that, without the backhoe and the second bulldozer, the road most likely would not be completed in time for cement trucks to get into the interior and lay the concrete foundation before the rainy season. He would, he promised, work the crew as efficiently as he knew how, while reminding her that men should not be expected to do the work of machines.

The minister of the interior was politely ineffective, as she'd known he would be, based on the background checks she had requested on all of the island's ministers and other top officials. His name was Roland Charles and he was a native of Martinique and a graduate of the University of the Virgin Islands and the Georgia Institute of Technology, where he'd studied engineering. He'd spent twenty-five years as a midlevel project manager with the Georgia transportation department, overseeing road construction in small towns throughout the state. But Roland apparently was quite thrifty, managing to save practically every dollar he'd ever earned in Georgia and retiring with a healthy, six-figure bank account and a pension that was wealth by island standards. He built his dream retirement home in a mango grove on Isle de Paix's southern end because it was cheaper than building in his native Martinique. And, Roland Charles told her with a tight smile and a slight bow, he was happy to help out President Collette in whatever way he could. Well, at least she knew now why the president himself met her at a construction site early in the morning instead of the interior minister.

He did offer one useful piece of information, however: there existed, in a warehouse in Little Haiti, an old backhoe that Roland believed to be operable. However, since he had left the warehouse key at home, she took specific directions from him and arranged to meet him there "before the cocktail hour" because, he said, his wife was expecting him home "on time." She drove back out to the construction site, sorely missing cell phones and pagers, and asked Paul Francois to join her later at the warehouse, hoping, she told him, that he could tell what repairs the machine would need and, further, hoping that he could make them. She didn't tell him that she harbored no confidence that Roland Charles could add a quart of oil to his car. Paul Francois contorted his face in mock surprise and marveled at the fact that she couldn't fix the thing herself. She replied, with equal exaggeration, that how to repair a backhoe was the *one* thing that she didn't know how to do. Then she really shut him up by climbing out of the Jeep, stretching, and running four miles in little more than half an hour. He was still eyeing her in amazement when they met at the warehouse three hours later. But Carole Ann's amazement was for Little Haiti in general, and the warehouse in particular.

Some four hundred expatriate Haitians lived in the tiny community up a rutted ravine off the South Coast Road, around the bend from Ville de Mer and Aux Fruits de Mer—a vibrant, active community of thatched, tin-roofed residential and commercial structures carved out of a tangle of dense vegetation. The warehouse, constructed of concrete block with a barnlike roof, was surprisingly well maintained and, even more surprisingly, dry; the broken-down equipment and tools within had been spared the insidious damage caused by salt air. Carole Ann wondered whether credit was owed to Henri LeRoi, but she cut short her mental congratulations as she strolled around the cavernous space. In addition to the backhoe, two dump trucks, a pickup truck, a police cruiser, and a school bus collected dust, along with a large assortment of farm tools and equipment.

"Are any of these vehicles functional?" Carole Ann asked the interior minister, who looked at her in astonishment, his face asking the question that his mouth hadn't: How should I know?

"Well, Madame Boss," crooned Paul Francois, "when you find out, will you kindly inform me? Those trucks—"

"I know, I know, I know!" She raised a hand to stop whatever he was going to say about the trucks and asked Roland Charles how many big-engine mechanics were employed by the government, and immediately regretted having spoken. She turned back to the rangy construction foreman, who was clambering about the backhoe like a kid on a playground, and she found herself releasing breath she hadn't known she was holding when, after his inspection, he pronounced the thing "fixable . . . if there are any tools."

Both she and Francois were halfway through their second beers before Carole Ann trusted herself to speak, and then she had to be very careful in her choice of words. "I will do whatever I need to do, and do it as quickly as possible, to see to it that those vehicles are made operable." He had determined that all three trucks and the police car had engines, though no keys were found for any of them, and the school bus belly was empty. Roland Charles had backed away from them as if he'd never in his life touched a dirty truck. Maybe, she thought, being charitable, twenty-five years of climbing in and out of dirty trucks was enough for one man in one lifetime. Maybe, she thought, turning vindictive, she'd make his life a living hell if he didn't get that equipment up and running.

Paul Francois had introduced her to a cafe-cum-bar that most charitably, since she was in that frame of mind, could be described as rustic. It was a mile or so down the Coast Road from Aux Fruits de Mer, into Little Haiti, and far enough inland that the sea was not visible. It was called Armand's and its patrons clearly were predominately working class—everybody from construction workers like Francois to hotel maids and waiters still wearing the uniforms of their establishments. The music was loud and heavily reggae-influenced, the crowd was lively, the beer was cold, and the appetizers, to Carole Ann's delight, were dried plantain strips.

"Do you really think you can find the keys to those trucks?"

"Somebody knows where the keys are, Paul. You saw how well maintained that place was—no moisture, no rust. Somebody has been taking care of it, and that somebody knows where the keys are. That somebody may even be a mechanic." She realized that she was sounding slightly plaintive, and took another swallow of beer to cover.

"And you think your president knows this mechanic and where to find him?" he asked with cutting disdain. "Because the interior minister wouldn't know the mechanic if he tripped over him. Which would never happen because it might get his shoes dirty."

She would not publicly share her own disdain for her employers. "If the keys can be found, I'll find them. In the meantime," and she tossed him a duplicate key to the warehouse, "as soon as you tell me what you need to get that backhoe cranked up and running, I'll get it to you. Do you have somebody you can leave in charge at the site while you're at the warehouse?"

He nodded and cast his glance across the crowded room. A tall, loose-limbed man with dreadlocks tucked beneath a knit cap was standing before the jukebox, swaying to the music. "Name's Joseph and he's good. I've worked with him before. But I'm going to need to pull one of the men to help me work on that thing," he said, referring to the backhoe.

"Do what you need to do," she said, reaching into her pocket and withdrawing several bills. "Buy the crew a drink," she said and stood up. As she made her way through the maze of tables to the front door, she noticed—felt—the combination of inquisitiveness and borderline hostility of the bar patrons. She was an outsider, which could, alone, be sufficient cause for hostility in some places. But she knew these people knew that she worked for the new president, the man who had replaced the man they presumably had put into power. What did they think of Philippe Collette? And if they disliked him or mistrusted him, was their enmity great enough to result in an attack on his life? She stopped in the doorway, turned, surveyed the room and the crowd, and was unnerved to find many staring back at her, no doubt as curious about her motives as she was about theirs.

The sun was setting when she walked outside, and the promise of velvet darkness hovered at the edge of the sky. She bumped too rapidly down the rutted road, anxious to reach the Coast Road before full darkness settled, aware of the tingle of panic she felt at the thought of being up a ragged, rutted road in the dark, submerging the memory of the last time she found herself in such a predicament. She slowed as she rounded the bend toward Aux Fruits de Mer, debating whether to stop, deciding instead to eat at home for a change. And as she drove, relishing the beauty of the sunset, she made mental to-do notes: find out who had been in charge of the island's maintenance shed and whether he had the key; find out whether the island government employed any mechanics; arrange a meeting with Marie-Ange Collette . . . no, not a meeting—lunch or drinks or dinner. And ask Jake why they hadn't given more thought and consideration to the social service issues of Isle de Paix.

"*Because* we weren't asked to do that and we still haven't been asked to do that! Goddammit, C.A.! Would you just get the damn road built and get the damn police department up and running so we can get paid and get the hell outta there! And for the record, I personally think every able-bodied man and woman resident of Isle de Paix ought to have a job and be paying taxes to the government before any hospital or clinic gets built down there. I think the same thing about up here, for that matter: no free rides, except maybe for old people and children and those who can't help themselves."

She knew better than to rise to that bait, and wished she hadn't even posed the question; wished she'd just come home and eaten dinner and gotten to work. So, after a lengthy silence during which they listened to each other breathe, she said, "Something's wrong here, Jake, and before you ask, no, I've got nothing to back up the feeling or the hunch or whatever it is."

"Wrong with what part?"

"That hurry-up-let's-build-a-school-and-clinic business. Nobody with good sense would start to build something nobody wanted, not even an eccentric, rich old man. And no politician with good sense would allow it."

"Could you be getting the wrong vibe, C.A.?"

"Of course I could. But I don't think I am."

"Is Collette double-dealing us somehow, telling us one thing, doing another?" He asked the question quietly and she could imagine that his eyes were closed to ward off the answer he didn't want to hear.

"I don't think so."

"Then his wife is."

Carole Ann didn't respond and Jake, surprisingly, didn't press her, changing the subject instead. He didn't want to think that any more than she did.

"Have you seen any more sleazeballs like the one St. Almain was talking to at that bar, or found out who that one is?"

"Nope. But then I haven't had time to go looking for them, either."

"And don't worry about making the time," he snapped. "Worry about getting that equipment running and let Messinger and the new chief worry about St. Almain and his sleazeballs."

She ignored that quip and changed the subject herself. "Will it be troublesome getting parts shipped in?" she asked, having allowed herself to imagine that the backhoe and the trucks would need to be entirely reconstructed.

"Not if the parts are available. But if that stuff is a hundred years old, then yeah, getting parts will be a bitch, though still easier and cheaper than sending in new equipment. Which reminds me, all your cop stuff is leaving here by boat tomorrow morning and should reach you by the middle of next week, at the latest. And I heard you change the subject on me a minute ago, so let me say this: I like that security minister and his new police chief, so be nice to 'em, C.A., please. Don't piss 'em off in the first hour."

She allowed herself a few uncharitable thoughts about her partner while she prepared and ate her dinner—not Viviene LeRoi's sautéed seafood, but a very passable pasta primavera. A nice Italian touch, she thought, in the midst of so many things French. "And a lot less work," she muttered to herself, pouring another glass of Chardonnay.

She finished her meal, cleaned the kitchen, brought the wine into the living room, and settled herself onto the couch. She'd have preferred working in the library, but she found the rows of empty bookshelves strangely unnerving. And she found the sofa in the office uncomfortable; it clearly was intended for brief business meetings and she knew she'd be several hours poring over the background reports on the island's ministers of government and sorting out the growing list of questions she needed to find answers to, Jake's pissy admonitions notwithstanding. Just because she didn't believe that Philippe Collette was a double-dealing dirtbag didn't mean that she thought he wore a halo. On the contrary, she thought the new president greatly flawed: something enormously ugly was afoot in his domain and he was completely unaware. Add to that an apparent inability to judge talent, if Roland Charles was any indication, and Jackie LaBelle's prediction of Collette as a one-termer was on the money. But just maybe Roland was the exception, she thought, as she reread the file on the minister of internal security.

David Messinger was an American-born white man, a Chicago cop who'd become a lawyer who had worked both sides of the table, as a prosecutor and as a defense attorney. He was a hard-liner—he didn't like crime or criminals—but he was without the us-versus-them view so many cops possessed regarding citizens. Messinger actually believed that police officers were, and should view themselves as, public servants. He abhorred the increasing violence bestowed on citizens by their law enforcement personnel, and when he quit his job with the police force, it was because, as the deputy chief in charge of the training academy, he had refused to issue the "two to the head, one to the chest" order to new recruits as their first response to being threatened. Like every resident of a big city, he was alarmed by the number of homeless people who were psychotic and generally deranged, but he didn't believe that they should be killed because they exhibited "threatening" behavior. He also didn't believe they should be allowed to sleep in the parks and the public libraries and hustle money on every corner.

"No wonder Jake likes you," she muttered as she reached the section of the report that detailed how Messinger, after he quit the police force, attended law school, entered private practice, and quickly grew disenchanted and disgusted with the revolving door that literally could return criminals to the street before the arresting officers completed their paperwork. So he became a prosecutor, a ruthless one who worked tirelessly to rid society of some of its most vicious and violent and incorrigible criminals. And then Messinger learned that the words of the law weren't necessarily the reality of the law; that innocent until proven guilty was a lofty goal and little more; that a poor person, particularly a poor person of color, was as good as convicted if charged with a felony; that the system didn't make mistakes. Nobody charged with a crime was ever innocent. And at the age of fifty-three, with his youngest child in college, David Messinger had allowed his Caribbean-born wife to convince him that retirement would be sweeter in her homeland. Then he allowed her to convince him to go to work for the new president of Isle de Paix.

"You don't sound like the kind of boss who wouldn't know where all the keys were," Carole Ann said musingly, dropping the Messinger file to the floor and opening the Casson file. She sat up straight. Yvette Casson was the new police chief. A woman police chief! OK, so perhaps Monsieur le Présidente wasn't a great judge of talent, but he was an equal-opportunity employer. She quickly paged through the other folders, learning nothing new.

She yawned and propped the yellow legal pad on her knees, wishing she had something to write, some notes or thoughts or observations, but she had received not a single hint that anyone on the island had a clue about who had killed the two constables. No one would discuss the matter beyond a display of horror that the attack had occurred, and not a soul believed that Philippe could be in danger. And yet Carole Ann believed that he was. She closed her eyes and envisioned the dead-end road leading to the presidential yacht: an isolated, secluded location in the dark, a perfect location for an assassination. She didn't believe for a second that Philippe's boat was boarded by accident or that the attack was random, nor did she have any way to prove her suspicions. "You've been here less than a week," she admonished herself. "Relax."

She stood and stretched and yawned again. She would get up early in the morning and go for a run, then perhaps do a few laps in the pool. Then, she decided, she would confront Roland Charles. She would make it impossible for him not to do his job. She would hound him until they got that machinery operable, in front of Philippe Collette if necessary. She gathered her papers and lugged them down the hallway and into the office and dropped the load on the desk. She stood there for a moment, shuffling through the mound of paperwork, wanting to be certain there was nothing she'd left undone that day. Then she turned off the light and went to bed.

She sat straight up, her heart pounding so hard her chest hurt. What the hell was that noise? The alarm! The damn motion detectors that Harold Collins had installed! Somebody was in the house. She snatched the pistol from beneath the pillow where she kept it when she slept and crept silently to the doorway, though it wouldn't have mattered if she'd stomped; the damn alarm sounded like a World War II air raid siren. She peeked around the corner, saw a shadow move, and bolted down the hallway toward it. She was barefoot and soundless and the shadowy figure trying to force open the French doors in the living room was unaware of her presence.

"Don't move, I have a gun," she called out, simultaneously pressing the light switch, illuminating the room.

Denis St. Almain turned to face her, his hands raised. "I am unarmed, madame," he said in his low voice.

"I am relieved," she replied dryly, lowering her gun. "And I'd appreciate your remaining where you are until I can shut off this horrendous noise." She went in search of the control panel, marveling at the absurdity of the entire scenario. Who could she tell it to who'd have the proper response, which would be to laugh? For, despite the howling of the alarm, the system wasn't monitored by any external entity and there were no police to respond even if it had been. And the intruder, who might or might not be a drug-dealing murderer, was standing by politely, as requested, while she disarmed the only security system that was at her disposal.

They both sighed when the house suddenly was returned to stillness. Denis St. Almain broke the silence. "I suppose I should have thought that you would have alarms," he said quietly and calmly, "though Henri never cared for security systems. I wouldn't have entered through the window had I known such a sound would result."

"The door would have worked just as well," she replied, and waited for him to explain why he'd broken in. "So?" she demanded sharply when no explanation was forthcoming.

"So what?" he questioned.

"Why did you break in here, Denis? Why not ring the damn bell and come in the front door, instead of breaking in like a criminal?"

He shrugged cavalierly though she read the hint of embarrassment in his face. "I wanted to find out exactly how much you know."

"So in addition to breaking and entering, you planned to rifle my office?"

He raised his hands, palms forward, to ward off her anger. "You're correct, of course, to be angry, and I apologize. For my rudeness, and for frightening you."

And she most certainly had been frightened. Carole Ann shuddered and looked down at herself. "Since we're being so polite, Monsieur St. Almain," she said dryly, "please have a seat. I'll dress more appropriately and return. There's food and drink in the refrigerator if you're hungry. You obviously know your way around." She heard him mutter something as she whipped around and hurried down the hallway to her bedroom, trying not to think how she must have appeared, standing there in panties and a tank top, pointing an unloaded pistol.

Of course, he hadn't known that it was unloaded and Jake would kill her if he knew. . . .

He was seated on a stool at the island in the kitchen eating the remains of her dinner salad with a baguette and a hunk of Camembert when she returned, wearing jeans and a T-shirt. She took a bottle of wine from the refrigerator and two glasses from the rack overhead. She opened the wine and poured it and he nodded his thanks, all the while chewing with an intensity that she found interesting. She couldn't tell whether it was a result of hunger or merely a manifestation of his personality. The surreal nature of the scene increased when she opened the drawer and removed the paring knife and he flinched. She slowly reached for the bowl of apples and pears at her elbow and he relaxed. She sliced the fruit, placed some on a napkin, and shoved it toward him and he, in turn, broke off a piece of cheese and shoved it toward her. And for several moments they ate fruit and cheese and drank wine as if they were friends and he an invited guest.

She watched him while he ate and he seemed not to mind; at least, he didn't seem to feel self-conscious. But then, she wasn't staring, she was observing. And what she saw confirmed her earlier assessment of him, based on the fleeting court appearance: he was a polite and well-bred man, soft-spoken, shy, almost. And if she had to, she'd guess that both Hazel and Simone had been correct in their assertions that Denis St. Almain was no criminal. But who was he?

"Odile Laurance told me what you said and I find it very difficult to believe, though I do believe it. Would you please, Miss Gibson, tell me everything? How did my mother come to ask for your assistance?"

She told him everything, beginning with Hazel Copeland's Sunday-morning visit and ending with her conversation with Odile Laurance the previous night. He listened intently if impassively, registering emotion only once, when she told of Simone's showing her and Jake the envelope with the DEA pay stubs inside. All the color drained from his face and he bit his bottom lip. Too hard, Carole Ann thought; he was struggling too hard to maintain control, and he bit his lip too hard.

"I am not a drug dealer, Miss Gibson. I did not kill Judge Campos. I was an undercover agent of the Drug Enforcement Administration until . . . I don't really know exactly when they cut me loose; they didn't bother to tell me. I didn't know that I was out in the cold until I was left to rot in that damn D.C. jail cell. No arrangements were made, as usual, for my release. Judge Campos had no idea that he was expected to reduce my bail; I know that now." He stopped talking and his breathing became shallow and audible. Carole Ann poured more wine in his glass and he gulped it like it was water.

"Who killed Judge Campos?"

He shook his head. "I don't know."

"Can you make an educated guess?" she pressed him and he shrugged and his eyes narrowed, as if he were looking into the distance.

"Perhaps, if I knew some things . . . no, I'm sorry, I can't. I don't know," he finally said, sounding helpless and exasperated. "What I do know is that I was cut loose and left to dangle in the wind. I did find out that the network of dealers that I had infiltrated—the real drug dealers—managed to get word of a major bust and not one of them was around when the raid went down. But I was around, and the drugs were in a storage locker rented in my name, and my prints were the only ones on the locker. Twenty million dollars' worth of cocaine and marijuana and I've got the key to the locker in my pocket and the house where I said the dealers would be with another million dollars in cash was empty and so clean the cops doubted that anybody had lived there in the last year." He rubbed his eyes, then his head, and he looked a little surprised to find so little hair there. She wondered how long he'd worn the dreadlocks.

"Who were the real dealers?" she asked. "People you'd known and associated with for a while?"

He shook his head. "I'd been in contact with them for about three weeks, and the only thing I knew about them is that they were Trinidadian, and I knew that because I know island people, not because my boss told me."

"So, if the DEA hung you out to dry, what would make them have a change of heart and arrange your release from jail?"

"There was no change of heart," he spat in his first display of real anger. "My mother begged and begged my father and he somehow raised the money. And then what do I do? Run away! His entire life savings and everything he could borrow thrown away! But once the judge was killed, I knew I had no choice but to leave."

"Of course you had a choice!" she retorted.

"Oh, give me a break! All you people who sit on the sidelines with your stupid 'just say no' mentality. I tell you, I had no choice!"

"Why did you come back here?" she asked, foiling his attempt to put her on the defensive, and failing in hers to put him there.

"Because the answers are here," he said simply, and her heart skipped a beat.

"Where?"

"I don't know," he said slowly, "and I need some time to figure out some things. And I need to go talk to my father. And I need your help, Miss Gibson."

She emptied her glass and stood up, shaking her head. "I don't know what you think I can do, and, in any case, I may not be able to help you, if your interests would be in direct conflict with the interests of my client."

"Of course. I'm sure the contract with Philippe Collette's government is much more lucrative than the one with Mom's hotel to find me," he replied bitterly.

"Damn right it is," Carole Ann snapped unapologetically and walked to the door, intending to open it and show him out. But something about his expression stopped her. "Look, Denis, I promised your mother and Mrs. Copeland that I would talk to you and, to the extent that I could do so without creating a conflict of interest with my other client, that I would help you prove your innocence. But if you're telling me that the answer is on this island, there's no way that whatever it is can't impact and endanger my contract, especially if illegal drugs are involved. I'm sorry, Denis."

"If you could just wait until I can meet with my father, Miss Gibson! Please don't make a decision until then. I need a few days, maybe even a week. Can you allow me that much time?"

"The time isn't mine to give you, Denis."

"But you have influence, Miss Gibson. You can buy the extra week that I need."

She shifted impatiently. "By now you've no doubt heard about the murders of the two constables." She made it a statement and not a question and waited for his reaction. He surprised her by smiling.

"And you want to know whether I'm responsible." He also made it a statement, not a question.

"I want to know who is responsible, yes. Do you know?"

He kept his smile in place but shook his head. "I don't know and I don't know anyone who knows. Unless, of course, you think *mes tantes* would have knowledge about such a thing." His smile faded and he locked eyes with her. She refused to react to his reference to Odile and Viviene as his aunts.

"Who is your father, Denis, that a conversation with him could prove so enlightening?" She intended the sarcasm to be as pronounced as it was, and she therefore was caught in a rare and unfamiliar position resembling embarrassment when Denis St. Almain responded quietly, gently almost: "Henri LeRoi."

Carole Ann was so wired the following morning, despite a four-mile run and a twenty-minute session in the lap pool, that she literally could not contain herself. That intensity manifested itself in behavior that, if pressed to put a name to it, she would have had to admit was bitchy. But Roland Charles was too refined to call her a bitch even though she had hounded him to the point that, by noon, she not only had the keys to all the vehicles in the Little Haiti warehouse, she knew the location of the storage shed where, Monsieur Charles assured her, she should expect to find a supply of engine oil and brake and transmission fluids, in addition to an underground gasoline storage tank. And, he'd added with a flourish and a chest puffed out with self-satisfaction, the former head of island maintenance, one Toussaint L'Overture Remy, would meet her at *la garage*—that's what he called the warehouse—at one o'clock that afternoon.

Toussaint Remy looked as ancient as the Haitian hero for whom he was named. He was gnarled and withered, his sparse hair snow white and hugging his head like a cap, his eyes watery and cloudy. And he spoke no English, only island patois that was so difficult for Carole Ann to understand that she first thought she'd need to send for a translator. In fact, she wished fervently that Warren Forchette were present. The Louisiana native who was part Creole and part Cajun spoke a version of French that she could understand only by listening very carefully, and demanding that he speak very slowly. What she discovered during her conversation with Toussaint Remy was that he could, if he chose, speak perfectly understandable French. He merely chose not to, in defiance of the upper-class, upper-crust snobs who looked down on people like himself. So, they reached an agreement of sorts: Carole Ann spoke to him in the French that she knew and which he understood, and he responded in the French that he chose to speak, sprinkling it with enough of Carole Ann's French that they could effectively converse.

What was immediately clear was that despite his age, Toussaint Remy was as physically fit as any man half his age, though she wouldn't dream of speculating what that age might be. Hell, she thought, men a third his age couldn't climb in and out of truck engines with such agility. And climb in and out of the engines he did, coaxing the two dump trucks to ignite briefly when he poured gasoline into their distributor caps, and insisting, with a gnarled finger pointed at her nose, that "his" trucks indeed would "catch fire and hold."

Carole Ann asked him if he wanted his old job back and he looked at her as if she were crazier than he'd originally thought her to be. He didn't have a job, he told her. He'd helped out LeRoi because he liked him, and because, the old man said, he liked trucks and engines. So then she asked him if he wanted a job, the job of being in charge of all the engines and teaching some of the young men how to take care of them. The old man's watery eyes narrowed and he squinted at her. "I don't like that pantywaist of a president," he said.

"Then we won't tell him," Carole Ann replied, and the old man's sustained cackle, revealing his almost toothless mouth, told her she'd just made her first hire. Then, she thought with a sinking feeling, how would she explain all this to Roland Charles? Hell, for that matter, how would she explain Roland Charles to Toussaint L'Overture Remy? If he thought Philippe Collette was a pantywaist, what would he make of the minister of the interior? She was wondering when Paul Francois arrived with two men in tow. She hurried over to him.

"Do you speak island French, Paul?"

"*Certainement,*" he answered with an elaborate shrug. "I live on the islands where people speak island French." And when she finished explaining about Toussaint Remy, he grinned widely, slapped her on the back, and hurried over to the old man, who was sitting inside the raised hood of one of the dump trucks. Their conversation was spirited and became more so when the two workers Paul had brought joined in, and she didn't understand a single word until Paul yelled over to her, "Hey, boss! Is it all right if Luc and Jean become Monsieur Remy's first pupils?"

"Sure, as long as losing them from the road crew doesn't put that work behind schedule."

"Au contraire! They'll be bringing us a backhoe and a dump truck! We'll finish the damn road ahead of schedule!"

She shared their enthusiasm, then sobered. "Do me one favor, Paul? Ask the guys to keep this to themselves until I have a chance to talk to my employers."

Paul sobered, too. "Do you think there'll be a problem? Will they resist?"

"Oh, no," she replied, more offhandedly than she felt. "I've just got to figure out how to ask them if I can do this instead of telling them that I've done it."

And before she could stop him, Paul told the men what she'd just said, and raucous laughter and cheers followed her out of the dimly lit warehouse into the bright sunlight.

Roland Charles couldn't stop preening. The story she'd told Philippe made it seem as if the entire plan was the brainchild of the interior minister, though she'd been prepared to claim ownership had the president been displeased. On the contrary, he was so grateful he was beaming. To not have to beg Hubert de Villages for his backhoe or import one from another island was a gift from heaven! the president exclaimed. But the ribbon on the present was being able to demonstrate to Henri LeRoi supporters that he, Philippe Collette, would indeed be president of *all* the people! He actually rubbed his hands together and danced a little jig when Carole Ann suggested that perhaps she and Roland Charles should sit down and draw up job descriptions with salaries attached.

Later, when they were alone together in his office, Roland Charles gave her a sly grin and extended his hand to her. "I'd certainly rather play on your team than on the opposing squad, Miss Gibson. Well done. I'll draft the job descriptions and have something ready for your review early next week, if that's acceptable." When she nodded, he continued: "And I intend to track down every piece of equipment and every tool belonging to this government. And I will learn every inch of this island." Carole Ann couldn't think of anything to say, so she offered him her hand again and headed for the door. He stopped her before she could cross the threshold. "By the way, Miss Gibson, island French was my first language. I'm looking forward to meeting Monsieur Remy."

She returned to her own office buoyed and confident, for a change, that her work in Isle de Paix was on the right track. She looked at her watch: after five o'clock. She still had time to inspect the now empty office that would become police headquarters in two days when David Messinger and Yvette Casson and ten new recruits arrived. The cops would share space in a renovated building with the also newly rejuvenated tourist bureau on the edge of Government Square.

It was Jake who had argued that having the police in the same building with the tourist board would comfort tourists and inspire confidence in the island's safety, and he had been absolutely correct. Even though the cops hadn't arrived yet, the activity in and around the building had increased dramatically. Carole Ann strolled down the street, aware that the energy was shifting from the frenetic, day-time activity of the crowds to the more relaxed mood of sundown and evening. Some early diners, already dressed for the evening in is-land-casual silks and linens, passed in and out of the boutiques or sipped rum drinks under brightly colored umbrellas on the patios of the restaurants. Within the hour, dinner would be in full swing. She looked up at the old stucco building, painted pale yellow and glowing as if lit from within in the late afternoon sunlight. ISLE DE PAIX BUREAU OF TOURISM read the letters of inlaid stone and shell at the top. And beneath, in smaller letters of the same construction, BUREAU OF IS-LAND SECURITY.

The glassed-in front door bore gilt-edged letters, again proclaiming this to be the Bureau of Tourism. And, again beneath those letters, an arrow, and the words POLICE DEPARTMENT ENTRY AROUND THE CORNER. Carole Ann walked around the corner to face a similar glassed-in door upon which, in simple black, block letters, were the words ISLAND POLICE. PLEASE COME IN. She unlocked the door and entered a large, square room with windows on one side, a wall-sized map of the island on the opposite wall, and a map of the Caribbean Sea and its islands occupying a quarter of the back wall. The rest of the space was taken up by a row of file cabinets with a fax machine on top of one and printers on top of three others, a scheduling board, and a door that led to a hallway. The first door on the right was the office of the chief of police. Carole Ann opened the door and looked in. It was fully furnished: desk, chair, worktable with four chairs, a huge bulletin board, three tall file cabinets, a computer, a telephone, and a fax machine. The room was large enough that it did not feel cramped or crowded, and bare enough to permit the new chief to impose her own personality.

Across and down the hall from the chief's office was the cops' combination toilet/locker room. Carole Ann had lost the argument for providing public toilet facilities. Jake's view that the only members of the public needing toilet facilities inside the police station would find them in the cells prevailed; and newly built on the rear of the hundred-year-old building was a two-cell jail with a toilet in each cell, and an enclosed shower stall. Philippe Collette didn't like having to admit it, but the jail was a necessity.

Isle de Paix was a large island with a deep harbor and a magnificent beach and coral reefs for diving and good restaurants and lodging to accommodate a range of budgets. The minister of tourism was getting the word out that this little bit of paradise no longer was governed by a dictator, and tourists were returning in droves, in turn attracting an influx of workers from the other islands. Add to that the annual Carnaval, and there existed the possibility of a variety of mis-behaviors that would respond to a strong law enforcement presence, as well as jail cells.

Out front, in the main room, were half a dozen desks, all with phones, though all the phones would not function for at least a year. She picked up each phone in turn and found that none of them worked now, which meant that none of the computers worked. She sighed but did not despair; after all, it wasn't Monday yet. There was a lot of open space in the room, and lots of light; Jake had insisted on it. It would, he said, allow the cops to make the room what they needed it to be, and light and space would make the public feel com-fortable and welcome. Carole Ann looked around and felt good about what she saw. There certainly was sufficient space here for the new chief and the first ten officers. And by the time the other fifteen cops came on board a year from now, the new police building would be built and this would be the Ville de Paix precinct.

If the road gets cut through and paved. *If* the new government cen-ter gets constructed. *If* the president doesn't get nailed first. For that matter, she thought, if *I* don't get nailed first. Suppose the intruder into her home the previous night had not been Denis St. Almain? Or suppose Denis St. Almain really was a drug-dealing murderer? Dammit, she needed somebody to talk to about the island, about the people, about what went on when the tourists weren't watching. Somebody on this island had killed two cops and nobody wanted to talk about it.

She left the empty police station, locking the door behind her, and looked again at her watch and then at the western sky. There was time for a quick shower and a change of clothes and the drive out to Ar-mand's, before darkness descended, to tell Paul Francois and the me-chanics-in-training that their work was sanctioned. She was glad that she'd parked the Jeep behind Government House instead of at home; she didn't feel up to the three-quarter-mile trek. She finally was feel-ing the effects of the night before on her mind and the morning's physical activity on her body, not to mention the adrenaline generated by the afternoon encounter with Toussaint Remy at *la garage*. She smiled inwardly as she realized that she'd come to think of the place as a garage instead of a warehouse. She also realized that she was anxious to learn what success the old mechanic had had coaxing life into the moribund engines. In truth, she admitted, that was her real reason for the trip to Armand's.

The Jeep bumped up the rough road, bouncing her around inside, making her bless the seat belt that kept her from feeling completely like a pinball. All the roads into Little Haiti and the other communities, she knew, were like this one, and while it was a nice note to his overall reform package that he planned to have these ruts paved, President Collette would do well to make that plan a priority. At the very least, she thought, the bulldozer could be brought in to smooth out the ruts; the pouring of asphalt could happen later.

That's what she was envisioning when she pulled into the crushed-shell and gravel apron that was Armand's parking lot. Paul Francois's pickup was there; she hoped that Luc and Jean were with him, though she realized that she didn't know enough about island protocol to know whether the men would be drinking together or merely drinking in the same bar. She opened the door and immediately removed her sunglasses. This was not Aux Fruits de Mer. It was both dark and smoky within, and she stood in the doorway for a couple of seconds to allow her eyes time to adjust to the dimness. She was glad she'd changed into more casual attire; the silk ensemble she'd worn earlier, though quite dressed down for a job in what would be comparable to the Executive Office Building back home in Washington, would have screamed "out of place" here. And Lord knows she didn't want to feel any more out of place than she already did.

"Over here!" Paul's voice called out over the reggae blaring from the jukebox, and she followed the sound and spied him at a corner table in the rear of the room with the three mechanics. Half the eyes in the room had followed the direction of her gaze, and an almost imperceptible path was cleared so she could make her way back to

Paul's table. The place was more crowded than the day before and, she thought, the energy slightly less hostile. Or was that merely wishful thinking? Paul was dragging over a chair from an adjacent table as she approached, and the four men scrunched themselves closer together at the small table to make room for her. She greeted each man by name and was greeted, in turn, with two smiles, a seated bow from the waist, and a half salute. Luc jumped up to get the beer that she requested, and Jean went in search of a bowl of plantain chips. They returned almost immediately and she thanked them and took a long quaff.

"Well? Good news or bad?" Paul asked, a smile in place but wavering, ready to widen or droop as necessary.

"Monsieur Remy is the new chief mechanic for the Ministry of the Interior and these gentlemen," she nodded toward Luc and Jean, "will be his first apprentices."

The grin widened and, in rapid-fire island French, Paul related to them what she'd said. The two younger men released simultaneous and spontaneous whoops of delight, and Toussaint Remy beamed. He said something that Carole Ann did not understand and Paul began to translate but the old man stopped him and spoke again, very slowly this time. Carole Ann leaned in close. He bestowed blessings on her and on her children and on her children's children, for many generations to come. He was grave as he spoke and she was grave as she thanked him for his blessing. Luc and Jean stood and grabbed their beers. They shook her hand and hurried off toward the other side of the room.

"By nightfall, everyone in Little Haiti will know what you've done. But tell me, how did it happen? Was it difficult to convince the minister and the president?"

"Not at all, thank goodness. They were very receptive. Now, you tell me: What condition are those engines in? Will you be able to get anything running anytime soon?"

He drew his hands together as if in prayer and cast his eyes heavenward. "Toussaint Remy is a genius. The man is brilliant! To call him a mechanic is to cheat him. He is an engineer! He is a surgeon!

He is a . . . he is . . . brilliant! It is as if he talks to engines. He studies them and listens to them and then studies them again before he ever touches them. They all will be up and running! All but the bloody school bus, which doesn't have a bloody engine!" He actually looked offended at the bus's transgression. Then he looked at Toussaint Remy and spoke to him and the old man blushed.

"Will you ask Monsieur Remy for a favor? The new police chief will be in town next week. Any chance of having the cruiser ready for her?"

Paul turned toward Remy and opened his mouth to speak, but stopped suddenly and whipped back around to Carole Ann. "Did you say *her?*"

"I said *her.* Yvette Casson. What's the matter, Francois, you got a problem with women on the job?"

"Not anymore," he said ruefully, then turned to the old mechanic and posed C.A.'s question. The white head was nodding up and down and then it stopped. Carole Ann had heard the word *femme,* and knew that Toussaint Remy now knew that the new island police chief was a woman. She wondered whether that was something that should be kept quiet, something that President Collette would want to announce at some special service or ceremony. She might have just blown it.

"Monsieur Remy says he hopes she's like you and yes, he'll have her car ready, and no, he won't tell anybody that she's a she—and neither will I—and he wants to know if you're married."

She was still smiling when she walked out of Armand's and into the velvety-smooth evening half an hour later, though her good humor was tempered by the reaction she'd received from both Paul Francois and Toussaint Remy when she asked what, if anything, they'd heard about the shootings. The old man's face closed up with tight finality and he shook his head back and forth as if warding off evil spirits. Paul Francois had shrugged and, while he'd heard the workers whispering among themselves, he didn't really know anything. "And it's not likely that anybody will tell me anything. After all, I am an outsider." It was a feeling that she understood all too well. She left them with fresh beers, feeling good about themselves, and stepped out into the night, almost bumping into half a dozen new arrivals. They all stepped aside to allow her to exit, and they all bid her good evening by name. She smiled greetings, bid them all a good evening, and walked out into the parking lot, grateful to have parked on the fringe.

She turned the key and gunned the Jeep's engine, not minding that it was almost too dark to see the road or that she hit one rut and bounced up so high that she hit her head on the roof. Feeling good feels good, she thought, and she liked the feeling. Liked it that Luc and Jean had called out to her as she left and waved at her. Liked it that the people around them had smiled and waved as well. Liked it that a man of Toussaint Remy's age and experience, not to mention his cultural background, respected her enough that he would accept a woman police chief based on his feelings for her. And the support of the island's Toussaint Remys certainly would make Yvette Casson's job easier. And make no mistake, the new chief had a tough job. Islands were paradise only in the tourist brochures. To prevent them from becoming complete hells, the islands needed the tourists to see paradise, to experience paradise for the seven or ten or twenty-one days of their visits. Which is why island presidents like Philippe Collette hired people like David Messinger and Yvette Casson. And Gibson, Graham International.

She squeezed the Jeep into the Aux Fruits de Mer parking lot, turned off the engine, and sat there, savoring the final, dramatic moments of the sunset. Surely this was paradise! Nothing ugly should reside here. The Caribbean rippled gently, to and fro, reflecting the fiery red of the setting sun. Gulls dove and hovered and soared and screeched, contemplating dinner, and, far out, sails flashed white and fishing boats plied the waves, continuing the ancient ritual of bargaining with the sea, just as the gulls did. And then one of the loud, ugly jet skis screamed into the portrait, spoiling it and the fantasy. Yes, there was ugliness here. It took the form of jet skis and drug dealers: the new forms of ugly. Slave traders and rum runners and pirates were the old forms.

A good portion of her good feeling drained away and she was left feeling merely drained. She wanted to eat but she didn't want the work of polite bantering or sparring with Odile Laurance or whomever else she might encounter. On the other hand, she was curious to see if Denis St. Almain was present and, if so, who would be in his company. And she was curious to see how she'd be received by Odile. She thought that Denis must have told her of his visit and she therefore would know that Carole Ann knew of her relationship to him. And that's why, she realized, Odile had warned that Philippe must never know of her association with Denis. Damn! but she was weary of the tangles and complexities of this island, and resentful of the rebuffs of her efforts to help.

"Nobody asked for your help," she reminded herself. "Nobody but you thinks there's a problem." But how could that be, she wondered, when so many signs and signals suggested otherwise? Paradise interrupted. "Maybe this isn't paradise to those who call it home, any more than Los Angeles is paradise to you." The thought stopped her cold as she conjured up the image of the thousands of Mexicans who daily risked their lives to cross the border into California. That was her home but she no more considered it paradise than . . . than residents of Isle de Paix considered their home paradise. "Go home and go to bed," she told herself, and she cranked up the Jeep and backed out onto the Coast Road for the brief drive home. An omelette and some cheese and fruit and what was left of the wine she'd opened for Denis St. Almain last night would do for dinner. And she would go to bed.

She drove slowly, paying close and careful attention to the activity on both sides of the road, for the beach side had its share of activity despite the fact that almost absolute darkness now had settled over the sea. Several small boats rode low on the gentle tide, and people waded in and out of the water, their voices floating outward but unintelligible. Cars and mopeds were tightly packed into the parking areas in front of all the stores and shops along the Coast Road, though only the eateries and bars were open. Who were these people? Tourists? Islanders? And were they all just out for a good meal, a rum punch, and romance under the stars?

As she was contemplating parking and strolling for a bit along the beach, the night quietude was punctuated by the rapid *rat-a-tat* of automatic gunfire. Yes, the sound was distant and distorted by the sea, but she did not doubt that it was gunfire. She stopped in the middle of the road, closed her eyes, and replayed the sound in her memory: *rattattattattattattat*. Seven. There were seven reports in rapid succession, followed by silence. No scream carried on the air, and certainly no siren. She jammed her foot down on the accelerator and the Jeep sprung forward with a screech of rubber. This stretch of the Coast Road was narrow, but it was straight, and she barreled up the road, heading north, directed by her sense of foreboding.

She cruised past the road construction site and slowed as the road rose and curved. Cliffs rose to greet her and the sea vanished as the lights of Deauville came into view. She slowed to a normal driving speed and coasted into the town. It was as alive as Ville de Paix and Little Haiti, though with a different, more subdued energy, and certainly with no suggestion that assault weapon fire had interrupted the night. She crept down the street. Couples strolled on the cobblestone walks and dined beneath canopies and on terraces overlooking the Atlantic. She stopped as a car backed out of one of the angled parking spaces, and she pulled in so she could turn around and head home, feeling both frustrated and a bit silly. She looked behind her, to see if the road was clear, then returned her gaze forward. And as she did, the door to the restaurant in front of her opened and Marie-Ange Collette swept out, followed by the dark, handsome man she had seen in Aux Fruits de Mer with Denis St. Almain.

Quickly and instinctively she shut off the headlights and simultaneously leaned down across the seat. Her heart was thudding and she was breathing heavily. "Holy shit," she muttered, sitting up. Marie-Ange was walking rapidly down the street, followed closely by the too smooth, too good-looking sleazeball. When they were far enough away, she threw the gear into reverse, backed out, and headed the opposite way from the direction in which Marie-Ange had gone, though she desperately wanted to follow, to assure herself that the wife of the president wouldn't do anything so foolish as to indulge an affair in public. By the time she arrived home, heart still pounding as if she'd been the one caught in a compromising situation, she'd convinced herself it wasn't her business. She took a bottle of Chablis and a bag of popcorn to bed and fell asleep to *Silverado,* her second favorite Western, wishing for an open-air gunfight instead of rapid-fire shots in the dead of night.

"The hydraulic lift is frozen." Paul Francois's tone was so mournful, so baleful that Carole Ann immediately wanted to sympathize. But she didn't know what he was talking about, and that admission didn't improve his disposition. "The damned hydraulic lift raises and lowers the platform on the damn truck!" he shouted, pointing to the dump truck, whose engine was idling as quietly as an engine in a dump truck can idle. "It's broken! And Monsieur Remy says that it *cannot* be repaired." He was almost whining now, and she was at a loss. Surely a broken hydraulic lift was relatively insignificant in the scheme of things? After all, the truck was running.

"Paul? You're going to have to tell me why you're so upset because I really don't know why."

"The damn truck runs and the damn backhoe runs but we can't get the backhoe on the truck and we can't get it to the site if we can't get it on the truck!"

"I see the problem," she said quietly, casting about in her mind for a solution, for she understood immediately that it would be virtually impossible to drive the backhoe from one end of the island to the other on the island's only paved road. It needed to be transported in something like a dump truck or . . . "Paul, if the truck can carry the backhoe, it can pull it, yes?"

"Well, of course!" he snapped. "But what does that—"

"Build a platform with wheels and a ramp."

"You're almost as brilliant as Remy! But it'll take all day. That thing weighs a ton and the truck's top speed is about ten miles an hour."

She thought for a moment. "Do it on Sunday. Start early in the morning. Unless you were planning on going to church, that is."

"When does the police chief arrive?"

"Monday. When will the car be ready?"

"Sunday," he shot back with a little smirk. "I shall deliver it my-self to the front door of police headquarters. *After* I've delivered the backhoe to the construction site. And by the way, there's only the one vehicle, yes? What will the other police use for transportation?"

"Bicycles," she said with a grin, enjoying having the last word.

The president was beaming again, and so congratulatory that she begged him to stop. She was, she insisted, merely doing her job. "We both know that your efforts have been above and beyond the call of duty, Carole Ann, and I'm grateful. You're even forgiven for bullying and intimidating me! And judging from the change in him, I'd say that Roland had a similar response to your, ah, persuasive tactics." He smirked a bit and Carole Ann grew wary.

"I'm not certain what you mean, sir."

"Ha!" The word exploded from his mouth and she realized that it was amusement that fueled it. "You should see Roland. He hasn't worn a suit since, what day was that? Wednesday? He wears guayaberas and sandals now, and spends most of the day 'out in the field,' as he says. He's conducting a survey of all the roads on the is-land—ruts, he calls them—and he's assessing beach erosion. He's drafting plans for training programs in several areas, inspired by your example with the mechanics."

"That was Roland's idea."

"Ha!" The explosion was louder this time. "Let us save the cha-rades for others, eh? Between us, Carole Ann, only the truth, eh, *bien?* Though I admire your motivation. Now. On to a matter of purely social consequences: Marie-Ange would be delighted if you'd join us for dinner tomorrow evening. You'll find that Friday and Saturday nights on the island are social, and not always stuffy and formal, as you will see. I think you'll enjoy yourself, and we'd certainly appreci-ate your company. After all, you're the talk of the town! And if the president can't produce the object of everyone's interest, then what good is he, eh?"

"I'd be delighted," Carole Ann responded in what she hoped was a tone devoid of relief and gratitude.

" I don't know what you're so happy about" was Jake's response. "You can't pump and grill the woman in her own home at her own party."

"I've no intention of pumping or grilling her, Jake, no matter what the venue," Carole Ann said sourly. "I merely want to talk to her."

"You're a lawyer, C.A., and lawyers never merely talk to people, you pump and grill. And besides," he growled nastily, "she owes you an explanation."

"She owes me nothing! She's a grown woman with a life of her own."

"Goddammit, she's the wife of the president, for Jesus Christ's sake, and she's got no damn business out in public with some fucking sleazebag!"

"We don't know he's a sleazebag, Jake."

"We know he wasn't her husband, goddammit!"

"Yes, we do know that much," she sighed, and brought him up to date on everything else, intentionally saving for last the details of Denis St. Almain's visit, hoping that he'd still be too pissed off about Marie-Ange to have the energy to light into her. But when he was eerily silent, she grew worried. She waited several moments for him to respond and when he did not, she wondered whether they had been disconnected.

"I'm still here," he replied in a strangely weary tone of voice. "Though I really do wonder how long you will be, C.A."

"Jake, I . . ." But she didn't finish because she didn't know what to say.

"I used to think that you went looking for trouble, C.A., but I don't think that anymore. I think trouble looks for you, but because you're who you are, you don't even think about trying to hide from it. You just rush to meet it head on, and that scares me."

She started to speak but he cut her off. "Look. It's Friday. You've got Marie-Ange's shindig tomorrow night, and I know the devil himself couldn't keep you away from the backhoe ride on Sunday. But aside from that, C.A., will you just lay back and take it easy? Please? Go lay on the beach, drink too much rum punch, watch movies, eat popcorn. Stay out of harm's way until Monday, then let Messinger and Casson handle things."

"Dammit, Jake, you think cops are the answer to every problem!"

"To the kinds of problems that find you, C.A.? Damn straight!"

"Cops wouldn't have stopped Denis St. Almain from breaking in the other night, Jake!"

"Yes, they would," he snapped, the steel in his voice a little frightening, "because they'd have had a tail on his sorry ass from the moment you saw him step out of those woods."

"Why are you so intent on believing the worst about the man, Jake? You have no cause."

"I've got every cause! He's either a drug dealer or he had a career masquerading as a drug dealer, either of which puts him in the company of some nasty sons of bitches, the kind who play with AK-47s. And we don't know that he's not a murderer but we do know that he's desperate to clear his name and save his ass from prison. That makes him dangerous, C.A. Dangerous enough to break into your house in the middle of the night to rummage through your office."

There was nothing left to say, so she changed the subject. She asked him for a status report on the shipment of police uniforms and guns and bicycles and he told her to expect the boat on Tuesday. Then she reminded him that the telephone lines in police headquarters still were not connected and he promised to correct that problem immediately. She spent the remainder of the day writing up a report of her first week's activities on Isle de Paix. She faxed one to Jake and delivered a copy to Philippe Collette's office. Then she went home and got a head start on the part of Jake's program that involved rum punch.

* * *

The Collettes' dinner party indeed was a relaxed affair, if elegant in the extreme, the two concepts not at all at odds with each other under Marie-Ange's ministrations. The crowd was smaller than Carole Ann would have expected—perhaps two dozen people in all—including the finance and tourism ministers and their spouses; the Collettes' eldest son, who was the island's only physician; several members of the yacht club; three French movie stars, who, judging by the way they were fawned over, must have been the equivalents of Robert De Niro, Susan Sarandon, and Denzel Washington; and house guests of the Collettes from New York and Paris. Marie-Ange was breathtaking in coral satin, a color that accentuated her deep copper skin; she was relaxed, at ease, and gracious, and every bit the wife of the president.

The food was extraordinary. Everything was grilled, though differently and unlike anything Carole Ann had ever experienced: the lobster was spicy, the fish sweet, the chicken fiery hot, the shrimp pungent, and the steak like melted butter. The panoply of island fruit was presented in its natural state—fresh and chilled—and as ice cream, sorbet, and juice. The seafoods, in addition to being grilled, were presented in a variety of salads and in sushi. And Marie-Ange seemed to be everywhere at once, like the spices in the food, a welcome ingredient in every conversation, never lingering too long, never dominating, always welcome. Carole Ann observed her discreetly. Her smile was genuine, as was her evident enjoyment and appreciation of her guests, and the feeling was mutual. Carole Ann had attended enough social affairs to recognize false smiles pasted onto yawns of boredom or grimaces of disdain. The affection and mutual appreciation evident between Marie-Ange and her guests were genuine. So was that between husband and wife.

Carole Ann, who found herself easily and comfortably engaged in conversation as she moved about, realized with no small degree of surprise why: they were intelligent, charming, gracious people, and good conversationalists. Despite their wealth and social status. In a rare acknowledgment of her own wealth, she chided herself for falling prey to the stereotype that wealthy socialites all were shallow and boring; and to demonstrate her own charm and grace, she engaged in a spirited dialogue with both the ministers, never once talking shop; and when the actors learned that she spoke fluent French, they pummeled her with questions about American film, and were so excited to find that she was a film buff, they commanded her attention until Marie-Ange shooed them away, rescuing her.

"They are irrepressible, yes? But delightful, I think, though you may rather discuss matters of government and policy."

"They're wonderful, Marie-Ange, as are all your guests, and I'd always rather discuss *anything* than matters of government and policy. I'd also rather dine at your table than any other place in the world. The food is art."

"You are very kind, Carole Ann, and I'm honored that you could take the time to join us."

Carole Ann, pleased that Marie-Ange had taken her arm and led her away from the crowd, now steered them even deeper into a quiet corner of the garden. Her effort to have a few moments alone with her hostess was aided by the fact that most of the guests now were dancing. A live, seven-piece orchestra, enhanced by steel drums, managed classic jazz, reggae, ragtime, and Broadway show tunes with equal aplomb, and it seemed that everyone decided at the same moment to dance off dinner.

"As wonderful as the evening is, I came specifically to see you. I've wanted to make time since I arrived—"

Marie-Ange interrupted with a bark of laughter that almost was a guffaw. "How like Philippe you are, Carole Ann! You've been here just a week and you've worked nonstop in that time, and you chide yourself for having no time to socialize. I don't expect that, as much as I would enjoy the chance to spend time with you."

"Then we'll make the time," Carole Ann said. "But what I wanted to say to you, Marie-Ange . . . what I want is to apologize for having to stop the work on the clinic. I know how important health and education issues are to you, and I assure you that on a personal level, I share them."

"Ah, but it is the business aspect, the financial aspect, that always assumes the importance, no?"

Carole Ann shook her head. "Too often, perhaps, but not always. And in the case of Isle de Paix, Marie-Ange, the issue really and truly is one of security."

"Yes, yes, yes. Philippe told me of your . . . your rules. Do you really believe that such extremes are necessary?"

"They are not extreme in the least, Marie-Ange, and yet extremely necessary. Please don't believe for a second that the murder of those two constables was random or accidental."

"What do you mean?"

"The assassins, and I believe there were two of them, boarded your craft specifically, and the constables stopped them—" The woman's reaction stopped Carole Ann. She gasped, horrified, and gripped Carole Ann's arm. "You didn't know that, Marie-Ange? Philippe didn't tell you?"

She shook her head, her whispered response all but inaudible, and tears glistened in her eyes. She produced a linen handkerchief and turned her back to the party long enough to restore her equilibrium. Carole Ann admired the strength and control required for such an effort, whatever the motivation—to preserve her image as a woman of grace and elegance, or to maintain the dignity of the president of a country, or, as her own mother would have it, to keep one's personal emotions personal.

"I'm truly sorry to have upset you, Marie-Ange. Please forgive me and let us talk of something less disturbing. At least I hope it will be less disturbing. Will you tell me about the health issues here that concern you, and about your son's work?" And she listened as Marie-Ange spoke passionately and nonstop for several minutes about rickets and scurvy and measles and chicken pox and whooping cough and polio, about premature births and low birth rates and infant mortality. Then Carole Ann talked for a while, with equal passion, giving voice to several thoughts and ideas that had occupied a corner of her consciousness for several days. And when she was finished, tears again glistened in Marie-Ange's eyes and this time she did not wipe them away. She embraced Carole Ann and whispered her thanks.

"Maurice will be so delighted, Carole Ann, and so relieved and so grateful. Words of thanks really are inadequate."

"They're more than enough, Marie-Ange, but if you would keep this between us . . ."

"Oh, but I must tell Philippe! I could never keep such a secret from him."

Carole Ann nodded. "Of course. I don't expect you to keep secrets from your husband," and she was startled to see embarrassment rise in the other woman's face. She quickly changed the subject. "I meant only that this is a matter for you and your family."

"Will you speak with Maurice now, Carole Ann?" Marie-Ange clapped her hands together in a child's excitement. "This is an imposition, I know, to ask such a thing during a party, but it would mean so much to him. And to me."

Carole Ann followed Marie-Ange through the garden and back into the house. The party was in full swing, inside and out. Maurice and his father were the animated center of an equally animated group holding court near one of the bars; but when Maurice spied his mother, he excused himself and walked quickly toward her. She embraced him and reintroduced Carole Ann and launched into a recitation of Carole Ann's interest in the Isle de Paix hospital. Maurice stopped her with a gentle hand to her shoulder.

"Madame Gibson and I will talk. You should see to Andre."

Marie-Ange blanched. "Andre?"

"He's upstairs," her son replied in an expressionless tone that was heavy with meaning. As Marie-Angie hurried away, Maurice led Carole Ann to a quiet corner where she repeated for him what she'd said moments ago to his mother. He was as effusive in his appreciation of her proposed largesse as was his mother, but Carole Ann was too distracted to be gracious. Marie-Ange had been surprised, annoyed, and frightened at Maurice's direction that she should "see to Andre." And, Carole Ann realized, his words had indeed been direction: Marie-Ange had had no option but to respond. Carole Ann excused herself with the promise to meet with Maurice at the clinic the following week, and went in search of Marie-Ange.

As she genuinely was tired, she covered her search for Marie-Ange by saying good-night to the company, beginning with Philippe and working her way through the ministers and the actors and, along the way, asking if anyone knew where their hostess was. But no one had seen Marie-Ange recently, which worried Carole Ann. A hostess with Marie-Ange Collette's concern for propriety did not—would not— disappear from her own party. She had worked her way through the house and the patio without a sign of Marie-Ange. She contemplated sharing her concerns with Philippe when movement in the far corner of the garden caught her eye. She stepped off the slate patio into the lush grass and strolled toward what she saw were a man and a woman. She halted when she recognized the woman as Marie-Ange and the man as a stranger. The tenseness of their conversation, even at a distance, was evident.

Marie-Ange took a step back from the man and covered her mouth with her hand, and Carole Ann moved quickly toward them, taking them by surprise. Marie-Ange struggled to recover her composure. The man merely stared at Carole Ann, his gaze demanding her departure. She ignored him. "Are you ill, Marie-Ange?"

"No, Carole Ann." Marie-Ange shook her head and produced a passable smile. "I'm quite all right, thank you."

"Forgive me for disturbing you, but I wanted to thank you for a wonderful evening."

"You're leaving so early?"

"Your husband is an exact taskmaster," she said almost idly, and so was gratified to catch Marie-Ange's companion completely off-guard when she whipped around to him. "Are you associated with the government, monsieur?" she asked.

He was a very pale man, with light blond hair and light blue eyes, so the flush that rose in his face was visible, even in the darkness of the garden. His jaw tightened, but he did not respond. He glared at Carole Ann and she laughed at him, intensifying the flush.

"This is Christian Leonard, Carole Ann. He is the director of the bank." Marie-Ange had recovered her composure.

"Not, I trust, the bank with which the government does business." Carole Ann held Christian Leonard's glare and watched it turn into something like hatred, certain that he understood the threat carried by her words. He turned on his heel and stalked away. As Carole Ann watched him depart, her concern for Marie-Ange increased. "A very unpleasant man," she said.

"Oui," replied Marie-Ange. *"C'est-ça."*

One thing that Carole Ann didn't do gracefully was handle glitches, roll with the punches. Especially when the glitch was the result of a well-crafted plan gone awry. Monday morning, which should have witnessed the arrival of Minister of Internal Security David Messinger and Director of Island Security Yvette Casson, instead brought ten new police recruits on the same boat from San Juan that contained their equipment, both cops and equipment a day early. When it became clear that airline scheduling problems would delay Casson and Messinger until much later that evening, Carole Ann assumed responsibility for the recruits, not failing to take notice of the fact that a boat kept a better schedule and arrived faster than a plane.

She found the young officers pleasant and excited about their new jobs: eight men and two women, all of them American-born children of native Caribbean islanders, half of them married, all of them veterans of police work. David Messinger and Yvette Casson had hired them all, but Jake, through GGI, had run all their background checks, as well as those on both Casson and Messinger. She asked their names and told them who she was and what her role was. And then, because she couldn't think of anything else to do, she walked them up the hill from the cafe to their headquarters, and they all participated in the unloading of their equipment with the excitement of children on Christmas morning. Since the bicycles were all the same, she assigned a bike to each recruit, matching names and serial numbers. And she parceled out their uniforms, hats, belts, and shoes, withholding guns, badges, handcuffs, name tags, and sticks for their boss to distribute. These items she locked inside the jail cells. Then she turned her attention to figuring out how to get the ten of them to their new residences, for they were scattered throughout the island. Then she remembered: the cruiser. And if Roland Charles would make available the pickup truck . . .

Not only was the interior minister willing to help transport the recruits and their bicycles to their new homes, he spent the afternoon showing them around the island via truck, car, and speedboat, and then brought them back to Government House for a tour of the square, an introduction to President Collette, and an elegant buffet supper, his compliments, on the terrace of Government House overlooking the harbor. "I am truly pleased to meet these officers, Carole Ann, and I can honestly say that I am comforted by their presence."

Carole Ann stole a quick glance at Roland, surprised at the fervor in his voice, then turned her attention to the recruits. Yes, she thought, they most definitely were cops. Even in a social setting, in casual attire, watching the sun set over the Caribbean Sea, there was about them an awareness, an alertness, an edginess. They reminded her of Tommy Griffin and Paolo Petrocelli and Jake Graham himself, the cops she knew best and loved as friends but whom she did not, in some fundamental way, truly understand. "I think we can all feel comforted, Roland." And in a curious way, she meant that. She believed that each of the new officers would take seriously the obligation to protect the island and its inhabitants and visitors. She knew that in the "real" world, police presence suggested stability. She also knew, from personal experience, that no amount of police presence ever deterred those determined to violate the law. And there was little comfort in that.

She strolled out onto the terrace and the conversation ceased as all eyes focused on her. If these were cops she knew well, she'd raise her hands and assume the position, but she was afraid, in this case, that the joke would not amuse. "I know that you all must be totally exhausted, so what I'm going to say is definitely *not* an order and definitely *is* for informational purposes only: I'm leaving in an hour for the airstrip to pick up the minister and the director. Anyone who wants to accompany me is welcome to do so, and anyone who wants to go home and go to bed is welcome to do that."

David Messinger and Yvette Casson stepped off the inter-island jet to be met by ten Isle de Paix officers in uniform, standing at attention. Carole Ann left the dozen of them two hours later, comfortably ensconced in their office, eating pizza and drinking beer and telling dumb-perp stories.

"Cops," she muttered, gently closing the door and walking around to the rear of the building where her Jeep was parked. It was late and it was dark, the only light cast on the street coming from the Bureau of Island Security office and the only vehicle parked on the front street the police cruiser. It was, she admitted to herself, a comforting sight.

And it remained comforting during subsequent days to see the officers patrolling on their bicycles as she walked to Government House or jogged in the mornings or drove up the Coast Road to monitor the progress of the road excavation; to see them at Armand's or Aux Fruits de Mer after hours; to see them walking up and down the beaches, up and down the harbor front. Since she spent practically no time in Deauville or anywhere else on the north coast, she could only speculate that the officers' presence was as well received on that end of the island, though she had gathered, from overheard snatches of conversation at the road construction site, that the cops had not been so well received in Little Haiti; in fact, there had been a hostile exchange between one of the cops and several young toughs, who, like young toughs everywhere, resented their presence. Then, Toussaint Remy had invited Yvette Casson to dinner. And she had gone, driving the cruiser, and had told everybody who would listen how the old man had repaired the car just for her. And as she was leaving, she told those still gathered outside the old man's house that he made the best pigeon peas and rice she'd ever eaten, and marveled at the fact that the women of the town allowed him to remain unmarried. By the next evening, according to the vine report, the toughs were tame as house cats.

"Nothing but good news for a change, Jake. The telephone lines function most of the time and the computer program is magnificent; please tell Patty, would you? In fact everything works, including the jail." He relished the story she told of the drunk-and-disorderly arrest that had christened the new jail the previous night. "Yvette said he hadn't thrown up on the floor—seems he was able to make it to the toilet. And because he ended up sleeping on the floor beside the toilet, the sheets weren't slept on and therefore didn't need washing."

"Hell, I'd better get down there soon, so I can see for myself a jail cell floor clean enough to sleep on, not to mention a drunk courteous enough to spare the floor *and* the sheets! Ah, the joys of policing paradise."

She returned him to the real world with a jolt. "Do you have any information for me on Christian Leonard, Jake?"

"Patty's working on it. Whoever he is, he's somebody, and he's got more than three sentences in his file."

Carole Ann was intrigued, but she moved on. "What's the latest on the paving material contract?" They had been searching for an acceptable source for sand, cement, gravel, and asphalt, and for a reasonable and affordable way to get it to Isle de Paix. They'd so far done very well purchasing and shipping out of South Carolina's ports but, Jake said, everybody everywhere wanted an arm and a leg for shipping road-paving materials.

"You're not ready to pave anything yet, are you?"

"Not even close," she replied, "but I've been working with Roland Charles to identify suitable sites on both ends of the island for material storage facilities, and he asked how much time he had before he needed to start worrying about it."

"He can rest easy for the next two or three weeks. And why does he want to store that stuff inside anyway? Why can't it just sit on a barge somewhere until it's needed?"

"Because hurricanes tend to blow things away."

"Oh. Yeah. Hurricanes. I keep forgetting about them."

"You wouldn't forget about them if you lived here for more than a week. It's amazing how quickly that reality becomes part of your over-all approach to life and living. I find myself not thinking in terms of how much longer I'm contracted to be here, but in terms of how much longer until it starts to rain every day. Then, there's the game people play with how many good days we could expect to have in August, be-cause nobody is willing to concede the entire month to bad weather."

"But you're outta there the first of August, right?" He feigned calm but she could hear the edge of panic in his voice.

"Definitely," she responded. "But I think I'd be OK and be able to get more work done if I needed to stay a couple of weeks longer."

"Well, let's cross that bridge when we get to it. Are you still going to visit your buddy Jennings?" His artful change of subject im-pressed her; she must be rubbing off on him.

"I am. Flying out Friday morning and back on Monday morning." Arthur Jennings was a new friend of hers but someone her mother had known for more than forty years. He was a contractor and devel-oper who had constructed the experimental community where Carole Ann had grown up in Los Angeles, but he had retired many years ear-lier and had moved to the island of Anguilla. She had met him the previous year during her investigation of a crime wave that endan-gered her mother, and they had become friends. When the Isle de Paix contract was finalized, she had called and promised the old man a visit.

"Why are you flying? That's too expensive. Why can't you take a boat?"

"Because the boat takes too long, Jake. The vacation is to be spent with Arthur Jennings, not getting to him. Besides, I'm using my own money. I'm not billing the company," she said with a sniff.

"Oh, lighten up, C.A. What's the phone number there?"

"What's the phone number where? . . . Oh, no, you don't! I don't need you calling me every day to make sure I'm all right."

"You can give me the number or I can find the number."

She gave him the number and hung up on him. He really was a pain in the ass sometimes. *All* cops were pains in the ass, including the ones she'd just met and didn't even know very well. Yvette Casson proved the point when she, too, requested the number in Anguilla where Carole Ann could be reached.

"I'm really sorry to disturb you, but I thought you'd want to know now instead of returning to it." The police chief's slightly accented voice was low, clear, and calm, but Carole Ann could hear the underlying tension and, within it, the struggle for control.

"What is it, Yvette? All of it, quickly." It was eight o'clock on a Sunday morning and she was on a holiday. Quickly was the best way to hear whatever the new chief had to say.

"The construction equipment on the new government road was destroyed. Sabotaged. Burned. And Carole Ann . . . there's a body. It may be Paul Francois."

She closed her eyes and gripped the phone. "When?"

"We got the call just after three this morning, and it was almost four before we could assemble a fire brigade. You know there's no firefighting equipment on the island—"

"About the body, Yvette—"

"Burned beyond recognition."

"I'll be there as soon as I can."

"I'm sorry, Carole Ann."

"What for? You didn't sabotage the damn site."

Fire damage, Carole Ann thought wonderingly, fueled a mixture of anger and despair. Certainly fire consumed and destroyed, but all too often it did not eradicate, but left stark reminders of what once was and, therefore, of what could have been. That is what she thought and felt as she pulled the Jeep past the devastation and parked it. She stepped out and immediately her eyes and throat began to burn. She ignored the pain and walked quickly back to what, forty-eight hours earlier, had been a fresh-cut entrance to the new government road and stood staring at the charred, smoking hulks of the backhoe and the bulldozer and the dump truck.

The backhoe resembled a creature from an old Japanese horror movie—something scary and threatening but decidedly unreal. The bulldozer was a wounded animal gone to ground, something immense and powerful, like a rhinoceros, suddenly rendered impotent but which the mind resisted thinking of as dead: nothing so massive could die so suddenly. The dump truck just seemed sad and pathetic—a big and no longer useful thing. And what had been a promising new road into a promising new future now was a riverbed of mud and ash. Her feet in their thin-strapped sandals sank into the mire and she felt herself sucked slightly downward. The trees were scorched twenty feet into the air, and the underbrush was burned away for several yards in all directions.

She looked around at the crowd that had gathered, some of whom obviously had been there for several hours and most of whom obviously had fought the fire: their faces and arms and clothes were wet and sooty, exhaustion etched in their faces. She was looking, she knew, for the faces of Paul Francois, of Toussaint Remy, of the mechanics Luc and Jean. She was looking for some assurance that the body that had been burned beyond recognition was not one of theirs. That meant, she knew, that she wished horrible death upon a stranger. But so be it. She was scanning the faces in the crowd, disbelieving eyes staring back at her, when her name was called from the opposite direction. She turned to see Luc, his face soot-covered and tear-streaked, crossing the road toward her. He was still weeping. She pried her feet out of the mud and met him in the middle of the road. He tried to speak but no intelligible words came. She wouldn't have understood them anyway, but she would have welcomed them. Instead he began coughing and she could almost see the acrid smoke in his chest. He raised a helpless hand and she took it between her own and squeezed and he winced. She looked down at the blisters and the seared skin and shuddered. Then she released him and sought out Yvette Casson.

Even if there had been vehicular traffic on the Coast Road on this

Sunday, it could not have gotten through; nothing could have moved the throng that stood staring in horrified fascination at the smoldering equipment. But the crowd parted to let her through, and then closed itself behind her. She spied the police chief, in full uniform, deep in conversation with Roland Charles and David Messinger. Carole Ann took a deep breath and, resigned to the destruction of her shoes, waded through the muddy ash underfoot toward them. But when she reached them, she found herself speechless. Helpless.

"We don't know for sure if it's Francois," Messinger said when he realized that she would not speak first.

"Has anybody been ruled out?" she asked. "Remy . . ."

Yvette Casson shook her head back and forth. "Definitely not Remy. He was here all night. I had somebody take him home and stay with him. He burned his hands trying to salvage the . . . the . . . I've been thinking of it as a dinosaur . . ."

"Backhoe," Carole Ann said dully. "It's a backhoe. It *was* a backhoe. Toussaint Remy brought it back to life."

David Messinger cleared his throat and Carole Ann looked up at him; he was a tall, thin man with a head full of still mostly brown hair. He clenched an empty pipe between his teeth and managed to talk around it, as pipe smokers somehow did. "All the officers are out canvassing. Maybe somebody saw somebody on the road, heard something . . ."

"And what if they did?" Carole Ann asked, her tone of voice as dull as her spirit. "What good would it do at this point?" She wanted to scream. For the first time in her adult life she didn't care about right or wrong or any component of justice. It didn't matter if somebody could be charged with the crime of destroying the backhoe and the dump truck or with the death—the murder—of whoever it was who was burned beyond recognition. The only thing that mattered was that the road would not be finished on time. And the fact that whoever was dead was probably somebody she knew and liked.

David Messinger interrupted her thoughts. "I asked who knew that you would be away for the weekend and that the crew would be working?"

She considered the question: quite a few people had known of her plans to leave the island for the weekend. It had not been a secret. "What do you mean the crew worked this weekend? Who worked? Doing what?" Something cold slithered down her spine and she shivered in the heat. The three of them stared at her. Their looks were briefly accusing, then disbelieving, before finally settling on confused; and all three wore the same expression, as if programmed by some diabolical computermeister. David Messinger and Yvette Casson began speaking simultaneously but Roland Charles, in an uncharacteristically raised voice, overrode them both.

"Do you mean to say that you didn't order the men to work on the road Saturday and Sunday? They were not working under your orders?"

"Certainly not," Carole Ann snapped. "There was no need for that." Nor was there a need for her anger or even for remorse or regret. No emotional reaction could alter the reality of the scene before her. Every sense was bombarded with the awfulness of the truth. "I assume that Philippe knows?"

Once again, they all responded as if directed. All three nodded assent and their shoulders sagged, as if suddenly weighted down with the burdens of the president. But it was David Messinger who spoke. "You only just missed him. He was out here fighting the fire along with every other able-bodied person who cared enough to get out of bed to come see what the trouble was. He was sweating and cursing and crying just like every other islander who was watching the flames kill their dreams."

Roland Charles squared his shoulders and sucked in his protuberant belly and Carole Ann noticed that he was wearing jeans and a T-shirt and sneakers. She wouldn't have thought that he owned such casual attire. But, as usual, there was nothing casual or informal about his demeanor. "The flames have killed nothing, monsieur," he retorted stiffly. "This is a tragic accident that will result in nothing more than a temporary setback. These men do not yet know how to use such sophisticated equipment, so we must teach them, in order to prevent further mishaps. And, of course, we must impose a punishment for the unauthorized use of government equipment."

"Accident?" Carole Ann's eyes bored into Yvette Casson. "I thought you told me—"

David Messinger put a hand on her arm. "Philippe is waiting for us back at Government House. I'll ride with you, if you don't mind, so Yvette doesn't have to take me." Then he turned to Roland Charles and touched his arm, too. "I know how upsetting this must be to you. My people will give you every assistance, beginning with keeping the onlookers out of your way." And as he spoke, he dipped his head toward the milling crowd that now was within touching distance of the backhoe. Yvette scurried away. Roland Charles thanked David Messinger and shook his hand and the security minister loped off down the road toward Carole Ann's Jeep. She followed, her shoes squishing with every step, wondering why the cops wanted the interior minister to think that the destruction of his equipment had been an accident. And she wondered about a few other things as well, like what the hell Paul Francois was doing digging on the road on a Saturday!

"Your place or mine?" David Messinger said once the Jeep was turned around and Carole Ann had managed to inch her way through the still milling crowd on the Coast Road.

Carole Ann was driving slowly enough that she could turn her attention away from the road and toward her passenger and she gave him "the look," the one that successfully unnerved most average human beings, Jake Graham being the notable exception. David Messinger had been a cop for a long time in one of America's toughest cities, but he blanched, even if only slightly. "Philippe's not expecting us." It was not a question.

He shook his head. "I wanted to get you away from Charles before you spilled the beans. And why don't we make it your place, since you obviously need to change your shoes."

She clenched her teeth and swallowed the angry retort that had started out of her mouth. Jake had specifically asked her to be nice to the new minister and police chief. New! She had to remind herself that Messinger and Casson had been on the island less than a week, and already were confronted with at least two major crimes that strongly were resembling class-one felonies. "Why don't you want Roland to know this wasn't an accident?" she asked, and hoped that she sounded considerably more conciliatory than she felt.

"I don't want anyone to know," he replied quickly. "Not even Philippe. Not yet. This island is too small to have people walking around talking about arson and murder."

She downshifted and turned her head toward him. "Are you sure that's what it is?"

"I'm sure," he answered and, after offering the caveat that he was no expert fire investigator, he proceeded to offer a very expert-sounding assessment of burn patterns on trees and grass, and of the properties of different kinds of accelerants, and meltdown. "Can you park behind your house?" he asked as they reached the Coast Road split. "I'd just as soon you not advertise your presence."

"Dammit, David, the whole island knows I'm back," she snarled.

"And they all think you've gone to a meeting with Philippe. And if they don't see the Jeep at Government House, they'll think you're at his home, and if they don't see the Jeep at his home, they'll think you're at Government House."

Without further response she turned the Jeep into the narrow lane that led to the rear of the house she called home. She had been back here only once, just to see where it was and how it was accessed, as part of her security check with Harold Collins. The density of the foliage would prevent the vehicle from being readily noticed—reason enough for her to park here instead of on the street, Harold had argued. She had ignored him and his advice and, as she hoisted her carryall out of the backseat and followed David Messinger up the path, past the lap pool, and into the courtyard, she knew that she'd park here from now on.

She stepped out of the muddy sandals on the porch and unlocked the door, entering first and disarming the security pad. She told Messinger to make himself at home and she left him in the kitchen and padded barefoot down the hall, first to her bedroom, where she dumped her carryall in the closet and slipped her feet into a pair of loafers, and then into the office, where she placed a call to Jake. He wasn't at the office and she sighed in relief at the sound of Grace Graham's voice on the home answering machine asking callers to leave a message. She did, saying she'd call later. She knew he'd cuss at her for not calling him on his cellular phone, but she didn't have enough energy to talk to Jake at the moment. She also didn't have enough information.

"I took you at your word," David Messinger said when she returned to the kitchen. He had found bacon and eggs and bread and butter and cheese in the refrigerator. The bacon was sizzling in a frying pan and he was measuring coffee into a filter. "I've been up since three and I'm starving."

"Of course," Carole Ann said, sounding as genuinely apologetic as she felt. "If you'd like to shower while I finish in here . . ."

The tired grin on his face was his answer. She directed him to one of the guest bedrooms and told him where to find soap and towels and the stash of clothes that she assumed once belonged to Henri LeRoi. Then she busied herself preparing a breakfast that she realized her stomach would welcome, too.

She was on her second cup of coffee when Messinger reappeared, clad in a khaki shirt and slacks that seemed to fit him perfectly. They ate in silence, devouring everything. Messinger helped himself to fruit and, while he was peeling a mango, filled her in on the events of early that morning, beginning with the call to the police station that was logged in at seven minutes past three in the morning.

"But here's the thing that's really bothering me in all this," he said, peeling a second mango.

"You mean arson and murder don't really bother you," she said sarcastically.

"Jake said you were funny, but that I shouldn't encourage you by laughing," he said, not laughing and cutting a piece of the mango and popping it into his mouth. "Here's the thing," he said when he finished chewing. "Old man Remy said that Francois made them bring all the equipment back to the main road when they got finished on Saturday. Normally, he said, they leave the 'hoe and 'dozer inside and drive the truck out, just so they don't have to walk out, and then back in the next day. But on Saturday, Francois *insisted* that they bring everything out."

Carole Ann watched him, waiting.

He watched her, waiting.

"Well?" he asked, after a long moment.

"Well what?" she demanded.

"Was Francois the kind of man who did illogical things?"

"Don't speak of him in the past tense. Maybe it wasn't him."

"It was him," Messinger replied, showing a flash of irritation. "I'm sorry, but it was him. Now, was he?"

"No, he wasn't."

"So, if he insisted on moving that equipment back to the road, it means that either he set it up to be sabotaged—"

"I don't believe that," Carole Ann replied coldly. "And I trust you have a good reason for making such an accusation?"

". . . *or*," Messinger continued, with exaggerated emphasis on the word, implicitly excusing her interruption, "there was something down that road that made him nervous. There was a reason that he didn't trust leaving the equipment in the forest."

They sat looking at each other for a moment; then they sat not looking at each other for a longer moment while each pondered the possibilities inherent in that bit of speculation. Carole Ann also was wondering not only how to tell Jake what had happened, but what to tell him, and when. She could not, she knew, just tell him that somebody destroyed the construction equipment and killed the construction foreman in the process. Yet, in truth, that was all she knew, all she could tell him. It wasn't nearly enough. Of course, she could report that the law enforcement system that he had developed was working quite efficiently, given such an extraordinary early test.

"Where are your cops?"

He looked at her through narrowed eyes, then looked at his watch, then told her where each of the ten cops was at that moment. She stood up, walked around the counter to where he was straddling the stool, and looked down at his feet. He was wearing slippers. "Were those the only shoes you could find?"

"Why?"

"Because I want to see what's down the new road and if whatever it is requires that we haul ass outta there, you won't get very far in those cute little slippers."

He stood up abruptly, causing the stool to slide and teeter before righting itself, and muttered something under his breath. "Do you have a weapon?" he demanded.

"Do I . . . what?" she sputtered.

"A gun!" he snapped. "Do you have one? Do you know how to use one?"

"Why?" she shot back at him.

"Because," he replied with a wintry grin that resembled something borrowed from a Halloween skeleton, "nothing makes me haul ass outta nowhere except an asshole with a gun. And if there's an asshole with a gun down the new road, there oughta be two mean sons of bitches with guns ready to give him something to run from. If you get my drift."

Carole Ann looked at him evilly from beneath hooded eyelids. "I hate cops," she muttered, striding from the kitchen down the hallway to the office, where she'd locked her gun in the desk drawer. The sound of his laughter pursued her. No wonder Jake liked him. They were just alike. Cops! She cursed them while she changed clothes, necessitated by the fact that the damn gun—which she hated any-way—wouldn't fit in the pocket or in the waistband of the slacks she wore. It did fit nicely, however, in the deep pocket of the navy cargo pants that she tucked into the tops of her leather work boots, which she carefully and tightly laced. If hauling ass indeed were to be part of her afternoon, she'd just as soon be comfortable. She pulled a Braves baseball cap snugly down on her head, grabbed her sunglasses and keys, and hurried down the hall to the kitchen.

She stopped short at the sight that greeted her there: David Messinger in full combat attire. Her mouth fell open.

"You really didn't know this stuff was here, did you?" he asked, incredulity creeping into his voice. "How could you live in a house and not explore its contents?"

"Snooping is not exploring," she said coldly. "I'm a guest here,

David; this isn't *my* house. I looked around when I arrived, and I knew there were clothes and other personal items scattered about in closets and drawers, but I didn't look in every drawer or check in every closet." She felt defensive and didn't like the feeling. She also didn't like knowing that, apparently, there was a full store of military apparel somewhere in the house. "Besides," she said, regaining her composure, "you look a trifle overdressed. After all, we're just going for a stroll down a dirt road, not to overthrow a government."

The charred hulks stood sadly alone when they arrived back at the construction site, the bright sun high overhead in the cloudless blue sky seeming to mock the burned-out patch of ugliness in the forest paradise. The birds and forest creatures had resumed their singing and chattering, and the sea breeze had blown away the acrid scent of smoke and molten rubber. Carole Ann pulled the Jeep off the road and into the brush just north of the site, so that it was not visible from the road. The foliage was dense enough that she didn't have to drive in very far, and she was grateful for that; she'd been struggling since they left with the very idea of driving or hiking into an unknown forest. The last time she'd done such a thing, it was dark and frigid and her mission had been to rescue the kidnapped wife of Jake Graham. She'd been terrified then. She was somewhat less than terrified now, feeling more anger and sadness at the potential long-term implications of the current mission. She locked the truck and pocketed the keys and they walked back down the road, sticking closer to the forest than to the road in an unspoken agreement that it would be better if they were not observed.

The mud at the site entrance was three or four inches deep and beginning to harden in the sun, and the area was a gash, an open, ugly wound, and no longer the clean beginning of something new and potentially wonderful. Carole Ann inhaled deeply and followed David Messinger through the mire and into the forest. Several yards in, the road became a smooth swath; the fire had been halted at this point and there was no mud, no ash, no scorched foliage. It was dark and cool within the forest, and silent; because they were traversing the hard pack of a new cut, Carole Ann and David made no sound as they moved forward. He moved quickly but cautiously, looking around, stopping and listening, moving forward rapidly again, before stopping again and listening and peering into the woods on either side. Carole Ann followed his lead, emulated his caution, and marveled at both the amount and the quality of work the dedicated crew had accomplished in so short a time. "We would have finished before the bad weather," she thought, and the anger and sadness welled up and threatened to spill over.

She slowed her pace, keeping Messinger in sight but falling behind. She was wondering how this project could be salvaged, wondering whether the Isle de Paix government could afford the extravagance of importing excavation equipment, when Messinger stiffened and stopped, unholstered his weapon, and dropped into a crouch. Carole Ann instinctively followed suit. The gun was familiar in her hand. So was the sensation of fear-fueled adrenaline combined with excitement. She eased off the road and into the edge of the forest and, in a duckwalking crouch, inched forward. Messinger had relaxed his stance and was standing upright by the time she reached him. His face was incredulous and surprised and he was shaking his head back and forth in either disbelief or dismay, she wasn't sure which. He whispered, "Holy shit," over and over.

"David, what is it?"

"Do you know what this is?" he asked, still whispering.

"What what is?"

He waved his arm at the forest in a left-to-right motion that encompassed everything before them. "Marijuana," he said almost reverently. "Acres of it. Maybe even miles of it. This is enough weed . . . do you know what this is worth? Son of a bitch! Do you know how many people, what kind of organizational structure . . ."

"This is why Paul moved the equipment back down the road," she said.

"I'd say so. I'd also say it's why he's dead and why the equipment is dead. Whoever runs this operation can't afford to have a road come through here."

She released a sigh of relief, a breath of worry she hadn't realized she'd been holding. "I suppose that means we can eliminate Philippe Collette as the responsible party. He was too anxious to have this road finished."

"Who owns this land? The government?"

She nodded. "From just north of here all the way south to the coast. That's partially why this site was chosen. Why? What are you thinking?"

"This is not a virgin crop, Carole Ann, this field has been here awhile. And this isn't the few plants of an aging hippie or even the cash crop of a Rastaman. This is big business. This is agribusiness. This is a farm, and an operation like this takes money to keep it going and power to keep the world away from it. You got any thoughts on who could be behind this?"

"As a matter of fact, I do. But I've got some questions and concerns, too, David, not to mention contractual obligations to the government of Isle de Paix. So do you, for that matter." She had spoken calmly and quietly, in a tone of voice devoid of emotion. In her best lawyer voice. David Messinger had been a cop too long to be swayed by the tone of voice or to be able to overlook a marijuana farm.

He grabbed her shoulder, his voice and eyes hard with anger. "If you think I'm going to turn a blind eye—"

She slapped his hand away then took a step toward him, causing him to blink and backpedal. "I'm an officer of the court and it's not my habit to break the law, but it won't help us to merely blow the whistle on this crop. We need to know who's behind this."

"And why the fuck do we need to know that?" His voice was low and controlled but he was so angry that spittle formed at the corners of his mouth.

"Because," she replied in the same calm, emotionless tone, "whoever is capable of something this large is a deadly threat to the government of this island. Destroying a marijuana field won't put that person out of business, which, I'm sure you would agree, would only make your job a living hell. You may as well have stayed in Chicago. Destroying this crop without destroying its owner is the same as arresting a street dealer, David, and you know it."

They stared at each other for a moment until his anger ebbed. "You're right," he said. "So who do you think could be responsible . . ." He stopped and sniffed the air as a stiff breeze wafted through the treetops, causing them to sway gently. "Do you smell that?" He tilted his head back, wrinkled his nose, and, animallike, sought to determine the direction of whatever smell had caught his olfactory attention. "It's fresh but it's unmistakable. And it's coming from over there," he said, his voice lowered to something less than a whisper, pointing toward his left. He raised the pistol that he still held in his right hand and took a step toward whatever he smelled. Carole Ann moved to follow and he turned toward her. "You may want to wait for me. If I'm right, what I smell is dead body."

She grimaced, backed up a step, and waved him forward, though she remained tense and on guard. She kept him in sight even as her eyes scanned the forest around her, focusing in wonderment on the marijuana. It seemed carved into the forest floor. David was right: a tremendous amount of work went into this enterprise, including, she imagined, the use of farm or other excavation equipment. That would have been practically the only way to clear this much forest for cultivation, and the marijuana plants seemed to stretch endlessly into the distance. For acres, if not for miles. And who on this island possessed sufficient money and power not only to imagine such an enterprise but to orchestrate it? Who on this island had access to a backhoe and a bulldozer? Two names came to mind: Hubert de Villages and Henri LeRoi.

She started at the sound of rustling foliage and focused her attention—and her eyes—on the direction where she'd last seen Messinger. He had disappeared.

"Damn," she muttered to herself, inhaling deeply and stepping off on her left foot in the direction he'd gone in search of what had smelled to him like a corpse. "Double damn," she muttered again, then swung back around right at the sound of rustling. It wasn't coming from Messinger's direction. She raised the gun just as Denis St. Almain stepped into view.

"I'm still not armed," he said quietly, raising his hands, "and I need to talk to you again. It's important."

"Damn straight it is," she snapped, aiming the gun at him. "But Yvette Casson is who you need to talk to."

He looked at her sadly and lowered his hands. "I didn't know you were bringing police to the island," he said with a shrug. "But it is you that I will speak with, not your chief."

They both jumped at the gun's retort, a sound so loud in the quiet forest it could have been a jet breaking the sound barrier. Then came Messinger's voice calling her name. For only a moment she locked eyes with Denis St. Almain, then she turned and ran the other way, toward the sound of Messinger's voice, calling his name as she ran, gun held out in front of her.

"Here!" He hadn't gone very far, but the underbrush that grew on the northern edge of the marijuana field was thick and the trees were ancient and massive. He was leaning against the base of one of them, holding his right arm with his left hand, the gun in his right hand dangling uselessly at his side. Blood oozed between the fingers of his left hand and there was a body at his feet. Carole Ann looked at him, at the body, and back at him. He shook his head. "I didn't do him. He's what I smelled. I didn't even see who shot me."

She gave him a disgusted look and shook her head. "What kind of shit magnet are you, Messinger? Not in town a week and you stick me with two murders, an arson, and major-league drug dealing. Any chance Chicago would take you back?"

"Jesus," he said with a grimace. "And Jake Graham told *me* to be nice to *you?*"

10

Carole Ann was exhausted. She'd been arguing nonstop with David Messinger for three days and she was tired of the continual confrontations and tired of him. She and Jake argued—sometimes for days on end—but their arguments served to refine their individual points of view and to bring them, eventually, to a consensus. The arguments with Messinger seemed to serve no purpose. They simply disagreed on most matters and they neither liked nor trusted each other enough for either to feel comfortable yielding to the other. She had initially thought that since they both had the best interests of the government at heart, that would serve as a bridge to common ground. When that failed, she held out hope that since he'd once been a criminal defense attorney, having a shared profession would instigate some desire for harmony. She no longer believed harmony possible. So, control of the situation was her only option.

She paced back and forth before Philippe Collette's massive desk, the attorney performing for judge and jury. David Messinger sprawled in a fragile-looking side chair, his long legs splayed out before him, and C.A. knew that if this were elementary school and they were children, he'd trip her in a heartbeat. But they were in the office of the head of state whom they both served, and decorum, if nothing else, would prevail. Messinger wanted to stage a series of raids, with help from the U.S. Drug Enforcement Administration and the coast guard, looking for evidence of marijuana cultivation, harvesting, packaging, and shipping. It would have to be a sizable operation, he'd argued, more than a couple of boxes of Baggies and a scale. And, simultaneously, while the raids were taking place, the marijuana field would be torched. Two birds with one stone, he said, effectively shutting down a major drug cultivation and distribution ring.

Carole Ann's first point of rebuttal—that even on a Caribbean island, cops didn't conduct raids on bicycles—drew blood, and she forged ahead, relentless. She reminded Philippe how close to impossible putting out the fire at the excavation site had been, and asked him to imagine the potential for disaster brought on by setting fire to a square mile of forest. And employing the alternative—chemical deforestation—posed danger of a different kind, she warned, pointing out that many islanders relied on the land and on the sea for food and that poisonous runoff could threaten plant, animal, and marine life for years. She warned that bringing in the DEA signaled that the island had trouble of the unmanageable kind, and that such a signal would most likely frighten off foreign aid—especially U.S. aid. And, further, any sign of such instability certainly would threaten tourism, not to mention the restoration of diplomatic relations with certain nations.

"What would you have us do, then? Allow the marijuana to grow unchecked? Allow it to be harvested and sent on to wherever it goes? That just is not acceptable, Carole Ann! Doing nothing is not an option!" The president pounded his desk with his fist, and several small items jumped.

"Of course it's not," C.A. replied reasonably. "But in its own perverse way, in this instance, doing nothing, for the moment, will be perceived to be an impressive action." Messinger snorted in disgust and she strode over to him. "Haven't you ever deliberately and intentionally *not* responded in the conventional or expected way as a ruse, as a tactic, as a means of throwing your opponent off guard?"

He nodded slowly. "Yeah. So?"

"They—whoever 'they' are—expect us to do something predictable: to attempt to destroy the plants, to thrash around in the woods looking for clues of some kind, maybe even to stage random raids. But two things they certainly do not expect: for us to make no mention of the marijuana and for us to keep digging our road."

The silence was deep and eerie, the kind that fostered self-conscious—and inappropriate—giggles. Carole Ann was fighting to keep control of the one that was lurking in her throat. Repeated swallowing wasn't working and she was on the verge of losing it when Messinger let go a wild bark of laughter.

"Just like cops don't stage raids on bicycles, nobody digs roads with picks and shovels anymore. And even if you could wave some magic wand and materialize a bulldozer, are you really thinking you can just plow ahead like nothing happened?"

She nodded. "What happened, exactly, David? There was a tragic accident that caused the destruction of some equipment, and the foreman, who shouldn't have been operating the equipment without authorization anyway, lost his life. Who said anything about marijuana or a dead body or the minister of internal security being shot?"

"Mon Dieu! I'd forgotten about the body!" Philippe jumped to his feet and rushed around the desk. "But surely you don't think whoever shot that man and left him there forgot about it?"

"That's not what she's saying." Messinger now stood, too, cradling his bandaged right arm in the palm of his left hand. "And you're not really saying that we should do nothing, are you? You're saying nothing happened. That is, whatever happened is what everybody saw happen, right? But since nobody but us saw the plants, knows about the body, knows how I got hurt . . ."

"Nobody but those responsible," Carole Ann replied.

"Yvette Casson knows," Philippe interjected.

"She's the chief of police, Mr. President. She's on our side," David shot back, carelessly unaware that he'd offended his boss. "But this doctor, the one who has both the bodies and who removed the bullet from my arm—"

"He's my son," Philippe replied. "He's on our side, too." He rubbed his hands together rapidly as if to warm them, then he shoved them into his pockets. Deep furrows creased his forehead and he chewed his bottom lip. "Surely it cannot be so simple, Carole Ann, to avoid such a large problem. Tell me what dangers we face if we proceed as you have proposed."

"The preeminent danger is that whoever owns that field will attack again—attack equipment and people operating the equipment and the police sent there to protect them and, therefore, that more people will die. There is the danger that somebody working on the road crew will recognize the marijuana for what it is, tell his friends, and spark a harvesting frenzy in the woods that will make Woodstock look like a Sunday-school picnic. There is the danger that word of this field will find its way outside the island, attracting competing elements and setting the stage for something too ugly to contemplate. There is the danger that what I propose is wrong and wrongheaded—"

"But you don't think so."

"No, Mr. President, I don't think so. I think that it is our best, if not, under the circumstances, our only option. We don't know what we're up against or who. Our best hope is to throw them—whoever 'they' are—off guard by not being predictable and hope to force some action or some behavior that will expose them."

"And that's all you want the police to do? To sit around waiting for whoever 'they' are to make a mistake? I'm not that kind of cop, Carole Ann." He turned toward Collette. "And I thought you hired me, sir, because of my expertise in law enforcement and because of my connections to law enforcement agencies. The DEA—"

Philippe cut him off with an iciness that shocked and surprised Carole Ann. "I will not have the DEA involved in the affairs of this government."

She stepped quickly into the space where David Messinger's anger was about to collide with Philippe Collette's. "I don't like sitting around very much myself, David. But there are times when sitting and waiting—and watching—can prove useful."

He jumped on that. "Watching? What do you have in mind?" He was exhibiting classic cop behavior, twitching and practically salivating, already having forgotten or dismissed his pique at not getting his way.

"I'd guess that 'they' will be anxious to protect any product that's ready to ship, especially if they're anticipating aggressive action on our part. So, watching the coast, especially on the north end of the island . . ."

Messinger grinned and it didn't require too active an imagination to see the feathers in his mouth. "I had planned to get acquainted with the coast guard commandant for this region."

Yvette Carson was easier to convince to play possum than her boss, but perhaps that was because she'd spent more time chasing street-level drug dealers than Messinger. The only part of the plan she didn't like was staking out the construction site at night. Although all the cops—herself included—had roots and ties in the Caribbean, she was the only one who actually had lived on an island. The others were city cops, from Miami and New York and Atlanta and D.C., one generation removed from Jamaica and Haiti and Trinidad. They could stake out an urban ghetto with no problem. But a tropical jungle, at night, in the dark? She shook her head. "They'd rather eyeball an AK-47 than a tree snake. And they're not the only ones."

Carole Ann shared the feeling. "Don't panic yet. First I've got to get something for them to guard."

Roland Charles was full of ideas on that score. He'd already contacted former colleagues at the Georgia Department of Transportation and had identified several pieces of surplus road-excavating equipment slated for the junk heap. The next step was to get the stuff donated to Isle de Paix. "The city and state governments donate surplus and used computers to Third World countries as a matter of policy, so why not surplus backhoes and bulldozers?" She found that she didn't have to worry that he had noticed the miscue between herself and Yvette on the day of the fire, or if he had noticed, he hadn't attached significance to it. He was completely convinced that the destruction of the equipment and the death of Paul Francois were tragic accidents, and accidents not to be repeated. To that end he had organized training sessions for the road crew, and the Toussaint Remy–led mechanics-in-training classes resumed, though the old man was resistant: because he'd burned his hands trying to save Francois and salvage his equipment, he now needed to rely on photocopied engine schematics and verbal lectures instead of his preferred hands-on approach.

Though her enthusiastic support for the interior minister's plans and programs was genuine, Carole Ann's relief was fueled by the knowledge that not having to keep an eye on him meant that she could freely pursue other avenues. Namely, those that would lead her to Hubert de Villages and Henri LeRoi. She was uncertain how to access the island's oldest, richest, and most powerful inhabitant, but she knew exactly what path she would take to its former dictator, the fact that he was thousands of miles away notwithstanding.

"What madness is this?" Odile Laurance, hands on silk-draped, substantial hips, cocked her head and literally looked sideways at Carole Ann. "Where do you get such nonsense, you Americans?"

Carole Ann was left momentarily speechless, which provided Odile time and space for an uninterrupted tirade against the presumptuous nature of colonists in general, and Americans in particular, which, under other circumstances, she might have found absurdly amusing. But Odile was genuinely disturbed and Carole Ann found herself genuinely annoyed. "It's what he himself told me, Odile, not something I invented."

"*He* told you *himself?* What you mean, he told you? That cannot be! Why would he say such a thing? It is madness! It is nonsense! It is a lie and you must not repeat it! It is a dangerous lie." She had spoken in a hissed whisper but her words had the impact of a scream, and Carole Ann again was rendered speechless, this time by the intensity of the woman's reaction and by the growing fear in her voice and her eyes. She and Odile were standing outside the kitchen door of the Aux Fruits de Mer in the lull between lunch and dinner, and Odile looked around to be certain that they were not overheard. Only half a dozen or so patrons remained in the dining room, lingering over a late lunch, and another six or seven were relaxing on the patio. The kitchen staff was eating at the bar with Viviene as their centerpiece—Carole Ann had greeted her and had been warmly received before being directed through to the kitchen, where she'd found Odile seated at a desk in an extremely well-organized and surprisingly modern office, checking receipts. Odile, too, had greeted her warmly if a bit warily, though the wariness quickly became fear-tinged annoyance when Carole Ann stated her purpose. Odile had jumped up from the desk, scattering papers and knocking her reading glasses to the floor, and looked hurriedly around the office as if it contained concealed recording devices. Then she had beckoned for Carole Ann to follow her through the kitchen and out to an enclosed, private patio. ·

"If Henri LeRoi is not Denis's father, why would he tell me he was, Odile?"

"He would not," she replied flatly.

She was out of patience, but Carole Ann knew that she could not react or respond with anger; to do so would send the other woman more deeply into her shell of denial. "But he did, Odile, and if it's not true, then I need to know why he lied. Or why he thinks it's true." She had spoken softly and calmly and her tone had the desired effect. Odile relaxed. Her shoulders dropped, she unclenched her jaw, and her face took on a thoughtful, musing expression. She smoothed her dress and the silk rustled gently, like a breeze in the tops of the coconut palms. As she retreated into thought, Carole Ann watched her, wishing that she could see inside the woman's head, to read those thoughts. For surely if she could know what she imagined Odile knew, she would have a chance at unraveling the mysteries of Isle de Paix. Or at least those pertaining to Denis St. Almain. And under the circumstances, that could prove extremely helpful, because she was beginning to believe that Denis was more than peripheral to the events on Isle de Paix.

She recalled their last conversation. Odile had warned her not to divulge that she was working on Denis's behalf while on Philippe Collette's payroll. Now she was being warned not to repeat Denis's own assertion that Henri LeRoi was his father. Why? Even though she was the man's sister, would she necessarily know whether he'd fathered Simone St. Almain's child more than thirty years ago, or was she merely protecting her brother's honor and reputation? And what difference did any of it make at this point? Henri LeRoi was in exile and Denis St. Almain was a fugitive. Jake's warning notwithstanding, Carole Ann was determined to understand why, especially in light of Denis's presence in that marijuana field.

"Odile . . ."

The woman shook her head. "I need to think more and to talk with Viviene and . . . and others. You will dine with us on Sunday. We do not come to the restaurant on Saturday and Sunday. Those are family days, and Sunday is the day for quiet time. It will be peaceful and we can talk. Come, I will tell you how to find us." Carole Ann followed her back into the kitchen and into the office where, on the back of a coral-colored *sélections du jour* menu from the previous day, she drew a map with detailed directions to her home, for which Carole Ann was grateful because, as she observed the lines that indicated roads she hadn't known existed, she knew she'd never find the place otherwise. She accepted the paper from Odile and took her leave.

She felt unproductive and restless and extremely out of sorts. What was she to do with herself? It was Thursday, late in the afternoon. She couldn't endure another moment with either Roland Charles or David Messinger, and there was no reason for her to see Yvette Casson or Philippe Collette—she had nothing to tell them and they had nothing to tell her and she desperately needed information, the kind that quenched her intuitive thirst rather than her factual hunger. For instance, she could pay a visit to Maurice Collette, the president's son, a doctor and the director of the Isle de Paix health clinic, and learn exactly what caused the deaths of Paul Francois and the unidentified presumed drug dealer. Which would serve no purpose whatsoever. She needed to know people's secrets, people's suspicions; and if she couldn't know what Odile Laurance knew until

Sunday, then the patrons at Armand's would be her next best source of information.

The dusty parking lot was full, as usual, indicating that inside it would be busy, noisy, and smoky—as usual. She removed her sunglasses and opened the door and was smacked hard in the nose by the pungent-sweet scent of marijuana. She faltered, momentarily thrown off balance. Had that always been the case here and she'd never noticed it? And did she notice it now only because she knew that enough pot grew on this island to keep everybody who'd finished college in the 1970s high for the rest of their lives? Or had the pot field been discovered? She recovered her equilibrium and stepped all the way inside.

She knew instinctively that every conscious being was aware of her arrival though only half a dozen pairs of eyes actually looked in her direction. Several men standing near the door stepped aside to permit her entry, and the crowd shifted imperceptibly as she made her way to the bar. She received greetings along the way—casual, off the cuff, and usually low voiced. And when she reached the bar, a man stood, without speaking, and walked in the opposite direction. She knew that he hadn't finished his drink because he took it with him. As she straddled the just-vacated stool, a bottle of Red Stripe and a bowl of plantain chips were placed before her. She smiled her thanks to the bearded, dreadlocked bartender, and he dipped his head in acknowledgment. But he did not smile or speak or in any way indicate any particular feeling about her presence. She could just as easily not be there. She took a long pull on her beer, then looked around, first left and then right. There were several vaguely familiar faces but she saw no one that she knew. And she realized that she felt the same thing here that she felt at Aux Fruits de Mer: less than rejection, less than acceptance. She would not be mistreated here or there, but neither would she be befriended. No patron of this bar would come and sit next to her and engage in conversation. About anything. She finished her beer, put some money on the counter, and left.

Sunday afternoon. And it was only Thursday. She sighed in frustration as she bumped in the Jeep down the rutted road, feeling a tinge of regret that her ambitious plans to pave this and the road to Little Haiti . . . Toussaint Remy! She could go see Toussaint Remy! Immediately her spirits improved. The old man would talk to her, and perhaps so would his neighbors. She wasn't sure exactly why she thought so, but she was proved correct almost immediately when she turned off the paved Coast Road onto the graveled secondary road that fed the rutted tributaries leading into the village of Petit Haiti: everyone she passed lifted a hand in greeting. Most were women, traversing the rutted road with bare feet and baskets balanced on their heads, reminding her acutely of her Peace Corps years in the West African village that this place so much resembled. By the time she finally found Remy—she'd made three wrong turns along the way—she was much more relaxed.

The old man's greeting was warm, though he did not even attempt to conceal his surprise at her presence. And she tried, though she suspected that she failed, to conceal her shock at his appearance. Both his hands and his right arm were bandaged and a large, ugly blister crawled across his forehead, and all the hair on the left side of his head was singed off. He walked with the foot-dragging shuffle of an old person. All the spryness and agility were gone. He'd been sitting on his front steps when she arrived and she had to help him stand, his bony arm fragile and light as air in her hands. She all but picked him up, then followed him into his home, a tiny, one-room structure that was spotlessly clean, ascetic, almost.

He waved her over to the table and into a chair, and she knew that he planned to feed her; but before she could wonder how he would manage, there was a quick knock and the door opened to admit a woman who introduced herself as Madame St. Georges, Monsieur Remy's neighbor for twenty years, and busied herself with plates and glasses, talking and smiling the entire time. And though she'd understood practically nothing that old woman said, it was clear by her manner that Carole Ann was respected in this quarter of Little Haiti, and that brought her some relief.

Toussaint Remy did not eat. He cupped his glass of ginger beer between his two gauzed hands and took tiny sips while Carole Ann ate delicious gumbo that she assumed had been made by Madame St. Georges. He pressed a glass on her and she understood him to say that he'd made the ginger beer himself. It was delicious—strong and sweet, though it was nonalcoholic and she wasn't certain why it was called beer. And while she ate, he talked to her, slowly and precisely so that she could understand him. Tears fell from his eyes and down his cheeks when he spoke of Paul Francois. Yes, the men had worked on Saturday, to compensate for the days lost waiting for the equipment—and because so many of them had been without work for so long—but they had stopped just before five o'clock and had not planned to work on Sunday. But Paul had insisted that they return the vehicles to the site entrance, and backing up in the woods is no easy task, the old man recalled with a scowl. No, they had seen nothing unusual, heard nothing unusual. And all of the equipment had been working perfectly!

She listened intently, concluding that Toussaint Remy knew nothing that she didn't already know, but she asked several questions of him anyway, which made him feel useful and her, slightly depressed. She made him smile and cry again when she told him that Roland Charles already had found new equipment and that they just had to figure out how to get it to the island, predicting that he'd be back to work in a matter of days. Then she left him, stopping to chat with Madame St. Georges and several other women who had gathered in the swept-clean, hard-packed–dirt enclave where they lived. They were eager to engage her and, utilizing a mixture of French and English, they enjoyed a spirited discussion of island life that lifted Carole Ann's spirits. She received an invitation to return the following weekend for dinner at Madame St. Georges's and was surprised at how moved she was by the delight in the women's faces when she accepted.

She was further surprised, at herself, by going directly home when she left Little Haiti instead of returning to her Government House office; but she still didn't feel the need or the desire to talk to Roland or David, or to Philippe, for that matter. She also didn't have the energy to talk to Jake if he still was in the surly, pissy frame of mind he'd been in since Sunday, but she had no choice. So, before changing clothes or pouring herself a glass of wine, she went directly into the office and called him, receiving still another surprise: his mood was relaxed and expansive. He received her report with little comment except to agree with her that, indeed, Odile Laurance's information seemed worth waiting for, and that torching a marijuana field in the middle of an island would be "a damn stupid thing to do," not to mention the detrimental effect it could have on their contract. He promised to find a barge "by hook or by crook" to transport the excavating equipment Roland Charles had succeeded in getting the State of Georgia to donate to Isle de Paix. "If they're giving it to him, I'll get it to him!" And in the meantime, he added, a hint of smugness in his tone attracting her attention, what he called "a little Cat" was en route to them via Charleston. He explained that when he made cancellation noises to the pavement and gravel supplier, who hadn't yet agreed on a final price for the shipment to the island, the owner all of a sudden not only fixed a price, but when he heard the reason for canceling the order, he threw in a small paver free of charge. "As I understand him, it's a little thing, C.A., not much larger than one of those big riding lawn mowers, but it's powerful and it paves and for the time being . . ."

For the time being it would help keep a dozen people busy and employed improving the island's secondary roads, and, by extension, improve Philippe Collette's reputation among his countrymen and -women. And it would provide Carole Ann with a reason for trekking about the island asking questions and looking for any remaining St. Almains; looking for likely associates of Denis St. Almain; looking for likely cultivators of marijuana; looking for places to hide marijuana until it could be safely shipped out. Because there obviously was more to Isle de Paix than she had realized. This fact flashed neonlike in her face when she remembered peering over Odile Laurance's shoulder while the woman drew the map to her home, realizing she didn't know where it was. And she bumped back and forth down the road to Armand's and into Petit Haiti, all but certain that there existed other roads and paths branching off these roads. Now,

with Jake's news, she had motive and opportunity for testing that belief, and she had Roland Charles to lend legitimacy to her quest.

He wanted to begin immediately but Carole Ann persuaded him to
wait until the barge hauling the gravel and the paver arrived. He understood that it would be preferable to have residents of a community
return home from work one day to find their rutted street smoothed
out and passable instead of promising that it would happen but not
being able to say when. Or worse, not being able to deliver on the
promise. What they could do, however, she suggested, was decide
where the barge would dock to offload its cargo of gravel, sand, and
asphalt, and where, consequently, the storage sheds would be built.
He agreed and they spent the next two days cruising the circumfer-
ence of Isle de Paix, exploring coves and inlets, discovering beaches
that were accessible only by water, and cruising in and out of the
caves that eons of tidal shifts and hurricane winds had carved into
the cliffs on the eastern side of the island.

The de Villages clan controlled this section of the island and had,
without interruption, for a century and a half. When Isle de Paix won
independence from France forty years earlier, part of the arrangement for turning over control of the island to its native inhabitants
specified that Deauville remain under the control of the de Villages
family, and so it had. Roland piloted their cabin cruiser skillfully
around the island's point, affording Carole Ann her first view of Isle
de Paix from the north, along with a breathtaking glimpse of the de
Villages manse. Though it appeared to be constructed of the same
stone or slate as the cliffs, it did not seem to be something that belonged naturally to or on the cliffs, and were it not in so magnificent a
location, the structure would be called ugly. It was vaguely castlelike,
though of no specific design or period, and it caused Carole Ann to
speculate that the first colonizer of this cliff might have been a man of
means, but obviously not one of taste. A pirate, perhaps? Or a smug-
gler? Or a drug dealer?

Roland steered the boat in closer to the coastline, revealing a
small, private beach and a steep stone stairway. She could not determine if it led all the way up to the house, but if it didn't, why was it

there? As they rounded the top of the island, Roland cut the engine and they bobbed in the wake they'd created like a piece of driftwood, Carole Ann still peering back at the cliffs, thinking that she'd glimpsed the red-tiled roofs of other Deauville buildings, when Roland made a sound that caused her to turn to look at him. Coming toward them, speeding toward them, was a craft substantially larger than theirs, riding high on the waves. They bounced up and down as the larger vessel circled them in tighter and tighter formation until, almost with a screech of brakes, it coasted up beside them, rising out of the sea above them, revealing half a dozen men pointing assault rifles at them.

"What is the meaning of this!" Roland Charles bellowed, startling Carole Ann and the pirates, for that was the first and most immediate thought that entered her mind when she saw them: they were dark-skinned, though not of African descent, and dark-haired and dark-clothed and, all except the spokesman and obvious leader, they wore dark glasses. They were modern-day pirates.

"You are trespassing on private property," their leader called out in island-accented English, and two of them, still cradling their weapons, clambered down into the smaller cabin cruiser. Carole Ann backed up a step and Roland stepped forward.

"You are mistaken!" he bellowed, rage causing the veins of his forehead to protrude dangerously. "And you will release us immediately or I will have you arrested!"

"This is the private property of Monsieur Hubert de Villages."

"Monsieur Villages owns the land, he does not own the sea, of that I am certain. I am the minister of the interior of this island and I assure you that I know exactly who owns what. And the government of Isle de Paix owns—if such a thing is even possible—the sea surrounding this island for five miles in all directions." Roland's voice, still quavering with anger, did not cease its bellowing. "You will remove yourselves from this craft immediately and remove yourselves from our path, as you are hindering official government business."

"And what business of your *government* . . ." his lips turned slightly downward when he said the word, not bothering to conceal the mocking contempt, "brings you to this end of the island, and so close to shore?"

More veins popped out in Roland's forehead and neck and sweat poured down his face. Carole Ann reached out but he slapped her hand away before she could touch him. "My *government* does not answer to you," he snarled, and in a movement so quick that she would not have believed him capable of it had she not witnessed it, he lunged for the nearest pirate and dropped him to the deck, seizing his weapon in the process. "I know how to use it and I will use it," he said, chambering a round to prove it. "You," he said, backing up and pointing the weapon at the second assailant on the boat, "drop your weapon, pick him up, and get off my boat." Without looking to his leader for permission, the man followed Roland's orders, and when both had reboarded their craft, its powerful engines whined and it shot forward, drenching Carole Ann and Roland in its wake.

Roland dropped the assault weapon and it clattered loudly and slithered across the deck as he hurried to restart the boat's engine. The smaller craft took off in the opposite direction, in just as much of a hurry, seeming to skim along the surface of the ocean, bouncing, occasionally, like a skipping stone. Neither of them spoke until they could see, in the distance, the Ville de Paix harbor and the comforting sight of the luxury craft moored there, including an enormous cruise liner, which dwarfed everything else. "It is here just for the day," Roland offered casually. "Once a week they will come just for the day, until we can convince them to—"

"Stop the boat, Roland. Please." She was too shaken to pretend that nothing had happened, that they had just barely missed being shark snacks.

He complied without hesitation and as the boat slowed, with the engines cut, a calming silence prevailed. That's when Carole Ann noticed that Roland's hands were shaking, that his lips were quivering, that he was swallowing over and over again, his Adam's apple bobbing up and down like the boat. And in recognizing his terror, she recognized her own. And along with it, the fact that she had reason for it. The pirate ship gave definition to the vague feeling she'd had that something ugly and potentially dangerous lurked beneath the surface of Isle de Paix, something uglier than the possibility that Denis St. Almain was a drug dealer; uglier than a field full of thriving marijuana plants; uglier, even, than a wealthy man's ego trip, because she was certain that the intimidation tactics they'd just experienced had little to do with Hubert de Villages' property line. She also was certain that she recognized the leader, that he was the man she'd seen with Denis at Aux Fruits de Mer and that he was the man she'd seen with Marie-Ange Collette. Ugly didn't begin to describe what this was shaping up to be.

"They will be punished, won't they?"

Carole Ann looked at him, squinting. The boat had rocked and bobbed and shifted direction so that they now were facing away from the harbor and toward the sun and the open sea. She contemplated which of the numerous responses that leapt into her mind to give him, and shrugged. "I suppose that's possible. Does our police department have a boat?"

He nodded vigorously. "Just like this one, though with a more powerful engine, I think. And, of course, it has lights and a siren."

Carole Ann smiled slightly. "One boat, one cruiser, and a dozen bicycles." She shook her head sadly, the feeling inspired by the look of utter defeat on Roland's face. Then she brightened. "And two automatic assault weapons."

Ville de Paix was overrun with tourists when they slid into Roland's assigned space at the dock, and she felt buoyed by the festive air. This is what island life should be, she thought, bright and festive and noisy, not dark and ugly and menacing. Her mission of the moment should not be fetching the chief of police to take possession of guns. She'd much rather be able to stroll along, like the tourists, in and out of shops, buying a trinket here, a bauble there, stopping now and again for rum punch and conch fritters. She realized she'd stopped walking and gave herself a nudge. Roland was waiting.

She was momentarily startled by the crowd in front of the police station until she realized that it was the tourism office drawing the attention. Two officers emerged from the station door and the crowd parted, pleasantly, to allow them to pass. The officers smiled and greeted people and their greetings were returned in kind. This is how life should be in paradise, she thought, cops in khaki shorts and shirts smiling and waving at the citizenry, who feel safe and happy. The two cops noticed her and simultaneously lifted their hands. She waved back, not remembering their names but knowing that one of them was from New Orleans and the other from Miami and both were now in Isle de Paix because they'd sickened of the random, inexplicable violence of those cities, violence fed and fueled by drugs and perpetrated by idiots with automatic assault weapons. The kind she was about to present as gifts to their chief.

"I've heard that the old man is an arrogant fool, but this is too much!" Yvette Casson was seated behind her desk in the office that she'd so thoroughly imprinted that any visitor would believe she'd worked there for years instead of days. She'd added three plants, a woven mat that covered half the floor, a rattan window shade, a framed poster of a Romare Bearden painting, and a half dozen family photographs, but the real focal point of the room was Yvette's persona. She was a tough, no-nonsense cop. This was her domain and there would be no confusion about that fact. She picked up the phone, punched a button, and summoned whoever was on the other end. Almost immediately there came a knock on the door and it opened to admit Officer Garrison, whose name Carole Ann remembered because he was from D.C.

"Ma'am," he said, saluting sharply. His eyes widened a bit when Yvette directed him to get two pillowcases from the supply closet and then told him what to do with them, but his only response was a barked, "Yes, ma'am," and another crisp salute. He closed the door silently behind him.

"You seem certain that I can and should keep those guns."

"I am certain, Yvette, on both counts. I'm certain that there will be no serial numbers on those guns, and I'm certain that as long as there are people on this island with them, you should have a couple, too.

Besides," she added wryly, "they can afford to buy new ones a lot easier than you can."

"No shit, Sherlock!" the chief exclaimed. "Of course, I wouldn't have a problem if I could convince Monsieur le Présidente to shift his cabinet ministers around. Give me Roland in place of David, and we'll go intimidate the hell out of them! We won't need to shoot 'em or torch 'em or outgun 'em or outrun 'em. We'll scare the hell out of 'em!"

They shared the humor of the moment, then got down to business. Carole Ann answered all of Yvette's questions and knew that she'd yielded precious little useful information: She'd seen no registry listing on the pirate boat; she didn't know what kind of boat it was, though she'd recognize a similar one if she saw it; she would not be able to identify any of the assailants except the leader, and then not if he grew a beard or a mustache or changed his hair; and she could assign specific ethnicity to none of them, except to suggest that they looked Indian or Pakistani.

"This has the makings of a perfect crime, carried out by the perfect criminals," Yvette said. "So, I'm guessing that you met some of the guardians of the pot field," she added in a musing tone, then sat up straight when Carole Ann did not respond. "You don't think so?"

Carole Ann was thinking of Marie-Ange and her assignation with a pirate, but she couldn't reveal that to the chief of police. "I honestly don't know what to think, Yvette. But I *do* know that whoever they are and whatever they're doing, we can't fight them and win, and we can't stop them from doing whatever it is they're doing. All we can do, it seems to me, is collect information and prepare to defend ourselves should that become necessary."

Yvette shook her head. "I'm not sure anymore. If that's what we're up against, and if you're still planning to go ahead with that road, I'm not inclined to send my people out to defend against an army. They're good cops and they're well trained, but none of 'em did duty in Vietnam, and I'll bet David and I are the only ones who know how to use that damn AK-47." She stood up and shook her head some more, more vigorously this time. "I don't know, Carole Ann. This thing stinks. We need to talk some more before you send Roland's people back into that forest."

Carole Ann nodded and Yvette scrutinized her, studied her face, looking for something to read, finding nothing. But she'd been a cop a long time in a tough environment and knew the significance of nothing readable in a face. "You know something that I don't know and I don't like that, Carole Ann. Why don't you tell me what it is so we can both know what I'm up against."

So Carole Ann told her about Denis St. Almain, told her everything. Yvette made one comment: "No wonder you didn't want to call in the DEA." And she asked one question: "Why are you convinced that he's not a murderer or a drug dealer or both?"

"Because he broke into my house in the middle of the night to tell me he wasn't." She wanted to add, "And because Hazel Copeland said so," but that was a story she didn't intend to tell.

"Do you think he's Henri LeRoi's son?"

"I think he thinks he is."

"But your gut tells you that Odile Laurance is correct?"

Carole Ann nodded. "She was truly horrified when I told her what Denis said. And besides, Yvette, you know as well as I do that in any community where everybody knows everybody else's business, if Henri LeRoi had fathered Simone St. Almain's child, Henri's sister would know about it."

"No shit, Sherlock," Yvette said again. Then she asked Carole Ann to come see her at nine o'clock on Monday morning to report on her meeting with the LeRoi sisters. She asked, didn't order, but there was no room for Carole Ann's refusal. The chief wanted and expected a full accounting of her Sunday tête-à-tête with Odile. They walked together through the sun-filled squad room and C.A. noticed that it, too, had begun to assume an identity and a personality. There were coffee mugs and water bottles on desks, a large potted palm in one corner of the room wearing a single Christmas ornament, and three different screen-saver patterns flashing across the operational computers. As they reached the door, it opened, and Officer Garrison entered, a strangely bulging pillowcase in each hand. He raised his arms and shot his boss a questioning look. "My office," she said, and followed Carole Ann out the door. "You watch yourself, Carole Ann. And call me if anything else weird happens." And she went inside, closing the door, heading immediately, Carole Ann knew, to inspect the two weapons.

The crowd was still thick in Government Square, the air still festive. Carole Ann stepped out into the street and found herself caught up and swept along, and decided to go with it. After all, dressed as she was, in a T-shirt, bell-bottomed slacks, and deck shoes, she couldn't very well present herself at her Government House office. Besides, she knew what awaited her: the preliminary autopsy reports on Paul Francois and the dead body David Messinger found in the marijuana field. But she already knew, because Messinger had called her at six-thirty that morning to tell her that both men had been killed by bullets to the head. She didn't need to read the words. So, why not enjoy an early dinner, watch the sunset, and go home and watch a movie?

She was following the crowd, looking for a likely place to stop, when someone caught her eye . . . Denis! But she knew that it was not Denis. She craned her neck, peering over the heads of tourists for a glimpse of the man. Was that him, in the green-and-white-striped polo shirt? Yes! She followed, craning for a good look. But this man was half a foot taller and, judging from the back of his head, he was white. "Get a grip," she heard Jake snap at her, and she marveled at his absence in her subconscious before now. Given the events of the day, he should have been barking orders at her constantly. Then she realized why he hadn't: it hadn't been necessary because she hadn't been the one to disarm the pirate. She hadn't put herself in danger. She hadn't even considered it, consciously or unconsciously. She had, she realized, stood openmouthed and flat-footed and terrified, staring at the men who were holding her at gunpoint, thinking absolutely nothing.

The black-and-white-striped awning of Le Bistro caught her eye, and she angled through the crowd to the sidewalk. She stood before the cafe, deciding whether to venture inside or take an umbrella-covered table outside and watch the world go by. The decision was made for her when a waitress approached and informed her that there was an interior courtyard with a view of the harbor. Despite the early hour, most of the tables inside the restaurant and in the courtyard already were filled, and Carole Ann assumed that spoke well of the food. Either that or tourists got hungry early. Without reading the menu, she asked for a large salad, a bottle of Chardonnay, and an appetizer of conch fritters. "If you have them," she added hopefully.

"They are a house specialty, madame," the waitress replied.

"Then bring a double order."

Sunday dinner at the home of the proprietors of Aux Fruits de Mer would not be fish. That was clear half a mile down the road that led to Odile's house—the scent of roasting meat wafted on the breeze, causing Carole Ann to salivate. She glanced at Odile's expertly drawn and detailed map and noted that her destination was at hand. And when she made the final turn onto the road that would lead her to Odile's house, it also was clear that Sunday dinner would be a well-attended affair. There must have been thirty people of all ages, shapes, and sizes ambling about in the clearing where the road terminated, and Carole Ann was momentarily confused: There was a swimming pool surrounded by a large patio, which, in turn, was bordered by a wide border of lush, green grass and brightly colored tropical flowers; it seemed to be the front yard of the three large houses behind it.

Still following directions, Carole Ann parked left of the pool, on a paved deck where half a dozen other cars were parked. Before she could get out and close the door, a gaggle of children, all chirping her name, appeared and demanded that she follow them. She did, in the direction of the pool. She saw Odile rise from a chaise lounge, drop the book she'd been reading, and walk toward her. The children hopped up and down, chirping, *"Tante Odile, Tante Odile, Grand-mère, Madame Carole Ann est arrivée!"*

Odile introduced her to each of the children by name, and each grinned and shook her hand. Then they allowed themselves to be shooed away as Odile identified them as nieces, nephews, and two grandchildren. Laughing at the look in Carole Ann's eyes, she explained that, yes, all were part of the LeRoi family. They lived in separate houses in what could only be described as a compound—a settlement of a dozen or more structures of various shapes and sizes on what Carole Ann realized was a private road, which is why it hadn't appeared on any of her maps. These three houses—the beginning or the end of the compound?—were larger than all the others, and were built on a slight rise that, she realized as she followed Odile up the hill, commanded a stunning view of the sea. She also realized that the fronts of the houses faced the sea and that the pool/garden area was the backyard. Which was where pools and gardens usually were . . .

Just beyond the parking deck was a stand of trees that Carole Ann learned was a fruit orchard. Odile's husband was a horticulturist who experimented with fruit trees, providing Aux Fruits de Mer fruit of rare and exquisite quality for the sauces, jams, and jellies that enhanced the restaurant's fame. The setting was lush and elegant without a trace of ostentation, like the LeRoi sisters themselves, causing Carole Ann to wonder again what Henri LeRoi was like.

"First you must meet Mother," Odile said, after having explained the lay of the land, and she led Carole Ann up the flagstone walkway and into the larger of the three houses on the knoll. They entered a kitchen that smelled of cinnamon and nutmeg and cloves, which made Carole Ann's mouth water. "Mother made the dessert today."

"And I wager it will be the best bread pudding you ever ate."

Carole Ann turned to see exactly how Viviene LeRoi would look in . . . how many years? For the old woman, the doyenne of the LeRoi clan, was so old that she made Toussaint Remy seem young. She had once been tall and straight like Viviene, but now she was bent with age. She was thin and the skin hung from her, and her hands, when they took Carole Ann's, were gnarled and crooked. Her eyes, however, were clear and sparkled with the energy and mischief that filled Odile's. This old woman had doled out equal measures of herself into her daughters, and Carole Ann wondered again, even more fervently, what Henri LeRoi was like.

"I am honored to meet you, Madame LeRoi, and of course the bread pudding is magnificent. You would not allow it to be otherwise."

The old woman cackled and waved them away as she shuffled down the hallway. Carole Ann followed Odile outside and across a brick walkway to the house next door. They entered another kitchen, huge and bright and smelling of herbs instead of spices. Viviene was seated at a table tucked into a window nook. She looked up from the paper before her and smiled. She was standing when Carole Ann reached her, and she received kisses on both cheeks.

"Please sit down. I hope you don't mind the kitchen. I can't seem to get out of one or the other."

Carole Ann smiled and sat across the table from Viviene; Odile placed a bottle of red wine without a label and three goblets on the table, then sat next to Carole Ann. Viviene poured wine for all of them. Then she looked directly at Carole Ann, her gaze clear and steady. She was her mother's daughter, in all ways, for it now was apparent, watching the two sisters together, that it was Viviene to whom Odile deferred, not the other way around; it was Viviene who would, if she had not already, inherit her mother's place as head of the LeRoi family. And it was Viviene who would answer Carole Ann's queries.

"Denis St. Almain is not our brother's son," Viviene said in her gentle but strong voice. "Though we love him as if he were. And Henri loves him as a son. But Denis is the son of Philippe Collette. Denis is the president's son."

Sunlight streamed through the windows, making rainbows as it refracted through the deep red of the wine in the crystal goblets. The voices of the children at play wafted in on the breeze, both breeze and children light and carefree and unfettered by ugliness or complexity. Carole Ann delighted in the rainbows and the children and felt strangely comforted in the presence of the LeRoi sisters though she remained alert and on guard. This place and these people reminded her of another extended family, who had first fed her and then shared with her their family secrets, secrets she ultimately used to destroy members of that family. Would that happen in this situation, with this family? She hoped not; but like that other family in that other time and place, she might have no choice. And so, she remained on guard.

Viviene already had walked her down memory lane, to the time, thirty-five years earlier, when they all were young—Henri LeRoi and Philippe Collette and Simone St. Almain and Odile LeRoi younger by several years than herself—Simone the most beautiful of the girls, Henri the most brilliant of the boys, Philippe the most handsome and wealthiest of the boys, Odile the most brilliant and wealthiest of the girls. Isle de Paix was newly independent, though still completely in-fluenced and largely controlled by the French, and marked by divi-sions within island society and culture based on proximity to things French. Consequently, those families of color most easily able to access a connection to French families of the same name occupied the highest social strata and, by default, the highest economic strata. In second place were the professionals and tradespeople who, despite having no direct tie to wealthy white French islanders, nevertheless managed to achieve financial success and stability. On the bottom, as always, were those without name, wealth, or education. And pilloried on the points of this dangerous triangle: Henri LeRoi, Philippe Collette, and Simone St. Almain.

"Henri adored Simone," Viviene recalled. "And why not? She was beautiful. She was beyond beautiful. She took the breath away, of both boys and girls. Even the prettiest girls—and Odile was among the prettiest—paused in admiration of Simone." Viviene looked to her younger sister for affirmation of the truth and received it.

"Simone was lovely," Odile said. "But, Viviene—we never have agreed on this point, and still do not, even after so much time has passed—she was lovely in the way an orchid is lovely or a bird of paradise or a cockatoo: strangely. In some way not normal. You have seen her, Carole Ann. Do you understand what I mean? How did she seem to you?" Then, as if struck, literally, by an afterthought, she added, "She is still beautiful, Simone?"

Carole Ann recalled her own impression of Simone as a beautiful tropical bird and agreed with Odile, though she easily could imagine viewing such arresting beauty through the naked eyes of youth rather than through the prism of maturity. She nodded. "Yes, she is still beautiful. But in a fragmented, put-together way . . ." She faltered, seeking the correct words, then relaxed as she noticed both Viviene and Odile nodding their heads in understanding.

"So you can imagine that she was pursued."

"But what she cannot imagine," Odile interrupted her sister with controlled vehemence, "is how foolish it was for Simone to dream, to say nothing of believing, that Philippe Collette would marry her! My God, it was madness! Yet, she believed that her beauty would be enough."

Viviene coughed gently and reached across the table for her sister's hand, halting her flow of words. "Odile and Henri always were best friends, just a year apart, he the adored big brother for her. And because he was older, he refused to accept her warnings about Simone."

"Even after Philippe used her for his amusement that one summer and impregnated her and left her, to return to school in Paris, Henri still would have her! Can you imagine? He would marry her and give a name to Philippe's bastard!"

"Odile!" Viviene hissed her sister's name but it resonated like a shout. "That is enough. Please. Denis is *not* a bastard. We care for him, and Henri loves him just as he loves his own children, and certainly Denis loves Henri."

"Yes," Odile replied, "enough to claim him as his father."

The three women drank deeply of their wine in the emotional silence that hung over the table and, after a moment, Viviene resumed the tale: A defeated and despondent Henri LeRoi returned to his studies in America, eventually becoming a lawyer like his father before him; Philippe Collette returned to his studies in Paris, eventually becoming a lawyer like his father before him; and Simone retreated, in shame, to her parents' hut on the north end of the island where her father worked as a cane cutter. Simone never returned to school and refused further contact with the people she had grown up with, including Henri and Philippe. Eventually, she was forgotten; and until Henri assumed control of the government and Denis began to appear periodically, it was not known that Simone and Henri had been in touch with each other. "So, I suppose that is why Denis concluded that Henri was his father," Viviene mused. "Why else would such a man interest himself in the affairs of Simone and Denis St. Almain? And, as we later learned, it was Henri who arranged for them to go to the States and for Denis to be educated."

Based on all that, Carole Ann accepted as logical Denis's belief that Henri was his father; and no doubt, Simone would rather he believe the fantasy than claim as the father of her child the man who had so callously abandoned her. But were Denis and Henri joined by any other bond or connection, the kind that involved drugs and the DEA? The kind that would result in Henri LeRoi's fall from power and Denis St. Almain's becoming a murder suspect? "Why did Henri leave?"

His sisters locked eyes across the table, their desire to protect their sibling as intense as if they still were children jockeying for playground superiority: the LeRoi clan against all takers. Carole Ann kept her eyes on Viviene, waiting for the answer. But it was Odile who answered. "Something to do with drugs. He said he had been tricked, used somehow, and he was afraid." Odile stopped talking and looked again at Viviene, who shrugged slightly, then nodded. "It—whatever it was—had something to do with Denis."

Carole Ann felt as if the air had been sucked out of her. "Philippe had nothing to do with Henri's decision to leave?"

Viviene frowned. "No. In fact, Henri made the arrangement for him to return. Philippe now boasts that he was planning all along to reclaim his family's 'rightful position' as governors of this island, but the truth is that Henri made it all possible."

"And you're certain that Philippe doesn't know that Simone's child was his child? Certain that he hasn't encountered Denis and made the connection?" Carole Ann asked. Thirty-five years ago, Isle de Paix would have possessed, even more than now, a small-town mentality; everybody knew everybody else's business. And if Philippe ever met Denis, he had to make the connection to his past, unpleasant and uncomfortable as that might be; the image of himself reflected in Denis St. Almain's face would guarantee it.

"Who would tell him?" Viviene asked with an eloquent shrug. "We had contact with them—the Collettes and the du Mas and the de Villages clans and the Chartres—only at school, and then only because, despite their names, they were not permitted to attend school with their French relatives."

"De Villages?" Carole Ann interrupted with a start. "There are de Villages other than the old man who owns everything on this island that the government does not own?"

Odile released a girlish peal of laughter and Viviene almost matched it, and through intermittent giggles, they explained that, indeed, there remained several direct descendants of the island's original colonizers, both Black and white, though the de Villages now were the wealthiest—they owned the biggest bank on the island—and, therefore, the most powerful, despite the fact that a Collette wore the official mantle of power. "But a de Villages still wears the unoffi-cial mantle," Odile added with a sniff and a giggle. "If one could ever get her out of her haute couture, one could argue that she wears the pants in that family."

"Odile," Viviene hissed at her sister again. "That is quite enough. The back-stairs intrigue does not help Carole Ann," and she looked to Carole Ann for consensus.

"I'm sorry, but I don't know what you're talking about."

"Marie-Ange!" Odile exclaimed.

"What about her?" Carole Ann asked, feeling very much like she was the only one excluded from the inside joke.

"Marie-Ange is the eldest granddaughter of Hubert de Villages," Viviene began, but stopped short as Odile rose quickly to pound Ca-role Ann's back to prevent her from choking on the wine that she'd swallowed too quickly, the wrong way.

" Well, at least now we know why Collette didn't want to be the one to tell old man de Villages to shove his school and his clinic up his ass!" Jake was enormously amused to learn of the president's fa-milial tie to the island's wealthiest man. Carole Ann was less so.

"It's also why the old fart thinks he can maintain the upper hand by controlling access to essential equipment, like that bulldozer, and get away with it. Jake, this isn't funny!"

"The hell it's not," he chortled. "I knew Collette had his hands full with Miss Marie-Ange, but I didn't know how much trouble the man was in. I wouldn't wish that kind of pressure on my worst enemy."

Carole Ann all of a sudden remembered Jackie LaBelle telling her how Marie-Ange had yelled at Philippe the morning that construction had been halted on the de Villages school and clinic and how she had not attributed major importance to the event—a power play between spouses, she had imagined. She also recalled the early meetings that she and Jake had had with the Collettes, how involved Marie-Ange had been, and how invisible she had become since Carole Ann's arrival. She now wondered whether Marie-Ange knew about her husband's connection to Simone and Denis St. Almain, whether she knew the truth of Henri LeRoi's demise and of Philippe's ascendancy, whether Hubert de Villages' "gifts" were really that, or diversions. "Jake, get me every bit and scrap of information on Isle de Paix and its history that's available, paying particular attention to the Collette, de Villages, du Mas, and Chartre families. And I need it an hour ago, when I needed the file on Christian Leonard."

She looked at her watch: she had fifteen minutes to make her nine o'clock meeting with Yvette Casson. She'd be late if she walked. She'd also be late if she had another cup of coffee, which she intended to do. She called Yvette, bought herself another hour, and walked down the hallway to the kitchen. She was about to switch on the light when she heard a sound in the living room. She stopped and listened: faint tapping that grew increasingly louder and more insistent. She hurried across the room to the window, her feet silent on the carpet. She pressed herself against the wall and lifted a corner of the curtain. She saw feet, and then a hand, tapping again, harder. She put her mouth to the window. "Come around to the kitchen door. I'll turn off the alarm."

Denis St. Almain slid in when she opened the door and looked frantically around. "You sent for me, which I don't mind, but I do mind you putting my aunts in jeopardy." He'd spoken quietly but harshly and she was surprised.

"I don't know what you're talking about."

"I'm talking about the police you have looking for me. Why involve Viviene and Odile if you'd already sent your cops? I don't want the police hanging around the restaurant."

"I have no idea what you're talking about; you can either explain yourself or get the hell out of here and let the cops find you, but I'm tired of your games, Denis. And if anyone is putting Viviene and Odile at risk, it's you."

He looked around the kitchen again, then stepped farther in. He was filthy, and he looked as if he hadn't slept in several days. "I'm rather tired myself, Miss Gibson. And if you didn't sic the cops on me, then who did?"

"*What* cops, Denis?"

"*Your* cops, dammit! The ones you brought here, in their khaki outfits and their twenty-speed bicycles. Three of them have spent the last thirty-six hours riding up and down every rutted road on the east side of the island looking for me. Fortunately, they were looking in the wrong places."

"Which should tell you that I didn't send them. If I had, they'd have found you," she snapped at him. "Now go take a shower, fix yourself some breakfast, and take a nap. I've got to go to work. Make yourself at home in any rooms but my bedroom and my office. I'll be back by noon." She turned away from him, then turned back, catching the look of bemused surprise on his face. And the look that confirmed for her that he definitely had been a cop and not, she thought, a bad one. "I'm going to lock you in and set the alarm. I need for you to be here when I get back."

He gave her a lopsided grin. "I'm too hungry, too tired, and too dirty to pass up the offer of respite in all those areas. Just don't make too much noise when you come in, all right?"

"I'd have given you a cup of coffee," Yvette Casson said by way of greeting.

"I don't drink cop-shop coffee," Carole Ann replied ungraciously. "Not unless I'm being detained."

"Which you have been, on more than one occasion," the chief shot back, her aim steady and true.

Carole Ann shrugged and changed the subject. "So, are you the proud owner of two AK-47 assault rifles?"

"You betcha," she said, imitating Chief Marge from the film *Fargo*. "Though the minister of internal security wanted to turn them over to the coast guard or the DEA. What's with him wanting to turn everything over to the federal government?" she groused, knowing but not caring that she was taking the impolitic step of complaining about her boss to, technically, an outsider. "I think he doesn't understand yet that he *is* the legal authority here. He doesn't have to bow down to anyone anymore."

Making no comment but offering a conspiratorial half smile, Carole Ann knew without asking who had ordered the search for Denis St. Almain. What she didn't know was why. So she took the initiative, telling Yvette as much as she dared about her conversation with Viviene LeRoi and Odile Laurance. Yvette paled a bit at learning of Denis's paternity. "The minister is going to faint," she whispered.

"Why?" Carole Ann jumped at the opening.

"He found out from his coast guard pals that there's a 'want for questioning' out for him—for Denis St. Almain—with the warning that he could be here, since this is home for him. David asked me to send out lookers." She paused, waiting for questions or comments, and continued when none came. "I didn't tell him what you'd told me, and I sent the lookers to the wrong side of the island."

"Why?"

"Because, despite the fact that you're a lawyer, you have a better street-cop nose than David. I'm sorry to say that because I like David. But I don't trust him, the same way I didn't trust the brass when I was on the street, you know what I mean? David's too much of a bureaucrat, and those are the dudes that can get you shot."

"Would you kindly tell Jake Graham, next time you talk to him, about my street-cop nose? He still treats me like a lawyer."

Yvette laughed and Carole Ann engaged in a three-second debate with herself over whether to mention that Denis St. Almain was, at that moment, probably taking a shower in her house, then decided not to. The woman already was guilty of withholding crucial information from her boss; no need to make her guilty of aiding and abetting a suspected felon as well.

The decision proved to be a wise one. David Messinger was on a tear, ranting and raving about murderous drug dealers being the scourge of the earth and deserving of death. He stomped up and down his office, a big cat on the prowl, Denis St. Almain his prey. "That son of a bitch had better not be on this island! And he damn well better not be who killed Paul Francois, because if he is, I'll hang his ass!" He stomped about some more, his anger surrounding him like an aura. Carole Ann took note of the fact that his rage didn't extend to the still unidentified corpse from the marijuana field; but, like Jake, like so many cops, his sympathies didn't extend to criminals, and the dead body now officially was considered connected to the pot. And like cops everywhere, there had come for David Messinger an end to any amount of tolerance for drug dealing, for drug dealers, particularly for those who commit other felonies during the course of their drug dealing. "They think they can go up to the States and learn how to deal and rob and kill like pros, then run back home to set up shop down here." He shook his head back and forth. "Those days are over. When we enact the death penalty here—"

"When you do *what?*"

"I've already discussed it with Philippe, and he's already signed the Inter-Island Memorandum of Agreement Against Drug Trafficking."

"Talk to me, David, about enacting the death penalty here. What do you mean?"

"Exactly that! There's a movement to restore the death penalty to the Caribbean nations, brought on specifically by drug dealing and the murders they spawn. Trinidad and Tobago led the way a couple of years ago by hanging nine of them."

"Nine? The government of Trinidad and Tobago *hung* nine people . . ."

"No, Carole Ann," he intoned sarcastically, "not nine *people.* Nine drug-dealing, murdering bastards who were responsible for a decade-long reign of terror in the region." He heaved an exasperated sigh, flicked his hand at her as if she were some kind of pesky insect, and hurried over to his desk. He riffled through a stack of file folders on top, retrieved one, and hustled back to her. "Here! Read this," he ordered, shoving the folder at her chest. She opened the folder and began to read, when he stopped her. "Not now. Take it home with you. If you're going to continue to advise us on matters of security, you need to know how we're thinking—"

"At the very least," she snapped at him.

"—and we're thinking," he continued as if she hadn't interrupted him, "zero tolerance for any drug-related crimes. We have models to follow—Trinidad and Tobago, Jamaica, Bermuda, the Bahamas—all have enacted tough laws with strong penalties, including restoration of the death penalty."

Carole Ann was silent. She didn't yet know nearly enough about how the criminal justice system worked in the Caribbean islands, though she did know that all the islands he just mentioned were governed in some way by a British council of jurisprudence, as they all were or had been British colonies, and she said as much to David Messinger.

"You're referring to the Privy Council," he replied coldly, "which finally conceded Trinidad's constitutional right to enforce its own laws, which is how those nine drug-dealing murderers ended up dangling from a rope. You really should read the documents in that folder." He looked down at her and she struggled for control, reminding herself that Jake wanted her to be nice to this man. What she wanted to do was . . . was . . . she didn't know what she wanted other than not to have to talk to him anymore today. Or until she no longer was harboring a fugitive, or until she knew who was, in fact, dealing drugs on Isle de Paix, whichever came first.

"I will read this, David, and very carefully, I assure you. But I do think talk of hanging is premature."

"Even after what happened to you?" He was incredulous. "You're held at gunpoint on a boat in the middle of the ocean and I'm being premature?"

"For crying out loud, David, I don't want them hung!"

"Then what should we do with them, Carole Ann? Send them to their rooms without dinner? In case it didn't occur to you, that was about more than trespassing. You don't use AK-47s to discourage trespassers," he snapped at her.

"The damn thing shouldn't be used for anything except war," she snapped right back, not caring that she was on the verge of being angry enough to say something to him that Jake might wish she hadn't said.

"You're entitled to your opinion," he responded stiffly. "But I'm responsible for the safety and security of *everyone* on this island, you included. And in case this thought hadn't occurred to you, imagine the uproar it would cause for you, of all people, to be assassinated here. I won't stand for it! A coast guard drug-interdiction craft will, at our invitation, pay a surprise visit to the north coast one day during the next week or so."

Now Carole Ann was alarmed. "David, we had an agreement."

"I knew you'd say that." He shook his head sadly, his worst fears come true. "Our agreement, Carole Ann, covered only activities and events involving construction of the new government road. I never agreed to ignore hostage taking, especially with a minister of this government being one of the victims. And if it happens—" he raised a hand to forestall her interruption "—*if* it happens that rousting that bunch of hoodlums affects the pot field investigation, then so be it." And he turned away from her and headed toward his desk. She headed out the door.

Fortunately, her meeting with Roland Charles was brief. Neither had any new or pertinent information for the other. She left him and went in search of Jackie LaBelle. She wanted to know more about that inter-island memorandum that had left David Messinger feeling so smug. Whatever it was, it would, Carole Ann reasoned, have involved or required some elements of diplomacy and protocol. After all, governments never just decided or agreed to do something and then did it. The rules and the language of protocol and diplomacy prevailed: who sits where during the discussion, who enters the room first, who leaves the room first, who takes the first drink of wine. Jackie was Isle de Paix's only diplomatic officer and Carole Ann fervently hoped that she had been involved in any discussion with other islands regarding the death penalty. She shuddered to think of David Messinger being the only voice heard on the subject.

She walked down the wide marble stairway to the first floor of Government House, then turned down the corridor that led to Jackie's cubbyhole of an office. The title of "diplomatic liaison" may have sounded impressive, but it carried with it no trappings of grandeur.

"If you're looking for Jacqueline, Madame Gibson, she is not here." Carole Ann turned to face a young woman she'd never seen before. She had emerged from a door upon which was stenciled, in black lettering, MINISTRY OF FINANCE.

"Yes, I am looking for Jackie LaBelle," Carole Ann replied, wondering how someone she'd never seen before not only knew who she was, but knew what she wanted. What else did she know? "Would you happen to know where I might find her, or when she might return?"

The woman was very young, not much more than twenty, Carole Ann guessed, and her clothes were not those of a secretary or other administrative personnel one would expect to find in a government building; nor was her speech that of a civil servant. This girl would be more at home at the country club if she didn't seem so sad and unhappy. She looked at Carole Ann with dull, expressionless eyes. "She went off-island for the weekend and is expected to return by noon." And she closed the door behind her and slouched off down the hallway, her posture a screaming testament to her unhappiness, her brushed-silk ensemble proclaiming just as loudly her misplacement in a government office building. Carole Ann watched her, a slight frown bothering her face. How and why would that young woman know how Jackie LaBelle spent her weekend? She added that question to the list she had for Jackie and hurried off down the hallway in the opposite direction.

She disarmed the alarm control panel when she entered the kitchen door. The fact that it still was on meant that Denis St. Almain had not tried to leave. Clean pots, pans, and dishes in the sink drain indicated that he had eaten. She trod quietly down the hall. The first door on the right was three-quarters closed. She stood listening for a moment, detecting light snoring, then she continued down the hall to the office. She wrinkled her brow at the pile of paper on the floor in front of the table. "What in the world . . ." She scooped up a handful and began reading and realized that it was the information she'd asked Jake to send, then quickly gathered up all the pages, anxious to begin reading. "Bless you, Patty!" she whispered, noting that the pages were numbered.

She plopped down in the desk chair, dropped her purse and brief-case on the floor, and began ordering the pages. There were thirty-seven of them. She began reading. It was fascinating and useful, the gist of it being that the LeRois and the Collettes had been trading positions at the helm of the Isle de Paix government for half a century, and that the Collettes and the de Villages had been wielding economic power for longer than that. She took a clean yellow legal pad from the desk and began making quick notes to synthesize the material.

Isle de Paix won independence from France in 1960. At the time, Reginald Collette was the last French-appointed territorial governor. At independence, he appointed Marcel LeRoi interim prime minister, pending the island's first elections, which LeRoi won, only to die in office a year into his term, plunging the island into chaos. There was widespread speculation of foul play in Marcel LeRoi's death, though no supporting evidence was ever produced. Hubert de Villages was appointed to serve out Marcel LeRoi's term and he held the office, without ever scheduling an election, for ten years, when he decided that he no longer wanted to be president. Andre Philippe Collette, the father of the current president, won the next election, in 1980, and remained in power until unseated in a coup by Henri LeRoi, the son of Marcel, the following year.

There they were—two of the four names that Odile and Viviene said controlled the economic destiny of Isle de Paix—de Villages and Collette. She thumbed through the papers, looking for "du Mas" and "Chartre," stopping to read when she found them, finding herself strangely disappointed to learn that the original du Mas and Chartre colonists had arrived in the Caribbean with land grants from the French king in the early 1880s, and little more. A Chartre had held a position of power in the government when de Villages was president, and a du Mas had served the first Collette government as finance minister. Both families left Isle de Paix en masse when Henri LeRoi overthrew Andre Collette and suspended what was passing for a democracy.

Carole Ann sighed and tossed the papers aside. All of it was interesting, none of it was enlightening. What she was in search of was a secret, or at least some bit of information that could be construed to be damaging, if not damning. But there seemed to be nothing secret about the fact that the French aristocracy had, for years, openly and publicly kept island women as mistresses and had, as a result, parallel families. It seemed, she mused, that it was only the Americans and the British who managed to be surprised by the discovery of Black family members carrying the same name and genes. So what that Marie-Ange was the granddaughter of Hubert de Villages? It seemed not to bother either of them; in fact, if island lore could be relied upon, the president's wife embraced her connection to the island's richest man. It mattered not that he was white and she was Black; they were family. And again Carole Ann was reminded of the Louisiana family that had become like her own, people of Creole and Cajun and African descent who traversed the bayous and swamps with one major difference: they knew about but never openly acknowledged their ties to one another.

Carole Ann shuffled through the final pages, learning that Henri LeRoi's father, Marcel, had been the first Black lawyer on the island, and that his mother, Antoinette, whom she had met Sunday, the first Black college-educated schoolteacher. She also was surprised to discover that Philippe and Marie-Ange were the parents of four children—two sons and two daughters. Maurice Collette, the physician, she knew, and she knew that one daughter was married and living in San Francisco and that the other daughter was a student at a Florida university. She had heard no mention of a second son, who, according to the information before her, would be the youngest child, at twenty-two, and named Andre.

Carole Ann sat up straight. Was this the Andre whose presence at the party had so startled Marie-Ange? And if so, why wouldn't he have been as welcome a guest as Maurice? She leaned back in the chair, musing on the nature of family. Everybody on Isle de Paix knew that the wife of the president had a white grandfather. Nobody in New Orleans knew that Warren and Lillian Forchette had a white grandmother, and they'd never have wanted Carole Ann to know; and she wouldn't have known, had that information not been crucial to the unraveling of a murder investigation. A missing sibling had been crucial to solving the murder in that case. And here, she thought with a sigh, was another unaccounted-for sibling, and one unknown-about sibling.

The fax machine beeped. She hurried over to it and stuck out her hand impatiently. She grabbed the first sheet and began reading, growing more concerned with every sentence. Christian Leonard indeed had impressive credentials in French banking. He also belonged to an extreme right-wing political party and had paid for the defense of a band of hooligans who had attacked a family of Iranians for moving into "their" neighborhood. And he publicly had espoused the belief that all persons of color should leave France. What the hell was a man like Leonard doing in a place like Isle de Paix?

"I hope that what you're thinking so hard about isn't turning me in to the gendarmes."

She raised her eyes and looked directly into those of the "unknown-about" sibling. He'd found clean clothes—a denim shirt and jeans, both of which hung loosely on his slight frame, but at least he wasn't wearing military camouflage—and she noticed that he'd shaved and given himself a manicure. But he needed a haircut and about twelve hours' more sleep. She put thoughts of Christian Leonard aside and returned to the desk.

"You certainly look better. Come in and have a seat." She gestured to the facing love seats but he looked toward the conference table and chairs. "Wherever you're comfortable," she said.

"You are one cool customer, Miss Gibson, I'll give you that," he said, his voice well modulated, his tone cool, his English completely unaccented. He pulled one of the straight-backed chairs away from the conference table, turned it to face her, and straddled it. "Thank you for . . . for not screaming bloody murder and calling the cops." He paused. "You didn't call them, did you?"

She shook her head, then told him what she'd learned from Yvette Casson and David Messinger, then sat silently and watched him process the information. Then, surprising her, he said, "I hope Collette isn't chicken-shit enough to enact a death penalty law here. Isle de Paix isn't that kind of place."

"Isn't what kind of place?"

"A haven for drugs and dealers."

"Oh, please, Denis. What are you?"

"Obviously not a drug dealer or a murderer, or I wouldn't have been eating your porridge and sleeping in your bed, now would I?"

"You're amused?"

"Not in the least," he replied wearily. "What I am, in addition to being exhausted, is terrified that with the possible exception of you, my mother, and my father, the rest of the world does think the worst of me, and I don't know how to prove I'm not a criminal."

"You can start by telling me what I need to know to help you prove it," she said quickly.

"Why would you help me? What's in it for you?"

"Successful execution of my contractual agreement with the government of this island."

"Bullshit!" he shot at her, standing up and striding across the room. "You could have come back here with the minister of internal security and done wonders for your contract. You didn't. Why?"

She shrugged, holding his gaze in hers.

"Why do you believe in my innocence, Miss Gibson?" He asked the question with childlike simplicity, and in an almost childlike voice.

"Because Hazel Copeland believes in your innocence."

His face opened in a wide, full smile, allowing her to see for the first time what a truly handsome man he was, and how very much like his father he looked. "And how did you come to have such trust in Tante Hazel?"

She smiled at his use of the term of endearment, but she wouldn't answer his question. "It's a long story, and of little interest to anyone but myself. It probably wouldn't even interest Mrs. Copeland." Which she knew was untrue the moment she said it. Then she shifted gears. "How long did you work for the DEA, Denis, and in what capacity?"

He stuttered and sputtered for a moment before finding his center. "For seven years, as an agent."

"How did you end up in that courtroom in D.C., and who killed Judge Campos? I believe I asked you that question once before and you said you didn't know, but I find that hard to believe."

He shoved his hands deep into his pockets and his shoulders slumped and his face clouded and he bit his bottom lip, making him look like a little boy in trouble. "I honestly don't know who killed the judge, but I ended up in his courtroom because the agency screwed me because they think I screwed them."

"You're saying the DEA set you up?" She couldn't keep the incredulity from her voice. No matter how little regard Jake had for the DEA and the FBI and the ATF and "all those other damn alphabets," she could not believe that a law enforcement agency would intentionally set up one of its own.

"I'm saying the DEA could have bailed me out of that mess and chose not to. I'm saying the DEA knows damn well that it wasn't me who killed that judge. I'm saying the DEA could clear my name any day. If it wanted to."

"And it doesn't want to?"

He shook his head.

"Proof?"

He shook his head again. "My word—a fugitive from justice— against that of a DEA section chief."

"I'll accept your word."

He pulled his hands out of his pockets and rubbed them together as if warming them, then ran them through his hair, standing it on end. "Short version, OK?" When she nodded, he continued. "I was in jail as part of a sting. It was a con we'd run three times before."

"'We'? You and the DEA?"

He nodded. "The DEA set me up in D.C. as this bad-ass dude from the islands, bringing in coke and reefer like I had a license. And I'm talking major shipments, not street-corner stuff. The people I sold to were the people with money: we're talking half-million-dollar deals. The plan was to work our way up the chain, tracing half a million dollars here, a million dollars there, all the way up to Mr. Deep Pockets, the real drug dealer. We weren't interested in those jerks hanging out on street corners selling a bag or a rock."

Carole Ann nodded to indicate that she was following, but she did not interrupt. "We'd done this deal three times, with me getting busted each time, along with one of the major players, then getting sprung on some technicality, walking out of the jail extolling the talents of my high-priced lawyer."

She nodded again, recalling Fritz Barber's cold imperiousness. "Was Fritz part of the setup?"

"Hell, no!" Denis exploded. "That money-grubbing son of a bitch. He's what's wrong with the legal profession."

Carole Ann nodded and noted the hint of surprise that registered in Denis's eyes; she didn't disagree with him. The Fritz Barbers of the bar and the way they practiced law were indeed a large part of what was wrong with the legal profession.

"After that third bust, the boys in the 'hood began to look at me strangely, questioning my continued good fortune, so it was decided to get me out of D.C. for a while. That's when my section chief came up with the brilliant idea for me to get some real experience down here, since I'd been pretending to be an islander." He laughed gently. "The stupid bastard first refused to believe me when I told him I was born in the Caribbean and that I didn't have to pretend to be what I am." The smile faded and his eyes grew dark and sad. "He didn't believe me until he checked my file. Then he sends for me and he has this big, cheesy grin on his face. He's sending me home, he says, on a special mission: the DEA is going to arrange for me to meet the 'commie dictator' on Isle de Paix—that's what they called my father, a commie dictator—they're going to arrange for me to meet him, and I'm supposed to convince him to allow them to use the island as a DEA staging area."

"You mean the DEA would bring drugs onto this island from other places . . . and do what with them?"

"You catch on fast. Drugs, dealers, guns, you name it, they'd bring it, then decide where it would go from there; that's how they put the sting in place. And in exchange for his cooperation, the CD—that's what I called Henri, to take the sting out of hearing them call him a commie dictator—if he went along with their plan, would incur the goodwill of the U.S. government, thereby winning for himself some much-needed U.S. aid."

"What went wrong?" Carole Ann asked.

"The way the operation was set up, if there were ever any glitches, Henri would be the guy on the point and there'd be no evidence of DEA involvement. And since there never was a dime in U. S. aid, he couldn't claim that's why he let himself be set up to look like a drug dealer. So, he quit. He sent for Collette and told him everything, but he made Collette promise not to honor any pre-existing arrangement with the DEA as a condition of handing over the reins of government. And then he planned Henri's revenge: Four boats from Trinidad arrived, loaded with Colombian coke. They slid into a secret cove on the north coast and right into the arms of the U. S. Coast Guard. The dealers thought the DEA had set them up, but the DEA knew Henri had screwed them, and they couldn't do a damn thing about it!" He released a short bark of bitter laughter. "The next morning, Henri's on a plane to Paris, Philippe Collette is the new head of state, and he tosses the DEA guy out on his ass when he shows up to complain."

Denis managed a real grin this time, a brief one, before it faded and he resumed his story. "I never successfully convinced them that I hadn't known what Henri was planning and that I wasn't a part of it. So, when I got back to D.C., they kept me on ice for a while. Then I was activated for this sting. Same kind of deal as before."

"Only this time, they left you holding the bag," Carole Ann finished, "as payback for the screwup here. And Steve Campos didn't know he was supposed to set a low bond, one that a working woman like your mother could make."

"As I said before, you catch on fast."

She leaned back in her chair and looked up at him. He met her gaze calmly and steadily. "So Henri LeRoi made your bail after it got reduced . . . but how'd it get reduced?"

"Well, there did occur something just a little bit underhanded. . . ."

"Something like what, Denis?"

"Something like simultaneous calls were made to the DEA and to Judge Campos, the result of which was that when the DEA tried to make a backdoor overture to Campos, suggesting that they wouldn't object to a reduction in bail, he smelled a rat and got really pissed off. He threatened to expose the DEA for dealing dirty."

"But he ultimately reduced your bail," she said musingly, "which he most definitely wouldn't have done without a compelling reason." She leaned back in the chair, propped her feet on the corner of the desk, and contemplated the possibilities. It would have taken a personal request from the United States attorney general to have made Campos reverse himself and reduce the bail of somebody like Denis St. Almain. Or the belief that an agency of the federal government had behaved badly or illegally. Despite his exile, Henri LeRoi obviously still wielded a pretty big club against the DEA. Why would he risk his own safety if, as Denis had described it, going public would expose him as a drug dealer? "I need to be in touch with Henri LeRoi, Denis, as soon as possible, and I need the names of your DEA supervisors and contacts."

He walked to the edge of the desk, rested his hands on it, and leaned his torso toward her, all but putting his face in hers. "Who are you?"

"I beg your pardon?"

"You must be some kind of spook or something, because you're not just some security expert here to help Philippe Collette figure out how to run the government."

"That's exactly who I am," Carole Ann replied. "I'm the 'Gibson' in Gibson, Graham International."

"That might be who you are now, or who you're pretending to be, but it's not who you are deep inside, and I'm not sure . . . I don't know how I feel about trusting you."

She stood up and leaned across the desk toward him, mimicking his action, forcing him to back up. "You don't have much choice, Denis. In fact, you've got no choice. You can walk out of here right now and have the dubious distinction of being the second guest in Isle de Paix's brand-new jail while you wait for extradition back to

D.C., or you can help me help you. OK, so you do have a choice: there it is."

He walked around the room in ever-widening circles, first worrying the hair that needed cutting, then rubbing his eyes like a kid needing a nap. "I tell you how to contact the CD and then what?"

"Then you go take a nap while I talk to my partner. Then I cook dinner, then we eat, we talk some more. And we wait."

"I wait here, with you? Locked in like a prisoner?"

"Unless you like sleeping and eating in the woods. And unless you prefer a real prison." She gave him a pad and pen and, after a long hesitation, he provided the information she requested and reluctantly turned it over.

"He's a good man."

"I don't doubt that, Denis."

Past being surprised or amazed at anything she said, he exhaled deeply. "Why not? You don't know him."

She smiled a real, if brief smile. "No, but I know his mother and his sisters." She picked up the phone and he headed toward the door. "Denis. One last question," she said as he turned around, an expectant look barely creasing the fatigue on his face. "What were you doing in that marijuana field?"

He grinned a lopsided grin. "I wondered when you'd get around to that. Pure dumb luck. I was checking out the fire scene; the stories I was hearing sounded suspicious, so I came for a look-see. I angled up through the woods from the airstrip and almost wet myself when I saw that stuff."

"So you don't know who our Farmer Brown is?"

He shook his head. "Not a clue. When I was in business with the feds, we imported the stuff, we didn't grow it."

She struggled to the surface of consciousness, groggy and incoherent, and for a moment, she could not place herself. Then, when she could, in that instant, she was fully awake and fully alarmed. "Who is it?" she demanded into the telephone.

"We got trouble." Jake's voice was quiet the way it was when something was wrong. She sat up and swung her legs around and dropped her feet to the floor, not speaking, knowing that he wanted her to listen. "The CD is broken," he said, and lapsed into silence.

She emptied her mind, then allowed to return only those thoughts that would help her understand his meaning. *The CD is broken.* . . . The commie dictator. "Beyond repair?" she asked, holding her breath in anticipation of the answer.

"Don't know yet. C.A.—" he began.

She cut him off. "I know, Jake. I know. I'm a shit magnet."

"Well, if you say so, but I was going to compliment you on your nose," he replied with a soft laugh. "You sure know a dung heap when you smell one."

"Just one of my many talents," she responded, only partially in jest, wishing for once that it weren't; wishing, as he had wished, that this could have been a simple, easy, lucrative job. Instead, it had turned into something as yet undefinable, but certainly ugly.

"What are you thinking?" he asked.

"That we're talking as if one of our lines isn't secure, and that I've got to do something with the CD accessory that I have, and that both thoughts make me nervous."

"I think the lines are probably OK," he said and, to prove it, offered a detailed explanation of how the Paris associate GGI had hired to talk with Henri LeRoi had interrupted the attempted assassination of the former dictator. "If we hadn't sent somebody to talk to him, he'd be history and we'd probably never know what the hell is going on down there."

"Who do you think went after him, and why?"

"Whoever killed Campos, and because he knows the 'who' and the 'why.' Now, how're you planning to get rid of your house guest and do you need me to come down there and help out?"

"No, I do not," she answered testily, and then told him in detail her plan for getting Denis St. Almain off the island.

"You don't know how to drive a boat, C.A." was his response after a moment of silence.

"I know," she replied. "I also don't have a boat to drive," she added, and hung up the phone. She dressed quickly—as quickly as possible in the dark, in a room that still was unfamiliar. Then she turned on the bed's table lamp and angled the neck as far down as it would go, providing just enough light to find the door. She slowly opened it and eased out into the hallway and bumped into a fully dressed Denis St. Almain, holding his shoes in his hand.

"What the hell are you doing! You scared the poop out of me!" she hissed at him.

"It's never good news when the phone rings in the middle of the night," he whispered back, "and I'm relieved to know that *something* scares the poop out of you. What's wrong?"

"Come in and sit down and be quiet for a moment. I've got to slow my heart rate." She stood back and let him enter the room.

He brushed past her with a smirk and settled into an armchair in the darkest corner of the room. She closed the door and went to stand beside him. She put a hand on his shoulder and told him what had happened to the man he believed was his father. She tightened her grip when he began to tremble, and talked to him about what she and Jake believed had happened and why, knowing that he blamed himself and hoping to alleviate his guilty feelings. "It still comes down to being my fault. He tipped his hand to get me out of jail."

She squeezed his shoulder again. "Your father made his deal with the devil long before you were part of this, Denis." The momentary funny feeling she experienced referring to LeRoi as his father vanished quickly. Certainly it was more natural than calling Philippe Collette his father. "Surely you don't think for a moment that whoever set up the game forgot who all the players were? They'd have gotten around to him eventually."

He nodded, accepting the truth, though not liking it. And he continued to nod his acquiescence if not his excitement as she described her plan to spirit him off the island.

"So this guy in Anguilla, where you want to send me, Jennings? He'll take me in just because you ask him to? And the yacht captain, Metier, he'll take me to the guy in Anguilla just because you ask him to? Lady, who the hell *are* you?"

"I told you: I'm the 'Gibson' in Gibson, Graham International."

"Right. And you're just doing what's best for your company and your contract with our little slice of paradise," he said sarcastically. And when she didn't respond, he hissed at her, "I don't believe you!"

"I don't care what you believe, Denis, just don't get in my way."

Jake called again at eight o'clock with the news that Henri LeRoi was still living and breathing, and he won the argument, for the second time, that prohibited her from telling his mother and sisters. "Whoever's behind this needs to think they still have something to worry about," he growled. "If they think LeRoi is dead or dying, they might go into hiding and we'll never find out who they are."

"And if they know he's not dead, and they think they've got something to worry about, they'll come after whoever can leverage him."

"And they can't get to St. Almain because you'll have him under wraps."

"But they can get to Simone."

"Nope," he answered smugly. "Already got her picked up and in hiding."

"Then at least let me tell Philippe," she countered, and when he didn't respond, she pressed her argument: "He knows enough of the story to be in danger, Jake."

"Yeah, but who else knows he knows?"

She paused. "Well . . . Denis."

"And who do you think he's told? Other than you? Look, C.A., telling Collette will either just give him more stuff to worry about, at best, and worst-case scenario, put him in unnecessary danger. Why not just hold this close to your chest until we see how it goes with LeRoi, and until you get St. Almain off the island?"

She finally agreed, able to find no fault with his reasoning, and hung up, after writing down messages to deliver to Roland Charles and David Messinger and relieved to note that both of them would be kept too busy today to want or need to interact with her: Roland, worrying about where to store the sand and gravel that was on its way to him, along with the mini-paver; and David, finalizing the police procedures manual for Isle de Paix. She left a note for Denis with the updated information on Henri LeRoi's condition and reminding him that he was locked in, and walked to Government House. She needed the time to think, to figure out how to implement her plan for getting Denis to Anguilla on Lionel Metier's yacht. And, she admitted to herself, she needed to be alone. Having another person in the house unnerved her. She'd been uncomfortable with other people in her space since Al died, her mother and brother being the two exceptions. And maybe Warren . . .

She quickly dismissed that thought and replaced it with a mental exercise that required all of her attention: she attempted to draw relational lines between all the players in this drama. She called up the name and face of every person she'd encountered since her arrival, scrutinizing the linear connections. And she found that some people didn't fit as neatly within the lines as she'd hoped. Paul Francois, for instance. She knew nothing about him, except that Philippe Collette had found him on the spur of the moment to replace the construction boss who belonged exclusively to Hubert de Villages. How had Philippe found him? And there was the man she had seen with both Denis and Marie-Ange, Mr. Too Handsome direct from central casting. Who was he, dammit! She stopped in her tracks and, for a moment, seriously considered going back to ask Denis, annoyed with herself for not having asked before. How could something so potentially important have slipped her mind? She thought of him as a drug dealer, but she didn't know *who* he was. Then, realizing she was standing in the middle of the road talking to herself, she sighed and walked on. She could ask Denis about him later; he wasn't going anywhere.

There were few tourists and little activity in the square; it was early in the day, and early in the week, and she found the relative calm as enjoyable, in its own way, as the energetic crush of the teeming crowds. Even the craft moored in the harbor appeared somnolent. She'd been in such a hurry to leave that she hadn't made coffee, so she spent forty-five minutes in Le Bistro, over coffee and fresh-baked brioche and reading the national edition of *The New York Times* an even earlier diner had left. It was just past nine-thirty when she entered her office, and the door hadn't closed fully behind her when there was a knock and it swung open again. Roland Charles rushed in. "I've been waiting for you!" He closed the door and hurried over to her, practically wringing his hands. "I saw him!" he hissed in an exaggerated stage whisper that would have been humorous were it not for the fact that he was seriously agitated and upset.

"Who, Roland? Who did you see?"

"From the boat! The pirate! I saw him!"

Truly taken aback, she pounced on his words. "Where? When?"

"This morning, at breakfast, of all places! That . . . that hoodlum was having breakfast at Le Bistro just like a normal human being! I was appalled, I can tell you."

Had he been there, at Le Bistro, when she was there and she'd not seen him? Was he in the courtyard having coffee and brioche and reading the newspaper, while she was inside, doing the same thing?

"What time was this, Roland? And was he alone, or was he with someone?"

He began shaking his head vigorously back and forth, something like panic spreading over his face, the agitation that had subsided once again directing him. "Nonono! He was not alone, and that is what is so disturbing, Carole Ann! We must tread very carefully—"

"Roland, Carole Ann, good. You're both here."

They whirled around, as if caught in some misbehavior, to see Philippe Collette in the doorway.

Roland quickly recovered himself. "Good morning, sir. You were looking for me?" He sounded almost guilty and Carole Ann, stealing a quick look at him, was surprised to see that he looked guilty.

"Both of you, actually, yes. Am I interrupting?"

"Not at all," Carole Ann interjected quickly, "and good morning. Would you like to talk here, or would you rather that we come to your office?"

"No, here is fine," the president replied, looking as harassed and uneasy as Roland looked guilty. "I just want to be certain that you're both comfortable proceeding with the road construction under the circumstances. I don't want you to feel obligated to place yourselves in danger."

"We feel no obligation at all," Roland replied stiffly, squaring his shoulders and sticking out his chest. "And I think I speak for Carole Ann as well when I say that we will not be intimidated by thugs and outlaws. We are committed to doing whatever is necessary to ensure the effective operation of this government. That is our commitment to you, sir."

Philippe raised an eyebrow and looked toward Carole Ann. She kept a straight face. "I concur wholeheartedly, and though you probably don't know it yet, Roland, that resolve will be tested very shortly. A barge with your name on it is on its way here."

"My paver? My sand and gravel and asphalt!" Without waiting for an answer, he hurried to the door, brushing past his boss. "Then I have work to do!" And he was gone.

For a brief moment, the island president relaxed his face and body and smiled a real smile. "Roland is a marvel," he said, affection filling his voice. "His enthusiasm really is infectious, and I have you to thank for that, Carole Ann."

She started to protest but he waved away her objections before she could voice them, and the action served to restore the heaviness he carried when he entered the office. He paced a few steps away from her, then turned back. "Is something bothering you, Philippe?"

"Yes, Carole Ann, quite a few things, none of which I'm able to resolve at the moment." He ran his hands through his hair, standing it on end, then smoothed it back down; a well-worn habit. "But you could help me sort out one problem, I think. About the DEA . . ."

"What about it?" She'd spoken too quickly, she knew, and she covered herself just as quickly. "Don't tell me they've somehow gotten wind of the marijuana?"

"No, no, not that. Another matter . . . an old matter . . ." His shoulders sagged and he swatted at the air in front of him, as if warding off an insect swarm. "But perhaps now is not the time."

"Philippe, may I ask you something?"

"Of course. What is it?"

"How did you contact Paul Francois?" she asked, and was taken completely by surprise at the look of embarrassment the question produced. He actually hung his head. "Philippe?"

"I . . . ah . . . he was referred by Henri LeRoi."

"By Henri . . . you've been in contact with Henri LeRoi?"

He bristled. "There is no harm in that! The man is not a criminal, after all."

"No, no, no. Of course not, and I did not mean to imply anything of the sort. I merely meant . . . did you telephone him, Philippe?"

"But of course," he answered.

"From the telephone here, in your office?"

"No," he answered, "from the telephone at my home." Carole Ann knew by the lengthening of his words and the falling timbre of his voice that he realized he'd made a mistake. "Has something happened to Henri?"

She ducked the question. "May I ask, Philippe, that you refrain from making any business calls from home? Any calls related to the conduct of Isle de Paix business, please make from the office here."

He nodded stiffly, then looked at his watch. "I must leave. I've a meeting with David and Yvette, which, by the way, means that *you* no longer have a meeting with David this morning. Sorry." He tossed a crooked smile at her from over his shoulder as he opened the door. "I'm sure you can find other amusements for yourself." And he was gone.

She waited exactly sixty seconds before hurrying to the door. She opened it and stepped into the hallway, relieved to find it empty, and turned left toward Roland Charles's office. There weren't very many people about and, in that instant, for the first time, she was conscious of the fact that there were no surplus or superfluous employees of the island government; therefore, everybody in Government House had a specific job to do and spent the hours of their workday doing it. When the president wanted to see her, he walked down the hallway to her office. When the minister of the interior or the minister of internal security wanted to see her, he walked down the hallway to her office. And when she wanted to see one of them, there was no phalanx of secretaries and administrative assistants to create a buffer or barrier to prevent her access. There were no faxes or e-mails or memos. She realized how much she preferred this kind of smallness, this kind of intimacy, to the trappings of big government, not to mention how much more work got done in the process.

Except, dammit, when the minister of the interior was not in his office. "But I just saw him not five minutes ago!" Carole Ann exclaimed to the nonplussed assistant.

"Yes, ma'am, he visited your office, then he rushed in here, read the faxed message from your Washington office, and out he rushed. I'm afraid he won't return until very late this afternoon."

"Does he have a phone with him?"

"I beg your pardon? A *phone?* With him? No, ma'am, he does not."

Of course he doesn't, she thought. Neither do you, for that matter, she reminded herself; and you won't, not as long as you're on this island. No cell phones and no pagers and no way to establish immediate contact with anybody. "Would you happen to know exactly where the minister was going?" she asked hopefully, and sighed her thanks and left when the assistant regretted that he did not. She regretted that she'd have to wait until sometime later that evening to learn the source of Roland's morning agitation—her interest was piqued by the fact that he had seemed more upset by the identity of the pirate's breakfast companion than by the pirate's presence. And the boat, dammit! She needed to ask him if she could borrow his—his agency's—boat. And if he could teach her to drive it.

"Carole Ann!" She turned to see Jackie LaBelle speeding down the hall toward her, her purse dangling from the crook in her right arm, her briefcase clutched in her left hand. She stopped and waited for the young woman, who was breathless and, to Carole Ann's surprise, slightly disheveled.

"Jackie . . ."

"I need a place of refuge! Are you very busy?"

"Are you all right?"

"If I could commit murder with impunity, I'd be much better," she said through clenched teeth. "Can we go to your office? I need to avoid mine." And without waiting for permission, she led the way to Carole Ann's office and closed the door decisively behind them. She dumped her purse and briefcase on the floor and began repairing herself: she smoothed her hair, tucked her blouse into her skirt, and adjusted her jacket.

Carole Ann waited while the younger woman regained control, wondering how long it would be before such displays no longer were part of her behavior—before she realized that cool, calm, and collected was the only acceptable demeanor for a diplomat to present. Jackie seemed to have read her thoughts.

"Guess I can't go around losing my temper like that."

"I wouldn't advise it."

"My cousin's wife is driving me crazy. But then, my cousin is driving *her* crazy, so, in a way, she's not totally responsible for her behavior. And yet, I cannot allow her to continue to interrupt my work with her whining and complaining. Look at me! I'm afraid to go to my own office. I saw her lurking outside the door, and I fled to you!"

"Young girl?" Carole Ann asked, suddenly alert. "Well dressed and sad-looking? In the finance ministry?"

Jackie looked surprised. "You've met her?" Carole Ann related the encounter of the day before. "She knows who you are, Carole Ann, because everybody knows who you are. And she knows my comings and goings because she spends more time at my house than at her own, though I can't blame her for that. If I were married to my cousin, I'd make myself scarce, too, even if it meant spending more time with the mother-in-law from hell."

"You're talking in circles, Jackie."

"I'm supposed to talk in circles. I'm a diplomat."

"Not funny. Explain the mother-in-law crack," Carole Ann ordered.

"Just imagine having Marie-Ange as a mother-in-law!"

"I had a version of Marie-Ange as a mother-in-law. What's that have to do with the girl downstairs? What's her name?"

"Nicole, and she's married to Andre, which Marie-Ange hates because she didn't arrange the marriage. In fact, she didn't know Andre was married until he came home with his bride a few months ago. And poor little bride, she expected quite a different life as the daughter-in-law of the president of a Caribbean island. She also expected quite a different life as the wife of Andre Collette, and that's why she has my sympathy. Cousin Andre is a world-class fuckup, pardon my French," she said with a big chuckle. "He thinks racing sailing yachts is a profession."

"It is, in some circles," Carole Ann offered.

"Not in his," Jackie snorted. "Everybody in this family has to work for a living these days, including Andre and his wife. No more living off the labor of the serfs. Unfortunately, the only credential Andre has to his name is expulsion from four universities—one French, two American, and one Canadian. Nicole is French-Canadian, by the way, and formerly enamored of the notion of living life as the wife of the president of a French-speaking Caribbean island."

"So that's why she's so unhappy working in the finance ministry?"

Jackie nodded. "But at least she can keep a job. Andre has worked for the tourist board, the bank, and now some privately owned property-leasing agency. Can you imagine how difficult it must have been to fire the president's son?" She grimaced. "Poor Nicole. I really do feel for her, but I'm also really tired of being the one to listen to her whine about Andre."

"So why doesn't she dump him and go home?" Carole Ann had quickly lost interest in Nicole and her problems; her mind already had returned to her own, namely to the telephone call Philippe Collette made to Henri LeRoi from his home telephone.

"She can't, exactly," Jackie replied slowly. "Which is yet another reason for my sympathetic feelings for her. See, she married Andre against her parents' wishes, and dropped out of school to be with him."

"So, kids make mistakes. Parents forgive them." Carole Ann was impatient, and anxious for Jackie to go away.

"Not if the mistake is marrying a Black man," Jackie said softly, and stooped to pick up her purse and briefcase.

Carole Ann stared at her. "It came as a surprise to them that Andre is Black?"

Jackie nodded. "Let's just say that Andre bears a striking resemblance to the de Villages side of the family."

"And has Andre's behavior strained his relationship with his parents, too?" Carole Ann asked, recalling Marie-Ange's reaction to his presence at the party.

Jackie gave a sad half smile. "His behavior strains his parents' relationship with each other. He's his mother's baby boy and the bane of his father's existence." She moved to the door. "Thanks for listening, Carole Ann."

"You're welcome. And Jackie? You've got to get both your temper and your bleeding heart under control, or else some steely-eyed, coldhearted, wing tip–wearing junior diplomat is going to have you for lunch."

"I've seen Madeleine Albright show emotion," she answered defensively.

"Perhaps. But you've never seen her bleed," Carole Ann shot back.

"Touché," Jackie answered, closing the door.

For a long moment, Carole Ann did not know what to do. There was no order to the thoughts swirling about in her head. There were too many questions with no answers, and too much potential for disaster due to all those unanswered questions. She dared not call Jake from the phone here; her paranoia was such that she would trust only the phone at home. She marveled at the absurdity of calling Henri LeRoi's former residence "home." He was in the hospital at death's door, and Paul Francois was in the morgue because Henri LeRoi had given him a job referral. And here she was standing in the middle of the floor wondering what to do next: go chasing after Roland Charles to ask permission to borrow his boat so that she could ferry a possible felon out to sea to rendezvous with a luxury yacht? Tell the police chief that there quite possibly was a rogue DEA agent operating on the island—or more likely, an *ex*–DEA agent? Or take her own advice—the advice that she so cavalierly had tossed to Denis—and go home, sit down, and wait?

She looked at her watch. She'd barely been here an hour. Did she need to be worried that leaving would cause concern? Suppose Philippe came looking for her? No. He would be tied up with David and Yvette for hours. Yet, remaining served no purpose. And what purpose would be served sitting at home and staring at a telephone or a fax machine? She could, she thought, easily justify going in search of Roland Charles. If he allowed her to use his boat, she could even practice driving it about . . . or whatever one did with boats. After all, how difficult could it be? She could drive a car, certainly she could drive a boat. And, she speculated, she had at least two days to practice, for she was certain that once Jake contacted Lionel Metier, the yacht captain would come as quickly as possible to pick up Denis and get him off the island.

"Once I'm rid of Denis St. Almain, I'll turn David and Yvette loose and let them shake all the trees and rattle all the cages they want," she told herself as she walked down the corridor and out the front door, and she experienced a sense of great satisfaction at the thought. Responsibility for Denis was a weight she no longer wanted. For the second time that morning, she strolled across the square in front of Government House, and, for the second time during one of those strolls, she was startled by a man whom she first took to be Denis St. Almain. Because the square wasn't crammed with tourists, she got a better look this time: certainly he was taller than Denis, though he was just as slim; but this man walked with a loose-limbed stride, looking straight ahead, whereas Denis walked slowly and observantly, like a cop. And though this man, she thought, was white, he eerily resembled Denis St. Almain. And Philippe Collette. Andre!

She looked quickly around to see if she'd been noticed, and set off after him, thinking that he could not lead her into danger. There were, after all, only a few possible destinations in the immediate vicinity of Government House, and if he was going to visit his wife, he was headed in the wrong direction.

Behaving very much like a tourist, which he easily could have been, dressed as he was all in white, his sunglasses hanging by an arm from the neck of his T-shirt, he strolled casually in and out of shops and stores, stopping periodically to gaze into windows. He looked once at his watch and continued his meandering ways. Then he stopped abruptly, stuffed his hands into his pockets, changed direction, and crossed the square, going back where he'd just come from. Carole Ann slowed her pace and glanced around in search of a reason that the man she believed to be Andre Collette would have shifted gears so suddenly.

He was standing in front of a jewelry store, peering into the window. He looked at his watch again, then put his sunglasses on. Carole Ann continued to scan the street, eyes shifting from side to side, taking in every building, including Government House, and every person on the street. Then she saw him. Coming out of the bank, the smoothly handsome man she'd seen with Denis St. Almain at Aux Fruits de Mer, had seen leaving the north coast restaurant with Simone Collette . . . who had held her and Roland at gunpoint . . . whom she thought of as a drug dealer. He, too, donned sunglasses and swiftly crossed the square directly toward Andre Collette, who, as the man approached, entered Le Bistro. The man followed him in. Carole Ann waited a moment, then entered the restaurant.

She waved away the hostess and began a slow circle of the restaurant, ending up, as she'd expected, out on the patio, in the far corner. She walked up to the table. *"Bonjour, Monsieur Collette. Comment ça va?"*

He stared up at her, ignoring her extended hand. "You look very much like your father, but, unfortunately, you have inherited none of his charm or grace. Or, as I understand it, his ambition. Though perhaps your proclivity for fast boats has some value to your . . . associate." Then, ignoring him, she turned to the other man. "I wish I could say that it was a pleasure to see you again, but, of course, that would be a lie." She held his cold, contemptuous gaze, not terrified as she had been that day on the boat with Roland. "You two make an interesting pair," she said, looking from one to the other, and then turning abruptly away from them. She all but ran the three-quarters of a mile home.

"I don't know who he is," Denis insisted. "I went to the bar and sat down. He happened to be who I sat next to."

"But you talked to him."

"Did I?"

"Goddammit, don't get cute with me, Denis. People are dead and lives are in jeopardy and whoever that man is, he has something to do with it." Carole Ann was coldly furious.

"I don't know the man, I'd never seen him before, I haven't seen him since."

"What did you talk about?"

Denis flinched at the cutting edge of her tone and backed a step away from her. "He asked me," he said, curling his lips in disgust, "if I wanted to score, like he was mocking me, like he knew exactly who I was." He spit out the words.

"Who were the local DEA contacts here? Other than LeRoi?" Carole Ann asked, ignoring his angst.

Denis paused and thought for a moment, put off-balance by how cold and exacting she had become. "There was a contact at the bank, I know, and possibly one other person."

"What do you mean, 'possibly'?" she pushed him. "Either you were a part of the operation here or you weren't. They had your father in the middle of it, setting him up to be the Thanksgiving turkey, and the best you can do is 'possibly'?"

"Listen, damn you! They were using me, too! I was as big a chump as the CD, walking around believing that I was playing a part in slowing down the flow of coke into the States." He rubbed his hands through his hair, standing it on end, not bothering to smooth it back down . . . like his father did.

"And weren't you?" she shot at him.

"Hell, no! That coke shipment the coast guard seized the night my father and Collette changed places was the only time I know of that dealers got busted and drugs got seized here. And the only useful thing I did the whole time was convince the poor, ignorant commie dictator to cooperate with the DEA. I never arrested anybody or seized any drugs."

Carole Ann began to pace. Andre Collette in cahoots with . . . who? The man she'd seen him with at the restaurant was, she was certain, the same man Roland Charles had seen him with, the same man who had held her and Roland hostage at gunpoint. She had no trouble connecting that man—the sleazeball pirate—to the murder of the two constables and, given his proximity to the president's wife and son, there easily could be a motive for wanting Philippe Collette dead. But who was he and what was the motive? "The one other person who 'possibly' was a DEA source or contact, Denis: Who was it?"

"I don't know exactly who, but I always thought it was somebody associated with Hubert de Villages."

The pirate—damn, she wished she had a name for him!—used Hubert de Villages as the reason for intimidating her and Roland. Hubert de Villages owned the bank the pirate left just prior to his meeting with Andre Collette. The school and clinic that were the reasons for delaying construction on the new government road were surprise gifts from Hubert de Villages. Marie-Ange Collette was his granddaughter.

The phone on the worktable rang, startling both of them, and when it rang a second time and she didn't move to answer it, Denis looked panicked. "Aren't you going to answer it?"

"It's the fax machine," she said, still distracted by thoughts of Hubert de Villages, who was well into his eighties and supremely wealthy. What did a man like that need or want with drug dealers and pirates? Of course, he wouldn't be the first rich, old bastard to be motivated by greed. More money, more money, more money. The mantra of contemporary culture.

"You've got a message," Denis said, gesturing toward the fax machine with his head.

"Thanks," she replied absently, crossing to the machine. She wasn't expecting anything today. She held her hand out to receive the paper and read with relief that Henri LeRoi was alive and recovering. He could not say who had attacked him, and he was forbidden from saying anything more for at least twenty-four hours. "Good news," she said to no one, for when she looked up for Denis to deliver the message, he was gone. She tossed the paper down and rushed out the office and down the hallway to the kitchen, to find her suspicion confirmed: she had not armed the alarm system when she returned. She called out to Denis, running back down the hallway to his room, knowing that he was gone. "Shit, shit, shit," she muttered, looking around. It could have been a hotel room newly cleaned by the maid after a guest's departure. The bathroom looked the same way. She wouldn't be surprised if he'd wiped the surfaces clean of his fingerprints. She left the room and slouched down the hall to the office, thinking that the positive spin on this debacle was that it eliminated the need for Lionel Metier and his yacht, and for her to know how to drive a speedboat to get Denis to it. Damn!

She didn't know what annoyed her more—the fact that she had al-lowed him to escape or the fact that he thought escape necessary. Es-cape from what? And why? Because she was pressing him about DEA contacts and activities on the island? Did he know more than he had admitted and therefore had lied to her? She was imagining Jake's re-sponse even as she sat down to call him. Yeah, it would serve him right if the cops picked him up and shipped him back to D.C., but it wouldn't solve her problems; in fact, it would only serve to validate the suspicion that murdering drug dealers had a foothold in Isle de Paix. And that two sons of the president—and possibly his wife— were involved.

Carole Ann knew that she had given insufficient attention to Deauville, the principal town on Isle de Paix's north end. She also accepted the unspoken reason for the omission: this was the domain of the wealthy, ergo, not the place to look for crime and criminals. It was a glaring oversight, a mistake she knew she never should have made, and one she was prepared to correct.

She studied the maps of the island. Although most of what was geographically designated as Deauville was privately owned and therefore outside the purview of the Isle de Paix government, because the town and its inhabitants accepted basic governmental services, the government maintained certain proprietary rights, including police functions. And police functions, to Carole Ann's mind, included enforcement as well as protection. She had talked with Yvette Casson and knew that the police patrols on that end of the island had been met first with suspicion, then with bemused wariness, and, finally, with open acceptance. "Free coffee and croissants anytime at the cafe, and free pâté and baguettes anytime at Le Bistro," Yvette told her. "Makes me wish I still walked a beat."

Reminded that Le Bistro also operated on the north coast, Carole Ann decided that a late lunch followed by a stroll about the town, window-shopping and stopping here and there to chat, would be a more productive entry into Deauville culture than in her official capacity as consultant to the government. Besides, if she spent her own money, she was on her own time, and therefore, for all practical purposes, a private citizen. So, in a manner that would have made Jake Graham proud, she assumed her wealthy matron guise, hopped into her Jeep, and aimed it north. From her house, turning left on the Coast Road, the route was achingly familiar: three miles along the road she reached the still-scorched site where Paul Francois had lost his life and saw amazing evidence of life's struggle to overcome death. Green was showing through the black, the new growth even beginning to encroach upon the cut into the forest. Roland had told her that he'd had the destroyed equipment removed, and its absence gave the area a look of desolation rather than of despair.

Carole Ann continued driving, though more slowly now. She was riding parallel to the marijuana field and she wanted to see if there was any indication of egress into the forest. She didn't expect there would be, and she was certain that Yvette and David already would have looked for something so obvious. Still, she looked. She also wanted to give visual credence to what she knew to be factual: that she was approaching the widest part of the island and that inland from here were the sugarcane and lumber plantations. She knew that the road leading to them was on the other coast—on the Atlantic side— but she wanted to fix in her memory a clear portrait of the terrain.

The road rose and curved inward, revealing an endless expanse of sea. She was looking due north. The Caribbean lay immediately before her and, in the distance, the Atlantic. Somewhere in between were Puerto Rico and Haiti and the Dominican Republic—that Siamese-twin island, half French and half Spanish—as different from each other as if they were placed in different oceans. Indeed, the single island that was both Haiti and the Dominican Republic was reflective of the dual nature of these islands: Caribbean on one side, Atlantic on the other; exclusive on one side, egalitarian on the other. At least here on Isle de Paix, she thought, the differences were not as stunning. Or were they, and she had chosen not to see them? As she had chosen not to assign the possibility of Deauville as the source of the evil lurking on the island.

She rounded the tip of Isle de Paix and began the descent down its Atlantic side. Tile roofs and turrets took turns vying with the shale cliffs for recognition on one side of the road, the Atlantic awesome on the other. And, once around the bend, Deauville itself, a tiny French village plucked from its European roots, airlifted across the Atlantic, and planted here, on this cliffside. The traffic, such as it was, all things being relative, was Frenchlike, too, Carole Ann noted sourly as she waited for a parking space. How could there be traffic congestion in such a tiny place? she wondered. And where did all these cars come from? There were more cars parked on this one street than she'd seen in all of Ville de Paix. Every other parking space was occupied by the same shiny, new American vehicle, something she'd never been aware of, she realized, squinting to read the manufacturer's name on the bumpers. Then she saw the rental-car logo and remembered that there was a car-rental agency at the airstrip.

"Dammit!" she exclaimed and smacked the steering wheel much too hard with the palm of her hand. "Damn," she said again, with considerably less emotion, massaging her hand. But the realization that had struck her remained sharp: there was a paved road from South Coast Road leading to the island airstrip and, according to one of the older maps, there once had been paved roads from the airstrip into the interior of the island, and a small community of cane cutters and log splitters living in the interior north of the airstrip. That community no longer existed, but some semblance of those old roads must remain, she reasoned, because that's how Denis St. Almain said he managed to reach the marijuana field without being noticed. She closed her eyes and pulled his words into memory: *"I angled up through the woods from the airstrip"* is what he'd told her. And he couldn't have managed it, given the density of the underbrush, without some kind of road. That, no doubt, also was how he reached her house undetected. She hadn't attached significance to his use of the word "airstrip." "Better late than never," she muttered to herself, not entirely convinced of the truth of that sentiment. Late could be deadly.

She swung into a parking space, climbed out of the Jeep and

locked it, the myriad thoughts clicking into places of logic and rationality. There were pieces missing, certainly, but there also was beginning to be form to the pieces that existed. She began to stroll, looking about in the casual way of a tourist but paying close and careful attention to every detail of the scenery before her. And it was lovely scenery. She had parked on Deauville's main street, which, in keeping with apparent island tradition, bore no formal name. Perhaps it didn't need one. Certainly it was the widest street in the village, and home to the trendiest of everything Deauville had to offer. Though the sidewalks were paved concrete, the street was cobblestone, like the main street in Ville de Paix.

Most of the shops and stores were fronted with French doors and windows, sparkling in the sunlight beneath sloping, rounded thatched roofs. She was not the only stroller; in fact, the sidewalks were crowded, as were many of the shops and most of the eateries. But she was aware of the difference in the crowd on this end of the island. There was less hustle and bustle, less energy, less electricity. No doubt part of it had to do with the fact that none of these people had just disembarked from cruise ship confinement. The other part had to do with the fact that those tourists who booked accommodations on this side of the island probably were not the kind to wear cutoff jeans and flip-flops to lunch. There was, she knew, a mammoth and exclusive resort half a mile from here, nestled into one of the low-hanging cliffs, and she expected that a good number of her fellow window shoppers were lodged there; the others, no doubt, were guests at one of the two dozen or so other hotels, inns, and guest houses of various sizes and degrees of elegance. She wondered as she surveyed the crowd which of the strollers might be a native, a permanent resident, perhaps even a member of the de Villages family? She had no way of knowing.

The end of the street narrowed and petered out into a lane of saltbox houses, reminding Carole Ann of every East Coast beach town she'd ever visited, from Georgia to New Jersey. The clapboard structures were painted white or gray, a periodic pastel thrown in here and there. There were at least a dozen of them, single-story and multistoried, and in the yards of most, one of the shiny, new rental cars. The tourists who rented these houses certainly enjoyed easy access to town, but if they came here to enjoy the beach, they needed a car. True, the view of the Atlantic Ocean was just at the end of the street. A dip in the brine was down a steep cliff and around a winding road.

She turned her attention away from the saltbox houses and back to the main street, aware, again, of the parallels between Deauville and Ville de Paix: here, at the end of the street, before giving way to the residential strip, were the post office, the bank—the de Villages bank—the money exchange, and the tourist bureau. All that was missing was Government House. She crossed over to the other side of the street, hoping that by the time she reached the end, the crowd in Le Bistro would have thinned and she could get a table. Her appetite increased as she passed a butcher shop that easily would have been at home in the Seventeenth Arrondissement, though she wondered where the meat came from. It had not occurred to her to eat meat when the seafood was so plentiful and the ways of cooking it so artful. She understood fully, in that moment, why tourism was so important to this and all the islands of the Caribbean: residents imported almost everything and could not afford to do so without the income from tourist dollars.

"Madame Gibson!"

She turned, startled, to see who was calling her, and she smiled when she spied Toussaint Remy's neighbor in the doorway of the butcher shop. "Madame St. Georges," she said, turning back. She greeted the older woman with kisses to both cheeks. "How nice to see you! How is Monsieur Remy? Are his hands healing?"

The woman shook her head sadly. "He acts now like an old man." She shook her head again, then brightened. "You are still coming to dinner with us on Saturday, yes?"

Carole Ann smiled, too. "Nothing could keep me away, Madame St. Georges."

"*Bon.* That is the only time he smiles, when he talks of your visit."

"I may even come early, then!" Carole Ann said and asked whether she could bring anything, hoping that she wasn't offending, then relieved that her offer was well received though politely refused.

"*Mais non, madame.*" Then she gave Carole Ann an appraising, head-to-toe glance. "You are working on the north end of the island today," she said, and it was a statement filled with both knowledge and understanding.

"I realized that I know very little about Deauville," she replied carefully.

"And I, madame, know *everything* about Deauville. Perhaps you will ask me questions and I will give you answers, eh?"

Could it be so simple? Carole Ann nodded without speaking, her immediate shift into lawyer mode only part of the reason. In truth, she could think of nothing to say.

"I am cook for Monsieur de Villages," the woman added in a low voice, "just as my mother was cook for Monsieur de Villages. And on special occasions, I also cook for Madame le Présidente."

Carole Ann continued her stroll along the Deauville main street, feeling relieved and lightened, as if a weight had been lifted. More like a veil lifted, she thought, believing that come Saturday, she would gain a glimpse of Isle de Paix's secret places. She stopped in a small gallery and admired the work of a couple of local artists. And she ate a hearty meal at Le Bistro, reluctantly denying herself only a glass of wine; that's how good she felt, that she'd seriously contemplate wine with lunch. She walked for a while more after eating, instilling in her memory the lay of the land. She wanted to know Deauville's main artery as well as she knew Ville de Paix.

Then, as she reached the end of the street, she wondered how the residents of the saltbox beach houses reached them. No cars could pass through the narrow end of the street to the lane. Could they? She turned around and walked back down the street, more briskly this time, as if on a mission. And to demonstrate as much, she strode into the Bureau de Change, removing her wallet from her purse. She waited in a short line, listening to conversations in French, English, Dutch, and German. When it was her turn at the window, she exchanged pleasantries in French with the teller, and traveler's checks for island currency. She left the building and stood outside the door, slightly off to the left, taking time to carefully tuck the cash into her wallet, and just as carefully tucking the wallet into her purse, all the while satisfying her belief that vehicular traffic could not enter the enclave from the main road. How, then, did the inhabitants get their cars back there?

She put her sunglasses on and turned toward the end of the street. She stepped carefully as the paved sidewalk gave way to a concrete-set gravel that was solid though uneven, and she found herself wondering whether this would be an effective and efficient method of paving the roads of Ville de Paix. She'd have to bring Roland up here to take a look. She hung her purse on her shoulder and, like a tourist, strolled along the lane, looking from side to side. It reminded her very much of the street on which she lived—on the street where Henri LeRoi had lived. Well-tended grass verges took the place of curbs and sidewalks, bordered by equally well-tended tropical foliage. But these houses were much newer than those on her street; in fact, she doubted that this development was more than five or six years old. And it clearly was a development. All the houses, though marginally different from one another, retained an inescapable similarity. They were designed by the same architect and built by the same developer.

She looked up at the sky, searching for the sun. She'd lost her bearings and she wanted to know in which direction she was walking. This development didn't exist on any map she'd seen, and she wanted to be able to place it. When she looked back down at the road and toward the nearest house, she caught her breath. From the house directly to her right emerged "the pirate" with another man. She willed herself to keep strolling, to keep behaving like a tourist. To stop suddenly would draw attention and she knew he easily would recognize her. But neither man glanced her way, and without looking at or speaking to each other, they got into a green compact car and, before the doors had closed, Carole Ann had turned around and was walking briskly the other way. She knew the car couldn't follow and she hoped that by the time it had backed down the driveway, she'd be too far away to be recognizable. She did regret, however, not being able to get the license plate number of the car.

"Not a problem," Yvette Casson said easily. "I think I can get a roster of all the rental cars on the island without too much difficulty. You'd be amazed at the spirit of cooperation afoot on the island these days," she added cheerfully.

Carole Ann returned a sour response. "But that won't really tell us anything, will it?"

The chief raised an eyebrow at her. "I'd call finding out who held you and Roland at gunpoint quite a bit of something, Carole Ann, especially if we can connect him to the guns that killed those constables. We may even be able to find out how long he's been on the island, and, depending on how many cars are rented out to that location, get some idea of how transient the population up there is. Or not, as the case may be. At the very least, we'll have a name that we can run through NASIS. And before you panic," she said, raising a hand at the look on Carole Ann's face, "I won't say a word to David—at least for a few days. He's off island anyway."

Carole Ann panicked. "Where is he?"

Yvette laughed. "Relax. He and his wife went to St. Bart's for the weekend. There's a jazz festival over there. I was thinking about going myself, but things are a little too squirrelly for us both to be away. Now, about these enclaves . . ." They spent the better part of the next hour discussing what might remain of the village of the cane cutters and loggers in the interior, and the origin of the new Deauville community, neither of which appeared on any of the maps in Yvette's possession. "Did you all order any new topographical surveys and maps?"

Carole Ann shook her head. "We worked from the most recent one, which is almost ten years old, and Philippe said nothing new had been built in the intervening years."

"You think he doesn't know about those houses?" Yvette sounded both doubtful and incredulous.

"I think he doesn't think about Deauville when he thinks about Isle de Paix," Carole Ann replied. "I think he thinks only about what he's responsible for."

"I've got cops up there!" Yvette responded hotly. "He thinks he's not responsible for them?" She bristled, and if she were a cat, she would have been puffed up to twice her size.

"You know what I mean, Yvette," Carole Ann said, trying for soothing.

"Yeah," she allowed reluctantly, sounding somewhat less than soothed, "I know what you mean. I'm gonna go bug Roland, see if he's got some closets and storage rooms I can dig around in, look for old maps and legends. I'd sure like to have a better lay of the land before I go traipsing around in there."

"And I'd like to have a lot more information before you go traipsing around in there," C.A. said quickly.

"Yeah, yeah, yeah, I know you would," the chief groused, sounding very coplike. "Now you're talking more like a lawyer," she said sourly, "and less like a cop."

Carole Ann thanked her for the backhanded compliment and asked to accompany her to visit Roland's closets and storage bins.

"Why, Carole Ann? What are you looking for? That means there's something you haven't told me, doesn't it?"

Carole Ann shrugged and offered a rueful grin. "I don't know what I'm looking for, Yvette. Really," she added at the chief's lifted eyebrow. "There are pieces that don't fit the puzzle and I suppose I'm hoping that I'll recognize one of those pieces when I see it."

"You're still talking like a lawyer," the cop said, then said no more, leaving it for Carole Ann to pursue or drop the matter. She chose the latter option. Whatever dust might be stirred up in an old closet wasn't worth antagonizing Yvette Casson, who, so far, had demonstrated a remarkable willingness to line up behind Carole Ann against her boss. That was luck too good to push since, technically, Carole Ann's line of authority extended to David Messinger and not Yvette Casson.

Carole Ann stood up. "And I'm a good enough lawyer to know when I've used up all my lawyer chits. Thanks for your help, Yvette."

Yvette shook her head ruefully. "You're good, Carole Ann, real good. I know you haven't told me everything you know, or think you know. I also know you're smart enough to tell me what it is before you run the risk of placing yourself in line for an obstruction of justice charge. I just hope you're smart enough to fill me in before whatever it is gets you—or somebody else—in trouble."

Carole Ann left the chief's office feeling more than a little out of sorts. She'd just received a not-so-subtle warning to tread carefully. The fact that Yvette Casson, too, believed that something sinister and dangerous lurked in paradise would not prevent the chief from holding Carole Ann's feet to the fire if that became necessary. She walked out into the sun-splashed square and stood watching the crowd, wondering how she could avoid conflict with Yvette Casson. The chief knew that Carole Ann was holding back, but she had no intention of sharing thoughts and suspicions and postulations. She needed facts, and the pursuit of them could get her in trouble with Yvette, and she didn't want that. So her options were limited to making the three-quarter-mile walk home and submitting to an evening of paperwork. She started walking, consoling herself with the fact that she could go for a run before dark and do a few laps in the pool, maybe even in the ocean, to compensate for the helpless, useless feeling that was making her so irritable.

She frowned at the sheet of white paper hanging from the latch of the front gate, and quickened her pace. She reached for it, opened it quickly, and released a relieved breath as she smiled down at the handwritten note from Roland Charles: of course she wanted to be on hand in the morning when the road crew resumed construction at the new government road site. She could feel his excitement emanating from the paper, though she couldn't muster enough optimism to share his belief that the road might be completed before the rainy season after all. A mini-paver, or whatever the thing was called, was a poor substitute for a bulldozer, a backhoe, and a dump truck, even though she knew that Luc and Jean, working under Toussaint Remy's close supervision, finally had succeeded in getting the second dump truck up and running. She wondered why she hadn't known that the equipment had arrived early—she hadn't expected work to begin again until Monday—but to raise the question would possibly dampen Roland's enthusiasm, and she didn't want that.

* * *

Not that anything she could do or say could minimize the enthusiasm of the three dozen or more people who greeted her at the work site the following morning. The atmosphere was nothing short of festive, though everyone there—women, men, and a group of young people—was hard at work. Roland bounded over to her, perspiration already making his face shiny, his T-shirt and khaki slacks already soiled. "I called the men back to work and their friends and families have come with them!" She recognized that such an outpouring was a marvelous display of community spirit, and said as much, to his obvious annoyance. "No, Carole Ann," he snapped. "I am not speaking of community spirit. The significance of this demonstration goes far beyond that! You must see that it means that no one associated with the job did the sabotage." He met her astonished gaze with one of guileless self-satisfaction.

"Truly, Roland, I had not for a moment entertained that thought."

"But . . . but . . . you and David wanted me to believe that it was an accident! If you didn't mistrust these workers, then why?"

She mentally kicked herself in the butt for so totally underestimating the man. "We didn't want to alarm you, Roland."

"But I was already alarmed! What could possibly be more alarming?"

"The fact that at the end of your road, there's a field of marijuana worth several million dollars."

His eyes widened and he tried, and failed, to find his voice. He turned away from her to survey the scene across the road: people wielding everything from garden shovels and pickaxes to broken pieces of stick were attacking and beating back the foliage from the entrance to the forest, once again revealing the beginnings of the new road. Several large burlap tarps were spread out on the ground and the cuttings tossed into them. Carole Ann watched, too, growing increasingly concerned for the safety of these people. "Did you tell Yvette that you were resuming work this morning?"

He shook his head. "No, the equipment isn't here yet. . . . Oh my

God!" he exclaimed, as the realization of the potential danger of the situation became clear. "I was just so excited . . . it comes tomorrow, to the port, and we will bring it up here on Sunday. . . . Oh my God! What have I done?"

"Calm down, Roland." She took his arm, then tightened her grip. Several people already had looked toward them at the sound of his exclamation. "No need for anybody but us to know that we have anything to worry about here," she said, sounding not at all convincing.

"What can . . . should we do?"

"I'll run back home and call Yvette." She had jogged to the site and had nothing but a door key in her pocket. "Are there people down the road, Roland? Near the marijuana field?"

He looked across at the crowd. "I don't know . . . I don't think so."

"Without panicking them, Roland, make sure everybody remains here, at the entrance." As she turned away to head toward home, he grabbed her arm.

"It would be faster to take my truck," he said, retrieving a key ring from his pants pocket. When she hesitated, he added, "It is parked on your street. You must have passed it, a white pickup."

She nodded, accepting the keys from him. She remembered seeing it. She ran up the road, then crossed over and ran toward the truck, hoping she appeared more nonchalant than she felt. Just as she reached the intersection, Yvette's cruiser arrived, lights flashing along with the chief's anger. Carole Ann slowed her gait, more because of the scowl the chief wore than anything else.

"What the hell are you doing?" the chief barked.

"I was on my way to get you," Carole Ann replied, trying to cover her surprise.

Yvette looked her up and down. "How fast do you run, exactly?" Her tone was dry enough to crack ice.

"Roland's," she said, dangling the keys, and Yvette actually looked around for the white pickup, relaxing when she spied it.

"Why didn't I know this was happening today?" Yvette's question demanded an answer, but she didn't wait for one. "I don't like surprises, especially the kind that jeopardize people's lives. This was supposed to happen on Monday."

"That's what I thought, too, Yvette," Carole Ann said, quickly explaining what she knew of the hurry-up work order.

"All those people and God only knows what lurking in the woods . . ." she muttered. "How the hell can I show up and secure the place without looking like a jerk or scaring the hell out of them?"

"Surely it's against the law," Carole Ann offered in a voice devoid of inflection, "for so many people to be gathered on a public road." And she tossed Roland's key ring at the chief, who caught it with her left hand. "Tell Roland I'll see him tomorrow." And she jogged off toward home.

14

The reception she received from the people of Little Haiti in general, and from Madame St. Georges in particular, made Carole Ann thankful that she had dressed as carefully as she had for the occasion, and that she had brought the gifts that she had. She had spent considerable time contemplating both and there was as much relief as thanks that she'd made the proper choices. Her white linen dress with its close bodice and flared skirt complemented the brightly colored silks of the other women, and they all wore sandals. Understanding the communal nature of Little Haiti, Carole Ann had brought two large wheels of cheese and, from her personal stash of necessities, two large cans of coffee, two boxes of tea bags, and several bags of popcorn. The women were delighted, and they quickly dispatched the several men in attendance to divvy up the bounty. Madame St. Georges beamed her pleasure at the five-pound bags of flour and sugar and the bars of French milled soap for her personal use.

After half an hour or so of small talk, all but three of the women departed, leaving Carole Ann and her hostess, Madame St. Georges, whose name, she learned, was Anne-Marie, to dine with Henriette, Louise, and Sophie. Were these the closest friends of Anne-Marie St. Georges? Or were there other reasons for their presence? Carole Ann wondered, and knew she could but wait for the answer. That she didn't mind, because the meal was worth waiting for: chickens slow-roasted over a spit; potatoes and corn and plantains baked in the coals of the fire and seasoned with the juices of the chickens; slices of fresh tomato and cucumber and onion; and gallons of sweet, tangy ginger beer, compliments of Monsieur Remy.

The meal was a comfortable affair. The women told jokes and stories and tall tales and giggled like schoolgirls. They revealed, without shame and with little evidence of pain, the difficult patches of their lives, and Carole Ann amazed herself by telling of the murder of her husband and of her gradual return to something resembling normalcy. She found she was not the only woman to lose a husband to sudden, inexplicable violence, and was moved to give thanks that she hadn't lost a child as well, as had two of the other women. She told them in great detail of the reason for her presence on the island when they asked, and she was humbled by the gratitude with which they received the news that the roads of Little Haiti were scheduled for paving. They didn't care one bit that the work most likely would not be completed before the rainy season; they understood why and they cared only that their needs were considered by the new government. And then, without feeling that she was prying or resorting to subterfuge, the things that Carole Ann wanted to know began to be revealed to her.

She learned that not all residents of Little Haiti were Haitian by birth—in the case of Madame St. Georges, only her husband was Haitian. Prior to her move "down island," she had lived, as a child, in the de Villages mansion, where her mother was the cook, and later in Sugar Town, and now, finally, here in Little Haiti.

"Sugar Town? I've never heard of that," Carole Ann said. "Is it here on this island?"

"Oh, *mai oui.*" Anne-Marie St. Georges giggled and her friends giggled with her. "We grow old, eh?" she said, the giggle fading, giving way to a smile of resignation, as she explained that Sugar Town was the name given to the village in the interior of the island where, decades ago, hundreds of cane cutters and loggers lived, as much to be close to their work as because villages like Little Haiti didn't exist. "Back then, there were only haves and have-nots, poor and not-poor," she said with a shrug. "And now, not even the cane and the trees can provide work for the poorest among us."

"Did you know Simone St. Almain?" Carole Ann asked, and held her breath.

"Simone!" exclaimed Louise, and the four of them erupted into a rapid-fire conversation in island French, not a single word of which Carole Ann understood. Finally, as it abated, Louise asked Carole Ann how she knew Simone.

"She lives in Washington, D.C., and I am acquainted with her and her son," Carole Ann replied carefully.

"Her son!" Sophie exclaimed, sending them off on another round of excited discussion.

"This son," Anne-Marie asked after calm returned. "How old?"

"Thirty-three, I think," Carole Ann responded.

"And Simone," Sophie said. "She is still beautiful?"

Carole Ann nodded, recalling the conversation with the LeRoi sisters. "Do you know Denis?"

They shook their heads in unison. "Not as a man," Sophie replied by way of clarification. "They left for the States when he—Denis, you say?—was but a boy."

"Got sent away, you mean," Louise interjected with a snort. "To save the embarrassment."

"You'll have to explain that one," Carole Ann said, and listened again with genuine interest to the thirty-plus-year-old debate over who had fathered Simone St. Almain's child: Philippe Collette or Henri LeRoi. "And which was it?" she asked.

The four island women shrugged as one. "Who knows?" Anne-Marie said, and nullified Carole Ann's suspicion that Denis could be hiding out in Little Haiti. Not only would this community have recognized a stranger, these women certainly would have recognized Denis as the son of Philippe Collette. "Though I think Henri because it was known that he loved Simone, and it was known that Philippe did not," she added.

"Philippe did not love anyone," Louise contributed with another snort, "which is why he's condemned to the hell of being married to Marie-Ange and that family of Mad Hatters!"

Sophie cackled; Henriette, the quiet one, covered her mouth with both hands, her eyes wide above them in shocked delight; and Anne-Marie issued a gentle admonition that Louise shouldn't speak ill of the unfortunate. Barely able to conceal her fascination and her surprise, Carole Ann asked who in Marie-Ange Collette's family was mad, and who among them was considered unfortunate, unleashing another round of giggles.

"I'm certain that none but us consider them unfortunate, though anyone who knows them knows they're quite mad," Anne-Marie St. Georges offered. And considering that she had worked in the de Villages' household all her life, Carole Ann was inclined to accept her assessment of the situation. But which family of Marie-Ange did they mean? she asked.

"Ah, madame!" Anne-Marie exclaimed when the laughter had died down, but still wiping tears from her eyes. "You are very precise. You must understand things just so, yes?" And she set about explaining, to Carole Ann's total amazement, that Hubert de Villages "was quite mad," as were his eldest son and eldest nephew; when she heard their names, Carole Ann recognized them as the first cousins who owned the lumber mill and the sugarcane mill. And as she listened to the women's descriptions of the madness of the de Villages family, she recognized the symptoms of Alzheimer's.

"I know of Madame Collette's relationship to Monsieur de Villages, but what has she to do with his illness?" Then she was struck with a thought that literally chilled her. "You're not suggesting that Marie-Ange, too, is ill?"

"No, no, no, madame!" It was Henriette who answered. "Madame Collette is quite well, thank God, but much of the burden of the old ones' sickness falls to her. . . ." Her strong voice trailed off into a whisper, and Carole Ann could almost see her mind working, could all but witness her battle with herself over whether to say more. "I am Madame Collette's cook," she said after a moment. "I live four days a week in her house and the other three here, in my own home, now that my children are grown up." She stopped again and looked toward Anne-Marie. "For the big parties, like the one you attended last weekend, Anne-Marie also cooks."

"You were in Deauville looking for what, madame?" Anne-Marie asked pointedly.

"There is something . . . ugly . . . on this island," Carole Ann replied slowly, watching them understand both her words and her meaning. "I find that I am concerned beyond the scope of my contract with the Isle de Paix government."

"This . . . ugly thing . . ." Anne-Marie asked, "it is in Deauville?"

"I wish I knew for certain," she replied. "I think it begins there, and I don't think that it has spread throughout the island. It is not here, in Little Haiti, and it is not inside the government. Not yet." She spread her hands palms up. "I would like to know at least one government that is not infected with ugly things," she said with a slight shrug, and folded her hands in her lap.

She sat, not uncomfortably, in the circle of silence that surrounded her, the eyes of the four women alternating between studying her and seeking something from one another, searching for permission from within to release long-held secrets. And, she was convinced, these were the women who knew the secrets. Odile and Viviene had knowledge, information. Sophie and Louise and Henriette and Anne-Marie knew the secrets.

"I am cook to Monsieur de Villages," Anne-Marie said. "And Henriette is cook to Madame and Monsieur le Présidente. And Sophie is housekeeper to Monsieur de Villages, and Louise for the Collettes." She looked at each woman as she called her name and revealed her role; then she locked eyes with Carole Ann, making certain that she understood the transgression that was about to occur. "And you are correct that something evil and ugly roams about the island. But it does not begin in Deauville. It comes from France and it comes from the States, from your dea."

Carole Ann's total puzzlement prevented an immediate response. She was aware of the tremendous trust being placed in her care, and she did not want to do or say anything that would jeopardize it. But she simply did not understand. "From whose idea?" Carole Ann asked. "I'm sorry, I don't understand."

"The 'dea' people," Louise insisted. "The people from the States who do the drugs," she said with such vehemence that Carole Ann flinched. "And whatever they did, they caused Henri LeRoi to go away."

"The D-E-A?" she asked. "Is that what you mean?" The sight of the four nodding heads caused dismay to spread throughout her entire body. She hadn't wanted to believe Denis St. Almain's charge that the DEA somehow was tainted, and she didn't want to believe these women. Denis was questionable. These women were not. "And what exactly did the DEA do?"

"They did something to Andre," Louise answered. "And Madame learned of it and was furious! She said he must never tell his father."

"Then she became frightened," Henriette added, "when the 'dea' man came to visit Andre. Oh, he was horrible!" And she shivered at the memory. "It was early in the morning. Monsieur le Présidente had just departed and Madame was eating her fruit and she had just said to me that when she was finished, she would awaken young Andre. 'He cannot lay about all day,' she said, and there was a pounding at the back door, the *back* door, you must understand, where never do visitors enter! And there was pounding that frightened me and angered Madame. 'What insanity is that?' and she rushed to open the door and then she was thrown back into the room—yes, thrown! And then he came in. . . ." Henriette shuddered again.

"How did he look, Henriette? Can you remember?"

"Oh, *oui*, madame, I will never forget! He looks like a god and behaves like a monster!" She described in perfect detail the man Carole Ann had seen at the Aux Fruits de Mer bar with Denis St. Almain, and whom Andre Collette had met at Le Bistro, and with whom she had seen Marie-Ange Collette leaving the north coast restaurant. "His name," said Henriette, "is Osborne, and he is from Trinidad."

Carole Ann chose her next words carefully. "You mentioned the problem also has connections in France?"

Four heads nodded in unison. Henriette spoke. "His name is

Christian Leonard and he came from Paris. Madame herself brought him and he treats her so!"

"'Madame'? You mean Marie-Ange? She brought him here?" Carole Ann was incredulous.

Louise sucked her teeth in disgust and picked up the story. "To be in charge of the bank and to be in charge of the business affairs of old Hubert. And do you know what he did?"

Henriette chimed in: "He cut off her stipend! Told her no more money from the de Villages!"

For the next hour, the four women shared with her the intimate details of the de Villages and Collette households, of a mentally incapacitated Hubert de Villages unable to protect the rights of the granddaughter who had cared for him; an increasingly distraught Marie-Ange Collette, suspended between a lazy, no-good, possibly drug-addicted son and a husband whose career and image must be protected at all costs, and mounting debts she was unable to meet because Christian Leonard had terminated her lifelong stipend from Hubert de Villages.

As she listened, Carole Ann recalled David Messinger's glee at relating how the government of Trinidad and Tobago had hanged nine drug dealers. She knew that Trinidad and Jamaica were the principal drug-trafficking centers of the Caribbean and, based on Denis's account, she knew that the DEA used island-born agents to infiltrate the island drug trade. She tried on a scenario: Osborne, a Trinidadian, was the DEA agent in charge when Denis was stationed here, and when an angry Henri LeRoi set up the DEA by having the coast guard intercept a shipment of cocaine bound for the streets of America, Denis St. Almain was not the only DEA agent blamed for that fiasco; Osborne, too, took a share of the blame, and either was fired or, like Denis, demoted. To retaliate, Osborne, making use of his Isle de Paix contacts, either now was a rogue DEA agent operating an illegal sideline in Isle de Paix, or he no longer worked for the DEA. Either way, he had ensnared both Andre and Marie-Ange Collette. And from what Carole Ann had seen of him, Osborne was the kind of man who would use them until there was nothing left, and toss them aside like garbage. Then the thought expanded itself, taking on a new dimension: the DEA knew about Osborne and his activities, and thought Denis St. Almain was part of the game. No wonder they were after him.

Her hostesses had sat quietly while she thought, though they had watched her carefully and, she knew, shrewdly, waiting for her to process what they'd told her. "Has he ever returned, Henriette? This Osborne?"

Henriette nodded, fear and hatred blending in her eyes. "He comes often, always just after Monsieur le Présidente has departed. Sometimes he comes to see Andre, and sometimes to see Madame. And . . . and . . ."

"He gives her money," Louise interjected, finishing the sentence that Henriette could not. "You see what has happened, yes? Because of Christian Leonard, she is forced to choose between her son and her husband. Not a happy choice, madame."

Not happy at all, Carole Ann thought, as she sat on the edge of the Aux Fruits de Mer parking lot waiting for a space to become available, a potentially futile exercise on a Saturday night. But she would wait, and she surprised herself with that decision. She had had no plan, leaving Little Haiti, to stop in at Aux Fruits de Mer, but she was too unnerved to be at home alone with her thoughts, and even the sardine-tight parking lot did not deter her growing desire to talk to Viviene and Odile. She heard an engine start and saw taillights glow red in the darkness and, with the agility and speed of a New York City driver, she propelled the Jeep forward and had eased into what was a very tight squeeze before the other car was even out of sight.

The restaurant was, of course, packed to the rafters, and the noise level so intense that she barely could distinguish the Ray Charles on the jukebox. She scanned the room and realized that she was looking for Osborne; that's why she was here. Instead, she saw Odile hurrying toward her, the forced half smile on her face an obvious mask.

"You have brought news of Henri!" Odile exclaimed, kissing Carole Ann's cheeks in the island way of greeting, her eyes dark with worry.

Carole Ann's own smile was genuine, as was her relief at being able to deliver good news. "He's fine, Odile. He will recover slowly but fully." She had received that news from Jake just moments before leaving for dinner in Little Haiti.

"You must go tell Viviene *tout de suite.* She is rigid with worry. I'll join you at my table momentarily."

Carole Ann made her way across the packed dining room, entered the kitchen through the private door, and immediately spied Viviene. Shocked at the furrows in her face and the tautness of her carriage, she rushed to her, speaking words of assurance as they embraced, repeating what she'd said to Odile. She felt the older woman relax, heard her whispered thanks, and left her to her work.

Back out in the dining room, Carole Ann made her way to Odile's table in time to see a couple leave and Eliane arrive with a bottle of wine in a bucket. The change in Odile was remarkable. Her smile was wide, her face was open and clear, her eyes sparkling. Carole Ann wished that she had ignored Jake and come immediately to tell these women that their brother was alive, though, before today, she could not have added "well" to the description.

"I'm glad to see you smiling, Odile, and I'd like for you to keep that smile in place while I share some information with you." She described Osborne and warned that he was dangerous. She saw the flicker of recognition in Odile's eyes, who had busied herself opening the wine.

"I know exactly who he is. He pursues Helene. I took an instant dislike to him, and Helene accused me of being an overprotective mother."

Carole Ann now had reason for the wide grin on her face. "But, Odile, mothers are never overprotective, they just are always right about everything!"

"Ha! Tell that to my daughters!"

"You're a daughter yourself, Odile, so you know: either we learn that Mother is always right about everything, or we learn to pretend that she is without argument." Carole Ann laughed gently, envisioning her own mother, who still dispensed advice on a regular basis.

Odile clutched her ample bosom in mock horror. "But I was thirty-five before I realized that! Must I endure for so much longer?"

They shared a laugh before turning serious again. Carole Ann told her in the broadest of terms why Osborne was dangerous. "I wouldn't worry too much about Helene at this point if you're certain she doesn't do drugs. But if you see Denis, tell him to stay well away from the man. Osborne, I think, is the reason for Denis's trouble, and for Denis to be seen with him would be dangerous."

"But I thought Denis was with you!" Odile quickly wiped the alarm from her face but remained tense.

"He left," Carole Ann replied without explanation. Then, "Odile, I need to ask you something and I cannot elaborate on my reasons for asking, and I need as honest an answer as you can give." When she nodded, Carole Ann asked, "If Marie-Ange were in trouble, to whom would she turn? Who would help her?"

"Why, Philippe, of course!" Odile exclaimed without hesitation.

"And," Carole Ann asked carefully, "if she could not turn to Philippe, then where?"

Odile gasped. "Not turn to Philippe! What are you saying? Of course she could turn to . . ." Odile froze and her face became a mask. "Andre," she whispered. "*Mon Dieu,* he will destroy them."

Questions asked and answered. Any other time would have found Carole Ann's spirits elevated by such a productive evening. Not tonight. She took only slight comfort in the fact that Yvette Casson had instituted around-the-clock police presence at the Collette residence, and at the front and rear entrances of Government House. Her khaki-clad bicycle cops were no match for Osborne's assassins with their assault weapons; if they wanted to get at one of the Collettes, they could do so, taking out the cops in the process. Besides, Yvette now was worried that her ten-person force was stretched to its limits; any emergency would take it to its breaking point. Carole Ann shared her worry.

Not that shared worry was necessarily comforting, she thought as she parked her Jeep on the roadside behind the president's sedan

Monday morning and sat inside the car for a moment watching Yvette's hunched shoulders as she paced up and down the road. Once again, the scene at the new government road construction site resembled nothing so much as a celebration; and perhaps it was. The new mini-paver sat in tiny silence beside the lumbering dump truck, both of them surrounded by the two dozen men and women whose job it would be to clear the forest in the absence of suitable machinery to do that grueling work. Toussaint Remy stood in the middle of the crowd, an arm draped proprietorially across the paver. Philippe stood stoically in the shadow of his police protector, chatting with David Messinger and Roland Charles, shaking the hands of the several residents bold enough to cross the cop's path to greet their president. Carole Ann kept her eyes on the police chief, whose eyes alternated between the president and the road. The reason for that became apparent as three bicycle-riding officers emerged from the forest and pedaled over to their boss. Yvette's face relaxed a bit as she listened to the cops, then she joined the president's group, said something to them, and moved away into the crowd of workers.

Carole Ann followed and listened to her ask that they keep off the road, that they exercise extreme care and caution with their scythes and hoes and sling blades, and that they drink plenty of water. "Not beer, water." And she laughed with them, at their appreciation of her understanding of who and how they were, finally getting around to telling them that one of the officers would be on hand all day, "just in case somebody didn't listen to me and needs a ride to the hospital." They laughed again, and set about the business of conquering a forest. Carole Ann followed Yvette across the road.

"Masterful," she said in an admiring tone.

Yvette raised her eyes heavenward. "And useless if they don't listen."

"They'll listen. They like you. Probably the first time in their lives they've liked a cop, but they like you, and they like what you're doing for them, Yvette."

"Yeah. That and a buck won't get me a ride on the New York City subway," she replied sarcastically.

"So you're pissed off at me; why?"

"What were you doing in Little Haiti yesterday?"

Carole Ann laughed. "Having dinner with Anne-Marie St. Georges and a few of the girls, if it's any of your business. Which it's not, but just in case you need to know, I've also been a guest at Odile Laurance's home, and at Philippe and Marie-Ange's. I've had a few beers at Armand's with Toussaint Remy and Paul Francois, and a couple of gallons of coffee at Le Bistro, usually alone. Though I'm duly impressed, Yvette, at the eyes and ears you already seem to have all over the island. You're the top cop, you should know what's doing in your domain. So, to save you the trouble: I'm going home from here. Then, I'm going to Government House for a meeting with Jackie La-Belle." She tossed the chief a salute, then strolled over to the group of men, to whom she sang the chief's praises in both major and minor keys. Their agreement was total and unqualified.

"So you'll agree that she needs a second vehicle as soon as possible," Carole Ann added.

"Already working on it," David Messinger snapped.

She smiled at him and turned to Roland Charles with a question. "If this is dumb, Roland, please don't laugh at me in public, all right?"

"You sometimes say outrageous things, Carole Ann, but never dumb ones. Ask your question."

"Would it be productive to drive the dump truck through the foliage? Is the truck large enough to knock down and trample the underbrush?"

Roland made a sound and rushed away. She saw him grab Toussaint Remy's arm and whisper excitedly to him. The old man looked at the truck, rubbed the back of his hand against the stubble of beard on his face, looked at Roland, said something to him, and both men quick-stepped over to the big truck.

"Good thinking, Carole Ann," Philippe said, sounding hopeful.

"Our biggest concern is not getting shot at," David said testily, "not knocking down foliage."

"I think we're all agreed on that point, David," Carole Ann replied dryly. "So, assuming that nobody gets shot—nobody else, that is—my concern is getting that road in before it gets cloudy. Getting the road in and the foundation poured. By any means necessary," she added darkly, knowing that the oft-used Malcolm X admonition would rankle the law-and-order man. And since there was no one else deserving of her ire, and because she didn't want to inflict it upon the innocent, she took her leave with a wave that encompassed and included everyone, including Yvette. Perhaps especially Yvette, who had every right to be suspicious of Carole Ann.

They both knew that Carole Ann was withholding information, and Carole Ann believed that they both knew why, though they obviously differed on the rightness of the reason. Yvette was a cop with a cop's sensibilities and responsibilities; the fact that she was less of a bull in a china shop than her boss didn't lessen that reality. Cops thought short-term: remove the immediate danger at once, no matter that the immediate problem may not be the ultimate problem.

Carole Ann climbed into the Jeep thinking that short-term solutions could only be temporary solutions, and wondering whether that fell into the "something's better than nothing" category. The two-minute drive home didn't allow much time to formulate an answer. She parked in front of the house instead of in back, since she'd be leaving in a couple of hours for her meeting with Jackie. Across the street, a new crop of tourists had just arrived at two of the guest houses to replace those who had departed on Sunday. They stood in the grass surrounded by their luggage, looking up at the palm trees and the magnificent blue sky, perhaps pinching themselves, assuring themselves that they were, in fact, in paradise. These arrivals were younger than those who had departed, and just as pale of complexion as any Americans or Europeans beginning a ten-day or two-week Caribbean visit. But forty-eight hours on Isle de Paix will cure that problem, Carole Ann thought as she opened the front gate and stepped into the canopy of coolness provided by the overhanging tree boughs.

Movement to the right caught her eye as she walked down the path, and as she turned to look, a figure shot from behind a stand of monkey grass and toward the gate. Without thinking, she turned around and lunged toward the figure, grabbing a handful of shirt. And then she saw the gun. She brought the side of her right hand down hard on the hand holding the gun and heard, simultaneously, bones cracking and the gun clattering to the stone walkway. He cried out in pain and she increased the need for it as she twisted one arm up behind his back while she kicked his feet from beneath him. Then the scream of the alarm shocked them both, and she released him.

He scurried away from her on his knees, cradling his injured hand, then rose to his feet and sprinted to the front gate. She picked up the gun and ran to the second gate, through it, and around the side of the house. The bullet whizzed by her head, missing her by inches. She dove into the shrubbery hugging the house and lay still. The screaming of the alarm prevented her from hearing anything else, so she lay there, counting: one-one thousand, two-one thousand, three-one thousand . . .

Before reaching ten, she rose into a crouching position and poked her head out of the shrubbery. She couldn't stand the wail of the alarm for another ten seconds, and neither, she ventured to guess, could whoever was trying to break into her house. She looked at the gun in her hand—some kind of automatic thing. She pulled back on the clip, dropping a round into the chamber, and released the safety. Then she stood up and, keeping close to the shrubbery, inched her way forward. She reached the door unchallenged and surmised that she was alone in the backyard. Her keys, thankfully, were in her pocket, and not in the purse she'd dropped in the front yard. But she found she didn't need them. The lock had been jimmied and the door stood open. She stepped in and disarmed the alarm pad. The silence was a blessing.

She stood still, waiting for her heart rate to return to normal, deciding on an immediate course of action. She rearmed the system, pulled the door closed, and walked around to the front yard to retrieve her purse, which lay where she dropped it. She shouldered it and walked to the gate, and noticed that a crowd had gathered across the street. She waved to them, calling out that everything was fine. They must not be Americans, she thought, since they immediately returned their attention to their own business. She stepped out of the gate, holding the gun down close to her leg, and walked around the side of the house, following the lane that led to the backyard. The area was dense with trees and shrubbery, obscuring the house as well as anyone who might be concealed there.

She inhaled deeply and stepped onto the path that led to the lap pool. She followed it all the way back and ducked into the vines that overhung the latticework that served as a fence, understanding for the first time how obsession with personal security occurs. College presidents lived in more secure environments than this. Hell, elementary school principals in some cities probably lived more securely . . . and no doubt needed to. To think that the president of an entire nation had lived here!

She had crept far enough through the vines to have a clear view of the yard and the back of the house. She didn't see anyone, and the alarm hadn't sounded again. She didn't go so far as to consider herself safe, but she did think that she was the only thing that walked on two legs in the backyard. She sprinted for the door and pushed it open. She unarmed the system, then hurriedly rearmed it and leaned against the wall, once again to allow her heart rate to return to normal. Then she checked the interior of the house as thoroughly as she'd checked outside, looking in every closet and behind every shower curtain.

She fixed the events of the past few minutes clearly and firmly in her mind. She had passed no cars on the short ride from the construction site home, and she had seen no cars on the street when she drove up . . . correction: She had seen the green van that shuttled tourists to and from the airstrip. It was leaving as she arrived. But nobody had crossed the road in front of her, and the tourists still were standing in the yards of the guest houses across the street when she got out of the Jeep. So, whoever her assailants were, they were here when she arrived. Had they been here when she left, or had they merely known that she would have been at the construction site and had not anticipated her unusually quick return?

Her heart still was thudding loudly, and her breath still was ragged. She pushed herself to continue to clarify events in her mind. While she hadn't clearly seen the face of the attacker in the front yard, she had a sense that he resembled the pirates—the men who had held her and Roland at gunpoint on the bow of their boat. He was dark, and his hair was straight and dark. Like Osborne. She had seen nothing of the one in the back, the one who had shot at her. Her heart increased its pounding. He had shot at her and had intended to hit her. He had not aimed wide. "You son of a bitch," she muttered, and her heart, which had begun to slow, accelerated again and a wave of fear washed over her. She almost gave in to the urge to run outside, jump in the Jeep, speed up the road, and tell Yvette what had happened. And accomplish what, except to give the beleaguered chief one more thing to worry about? Besides, if she started talking to Yvette, she'd have to continue until she told all, and that she wasn't ready to do. Not yet. Not until she knew precisely what hold Osborne had over Marie-Ange Collette, and to what extent her knowledge of Osborne's activities had resulted in her being shot at. "You son of a bitch," she said again, and she continued to cuss as she stomped down the hall to the office.

She rushed over to the fax machine when she saw the pile of papers on the floor. She bent to scoop them up and realized that she still was gripping the gun. Her initial instinct was to hurl the thing across the room. Instead, she unchambered the round and set the safety. Then she dropped it into her purse, and hurled the purse across the room to the love seat. Then she gathered the papers off the floor and took them to the desk. She read for a long time. When she finally stood and stretched, she realized that she was hungry. She cooked and ate scrambled eggs with cheese, toast, and two mangoes. Then she took another shower. She gave longer than usual consideration to what to wear, finally settling on a pair of baggy beige linen slacks with deep pockets and a matching blazer. She added a coral silk T-shirt and a multicolored scarf and slipped her feet into brown flats.

Carole Ann mentally strategized her meeting with Jackie as she packed her briefcase. She unlocked the desk and withdrew her own gun from the drawer, dropping it into her pants pocket. Then she grabbed her purse from the love seat and found herself comforted by its weight: she intended to keep the automatic, at least for the time being. She stopped in the bedroom and studied her reflection in the long mirror: the gun in her pocket was not noticeable and she almost didn't care if it was. She had no intention of being an unarmed target again. Then, realizing that she was on the verge of being late, she rushed down the hall to the kitchen. She disarmed the alarm pad and opened the door. She stuck her head out and looked both ways, like a kid about to cross the street. She rearmed the system, stepped outside, and closed the door. She hung her purse on her shoulder, transferred her briefcase and carryall to her left hand, and stuck her right hand into her pants pocket. Then she walked around the side of the house, through the first gate into the front courtyard, through the front gate to the street. She again looked both ways, and then at her watch. "If I break the speed limit and run a couple of red lights, I'll be on time for my meeting," she muttered.

"**Well**, dammit, it's not fair, Carole Ann! It's wrong! And it's wrong of you to expect me to accept this . . . this . . . well, it's an affront is what it is!" Jackie LaBelle was having a tantrum. Carole Ann sat quietly, extending both personal and professional courtesy. In an ideal world, the young woman would be entitled to her rage. In the real world, the sooner she got over her anger and settled down to make a deal, the better. But Carole Ann vividly recalled being young and idealistic. In fact, she still, occasionally, was guilty of idealistic thoughts and behavior, though she usually could manage to return to reality in a matter of seconds.

Jackie's tirade already had exceeded that limit, the cause of her ire the realization that the U.S. government's Agency for International Development was withholding approval for Isle de Paix's much-needed satellites pending the outcome of the GGI report on the island's drug-interdiction program.

"If you could settle down, Jackie—"

"Don't talk to me as if I were a child!"

"Then stop behaving like one," Carole Ann snapped, "and let's get down to business."

"We're supposed to do business with you while you're holding us hostage? How's that work, Carole Ann?"

"Oh, grow up, Jackie! If we hadn't intervened, you'd be sitting here five years from now wondering why AID hadn't approved your request for the satellites, and Isle de Paix still would be waiting to join the twenty-first century. Instead, you'll most likely have your satellites and the ensuing links to the rest of the world by year's end. Now. Would you rather learn how to go about picking up the phone and getting the most useful, most truthful answers to your questions or sit here playing at diplomacy?"

Jackie's expression alternated between appalled and pained; she couldn't decide whether to be furious or wounded. Carole Ann didn't care. The anger that she thought she had suppressed—the anger at having been shot at—had grown. She was furious, and in no mood to placate Jackie LaBelle. "Tell me exactly how you learned of AID's position," Jackie demanded.

"We called 'em up and asked 'em where the hell were the satellites we asked for months ago," Carole Ann drawled, thinking that it wasn't a complete lie, and that nobody associated with the Isle de Paix government ever would know the truth.

"And somebody at AID just said, 'Oh, we won't give any satellites to Isle de Paix until we're certain they don't condone drug trafficking.' Is that what I'm supposed to believe?" Jackie's lips curled as she spat the words out.

"It wasn't just 'somebody,' it was a high muckety-muck on the Caribbean desk, who happens to be a good buddy of one of our technology experts, the one who's whining and moaning about not being able to finish her work on the Isle de Paix contract until the satellites exist. She's worked in Washington for thirty years. And you spent enough time in Washington, Jackie, to understand what that means. So, she called her buddy and asked the right question and got the right answer. Now, I'll ask *my* question again: What do you want to do about it?"

"What is there to do?" Jackie snapped, not willing to be so easily placated.

Carole Ann stood up. "You can make a formal complaint through diplomatic channels, Jackie. That's always an option. And you'll have a white Christmas here before you get a satellite link from the U.S. government." She turned to leave. Jackie stopped her.

"You've missed your calling, you know. You'd be right at home in diplomatic circles, the way you've mastered the art of the bluff."

Carole Ann sat back down and faced Jackie across the desk. "Practicing criminal law relies heavily on mastering the art of the bluff, Jackie. And I'm a very good criminal defense attorney. What I'm not good at is diplomacy, as you no doubt can tell." And they both relaxed as Jackie smiled.

"At least you're acquainted with your faults," she said, unable to resist the tiny jibe. "What do you want to know?"

"I need to know how the islands relate to each other on the matter of illegal drugs, and I need to understand the legal aspect as well as the diplomatic one." As she listened, she realized that the young woman seated across from her one day really would be a tremendous asset to her government. She possessed a vast store of knowledge, and, when she was calm, she presented her facts in an orderly, concise, and precise manner.

"So," Carole Ann said slowly, when Jackie was finished. "Let's imagine that there's a Jamaican drug dealer hiding out here who's wanted both in Jamaica and in the U.S. What do we do?"

"That depends," Jackie said slowly, sucking in her bottom lip and twirling a pen round and round in her fingers. She stopped her thinking behavior and met Carole Ann's gaze. "Has he violated any laws here?"

C.A. nodded. "He's trafficking in drugs, using Isle de Paix as his base of operations, and maybe you could attach a first-class felony or two to him."

"Well, Yvette could lock him up and toss the key into the sea . . ."

"Which uses up half your jail capacity . . ."

". . . or our internal affairs minister could notify their internal affairs minister, and our minister could agree to permit Jamaican authorities to make an arrest here, provided, of course, that we know where this . . . fictional character resides."

"And," Carole Ann asked, ignoring the snide tone of Jackie's voice, "how would the Jamaican authorities explain their capture of this fugitive?"

"Explain to whom?" Jackie asked dryly. "He's a fugitive, didn't you say? He'd be the one doing the explaining."

"Suppose Yvette arrested him. Could Isle de Paix notify Jamaican authorities after the fact?"

Jackie nodded. "Certainly. And there are circumstances where that would be preferable. For example, assume the recovery of contraband associated with the arrest: illegal narcotics and cash and weapons and . . . and . . . a bag of diamonds. The drugs we'd turn over to their government, the cash, weapons, and diamonds we could retain as reparations. Now, perhaps you wouldn't mind explaining what a fictitious Jamaican drug dealer has to do with our satellite uplinks?"

Carole Ann grinned at the young woman across the desk, gathered her belongings, and stood up. "There's an old saying, I don't know how old or where it's from: If you can't dazzle them with brilliance, baffle them with bullshit. AID will be baffled by the time we finish with them."

"I'm baffled now," Jackie managed through a howl of laughter, and the sound followed Carole Ann halfway down the hall.

She was met at the entrance to Philippe Collette's suite by a uniformed officer who smiled and saluted her and asked whether she had an appointment. Apologizing that she did not, and offering to make one, she turned to go, terrified that Yvette might have installed a metal detector in the president's suite that she didn't know about. "Miss Gibson. Ma'am," the officer said a little sheepishly, "I'm supposed to ask but I know he'll want to see you. Will you wait a minute?" He opened one of the double doors and disappeared inside, leaving Carole Ann more and more impressed with Yvette Casson, if nervously caressing the gun in her pocket and wishing now that she didn't have the one in her purse.

The door opened and the officer stepped out into the hall and a secretary stepped into the opening.

"*Bonjour, madame. Comment ça va?*"

"*Ça va bien, merci. Et vous?*" Carole Ann exchanged pleasantries with the woman and followed her into Philippe's inner sanctum, and he stood to greet her. "I'm so sorry to drop in unannounced."

He waved off her apology. "I'm glad for the respite from the paper-work. Do you have time to sit?"

She shook her head. "I just came to tell you that Henri LeRoi is re-covering. . . ." She paused, noting that he needed a moment to com-pose himself. This was rough terrain for the president—had been since she told him of the attack on his predecessor.

"I feel responsible. It never occurred to me that the telephone lines in my home could be compromised. Or that I would need an armed escort everywhere I go. In Paris, perhaps, or in London or in Washington and New York. But in Ville de Paix? In Deauville? In Pe-tit Haiti?" He shook his head and walked to the French doors that overlooked the harbor.

"You're not responsible, Philippe—"

"Then who is?" His anger flashed sharply and dissipated quickly. "I apologize. Of course you can't possibly know that."

She smiled and shrugged noncommittally. "I just wanted to let you know that in case you were concerned that you or the government had any lingering obligation to the DEA, rest your mind. Monsieur LeRoi's, ah, shall we say, arrangement, was unofficial and therefore has no standing." She turned away from him, not wanting to be privy to the naked relief that washed over his face. She turned back when she reached the door, to find him composed. "By the way, how is Marie-Ange? I've wanted to stop in and say hello, but time keeps get-ting away from me."

His expression was closed, guarded almost. "I'm sure that Marie-Ange would be delighted to see you," he replied stiffly, and looked down at the papers on his desk.

There was no guard posted at the door of the finance minister, though there was one at the end of the hall, who saluted Carole Ann as she passed by. She returned the greeting with a wave of her hand and opened the door, expecting to see Nicole Collette, and finding herself slightly disappointed that she wasn't one of the occupants of the four desks in the room. She identified herself to the woman who stood and came forward, apologized for not having an appointment, and asked if Madame le Ministre could spare a few moments. While she waited, she perused the room. It was large and square and brightly lit—there were tall lamps in all four corners of the room, halogen lamps on each of the desks, and fluorescent strips in the ceiling. She finally understood that this was one of the few interior rooms in the building—a wise choice for the finance ministry. She noticed also a computer at each of the desks. Another wise choice, and a wise use of the few telephone lines on the island.

"Miss Gibson."

She looked up to see the imposing figure of the finance minister in the doorway, and crossed quickly to greet her. "Thank you for seeing me, Dr. Anderson," she said, and followed the woman into her office—the office of a popular, overburdened, absentminded college professor, which is exactly what she was.

Carmen Anderson was a retired economics professor and an economist of note, who had served three American presidents between tenured stints at Columbia University and Boston College. She was the only non–French speaker in the government, and the only high-ranking official without a connection, direct or indirect, to Isle de Paix or any Caribbean island. Carmen Anderson was here because, at the age of seventy-two, she still knew more about finance and economics—about money and where it comes from and where it goes—than most people, and she had grown bored with retirement.

"I'm certain this is no social call, Miss Gibson, but I'm delighted to see you. The entire government is abuzz with your activities and exploits and I'm all aflutter that you've come to see *me!* Sit down! Sit down!" she chirped, waving in the direction of several armchairs, all of them piled high with papers and books.

Carole Ann privately enjoyed the thought of Carmen Anderson all aflutter. She conjured up visions of Washington's power women: Madeleine Albright, Alice Rivlin, Alexis Herman, Janet Reno—and tried to imagine any of them aflutter. She looked from chair to chair and, remaining standing, delivered her message. The professor listened, her face a mask of impassivity. Pity the poor doctoral candidate defending a thesis before her! As she finished, Carmen Anderson's eyes narrowed slightly—Carole Ann could tell because her thick lenses magnified them—and she leaned back in her chair, silent and impassive. Carole Ann stood the same way. It was like waiting for a jury to return: nothing else to do but wait.

"Are you sure we can keep it?" the finance minister asked after her long silence, and Carole Ann laughed out loud. She couldn't help herself. Here she'd just laid out a money-laundering scheme that involved both the banks on Isle de Paix and the finance ministry itself, and detailed a plan for stealing the bad guys' money, and one of the most erudite scholars in the world wanted to know only if she legally could keep the money! Carole Ann nodded and received a warm embrace from the professor, and left Government House in a better frame of mind than when she had arrived.

She lifted her face to the sun as she strolled to the bank, and she spent a few moments appreciating the architecture of the structure. Like many of Isle de Paix's older buildings, it had a faint Moorish cast, though it didn't claim membership in any particular school or period, and it had been beautifully restored and maintained. It gleamed white in the sun, the gold lettering on the door reflecting the light. She pushed open the door and was surprised at how cool it was inside—the kind of cool delivered only by a powerful air-conditioning system. She crossed the lobby toward the offices in the rear, musing that the de Villages, owners of the bank, certainly could better afford cool air than the beleaguered government of Philippe Collette.

Christian Leonard did not bother to feign politeness when she was ushered into his office and thanked him for kindly agreeing to see her without an appointment. "Of course I remember who you are, Madame Gibson, but as you and your government have no business with the bank, I cannot imagine why you are here." He was a thin man, and he looked older than when she had seen him before. His fair hair was thinning, and a virtual absence of lips and chin, and a pasty complexion Carole Ann would have thought impossible in such

a climate, made him altogether unappealing. He spoke heavily accented English, and he refused her offer to converse in French, assuring her that their conversation wouldn't last that long. "What is it
you wish of me, madame?"

"I'd like for you to permit the government to use the construction
equipment owned by Monsieur Hubert de Villages and his son and
nephew."

He raised an eyebrow at her and stretched his thin-to-nonexistent
lips in a slit of a smile. "And why are you making this request of me,
madame?"

"Because you have power of attorney for them, due to their mental
incapacitation," she said, still standing across the desk from him and
thoroughly enjoying his momentary inability to settle on an emotion.
His features displayed surprise, wariness, anger, and something close
to fear.

"You have no right," he hissed at her, having settled on a cold
anger.

"I have every right," she responded calmly. "I represent the government of Isle de Paix and I serve the interests of the government,
and securing access to that equipment would benefit the government,
so I not only have a right, I have a duty to make a request on behalf of
my client. As to whether inherent in that is the right to make a request of you . . ." She shrugged and raised her palms, gratified to note
that she had succeeded in both annoying and confusing him. He obviously didn't understand English any better than he spoke it, and his
arrogance at refusing to accept her offer to converse in French had
got him in trouble. And Christian Leonard was not the kind of man to
admit an error, or to rectify one.

"How do you know this?" he demanded.

"How do I know what, Monsieur Leonard?"

He sputtered. "About the messieurs! That they are . . . ill."

"Oh, is it a secret?" she asked, then shrugged. "I suppose that
here, on a small island, Alzheimer's would be kept secret, whereas in
the States, it is widely discussed as cures are sought and treatments

tested. We even have a former president who is afflicted. He and Monsieur de Villages are, I believe, about the same age—"

"Get out of here!" he hissed at her, a fine spray of spittle aimed at her along with his fury. "And never return!"

She closed the door to his office as she left, certain that he would not follow her into the lobby of the bank, certain that he was not the kind of director who advocated or engaged in camaraderie, though she dropped her hand into her pocket and grasped the gun, just in case. She stopped at the first desk she reached and asked who was handling Andre Collette's customers since his departure, and learned that the director himself, Christian Leonard, had assumed Monsieur Collette's accounts.

Her sense of well-being increased as she stepped once again out into the warm sunlight. She crossed the square, putting distance between herself and Christian Leonard and his bank, and stood peering in the window of the jewelry store as she decided what to do. There was one other visit to make. It could wait until tomorrow, but why should it? If she did it today, now, then she could spend all of tomorrow at her desk, completing her reports. She owed Jake a clear and concise view of her assessment of the state of Isle de Paix. She also needed to tell him what she had set in motion, so that if her assessment proved to be incorrect, which she didn't think likely, he would be prepared to deal with the fallout. Which would be significant. And that thought helped make up her mind.

She took the long way around to the rear of Government House where her Jeep was parked so that she could stop in police headquarters and speak to Yvette. She was surprised to find only one cop in the office, until she remembered the new postings. They really did need to get the road paved and the new government building constructed so the other cops could be hired. She recalled thinking that twenty-five cops for this island was overkill. She winced, remembering that she had used those exact words. Jake had told her to mind her own business; cops were his business. And, of course, when it came to cop business, he was right every time.

"Do you need to see me, Carole Ann?"

She was startled to find Yvette at the door speaking to her. She shook her head. "Nothing important. I was just leaving Government House and thought I'd check in with you. Smooth sailing at the site?"

Yvette nodded. "Thank the dear Lord. But tomorrow, as they say, is another day."

"I've got a ton of paperwork to do in the morning, but I can help out in the afternoon, if you like?" She made it a question to give Yvette the opportunity to gracefully decline her assistance, and was pleased when she didn't.

"Thanks, Carole Ann. We could use you. I'm strained to the breaking point."

"I know you are, but I can't commend you enough for the precautions you've taken and for the way you've deployed your officers. It's really very impressive."

She relaxed a bit. "Thanks. And thanks for the plug this morning." When Carole Ann looked clueless, she added, "David wanted me to know that it was *his* idea that I get a new cruiser, not yours, and that *he,* not Roland, pulled the strings that will get it here next week, if you can believe that!"

"It really was David's idea. Where's he getting it?"

"Tampa. We're somehow at the top of the list to get their surplus cop stuff. He promises a couple of scooters, too. Not the monster Harleys, mind you. The kind the ticket writers use. But they're faster than bicycles."

Carole Ann was relieved to be able to share laughter with Yvette again and, after agreeing to "come on duty" at the construction site at one o'clock the next afternoon, she left, walked around the building, climbed into the Jeep, and headed toward the Collette residence, certain that Philippe misspoke when he volunteered that Marie-Ange would be pleased to see her.

Louise's eyes widened when she opened the door, then narrowed as Carole Ann introduced herself, apologized for her rudeness in arriving without an invitation, and suggested that Monsieur le Présidente might be to blame for her impromptu visit. "Please follow me, madame. I will see if Madame Collette can come to talk."

"If she is too busy, I understand," Carole Ann added, as Louise led the way from the entry foyer down a wide, chandeliered and Persian-carpeted hallway to what she knew, from her previous visits here, was a small parlor or sitting room to the left of the grand staircase. In her crisp white blouse and tailored black skirt, withdrawn and formal, this Louise was the antithesis of the shy but warm and funny woman Carole Ann had spent Saturday evening with, though she understood as well as anyone the nature of and need for a work persona.

"Have a seat, madame," Louise said, standing aside so that Carole Ann could enter the sitting room. It was a lovely room, with floor-to-ceiling windows on two walls and furnished casually though elegantly in Asian-influenced rattan furniture, silk pillows and ottomans, and Oriental carpets. Travel and food magazines fanned out across the coffee table, and two large potted plants flourished in front of the windows. There were, however, no framed photographs or any other personal, intimate touches in the room, detracting, Carole Ann thought, from its beauty. And it was just such an omission that fueled Jake's dislike of Marie-Ange. He found her cold, distant, and pretentious. Carole Ann understood her. Just as she refused to allow guests at her party to see her cry, she would refuse to display her family in a public room. And for the first time, Carole Ann understood that for Marie-Ange, perhaps Philippe's presidency would prove to be too costly; that she certainly would have been happier to remain in Paris.

"Carole Ann!" Marie-Ange swept into the room, as beautiful by day as by night. Unlike the bank director, she took full advantage of the climate: her skin was burnished bronze and gold, and her hair—truly her crowning glory and her most identifying feature—was an unruly mane of red, gold, and silver. Her only makeup was lipstick, the same cherry color as her brushed-silk shirt and capri pants. The president's wife had not, Carole Ann thought, dressed to receive an unexpected and uninvited guest. She already was dressed, either to go out, or she had just returned from an outing.

Carole Ann rose and exchanged the traditional European-style greeting with Marie-Ange. "Thank you for seeing me, and, I hope, for forgiving my presumptuousness."

"No need for apologies, Carole Ann. Please, have a seat. I'm delighted that you could find the time to visit me. I hear from people all over the island how very busy you are, how much a part of the fabric of life here you have become."

"An easy thing to do, Marie-Ange. This island truly is a paradise, and the people are wonderful. I've enjoyed this work more than any in recent memory," Carole Ann replied with total honesty, realizing that she did. "And I really don't want to intrude. You appear dressed to go out. . . ."

Marie-Ange waved a dismissive hand. "Nothing that can't wait for a few moments. So, tell me, what brings you here?"

Carole Ann met and held the other woman's gaze before she spoke, and then she proceeded cautiously, knowing that she was about to offend but wanting to make it clear that that was not her desire or her intention. "I am in possession of some facts, some information, Marie-Ange, that could present difficulty for you and Andre."

"I can't imagine that any fact in your possession could have any bearing on me or my son," she replied haughtily.

"It concerns Osborne."

The color drained from her face and the breath caught in her throat, and her hands, resting on her knees, curled into tight fists. She held Carole Ann's gaze but did not speak; indeed, did not breathe.

"I'd like to help, Marie-Ange—"

"Then leave here, leave this island, leave my son alone, leave me alone." She had whispered the words but Carole Ann felt as if she'd been slapped.

"That I cannot do."

Marie-Ange shrugged. "Then how do you think you can help? For the only help can be to never speak of it."

"You know, Marie-Ange, that is impossible."

"Of course." The president's wife stood but did not pace or leave the room. She merely stood looking down at Carole Ann. "You have a commitment to Philippe and you therefore must tell him everything, no? So, why haven't you told him these . . . these facts you have, this information you have? Why come to me?"

"Because I want to help you, Marie-Ange, if I can. And if so, there will be nothing to tell Philippe."

"You cannot help. The damage is done."

"Not yet, Marie-Ange! There is no damage done yet."

Now her anger flamed. She raised a hand as if to strike and Carole Ann flinched but did not move. "You think only of the government, only of Philippe. Damage is done, madame, to my son and to me! Damage that cannot be repaired. And because that is so, damage also is done to my husband and to the government he serves—" She was interrupted by Louise bursting into the room.

"Please excuse me, Madame," she said in English, then, continuing in rapid French that Carole Ann barely understood, she imparted the information that a very upset Andre Collette had just arrived and, upon learning that his mother had a guest, and who that guest was, demanded that his mother get rid of Madame Gibson as quickly as possible. And then Louise herself left as quickly as possible.

Carole Ann sat impassively for a moment as Marie-Ange struggled for control of her emotions. Then she stood. "I'm leaving now, Marie-Ange. If you change your mind, please call." She was about to follow Louise when Andre Collette sprang into the room like a prowling cat, hissing and spitting.

"You have nerve to come here and upset my mother!"

"Your mother is upset because of your actions, Andre, not mine. It's you who placed both of your parents in danger. Your friend Osborne has tried to kill them both, you know, and he tried to have me killed this morning."

"You're a liar! Get out!" Andre screamed at her, and lunged. She saw it coming and sidestepped him, reaching out and grabbing his left arm as he went past, then twisting it behind him. He whimpered and begged his mother to order Carole Ann to release him.

Marie-Ange looked in horror at the tableau before her, turned away, and fled. Carole Ann dropped Andre to the floor and left the Collette residence.

"*I'm* telling you, Jake, the woman was terrified."

"She damn well should be, C.A.! The lady and her baby boy are in hock to a major-league piece of scum like Nigel Osborne, fear is the best response."

"He's got them trapped, Jake! First he hooks Andre. Then, because that Leonard asshole cut her off, he's able to hook Marie-Ange. Even if Philippe ever found out what was happening, he'd be powerless to stop it. All because Osborne believed he was set up," she said, more disgusted than she'd ever been. From the moment she read the GGI reports on Nigel Osborne, and the transcripts of the interview with Henri LeRoi, she knew with certainty that the ex–DEA agent was the source of the trouble on Isle de Paix. It was Osborne who had set up LeRoi, and then had attempted to bribe him into submission. LeRoi had complained, through diplomatic channels, to the U.S. government, and Osborne had been fired. But no other action was taken—Henri LeRoi still looked like a crook, Nigel Osborne still moved about the Caribbean with impunity, and Isle de Paix still was his base of operations. "And more than being in debt to him, I think Andre is part of his operation."

"Aw, shit," Jake muttered. "And how are we supposed to tell the president that his son is a drug-using, drug-dealing piece of crap, and that his wife is almost as bad?"

"Somehow, Jake, I don't think it will come as a huge surprise," she replied, recalling Philippe's response when she asked him about Marie-Ange.

"I disagree," Jake said. "I think he knows the boy is a flake who'd rather play than work, but I don't think he knows the boy is in danger, and I don't think he's capable of imagining the trouble his wife is in."

"Maybe you're right," she said, thinking that perhaps Philippe thought, as she had initially, that Marie-Ange was having an affair.

"This whole thing sucks," she said indelicately and hung up the phone.

She cooked and ate dinner while she watched the news on CNN. Then she took a bottle of wine and a bag of popcorn to the desk. She had told Jake everything about what she believed to be Nigel Osborne's role in the drug trafficking taking place on and around Isle de Paix, but she hadn't told him of the mechanisms she had put into play to flush him out—of setting up Nicole Collette by alerting the finance minister to her possible involvement; of antagonizing Christian Leonard at the bank; of visiting Marie-Ange and accusing Osborne, in her and Andre's presence, of the attempts on her life and on theirs. And just in case some piece of the puzzle didn't fit, or in case something happened that prevented her from telling the whole story, she began to write and she wrote until midnight.

She shut off the computer and turned out the lights and went into the bedroom, where she changed into shorts and a T-shirt. She set the alarm, turned out the lights, and went into the bedroom down the hall, the one she'd come to think of as the guest room. Harold Collins, the GGI technician, had slept in this room, as had Denis St. Almain. She would sleep here tonight, guns under each of the pillows on the bed. Because if she was correct about who and what Nigel Osborne was, she knew that she was in danger.

She arrived an hour early for her duty shift and found everyone at the construction site having lunch. Though there were thirty or forty people hard at work, not much remained of the festive air. These people were exhausted, and Carole Ann could see why: there was a gaping opening in the forest, and the road-to-be was cleared and flattened.

Roland Charles rose from the group surrounding him and walked across the road to greet her. "Yvette told me you would be here," he said, first leaning in to kiss her, then withdrawing. "Look at me!" he said, looking down at himself, indistinguishable in dress and degree of cleanliness from any of the crew.

"You look absolutely fetching," Carole Ann replied, offering her cheeks to be kissed. "And I can't believe how much work you've gotten done!"

"Come, let me show you!" he exclaimed, hopping about from foot to foot like a little kid, and he sped off across the road. She followed.

She greeted the workers—Monsieur Remy, Luc, Jean, and Joseph—by name and grabbed Roland's arm. "Why don't you finish your lunch? I'll just take a stroll down the road here," she said with a flourish and a bow to the crew. And stroll she did. The road, for it legitimately could be called that, had achieved a uniform width of ten feet, for a distance of one hundred yards or so. The effort that this had required made her curse Christian Leonard. Knowing that neither Hubert de Villages nor anyone in his family was responsible for withholding the construction equipment from the government's use somehow made the action that much more reprehensible. The aristocracy often behaved callously, either not recognizing their behavior as callous or not caring that it was. But who the hell was Christian Leonard to wreak such havoc on people's lives!

"You bastard," she muttered as she noticed, finally, the boards embedded in the earth, keeping the road straight. With the proper equipment, this road could be completed ahead of schedule. But a dump truck, thirty or so scythe-wielding women and men, and a mini-paver were giving the forest a run. And the marijuana! The road had penetrated well into the field and, Carole Ann noticed, the workers had not only moved forward through the plants, but had hacked them away for several feet on both sides of the road. No doubt an effort on Roland's part to minimize the obvious. She wondered when he'd done this. Then she shuddered as she wondered whether he'd acted alone.

She finally reached the end of the road. The dump truck, the paver, a mounted circular saw, a surveyor's tripod, and a load of lumber met her. She frowned and reached into her pocket for her gun. She should have been met by one of Yvette's cops.

"Here I am, Miss Gibson."

She peered around the truck and saw him standing on the hood, facing her, his back to the forest, and her heart skipped a beat. "Wouldn't you be better protected inside the bed of the truck?"

"Protected, sure," he said, his face serious, "but then I couldn't see the enemy approach."

"You didn't see me approach."

"Sure I did," he said, holding up a pair of binoculars in his left hand, along with the Glock automatic he held in his right hand. He jumped down from the truck's hood in a fluid motion, landing in a crouch. He looked all around him before he straightened and came silently toward her. He holstered his gun and extended his hand, which she took. His name, he said, was Charles, and that was the extent of his small talk. "You have a weapon, right, Miss Gibson? And you're trained to use it?" She felt his relief when she nodded. "The chief thanks you, and I thank you. I'll manage to get ten or eleven hours of uninterrupted sleep before reporting back here tonight."

"You're here all night?"

"Yeah, me and one other guy. And thanks to you, we'll both be able to stay awake." He gave her the binoculars. "Leave 'em in the cab when you take off," he said, and, tossing her a hasty salute, he ambled off down the road.

She hung the binoculars around her neck and, using the tire as a step, climbed up on the hood of the dump truck and sat facing the forest. She could easily see right and left and, without too much effort, she could swivel around and see behind her. "You live and learn," she muttered, adding, "Cops."

She heard the returning crew long before she saw them, and found relief in their presence. She also found herself more vigilant than she had imagined. She wasn't certain what she had expected when she volunteered for this duty, but she found herself constantly scanning the forest ahead and on both sides, and taking periodic looks to the rear. The binoculars were powerful, providing amazing distance and detail. When the work stopped at five o'clock, Joseph walked up the road and returned with what she recognized as Paul Francois's pickup truck. She hadn't seen it since his death. The circular saw, all the tools, and most of the workers were loaded into the back. Carole Ann noticed, as she watched it depart, that the ride was smoother than on any other road on the island except for the Coast Road.

She turned her gaze forward again and peered into the wide expanse of the forest. In another hour, it would be dusk in here, and probably dark by seven o'clock, despite the fact that it would be full daylight over the ocean for two hours longer. She looked directly above, into full sunlight. She looked ahead again, into dimness. Then she understood: the forest had been cleared for the cultivation of the marijuana. Where the trees loomed marked the end of the pot field. She looked north and attempted to calculate the distance to Sugar Town. She looked south and wondered how far to the airstrip. Off to either side of the truck, and slightly ahead, men were pounding stakes into the ground. Torches, she saw, seven or eight feet tall. Hearing activity to the rear, she stood up and looked behind her.

Roland and five other men, including Toussaint Remy, were parking the paver hard on the dump truck's rear tires. Then they climbed into the bed of the truck and stretched out on a quilt-covered pile of leaves and dirt. Here they would remain until the officers returned at eleven. "You are not expected to remain here so late, Carole Ann," Roland said, settling himself on the leafy pallet.

She had clambered onto the cab of the big truck and sat there looking down at them in amazement. "You've been staying here until ten or eleven at night?"

"What else can we do?" Roland asked.

"With all due respect, Monsieur Remy, is your health able to withstand such a regimen?" she asked and was met with a roar of laughter.

"He is younger than all the men," a much younger man she had never seen responded. "All the women say so!" They dissolved into laughter again, Toussaint Remy laughing louder and longer than all the others.

"Come down and have dinner with us," the old man said, wiping his eyes and extending a hand to her. Two of the men stood and caught her arms, lowering her into the truck's bed. She sat and found herself surprisingly comfortable. She found herself surprised again when they opened a built-in metal box that ran half the length of the truck and withdrew several pails and containers of food and bottles of cold beer. And a gallon jug of Monsieur Remy's ginger beer. She had a bowl of fiery gumbo and several cups of water. The men ate more heartily and, one by one, climbed down and disappeared into the forest to relieve themselves. She kneeled in the bed of the truck, peering nervously after them, ignoring their claims of bashfulness and modesty. Very shortly thereafter, they settled down and gentle snoring joined the cacophony of the forest's night noises.

Carole Ann climbed back up the cab and resumed her duty station on the truck's hood. The forest animals sang louder as it got darker, and the exhausted men in the back of the truck snored louder. She found herself less tense than she would have expected. At exactly eight o'clock, one of the men clambered down from the truck and went forward to light the torches, using a long taper. She didn't know how he knew it was time—she hadn't heard an alarm. But then, she never overslept, either, when she had important work to do. He waved at her and returned to his bed.

Almost without her realizing it, full darkness descended upon the forest. The torches were strobe lights that flickered and cast *Tyrannosaurus rex*–sized shadows in the distance. She found the scene beautiful and peaceful. Only the mosquitoes prevented it from being idyllic, finally forcing her down off the hood and into the cab. Where she dozed, because she awoke to pitch-black darkness and shouts from behind her: "What the hell . . ." Grabbing her gun, she opened the cab and jumped to the ground. Three figures scurried away from the back of the truck. She fired a round above them, ordering them to halt. Two stopped running. The third turned and fired. She ducked and returned the fire and all three disappeared into the darkness. She pursued them for several paces, realized the futility and danger of that, and ran back to the truck. "Roland! Monsieur Remy! Are you all right?"

"My God! These people are animals! They are insane!" Roland was shaking with rage and fear. Carole Ann was overcome by guilt. The attack occurred because she had fallen asleep.

"Is anyone hurt?"

"No," he growled, and jumped down to the ground. "But I hope you hurt one of them!"

She hadn't shot anyone. She hadn't aimed at anyone. She had fired off the rounds to demonstrate that the truck's occupants were not helpless, were not defenseless, though that was exactly how she felt. "What were they trying to do?"

"Destroy our equipment again!" Roland growled through clenched teeth. "They came right here, to the back of the truck. And they left something to remember them by." She looked where he pointed and saw the shape of a metal gas can and shuddered. Then she looked at her watch but could see nothing in the darkness. Roland whispered that the officers were due in half an hour.

"We need to get those torches relit," she whispered back. The men were clustered around her, seething with anger, the dangerous kind. The kind that would prompt them to go off into the night seeking revenge and retribution. She asked the one who had lit the torches not three hours earlier whether he'd be willing to light them again, with her standing guard beside him. "The light will make you a target," she warned him.

"We are prey for those animals standing here in the darkness," he replied, reaching into his pocket and withdrawing a lighter. He whispered something to the group and, after a bit of scurrying about in the darkness, he was given the long taper. He strode toward the front of the truck and into oblivion. Carole Ann rushed to overtake him. She stood in front of and to the right of one torch, chambered a round, and extended the weapon out in front of her in a two-handed grip. She tensed when she heard the lighter flick, inhaled at the first faint glow of light, and tightened her grip on the gun when the forest burst into artificial daylight, startling the night creatures into silence. She kept her grip on the gun but exhaled and followed the flickering taper to the other torch, keeping her eyes trained on the forest spread out before her. The second torch ignited and she heard rustling off to her right. She fired two rounds into the air and the rustling became feet running through the tangled brush.

An audible though restrained cheer rose from the men. Roland squeezed her arm and Toussaint Remy patted her shoulder in a fatherly fashion. She resumed her position atop the truck's hood, binoculars in hand, wide awake and totally unaware of any mosquitoes. The men took up positions in the truck's bed, all of them awake and alert. Stillness and silence prevailed. Then, at virtually the same moment, each of them became aware of a sound—at first a distant hum, then, growing closer, the distinctive roar of an engine. A vehicle was speeding down the road toward them. Carole Ann slid down the hood of the truck to the ground and raced around to the rear. Headlights were visible and approaching rapidly. She dropped into a crouch and backed off the road, eyes on the approaching vehicle, arms extended.

"It's our guys," one of the men called out, as the cruiser skidded in the dirt. The passenger door opened before the car stopped completely, propelling Officer Charles and a second cop into their midst.

"Is everybody all right? What the hell happened out here?"

"We're fine. How do you know anything happened?" Carole Ann asked, then grinned sheepishly as he brandished a two-way radio. Then she noticed that he looked more sheepish than she did.

"Our guys on stakeout on the other end heard gunfire and then a bunch of the rats came scurrying home, so he called me—called this radio," and he held it aloft. "The one I forgot to leave with you. The chief reamed me a new asshole—"

Carole Ann stopped him. "This isn't your fault. What stakeout on what other end?" she demanded.

"At that camp . . . it used to be a logging town, I think, but now it's a camp and HQ for the bad guys," Charles explained.

"And the chief's got people in there?" Carole Ann could barely breathe, her heart was pounding so hard.

He shook his head. "Not 'in,' near. We've been watching it for a few days. Lots of coming and going, I hear. But this is my detail, so I don't really know."

Her heart ceased its pounding and sank down to her kneecaps. If Nigel Osborne or Andre Collette thought they were under surveillance, if they spooked and ran . . . The crackle of the radio stopped her thoughts and her heart. Officer Charles spoke into it and then listened. He grimaced, tried and failed to convert it to a smile, spoke into the radio again, then listened for another brief moment, and shut it off. "They're on the run," he said.

She knew which "they" he meant. She felt paralyzed, useless, drained. Everything she'd put into place was about to unravel. Nigel Osborne would get away with murder—with four of them, at least—and with probably millions of dollars in cash. And Philippe Collette would be left with egg on his face; not in as much disgrace as Osborne had planned to have befall Henri LeRoi, but embarrassed and disgraced, because Andre Collette would not be allowed to escape. His usefulness had come to an end. "Shit," she muttered under her breath, and turned away from Officer Charles. She lifted a hand toward Roland and the other men, and started off down the road. The officer caught up with her. "Where are you going?"

"Home."

"And then where?"

She stopped and looked at him, the light from the torches now too distant to illuminate his face and instead casting flickering shadows. "I beg your pardon?"

"I know who you are, Miss Gibson," he said, rushing the words. "I was in New Orleans when you brought down the dirty congressman, and I read about what happened in L.A. If you're going active, I want in."

She leaned in close to him and peered into his eyes. Not a flicker. She couldn't outrun him and it wouldn't make sense to knock him down and disable him. And besides, he no doubt was a better shot than she was, and had few qualms about aiming at a subject when he fired his weapon. "Come on, then." She turned away from him and began to jog down the road.

Officer Charles ran over to his colleague, whispered quickly and urgently to him, and followed Carole Ann. Running now, they reached her house in less than ten minutes. The Jeep was parked out front. She had the keys in her hand when she reached it and quickly unlocked the door and jumped in. She reached across and unlocked the door for her new partner. He had the radio tight against his ear when he climbed in. "Do you know where something called the 'Seaview' cottages are?" he asked.

She shook her head. "Never heard of them—" she began but he cut her off.

"Sea*cliff*. Not *view*. Seacliff cottages . . . up on the north coast, in Deauville . . ." Still listening to the radio, he transmitted information to her as he heard it. "Some private beach cottages up on the hill . . ."

"Yes!" she exclaimed, remembering the saltbox houses at the end of the Deauville main street. "I know them! I didn't know what they were called, and I'm not sure how to get there. How to drive in, that is. I know how to walk in . . ." She stopped herself. She was babbling, but he didn't seem to notice, so intent was he on the information coming from the radio. She kept her eyes on the road and listened.

". . . from a private road through the de Villages estate . . . guests have some kind of key card that opens a gate."

Carole Ann jammed her foot on the gas pedal and kept it there until they rounded the crest into Deauville. She didn't know the de Villages estate was private and didn't care. "We'll go in on foot." And stand out like gate-crashers at a White House state dinner, she thought, turning onto the main street. It was sedately lit, by candles on the tables of outdoor cafes and by four towering gas lamps on the four corners of the street. No other traffic moved, and she parked the Jeep. Elegantly clad diners strolled in the middle of the street, just like the tourists in Ville de Paix, in Government Square. There, however, dressing for dinner meant wearing enough clothes to cover the crucial body parts; here, it meant jackets for the men and dresses for the women. Carole Ann, in baggy cargo pants, a T-shirt, and running shoes, appeared grossly out of place. Officer Charles, in the uniform of the Isle de Paix security force, looked . . . comforting.

"Where's this Seacliff place?"

"End of the street," she answered, and reached into the backseat of the Jeep for her baseball cap. She jammed it onto her head, pulled the bill down over her eyes, ducked her head, and began walking. She wasn't so foolish as to hope she wouldn't be noticed, but she prayed not to be recognized. They'd have difficulty enough being unobtrusive on Seacliff's narrow lanes without attracting attention before ever getting there.

Thankfully, just before they reached the end of the street, three couples emerged from the patisserie on the left and, talking and laughing a little too loudly, they jiggled and jostled their way into the enclave. Carole Ann and Charles followed as closely behind as they dared. She removed her cap and finger-combed her hair, and he dropped a few paces behind her, locked his hands behind his back, and whistled tunelessly under his breath. A beat cop on the job, doing his job. The six Germans—snatches of their conversation had wafted back on the gentle breeze and Carole Ann had heard enough to identify them—turned into the house across the street from where she believed Nigel Osborne lived. She slowed a bit and looked toward the house. No light at any of the windows. She continued to walk, past the house, swinging her arms, glancing from side to side and occasionally up at the sky. She didn't know whether any of Nigel Osborne's associates lived here; she didn't know anything, she realized, for Yvette Casson hadn't told her what, if anything, her search of the rental car records had revealed.

There were lights glowing in most of the houses, and noise emanating from many of them—music, laughter. After all, this was a resort and people were on vacation. Then she heard the sound of tires screeching. She stiffened and glanced quickly behind her; Charles had heard, too, and had stepped off the road, toward one of the houses. Carole Ann followed suit, just in time to see headlights approaching. The car definitely was traveling too fast, and its driver almost lost control of it as it screeched into the driveway of the next-to-the-last house on the lane. Carole Ann had stopped walking and Officer Charles was nowhere in sight. She ducked into the yard of a darkened house and chanced walking onto the porch, giving her a view of the car four doors down, but obscuring her from their view. The passenger door of the car opened, but no one emerged. Then the driver's-side door opened; a figure jumped out and slammed the door shut, and rushed around to the passenger door. It was a man and he reached into the car and pulled.

The screamed "No!" split the air like cracked crystal, the sound high-pitched and shrill for one instant. Then it faded. The man looked around, pulled again, and a woman flew out of the car. Carole Ann caught her breath: Andre and Nicole Collette. He shoved her up the walkway toward the house, then opened the back door of the car and emerged with two satchels or duffels . . . she couldn't be certain in the dark. Nicole was huddled on the porch and Andre stormed after her, cradling the two bundles close to him as if they were babies. He dropped the bags, unlocked the door, shoved Nicole in, picked up the bags, followed her in, and slammed the door. Carole Ann remained motionless on the porch for a full minute, then hurried down the steps and, keeping close to the edge of the lane, back toward where she'd last seen Charles. A shadow moved and she froze. It beckoned to her. She peered into the space between two of the houses and saw a form that she could not positively identify as Officer Charles.

"Miss Gibson!" Her hissed name came from the direction of the shadowy form. Still uncertain, she was debating what to do when the slam of a door diverted her attention. She looked over her shoulder to see Andre Collette running down the steps of his house. Without another thought, she ducked into the shadows. Andre sped past and Carole Ann knew that he was headed for Nigel Osborne's, apparently expecting him to be at home. Was Andre panicked and making mistakes, or was Nigel otherwise detained? Andre's rapid, insistent knocking continued for several seconds, then abruptly halted. He ran back toward his house, bypassed it, reaching the end of the lane, and disappeared. "What the hell do you suppose that was all about?" Charles whispered.

"Where the hell is he going?" Carole Ann whispered, understanding very well the meaning of the Collettes' actions, and wondering how much, if anything, to reveal.

"He's probably headed down to the cove, but why would he go down there this time of night?"

"What cove?" Carole Ann demanded, though she thought she knew very well which cove. "There's no road to the beach from this end . . ." And in the same instant that Charles mentioned the stone staircase, she remembered it.

"You clever bastard," she whispered, more to herself than to the cop lurking in the shadows beside her.

"Nothing clever about that silly little fuck, with women screaming and doors slamming and him stomping up and down the street like a jerk. I'd like to arrest his ass just for being stupid."

"And I'd like to know where he's going," Carole Ann said, hurrying down the lane after him.

"You can't do that!" Charles caught up to her in one stride and grabbed her arm. "You don't know who that guy is or what he's doing!"

"Let go of me, please."

He dropped his hand from her arm. "The chief is going to kill me if I lose you tonight." He was close to whining.

"The chief is going to kill you anyway for being out here with me," she replied. "I'm going to find that cove."

"You know who he is, don't you? The guy and the girl?"

How much did she owe him? Without him, she'd have probably gotten lost looking for Sugar Town in the dark instead of having a bird's-eye view of the unraveling drug cartel. She sighed deeply. "Nicole and Andre Collette."

There was a long silence; too long. She began walking down the lane toward the road that she knew must lead to the stone stairway, which would take her down to the beach and the cove. Is that where Nigel Osborne was? "Collette? As in President Collette?"

She nodded and kept walking, faster now as she reached the end of the lane. Andre had turned left, she thought, so she turned left, Officer Charles hard on her heels. "Who is this guy? Who are these people, exactly?" he hissed into her ear, walking with her step for step.

"The president's son and daughter-in-law."

"The chief is going to kill me. Then she's probably going to fire me."

"That's if you're lucky," Carole Ann muttered, squinting into the darkness. There was no more road and no sign of the stone steps. There was another cluster of the saltbox houses to the left, facing the sea, and, to the right, a cabana of sorts: tables with umbrellas and chairs and chaise lounges. A sunbathing deck for those not requiring direct contact with the ocean. But that didn't make sense . . . She angled off to the right, walking slowly, head down, eyes searching the dark. She stopped, closed her eyes, and tried to envision the cove and the stairs as she and Roland had seen them that day from the ocean. "Where are the damn stairs!"

"I think you're going the wrong way."

"And why do you think that, Officer Charles?" Carole Ann asked through clenched teeth, aware of the time and energy she was wasting.

"Because Donna Creighton, she's our harbor patrol squad, says you can see the stairs just after you pass all the beach umbrellas and naked bathers. And there's the beach umbrellas and I can imagine the naked bathers . . ."

"And the steps angled slightly," Carole Ann said, running in the opposite direction, toward the cluster of houses that faced the sea. The road was uneven at this point, and she lost her footing momentarily. She looked down. The path now was white stones and gravel—and the path led to the stairs. She ran forward, Officer Charles close behind.

The steps were steep and narrow, though there was a wooden railing at regular intervals. Even with the railing, it was not possible to do anything but proceed slowly and cautiously. When she reached the bottom and her feet touched sand, Carole Ann pressed her back into the cliff wall and moved to her left. Charles followed. They stood looking up and down the beach and out to sea, finding nothing but darkness. "The cove is north," she whispered; he nodded, and they sidled along the cliff wall for several yards, gaining confidence and moving more quickly.

"Wait!" Charles hissed, grabbing her arm. They stood in the darkness, listening. She closed her eyes and heard it: the whine of a boat motor; not a large one, but a powerful one opened to full throttle. But the sea played tricks with sound and they didn't see the speedboat until it was upon them, coming from the south and riding high up on its stern, the bow out of the water. And it was running without lights. As it approached them, the engine was cut and the craft bobbed in its wake briefly, then drifted to shore. There was one passenger: Nigel Osborne. He jumped out of the boat, in water up to his knees, and waded in to shore. The boat seemed to follow him in. He stopped in the sand and removed his shoes, then began to run up the beach. They let him get fifty yards ahead and followed, staying close to the wall, keeping him in sight.

"I suppose you know who he is too?" Charles whispered.

"Ex–DEA agent," Carole Ann answered. "He was dirty when he was on the job, and he's worse than dirty now."

"Oh, Jesus, what have I got myself into? Maybe I'll just kill myself, save the chief a slug. What do you think, Miss Gibson?"

"If we do this right, Charles, you'll get a promotion and a couple days off. Especially if you blame it all on me."

"I was going to do that anyway," he drawled sourly, then halted suddenly, just as Carole Ann did. They both saw the lights in the distance, on land and on the schooner that loomed in the cove. "Looks like somebody's planning a vacation."

"But who?" she asked. "Can you tell? Do you see Andre? Or Osborne?"

He was shaking his head back and forth, whether exasperated and frustrated with the situation or with her, she couldn't determine. Then, "There, isn't that Osborne? Walking toward the yacht?"

"Damn! If we lose him now—" She was stopped midsentence by yelling. Osborne stopped, too, and looked over his shoulder. Carole Ann followed his gaze. Someone was running toward Osborne and the schooner in the cove, running and yelling. Still holding his shoes, Osborne paused for a moment, then began to walk toward whoever was coming toward him, yelling. The words were indistinguishable but the fury was unmistakable. Andre! It was Andre Collette, and he had stopped running but continued to rail and wave his hands. Then Nigel Osborne raised his hand, his right hand, in which there no longer were shoes. And because of the way the sea plays tricks with sound, Andre Collette was sprawled on his back in the sand before the retort of the gun reached their ears, and Nigel Osborne was striding toward his yacht.

"My God!"

"He just killed the president's kid?" Charles made it a question, but the answer was obvious.

Carole Ann sprang forward. Charles grabbed her before she'd gotten two strides ahead, her running shoes dragging in the sand. "We've got to do something, dammit! We can't just let him sail off!" She pulled away from him.

"You think you can outrun him?" Officer Charles challenged, his shoes already off and his Glock in his hand. He was sprinting toward the cove, his feet kicking up sand in his wake. She bent quickly and untied her shoes and kicked them off and was about to follow when a high-pitched scream cut through the gentle night. A high, piercing, blood-chilling scream. A woman's scream. She looked up the beach. Charles was running harder and the schooner was backing up in the water. Another scream, and Marie-Ange Collette ran toward her son's corpse. She knew it was Marie-Ange because of the hair—even at this distance, at night, the red and gold and silver mane gleamed and glittered. She screamed again.

Carole Ann wanted to sit in the sand and weep. Instead, she turned and ran toward the motorboat that Nigel Osborne had left drifting in the surf. It still was bobbing up and down, though it was farther out to sea now. She waded into the water and winced as rocks and shells cut into the soles of her feet. Swimming would be faster and less painful, but her guns would get wet. She dug the automatic out of her pants pocket and stuffed it into one of her shoes, then unstrapped the waist pouch that held her own gun. Holding them aloft, she waded farther into the Atlantic, toward the bouncing boat, which seemed to taunt her by drifting even farther from shore.

"Would you like a hand?"

She froze and her heart stopped. She turned toward shore and saw Denis St. Almain jogging toward her, shoes held aloft. "Damn you, Denis St. Almain! You keep scaring the poop out of me!" She yelled at the top of her lungs, releasing fear and tension and the sorrow she felt for Philippe Collette.

"Serves you right," he shot back as he plunged into the surf. He threw his shoes into the boat and dove into the surf, reaching the boat in a few, expert strokes. He clambered aboard, started the engine, and eased toward her. He kept it steady as she tossed in her shoes and waist pouch, and he extended a hand to help her aboard. "Where to?" he asked, and she got her first good look at him. Thank goodness she had recognized his voice.

She pointed toward the running lights of the quickly disappearing schooner.

"You're kidding!"

"Goddammit! Either you drive the boat or I will!" she screamed at him. He pulled back on the throttle and the boat shot forward, riding on its stern and bouncing hard on the water. "Slow down," she yelled into his ear, pointing at Officer Charles running in the water toward them.

"That's a cop! Are you crazy?"

"You've got nothing to worry about, Denis. Besides, you look like shit. Nobody would recognize you anyway." She couldn't hear what he said as he cut the engines and drifted toward shore to pick up Officer Charles.

"I called the chief," he said, brandishing the radio, "and told her what happened out here. She and Donna Creighton took our boat and a coast guard cutter is heading this way." He looked out at the sea, shook his head, and looked back at her. "We're supposed to stay with the body. And I'm supposed to keep an eye on you."

"Good luck," Denis drawled and beached the boat. They jumped out and Denis caught her arm. "Aren't you forgetting something?" he whispered. At her blank stare, he added, "Your shoes and your pouch." She reached in the boat and retrieved her weapons. "You'd make a lousy cop," he muttered, but she didn't hear him. She was running across the sand toward Marie-Ange and Andre Collette, reaching for the words she'd offer in the presence of sudden, inexorable death. She could help the other woman grieve that loss. But what words were there to assuage the horror of betrayal? Hers and his.

"Just exactly what in the hell *were* you thinking?" David Messinger had been sneering and snarling at her for close to four hours. For the first two or so, she'd been too numb with shock and grief for his nastiness to register. Now, however, she was growing weary of him, of his posturing, of his refusal to see the larger picture. She turned to Yvette, who, so far, had listened in silence.

"As I've said before, at least half a dozen times, I was thinking that it was possible to flush Osborne out into the open. I was thinking that it was possible to separate him from Andre and Marie-Ange, to isolate him and apprehend him and then to deal . . . to let Philippe . . . President Collette deal with his family. And I was thinking—I was hoping—that perhaps the worst thing Andre was involved in was the marijuana, that perhaps the field was his. I was even thinking that perhaps Andre had something to do with the refusal to allow the government to use the de Villages' construction equipment—before I learned of Monsieur de Villages' illness and Christian Leonard's involvement. But I honestly never once really suspected Andre Collette of involvement in Paul Francois's murder, and I most certainly never suspected or would have believed Marie-Ange Collette to be a willing participant in illegal drug trafficking. I would have responded very differently had I known."

"A little late to be having second thoughts, isn't it?"

"Perhaps you misunderstood me." She turned back to the minister. "I'm not having second thoughts about any of my actions, David. I am, however, wishing that I had known, wishing that some tiny piece of information had pointed to Marie-Ange, because then I could have gone directly to Philippe." She smiled tightly at his reaction. Surely he couldn't think she'd trust him with such a delicate suspicion. Yvette, perhaps, but never him.

"You spend a remarkable amount of time outside the bounds of the law for a legal practitioner."

She finally laughed at him. "If you remember anything about being a lawyer, David, perhaps you'll recall the bit about one's responsibility to one's client. Philippe Collette and the government he runs are my clients. My first duty is to him and his government, not to you. And maybe if you had put the interests of this government ahead of your own petty interests, you'd have had some sense of what was happening here."

"What the hell is that supposed to mean?"

"It means that your time would have been better spent helping out Yvette and her cops, all of whom have been pulling double shifts these last few days, instead of hopping from island to island looking for permission to hang people!" She was fully, coldly furious, and she made no effort to hide or control her rage.

"And after all he's done, you don't think Nigel Osborne deserves to hang?" He was incredulous. "He most likely ordered the murder of that judge in D.C. He most likely murdered Paul Francois himself. And you saw him murder Andre Collette. For God's sake, woman, why can't you see that hanging is the best thing for scum like him!"

"Because, David, I'm looking at the larger picture. Hanging Nigel Osborne will not necessarily kill the root of the evil here on this island. He tried and failed to corrupt Henri LeRoi. He tried and succeeded in corrupting Andre and Marie-Ange Collette. That's all we know about his actions."

"And that's enough!" he thundered.

"No, it's not!" She slammed her palm down on the top of Yvette's desk, rattling her coffee cup. "Unless you can be certain that every connection to Nigel Osborne is severed, you're going to have trouble here. And right now, I'm not certain of that. So if you hung him at noon today in Government Square, somebody would be dealing drugs in Seacliff and Little Haiti tonight. Don't forget, David, that Osborne was using Isle de Paix primarily as a staging area—drugs come in here wholesale, to be packaged and shipped out for retail sale. The couple of million annually from the pot field is just gravy."

He scowled at her through narrowed eyes. "Are you saying you don't think we got them all? Osborne and that bunch on the boat and those holed up in that camp, and Marie-Ange and Andre Collette? That's not all?"

Carole Ann shook her head. "I don't think so."

"I don't either." Yvette stood up, wanting to pace, but David Messinger and his energy were occupying too much of the room's space. She sat back down and said, "We haven't turned up any cash, David. There's always cash and guns where there's drugs. The guns we got, but where's the money? The coast guard didn't recover any when they seized the boat, and we didn't recover any from Osborne's house, or from either of the Collettes' residences, or from that compound in the woods. Somebody's got the money."

David was waving his hand back and forth, dismissing her words. "The money could be anywhere."

"Dealers are never far from their money," Yvette said. "This was his base of operations; this is where the money should be."

"Then you'd better look again at that St. Almain character. If one DEA agent could go bad, so could another one."

Neither Carole Ann nor Yvette bothered to respond to so patently ridiculous a suggestion. The DEA finally had come clean regarding Denis, totally exonerating him, once it was clear that an airtight case could be made against the rogue Osborne. All the pieces were finding a fit, all the loose ends were being knotted. All but a couple, and Carole Ann was beginning to be worried about them. She also was worried that those loose ends represented information that she still was withholding from David and Yvette. Her horror and sorrow over Marie-Ange, coupled with her fatigue, caused her to question the wisdom of her actions. And since they were discussing money, this would be an appropriate time for her to come clean, as it were. She mentally shook herself. She had a plan, she would stick to it, despite the fact that her thought processes were feeling as if they were made of spaghetti. Clarity occurred, it seemed, only when she was furious with David Messinger. Maybe he'd say something else stupid that she could react to. Otherwise, she'd fall asleep.

There was a knock and the door opened and Officer Charles stuck his head in. "Excuse me, sir, ma'am, ma'am," he said, with extra emphasis on Carole Ann's "ma'am." "The finance minister is here to see you."

David Messinger jumped up from his chair, his face full of surprise. Yvette Casson rose more slowly, her brow furrowed. Carole Ann kept her seat; the fatigue had taken control. Carmen Anderson bustled into the office. She grabbed Carole Ann up into a standing position and a crushing embrace, alternating between thanking her and praising her brilliance. "Did you tell David what you did?" she chirped.

"You mean she's done something else?" the minister of internal security snapped at his peer.

"Professor Anderson," Carole Ann said sweetly, ignoring him, "have you met our chief of police, Yvette Casson?" Yes, the two women had met, and they exchanged pleasantries, and Yvette offered the minister of finance the chair at the table formerly occupied by the minister of internal security, who was standing in the corner rubbing his hands together, a worried look on his face.

"Delighted to see you, Carmen, of course, but what has our Miss Gibson done to bring you to police headquarters so early in the morning?"

And, as if giving a lecture on not-so-advanced economic systems, the professor, eyes wide and shining behind her thick lenses, told them of the deposit made that morning when the bank opened of more than seven hundred thousand dollars to the personal account of bank manager Christian Leonard by Nicole Collette; a deposit that, by law, had to be reported to the finance ministry because any deposit in ex-cess of ten thousand dollars had to be reported by the bank to the finance department. But it had not been reported. And, because she'd been advised by Carole Ann to check accounts and records, she discovered quite a few heretofore unreported deposits of large sums of money to accounts held by Monsieur Leonard, Madame Marie-Ange Collette, and several accounts in the names of Hubert de Villages and members of his family but controlled by Christian Leonard. In accordance with the finance laws of the island, she had, she said, confiscated all of the money—totaling more than four million dollars—which, if found to be the proceeds of illegal activity, reverted to the Isle de Paix treasury.

Carole Ann, Yvette, and David sat in stunned silence, staring at the finance minister, who beamed back at them. Then David and Yvette simultaneously turned their focus to Carole Ann, who had begun shaking her head. "I didn't know. I swear to you that I didn't know."

"Bullshit, Carole Ann!" David Messinger thundered. "Dr. Anderson just said you told her to check—"

"I told her, David," Carole Ann snapped, her cold fury overriding his hot anger, for now she was both alert and furious, having been caught by surprise again, "to monitor any deposit made by Nicole Collette, thinking, believing, speculating that it would be in Nigel Osborne's name, or in Andre Collette's name. I had no idea that Christian Leonard was involved!" She closed her eyes and massaged her temples while this new bit of information took its place among the bits and pieces and loose ends. When she opened her eyes, Yvette Casson was looking into them, a flicker of satisfaction in her own.

"He's the last connection to Osborne. He's the money, and probably the brains."

Carole Ann nodded agreement though her face bespoke her confusion, and Yvette questioned her. "I think you're right about Leonard, but I don't get it. The man's a right-wing, racist bigot. Why would he even accept a job here? Why would he go into business with Osborne?"

"Greed," Messinger, Casson, and Anderson replied simultaneously, and Carole Ann knew they were correct. Greed overcame prejudices of all kinds.

"So," Yvette said, "I think that's it. I'll have Nicole picked up and then I think we got it all," and her voice echoed the relief that Carole Ann felt.

"Got all what?" David demanded to know, sounding both irritated and hurt, as if he hadn't been included in something.

"The cancer that was growing here, David," Yvette replied since Carole Ann was ignoring him. "The evil, the ugliness, the danger. Of course, we will have to burn that pot field and stage raids on Armand's and a couple of the other local watering holes, and the sooner the better."

Carole Ann welcomed a reason for levity, and she smiled. "I knew some of that crew seemed a bit too eager to go to work. Who was it, Joseph?"

"And Luc and Thomas and Lise and half a dozen others," Yvette said, allowing a smile of her own. After the specter of Nigel Osborne, she probably could find humor in a little marijuana . . . as long as it was only a little. She stood up. "Dr. Anderson, would you be kind enough to walk with me over to your office, and walk me through, on paper, what you just told us? And, David? Do you want to handle the arrests of Nicole Collette and Christian Leonard, or shall I get a couple of the troops?"

He cleared his throat, straightened his back, and squared his shoulders. "I think I can still make an arrest." Then he turned on his heels and left them.

She didn't know how long the pounding had been going on, only that ignoring it didn't make it go away. Carole Ann stepped into a pair of shorts and pulled a T-shirt over her head and, still yawning, padded down the hallway to the door. She opened it to see Denis St. Almain's back rounding the corner. "I'm awake now, Denis, thank you very much. You may as well come on in," she called out, suppressing a yawn.

He was grinning when he turned back toward her. He looked more rested than she did, though he couldn't have gotten much more sleep than she had. But, of course, he now no longer was a fugitive, and no doubt having that weight lifted allowed for this new aura of calm. He also was cleaner and better dressed than when she'd last seen him. "How can you sleep in the midst of so much excitement?" he asked, following her into the kitchen, where he took a stool at the counter.

"Excitement. That's what that was!" She yawned again and opened the refrigerator. "I suppose I should thank you for waking me. I've never heard of anybody succumbing in their sleep to hunger, and I am ravenous."

"Then put on some clothes and let's go! Dinner with the aunties, my treat!"

On the drive to Aux Fruits de Mer, and over dinner at Odile's table, he explained how he'd ended up on the beach the previous night. He'd been living in the woods, he said, watching Osborne's drug camp for several days, and he could tell by the frantic activity that a major move was under way. He knew he couldn't prevent it, but he wanted to amass enough information to lead to the arrest of whoever was in charge, with the hope that that would help clear his name. He explained that he knew Nigel Osborne's name from his DEA days, but that the two had never met because Osborne was undercover, and he was based in his home country with the entirety of the Caribbean as his turf, while Denis was undercover only in Washington, and Isle de Paix was his only island assignment. "I got sick to my stomach when I realized that Nigel Osborne was who you were asking me about. But once I knew who he was, I knew who his connections were in D.C. They may have cut him loose, but knowing how the agency works, I knew that nobody wanted their name used in the same sentence with his."

"So, you were planning to blackmail the DEA into exonerating you?"

He scowled. "And you had a better idea?"

She shook her head at him. "Catch the bad guys and make them come clean, which, by the way, we did, Denis."

"Yeah, after I'd been living in the woods eating nuts and berries for what seemed like years! I'm just glad you caught them before the rainy season," he said darkly, and she laughed.

"Osborne did admit everything, you know," she added.

"Of course he did! The bastard is going to hang! He'd say anything to save his neck at this point, including telling the truth, for a change." His scowl deepened, then, abruptly, his face relaxed into a more thoughtful expression. "I'd like to have been a dust ball in the corner when he realized that the new government here not only wouldn't play ball with him, but it had cops that were looking to lock his ass up! That Chief Casson is really something," he said admiringly. "And that Messinger is one tough customer. I heard that he refused to allow the coast guard to bring Osborne and his crew back here, had them delivered directly back to Trinidad, at the expense of the Trinidadian government!"

Carole Ann found herself enjoying a view of David through the eyes of another. She'd probably get along much better with him when she and Jake returned in January, and he had the day-to-day contact with David while she worked with Roland Charles and Jackie La-Belle. She felt the tug of pain and grief that she knew would nudge at her for a long time whenever she thought of Philippe Collette, who easily would have been excused had he terminated the GGI contract. "I have no just cause," he had said when she presented the opportunity. "You and your company have served this government well. I hope you will continue."

"You suddenly look sad," Denis said.

She shrugged and changed her expression and the subject. "What are you going to do with yourself now that it's safe to come out of the woods?"

A sudden boyish look overtook his face and he ducked his head. It was a moment before he met her eyes. "I asked Chief Casson for a job."

Her surprise was complete, and so was her approval, and she

promised him a good reference if he needed it and if Yvette wanted it.

"President Collette is the one you'll have to convince," he said darkly. "He knows I'm not dirty, but he's thinking that anybody with any connection to all this . . ." He trailed off, looking again like a young boy. "Anyway, the chief said it would be up to him and she's hopeful, since he hasn't said no."

"I'll be happy to speak with Philippe," she said, "and once you meet him . . ."

"Once I meet him, what?" Denis pressed, looking at her curiously.

Once you meet him, you'll know that Henri LeRoi is not your father, she thought. And coming face-to-face with the man at a job interview is not the time and place for such a discovery.

"Carole Ann, what's wrong?"

"May I make a suggestion?" she asked, and when he nodded she continued. "Before you meet with President Collette, ask your fath . . . ask Monsieur LeRoi his opinion. Tell him you'd have to meet first with President Collette before getting a job here, and tell him why. I think his very unique perspective will be valuable to you."

He looked at her strangely, but agreed to do as she asked. He extended Henri LeRoi's thanks to her, as well as that of his mother and Hazel Copeland. Then he raised his glass in a toast to her, and he thanked her for himself.

She found herself, in subsequent days, unable to categorize her feelings about being thanked for doing her job. Certainly, back when she still practiced law, clients thanked her if she kept them out of jail, but she received those words with little sentiment attached. She was paid extremely well to defend the accused and she was good at it. She expected to win, and more often than not, she did. But being thanked by Denis and Henri LeRoi and Odile and Viviene and Carmen Anderson and, after a fashion, Yvette Casson . . . what did that mean? Whatever they were grateful for had accrued as a result of her doing her job, even if they were not directly her clients. Did she warrant gratitude? Even Philippe Collette had thanked her, for her service to his government, if not on behalf of himself, for she had effectively destroyed a significant segment of his life.

She recalled in detail her meeting with him. Indeed, she'd most likely never be able to forget it. He was formal and gracious, as always, and so sad that tears came to her eyes when she looked at him. It was the kind of sadness she knew too well, and she had caused it. She had apologized and he had brushed it aside. She'd asked how Marie-Ange was and he'd closed his eyes for a moment, then said that she was heavily sedated, that Maurice never left her side. And, Carole Ann had asked, what will happen to her? He had looked at her for a long moment before answering: "Nothing." She had waited for him to explain and he had not. So she had asked how that was possible. He had told her how, in exchange for extradition home to France to face charges rather than execution in Trinidad, Christian Leonard would testify that he and Nigel Osborne were in the drug business together, that it was Osborne who bribed Andre and killed the constables and Paul Francois. Marie-Ange would not figure anywhere in the equation.

"I've lost a son and some of my will to live, and my wife would rather be dead. But she is not, and if that is all that I can salvage from this, I accept it as sufficient." Then he had turned the tables on her: if GGI no longer wanted to work with him and the Isle de Paix government, he would understand and release them from the terms of their contract.

"He's gonna be pretty good at that president stuff" was Jake's reaction, along with his unmitigated desire to continue with the contract, over Carole Ann's halfhearted reservations.

"He's violating the law, Jake."

"And you didn't when you went after the bastard who murdered your husband?"

To that she had no response, only thoughts of violence and vengeance that would not leave her alone.

"You don't like those thoughts? Change them!" she heard Al's voice whisper in her ear. My husband the Buddhist, she thought, with the hitch in her heart she felt each and every time she thought of him.

Right again, Al. Almost. She would not think about Nigel Osborne or his fate, but she would think about Philippe Collette and how he would live with his decision to save his wife. And she would think about Marie-Ange, who couldn't live her Parisian life on Philippe's Isle de Paix salary once Christian Leonard stole her inheritance, and wonder why he hadn't kept his hatred at home. And she would think about Andre. She also would think about Roland Charles completing his road ahead of schedule once the government moved to confiscate the de Villages' construction equipment.

And she would think about the first time Philippe Collette and Denis St. Almain looked at each other and saw themselves.

{ FLiP-iT-OVeR }
GUIDES TO TEEN EMOTIONS

A Guys' Guide to

Stress

Travis Clark

Enslow Publishers, Inc.
40 Industrial Road
Box 398
Berkeley Heights, NJ 07922
USA

http://www.enslow.com

Library of Congress Cataloging-in-Publication Data

Clark, Travis, 1985-
  A guys' guide to stress ; A girls' guide to stress / Travis Clark and Annie Belfield.
      p. cm. — (Flip-it-over guides to teen emotions)
  Includes bibliographical references and index.
  ISBN-13: 978-0-7660-2857-9
  ISBN-10: 0-7660-2857-7
  1. Stress (Psychology)—Juvenile literature. 2. Boys—Life skills guides—Juvenile literature. 3. Girls—Life skills guides—Juvenile literature. I. Belfield, Annie. II. Title. III. Title: Guys' guide to stress ; A girls' guide to stress. IV. Title: Girls' guide to stress.

  BF575.S75C545 2008
  155.4'18—dc22

                              2007026458

Printed in the United States of America.

10 9 8 7 6 5 4 3 2 1

Produced by OTTN Publishing, Stockton, N.J.

To Our Readers: We have done our best to make sure all Internet Addresses in this book were active and appropriate when we went to press. However, the author and the publisher have no control over and assume no liability for the material available on those Internet sites or on other Web sites they may link to. Any comments or suggestions can be sent by e-mail to comments@enslow.com or to the address on the title page.

Photo Credits: © Digital Vision, 1, 25; Corbis Images, 7; © 2008 Jupiterimages Corporation, 10, 33, 34; © OTTN Publishing, 16; © iStockphoto.com/4x6, 49; © iStockphoto.com/Joshua Blake, 3, 12; © iStockphoto.com/Ana Blazic, 4; © iStockphoto.com/José Luis Gutiérrez, 42; © iStockphoto.com/Justin Horrocks, 26; © iStockphoto.com/Filip Kaliszan, 22; © iStockphoto.com/Georgy Markov, 29; © iStockphoto.com/Aldo Murillo, 48; © iStockphoto.com/Sherrie Smith, 36; © iStockphoto.com/WinterWitch, 50; © iStockphoto.com/Lisa F. Young, 30, 38; Used under license from Shutterstock, Inc., 11, 15, 40, 44, 46, 53, 54, 57; © Stockbyte, 27.

Cover Photo: © Digital Vision

CONTENTS

CHAPTER ONE

Stress and Stressors

It was the night before a huge test, and Philip was over at his friend Tim's house. They had been studying all afternoon for their European History test the next day. Both of them wanted to do well. But there was a lot of material to cover. Even though they studied for several hours, both felt nervous about how they would do.

The feeling that Tim and Philip are dealing with is called stress, which is the body's reaction to an external force or event. In Tim and Philip's case, that outside event is the test they face the next day. The test is their *stressor*—the term used to describe something that causes stress.

A stressor can be several different things—a project, a job, a large crowd, an illness, an immediate danger, or even hunger, just to name a few. Generally, any type of change in a person's normal routine can cause stress. When stressful situations occur, the body prepares to deal with a challenge or tough situation by increasing alertness and focus.

Up until the mid-1930s, the concept of stress did not even exist. Around that time, a physician named Hans Selye first noticed that his patients shared many of the same symptoms, although they suffered from

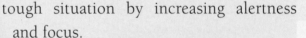
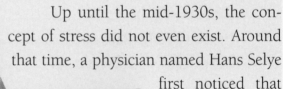

You and Your Emotions

A part of everyone's personality, emotions are a powerful driving force in life. They are hard to define and understand. But what is known is that emotions—which include anger, fear, love, joy, jealousy, and hate—are a normal part of the human system. They are responses to situations and events that trigger bodily changes, motivating you to take some kind of action.

Some studies show that the brain relies more on emotions than on intellect in learning and in making decisions. Being able to identify and understand the emotions in yourself and in others can help you in your relationships with family, friends, and others throughout your life.

different diseases. These complaints typically involved aches, pains, and nausea.

When Selye investigated the biological causes of the symptoms, he came to the conclusion that something within the body was causing it to react, or adapt, to illness. Through further research Selye learned that the body responded the same way, whether it was reacting to an illness, the injection of foreign bodies, or some other external force. Selye referred to this ability of the body to react and adapt as general adaptation syndrome. He would later call it stress.

Stress can involve many emotions, ranging from excitement to anger, fear, embarrassment, guilt, or shame.

Selye's research has led to a greater understanding of how the human mind can cause changes in the human body. He has also helped future generations understand why the body reacts to outside forces in different ways.

Everyone responds to stress differently. Some people may be very bothered by having a major test, while others feel completely confident. On the other hand, the confident test-taker may fall apart when having to give a speech in front of a group

Common Stressors for Guys

Can you identify with any of these stressors and the emotions they cause?

1. Starting at a new school
2. Trouble with family and friends
3. Overloaded with school work, job, chores
4. Highly competitive athletics
5. Lack of rest
6. Desire to fit in
7. Birth of a new brother or sister
8. Tests or exams
9. Death of a family member or friend
10. Big social event, party, or date
11. Body changes of puberty

Keeping on top of homework can remove a major stressor from your life.

of people, while the nervous test-taker can easily speak before the whole student body. Similarly, the amount of stress that people can handle varies from person to person.

While a little bit of stress in your life can help you be at the top of your game, too much stress in life can cause health problems. That's why it's a good idea to learn how to manage stress. You can do this by learning how to identify your stressors and why they make you feel stressed. That way, you can know when it is time to make changes or take action to reduce stress in your life—and keep it from overloading your system.

CHAPTER TWO

Your Body's Response

> The auditorium was full for the school assembly. The entire high school had filled the 1,000-seat auditorium and the crush of people was really starting to bother Will. He didn't like large crowds, but was okay when he could talk with his friends. However, they had decided to skip the assembly, leaving him stranded. As Will looked around the auditorium, he grew more uncomfortable. Waves of nausea began washing over him, and he started to sweat. Unable to bear his feelings any longer, Will stumbled out of the auditorium. He made it to the hall, where he sank to the floor and tried to collect himself.

Because crowded environments bother Will, he responded negatively to the stress of being in the auditorium. He broke into a sweat and felt sick to his stomach. Why was he feeling this way?

Will's body was responding to stress. The physical symptoms can range from a headache, to nausea, to a rash, to an anxiety attack. (An anxiety attack is when you feel overwhelmed by apprehension and fear. Symptoms include sweating, rapid heartbeat, and tension.) Anxiety often involves a number of different emotions, including fear, shame, and sometimes guilt. Feelings of anxiety commonly occur as a result of overstress, which occurs when your body is exposed to a high level of stress.

"Worry and stress affects the circulation, the heart, the glands, the whole nervous system, and profoundly affects heart action."

—Charles W. Mayo

Science Says...

Hans Selye theorized that the body goes through three different stages when exposed to stress:

Alarm reaction: This is the body's initial excitement after recognizing the stressor. In a response known as "fight-or-flight," the body prepares to take action. This causes a high level of activity within the body: the muscles tense, blood pressure rises, and the rate of breathing increases.

Resistance: The body begins to deal with the stress. Depending on the stressor, the body will react in various ways. But it is also attempting to move back to normal.

Exhaustion: If the body has to endure a high level of stress for a long period of time, its ability to cope or resist will be worn down. The result can be a weakened immune system and illness.

In his research, Hans Selye examined how the human body physically responds when under stress. He eventually identified an internal stress-causing system, known as the hypothalamus-pituitary-adrenal system. The stress response starts in the brain, where the hypothalamus is located. The hypothalamus directs the pituitary gland, which is also in the brain, to send a message to other organs in the body. As a result certain chemicals, called hormones, are released into the bloodstream.

Two hormones that increase in response to stressful situations are adrenaline and cortisol. These stress hormones come

Physical Symptoms of Stress

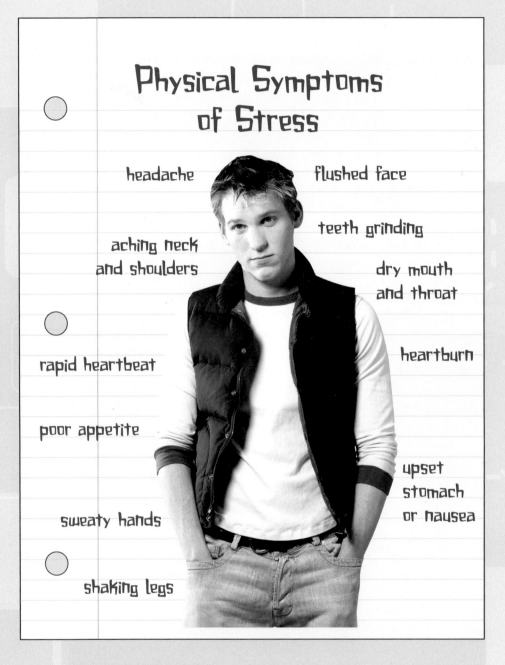

headache

flushed face

teeth grinding

aching neck and shoulders

dry mouth and throat

rapid heartbeat

heartburn

poor appetite

upset stomach or nausea

sweaty hands

shaking legs

from the adrenal glands, which are located on the top of the kidneys. The additional amounts of adrenaline and cortisol cause the amount of sugar in the bloodstream to increase, resulting in a feeling of extra strength and energy. The adrenaline and cortisol can cause many other body changes, including a rapid heartbeat, sweaty hands, and upset stomach.

In Will's case, the stress of being in a hot, crowded room triggered extreme feelings of discomfort, nausea, and nervousness. His response was to remove himself from the environment—that is, to flee from it.

This response to stress is known as the fight-or-flight response. When the body senses danger or some kind of emergency it prepares either for fighting or for fleeing from attack. The fight-or-flight instinct dates from prehistoric times, and helped ensure that early humans could survive in a dangerous world.

Although humans no longer need this survival instinct to fight or escape from wild animals, the automatic reflex remains. The body has the same reaction whenever you are actually facing a dangerous situation or simply catching yourself as you trip on the stairs. Stressful situations as well as emotions such as anger will also trigger the stress response.

Emotional reactions to stress include anxiety and depression.

CHAPTER THREE

Messed with Stress

Scott was upset. As he walked home from school, he tried to figure out how he was going to get everything done. He knew that he had to read fifty pages for his American Literature class, study for a biology test, and finish a project that he had been working on for history. On top of all that, in thirty minutes he had to be at a three-hour practice. How in the world would he be able to fit in all the work he had to do?

Scott has a lot on his plate, and he's feeling stressed. Sometimes "achievement overload"[1] can cause kids to feel stressed out (feeling exhausted and physically ill because of overstress). This happens when teens try to include as many activities into their lives as possible. In addition to carrying a busy school workload, they are trying to balance numerous extracurricular activities—such as dance or music lessons, volunteer work, part-time jobs, and various sports. The pressures that come with taking part in so many extracurricular activities can have a negative effect on their health.

"Adopting the right attitude can convert a negative stress into a positive one."

—Hans Selye

How Stressed Out Are You?

Count up the number of sentences you agree with. Then evaluate how stressed out you are.

1. I often feel tense or anxious.
2. I frequently have stomachaches.
3. My family often makes me feel upset.
4. I get nervous around people at school.
5. I often get headaches.
6. I have trouble falling asleep at night.
7. I worry about school.
8. When I get nervous, I tend to snack.
9. I have trouble concentrating on one thing because I'm worrying about something else.
10. I have considered using drugs or drinking to relax.
11. I have a full schedule of responsibilities at school and at home.
12. I have trouble finding time to relax.
13. I often feel guilty that I'm not getting all my work done.

6 or more = stress level quite high
2 to 5 = stress level average
1 or 0 = stress level below average

Stressor Scenarios

The next time you feel stressed out about a situation, keep in mind that there are many different ways you can respond. Which of the following solutions do you think would produce the best results? Which could cause even more stress?

1. Martin is running for class president. Winning the election is a big deal for his parents, who want to see him succeed at all costs. Martin is uncomfortable with their attitude. What do you think he should do?

    A. Talk to his parents and let them know that they are putting a lot of pressure on him.

    B. Go all out and spend all available hours of the day preparing for the election. Put posters up all over the school; create buttons and stickers to promote his campaign.

    C. Crumble under the stress and drop out of the election.

2. John is playing in his first basketball game for the freshman team. He's nervous and becoming stressed out the night before the next game. What should John do?

    A. Go to school the next day and pretend that nothing is bothering him. Trying to forget it will make it go away, right?

B. Get to school early the next day and try to shoot the ball around before homeroom. This will give him more confidence and get him excited for the game.

C. Go to see the coach the next day and quit the team.

3. Mark is failing his class and has to get an "A" on the next test in order to bring up his grade. What's Mark's next move?

A. Work hard every night prior to the test, studying and making flashcards, and get his parents to help him study. Go in to see the teacher for extra help.

B. Watch TV every night instead of studying. Casually flip through the textbook the night before the test.

C. Decide that he is a failure in life and give up.

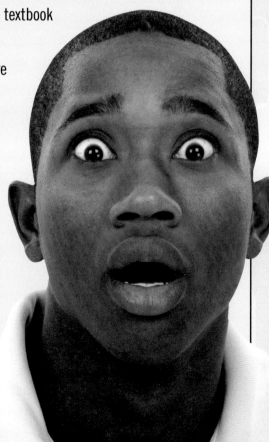

ANSWER KEY		
Question	**Less Stress**	**More Stress**
1.	A	B, C
2.	B	A, C
3.	A	B, C

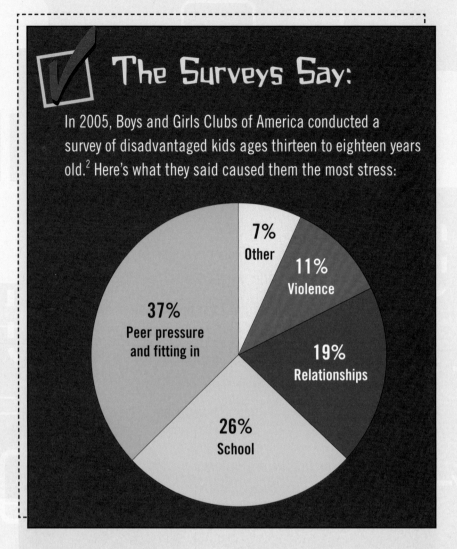

The Surveys Say:

In 2005, Boys and Girls Clubs of America conducted a survey of disadvantaged kids ages thirteen to eighteen years old.[2] Here's what they said caused them the most stress:

7% Other

11% Violence

37% Peer pressure and fitting in

19% Relationships

26% School

Like Scott, you may be trying to do well at school while participating in lots of extracurricular activities. It can be difficult to deal with tests, projects, and other challenges of education without feeling stressed out.

Make a plan. Don't let your schoolwork overwhelm you too much. Pulling all-nighters before a big test or doing nothing but studying will cause even more stress. Set aside time to do your homework, and be sure to give yourself a break every now and then. However, that doesn't mean you should treat academics lightly, because it is important to always try to do your best and to be prepared for school.

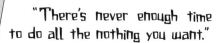

"There's never enough time to do all the nothing you want."

—Bill Watterson, Calvin and Hobbes

The way you respond to the pressures of school can either help you relieve stress or make it worse. In Scott's case, he could simply sit down and figure out the best way to take care of his work that night. For example, maybe he could skip his sports practice. This would be taking a direct action to deal with his stress. Deciding to stick to a plan of getting home from school, taking a short break, and then immediately settling down to work would be another way for Scott to get everything accomplished. By coping with his stress directly, Scott could avoid problems that might occur if he didn't get his work done. Sometimes, not taking immediate action to deal with a busy schedule will lead to even greater stress.

Set priorities. If you are putting too much pressure on yourself to a point where you are feeling overwhelmed, you need to stop and think about whether you are overcommitting yourself. Take a moment to prioritize what is important to you. Think about what you like to do best and put that at the top of your list. You may have to make a hard decision and stop guitar lessons so you can make all the necessary basketball practices. Remember that you need to make time for yourself in order to feel better about yourself.

Remember that stress can affect your health, behavior, thoughts, and feelings.

CHAPTER FOUR

Learning to Cope

> Drew was trying out for the school soccer team. Even before tryouts started, he knew that making the team was going to be difficult—there was a lot of competition. However, he managed to survive the first two rounds of cuts. Now it was down to just him and two other players.
>
> As Drew tried to sleep the night before final tryouts, he was feeling nervous. He imagined himself making the team (and how great that would be) and he thought about what a big letdown getting cut would be. For the past few weeks Drew had spent so much time thinking about soccer that he hadn't been able to concentrate on anything else, including his campaign for class senate and the big assignment in English that was due in three days.

Drew's stress is normal. He isn't going through anything out of the ordinary for most student-athletes. However, he needs to figure out a way to deal with everything that is causing him stress.

One way for Drew to reduce feelings of panic or anxiety is for him to focus on the potential positive outcome. A positive outcome in this situation—making the soccer team, winning a spot on the class senate, and turning in the assignment on time—would boost Drew's confidence. And it would reduce any feelings of stress. If his thoughts focus on

People who are optimistic and think positive thoughts can handle everyday stress better than negative thinkers.[1]

> **Acute stress** is the immediate reaction to a stressful situation.
>
> **Chronic stress** is stress that builds up when you have to face one stressful situation after another.

a negative outcome—failing to make the team, losing the election, or forgetting to turn in the assignment—it's likely his feelings of stress would increase.

Acute stress and chronic stress. There are two types of stress—acute and chronic. Acute stress occurs when the fight-or-flight response is triggered but quickly resolves, allowing the body to return to normal. Acute stressors include crowded areas, noise, isolation, hunger, immediate danger, or anything that can overload you in a short amount of time. These stressors trigger the fight-or-flight response. The heart beats faster, the breathing rate increases, and the blood pressure rises. This is why acute stressors can be dangerous, especially for anyone with heart disease. The sudden increase in blood pressure can cause serious heart trouble.

Chronic stress is stress that is continuous and that accumulates over time. Chronic stressors can include having a large amount of work at school, trying to balance school and job responsibilities, having relationship problems, or feeling lonely or isolated.

With chronic stress, the stress response doesn't shut down. Stress hormone levels in the bloodstream remain high, and that can have a negative effect on the immune system (which protects the body from disease and harmful substances).

Tips for Coping with Stress

Identify and manage your sources of stress. Try to deal with the problem at the beginning. For example, if you are having a conflict with a teammate on your soccer team, think through the issue first. Then, try to come up with a healthy and direct way of resolving the problem.

Follow stress-reducing activities. If schoolwork or studying is causing you a great deal of stress, give yourself a break every hour or two. Try a stress-reducing breathing exercise like the one shown on page 23 or go outside for a short run.

Connect with other people. While friends and family can be the cause of some stress, they also can relieve it. Sometimes you need to hang out and spend time with friends. Go see a movie, hang out, play a sport, and take your mind off what is stressing you out.

After completing a hard task or getting yourself out of a tight spot, reward yourself. Go do something that you truly enjoy and that will help you relax.

As the body deals with pressure from long-term stressors, it can become worn down and less able to combat illnesses.

Learn to recognize your stress signals. Like Drew, you may have a lot going on in your life. And your body may be telling you that it is stressed out. That knot in your stomach, feelings of irritability, a reoccurring headache, or difficulty concentrating can all be symptoms of chronic stress.

Identify your stressors. Are you bothered because a friend is pressuring you to do something you don't want to do? Are you worried about money? Are you having trouble getting along with your parents, your brother, or your sister? Are you feeling overwhelmed by having too much schoolwork? All of these are stressors that teens have identified in their lives.

Once you can identify the conflict or issue that is causing you stress, you can take steps to do something about it. Try to come up with a way to deal with the situation or change it. For example, if a homework assignment is bothering you, you can talk to the teacher who assigned it. If your kid sister is teasing you all the time, ask her what is really bothering her. If she won't talk, tell her if she doesn't stop teasing, you're planning to let your parents know what's going on if she doesn't stop.

Other Ways to Relieve Stress

- Spend some time alone.
- Listen to your favorite music.
- Work on your favorite hobby or start a new one.
- Play a musical instrument.
- Shoot some baskets or join friends in a pickup game.
- Review your commitments and give at least one obligation up.

It's perfectly normal for you to feel stressed, but whenever possible you should try to reduce stress by dealing with its causes in a direct way.

One Way to De-Stress

If you come home from a stressful day at school, try to identify what went wrong. On a piece of paper, write out your feelings by finishing these sentences:

I felt angry when . . .

I felt troubled when . . .

I was offended when . . .

I felt hassled when . . .

I was frustrated when . . .

I got anxious when . . .

This exercise will help you think through why you felt stressed out. When you take time to stop and think about your problems, you can put them in perspective. And evaluating your stress can help you figure out ways to lighten the load you are placing on yourself.

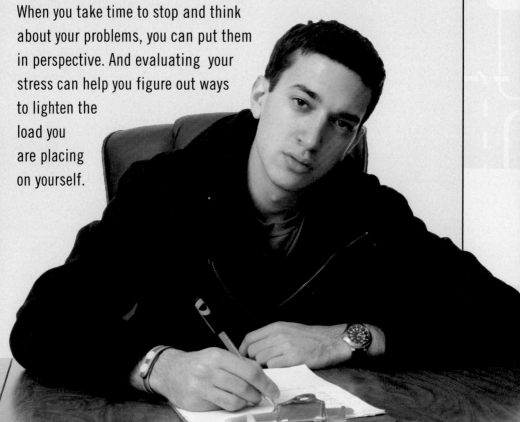

Stress Reducer: Breathing Exercise

When you're under a lot of stress, you breathe rapidly. To help yourself calm down and relax after a stressful experience, try the following exercise:

1. Inhale through your nose slowly and count to ten.

2. As you breathe, expand your stomach and raise up your abdomen but make sure your chest doesn't raise up.

3. Exhale through your nose completely and slowly, counting to ten.

4. Block out everything else by concentrating on breathing and counting.

5. Repeat five to ten times.

Keep yourself healthy. You will be better able to cope with or reduce stress in your life if you are healthy. Simply following a healthy lifestyle—eating a proper diet and exercising regularly—will help you keep stress levels down.

Eating a healthy diet means eating three meals a day, and sticking with nutritious foods. (See the suggestions for a healthy diet on page 24.) And be aware that certain foods can make stress worse. Among them are caffeine-rich foods such as coffee, certain sodas, and chocolate. Caffeine is a drug that causes a release of adrenaline—and feelings of stress. Other foods to avoid are sugary treats. Although they provide a sudden boost of energy, foods that are high in sugar can wear off quickly and cause irritability and poor concentration.

Eat a Healthy Diet

According to the U.S. Department of Agriculture, a healthy diet should include an assortment of foods from the following categories:

- Grains—particularly whole grains and brown rice.
- Vegetables—dark green (such as broccoli and leafy lettuce); orange (such as acorn squash, carrots, and sweet potatoes); starchy (including corn, green peas, and potatoes); and dry beans and peas.
- Fruits—any fruit or 100 percent fruit juice.
- Milk and dairy products—including low-fat milk and cheeses.
- Meats—lean cuts of meats such as beef and pork, as well as fish and shellfish.
- Oils—including canola, corn, and olive oil.

For more information, check out the food and nutrition link at the U.S. Department of Agriculture Web site.[2]

A great stress reliever is exercise. Spending time exercising will not only help you take your mind off your stressors but also relieve any tension building up inside. Make time for an activity you really enjoy and exercise three times a week for at least thirty minutes at a time. Exercise relaxes tense muscles and has a positive effect on mood. That's because when you exercise, your brain releases chemicals called endorphins—natural substances that make you feel good.

> "Rest is not a matter of doing absolutely nothing. Rest is repair."
>
> —Daniel W. Josselyn

Make sure you get enough sleep, too. It's easy to run out of time for something like sleep if you are involved in a lot of activities such as sports and clubs or have responsibilities like a part-time job, house chores, and homework. Regardless, it is important that you figure out a way to budget your time to get at least seven to eight hours of sleep each night. Getting a healthy amount of sleep will help you stay focused and keeps you energized. And that can be especially useful before a big test, game, or other potentially stressful event.

Of course, you do want some stress in life. Otherwise, you might find it hard to motivate yourself or feel a sense of worthiness. But too much stress is a bad thing. What is important is knowing how to manage your stress. You know yourself best and are the only one who can determine what stress you are able to sustain and what stress causes you pain.

CHAPTER FIVE

Unhealthy Ways to Cope

> "I stomp around the house and pound on my brother."
>   (Tim, age fifteen)
>
> "I drink and smoke." (Aaron, age sixteen)[1]

These comments reflect the ways some teenage guys cope with stressful situations. However, their methods for dealing with stress do nothing to fix the problem. In fact, these responses are all harmful. Unfortunately, there are many negative ways in which people deal with stress.

Overreacting and venting. Lashing out at others because you're under stress does nothing to get to the heart of your problem. In fact, the people who are the object of your anger or yelling are likely to respond with similar actions. They're going to yell and scream, too. Overreacting and venting can also lead to violence.

Suppressing, avoiding, or ignoring. Many times, people avoid thinking about their problems as a way to escape from their stress. Others zone out by listening to music. While this can be one way to

Venting your anger won't make your stress go away.

cope with short-term stress, if you are constantly plugged into your MP3 player, you are avoiding having any contact with others. And those people could be helping you resolve some of your problems.

Abusing harmful substances. Cigarettes and alcohol are two common "quick fixes" that younger people turn to in order to relieve stress. In 2005, the National Institute on Drug Abuse reported that 68 percent of high school seniors had used alcohol in the past year.[2] The report also showed that 23 percent had used cigarettes within the last thirty days.[3] The kids who drank or had a cigarette did not necessarily do so because

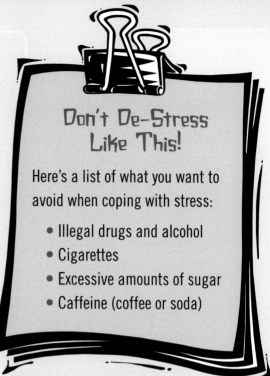

Don't De-Stress Like This!

Here's a list of what you want to avoid when coping with stress:

- Illegal drugs and alcohol
- Cigarettes
- Excessive amounts of sugar
- Caffeine (coffee or soda)

Cigarettes contain many substances that poison and damage the body.

How Susceptible to Stress Are You?

Your lifestyle can affect how much stress you can take. How many of the following statements do you agree with?

1. I eat a least one hot, nutritious meal a day.
2. I get seven to eight hours of sleep per day.
3. I exercise hard at least twice a week.
4. I don't use tobacco at all.
5. I am the right weight for my height.
6. I have one or more friends whom I can confide in.
7. I am in good health.
8. I do something for fun at least once a week.
9. I am able to organize my time well.
10. I have an optimistic outlook on life.

The more statements you can agree with, the less likely you are to have problems when dealing with stressful situations.

they were feeling stressed. However, stress probably was a factor in one way or the other.

Some kids use cigarettes and alcohol because they think it helps them relax, slow things down, and forget about whatever is stressing them out. Dealing with your stressors by using alcohol and drugs allows you to artificially calm yourself down. But you run the risk of becoming addicted, and essentially are doing nothing to solve your problems. In addition, alcohol use by anyone under the age of twenty-one is illegal, so you also run the risk of getting in trouble with the law. If you use tobacco, alcohol, or other harmful substances to relieve stress, you may become dependent. Addiction is an unhealthy habit and when developed at an early age can be hard to break.

Poor eating habits. Another unhealthy way to de-stress (relieve tension) involves using food to take your mind off your stress. However, constant snacking as a way to de-stress can have negative effects. While you may get a temporary boost of energy from a sugary snack, the reaction doesn't last long. The effects will quickly wear off, and you will be right back where you started, and yearning for more.

In some teens, chronic stress can lead to eating disorders. Some turn to overeating, or binging, to deal with their emotions. The resulting weight gain can be unhealthy. Others may lose a great deal of weight because their stress makes them lose the desire to eat.

The quick pick-me-up provided by using alcohol, cigarettes, or sugary foods only masks the symptoms of stress. Their use can lead to a roller coaster of emotions, in which you experience temporary highs, then come back down once the effects wear off.

Dealing with stress by overeating can lead to additional health problems caused by obesity.

Learn how to manage your stress level without resorting to these unhealthy methods. By developing healthy habits early on, you will be ready to deal with stress for the rest of your life.

CHAPTER SIX

Stress in the Family

> Kyle's brother Zach is the star player on the high school basketball team. Although he works a part-time job, Zach sill manages to get top grades in all his classes. However, Kyle doesn't play basketball as well as his big brother, and the classwork in his middle school is hard for him at times. Last week, when Kyle brought home his report card, his parents got angry with him, even though he managed to get B's in all his classes. "Why can't you do as well as Zach?" his mother demanded. Kyle didn't know what to say.

Some of the most important people in life are the members of your family. Your parents, brothers, and sisters often are a huge part of your life. However, like anyone whom you spend a lot of time with, family members can also be great stressors.

Parent pressures. Sometimes, as in Kyle's case, stress can come because you believe your parents expect you to do as well as a high-achieving sibling. If you feel that your parents and family are

Sometimes parents can become a source of stress. If you think their demands are unreasonable, don't give them the silent treatment. Talk with them about your concerns.

Tips on Talking to Parents and Other Adults

Bring up your issue when the adult has the time to listen. Don't try to talk to your parents when they're busy with something or someone else or rushing out the door. Say, "Is this a good time for you? I have something important to discuss."

Be aware of your body language. Don't roll your eyes, cross your arms, or clench your fists. Look the other person in the eyes and try to remain calm.

Use respectful language. Don't use sarcasm, insults, or put-downs when explaining your point of view. Snapping something like, "That's a stupid reason," will only make the other person angrier.

Be honest. Tell the truth about how you feel or what has happened; your parents and other adults want to trust you.

Listen to the other side of the issue. The adult will be more likely to show you the same respect.

creating an unhealthy amount of stress for you—for example, they want you to get all A's, star on the basketball team, and win a music scholarship—you need to let them know if their expectations are reasonable or unfair.

Be sure to talk about the effect this pressure is having on you. Don't be afraid to talk to your parents and explain to them how you are feeling and why. It can make a huge difference and will make you feel good to get your side of the story off your chest.

Sibling conflicts. In other cases, stress can occur because you and your brother or sister simply don't get along.

Tips for Getting Along with Brothers and Sisters

Spend some time together. Invite your younger sister to play a board game with you. Ask your older brother to kick the soccer ball around. If you spend a little time together, you'll get to know each other better. And you can better understand what he or she is thinking.

Go out of your way to give your brother or sister a compliment. Positive communication is important in building a strong, healthy relationship.

Show an interest in your sibling's hobbies and interests. Attend his or her sporting events, dance recitals, and other activities and invite your sibling to your games and events.

Pick your battles. If your sibling did something deliberately to hurt you or make you angry, then you need to let him or her know that you are bothered. But try not to lose your cool and get mad if your brother or sister has said something wrong or broken a possession of yours accidentally.

If you find yourself becoming irritated over something your sibling has done, walk away from the situation and take time to cool down. Try to calm yourself down by taking a deep breath and counting to ten. When you can think more calmly, come back and talk things out. Keep your voice low and calm when telling your side of the story.

A hostile sibling relationship—with constant fights, complaints, and negative comments—can not only make your life miserable but also stress out everyone else in the family.

Be aware that you can help relieve stress for everyone simply by making the effort to get along with your brother or sister. When a sibling does something to make you upset, don't keep your bitter feelings inside until they escalate into full-fledged conflict. Use a calm quiet voice to let your brother or sister know that you are bothered. Try talking with him or her so you can work out your differences.

Fights between siblings can make life miserable for parents as well as kids.

After all, the relationship you have with your brother and sister is unique. You share memories that no one else does. When your brother takes your hockey stick without asking—and you planned to use it that day—or your sister scratches your favorite CD, you have a reason to feel angry. But don't respond to the situation in an unhealthy way. Stay calm, be up-front, and try to solve the issue early on. That way, you'll reduce your own stress as well as that of your parents and siblings.

CHAPTER SEVEN

Peer Pressures

> *Dave and Anthony are best friends. They have grown up together and lived on the same street their whole life. When it came time for homecoming, however, they had a little bit of a conflict. Neither of them had dates to the dance, and both had their eyes set on the same girl— their neighbor Lindsey.*
>
> *One day, while at Anthony's house, Dave brought up the topic. "So dude, did you ask Lindsey to the dance?" he asked. Anthony's nonchalant reply of "Yup" didn't bother Dave too much at the time. But as homecoming came closer, he found he was bothered. After all, he had wanted to take Lindsey to the dance. And Anthony knew that.*

Friendships can cause a great deal of stress. The amount varies, depending on the situation. But even little things that friends do can bother you. Maybe your friend took the girl to a dance whom you planned ask. Perhaps he joked with you in a way you didn't like, or maybe he borrowed your basketball and left it at the court. Sometimes little things that cause tension between you and your friends can pile up and stress you out.

Friends can unintentionally do things that make you upset, angry, or disappointed. When you are not honest with them, and let them know how you feel about an issue, you will have much more stress than you

Resolving Stress-Causing Conflict with Friends

Friends can cause problems and stress that you don't want to deal with sometimes. It is important, whenever possible, to work out your problems or disagreements. You will become better friends if you make this effort.

- If your friend has said something that upsets you, pull him aside and tell him how you feel. For example, if he is constantly teasing or making fun of you, let him know you don't like it and ask him to stop.

- Make sure that you remain calm when you talk with your friend. If you are feeling bitter or angry, stop for a moment. Take a few deep breaths. This will give you some time to calm down before trying to talk.

- If you think another point of view will help, go to an adult or a friend who will help the two of you solve whatever is causing the conflict.

- Be willing to forgive if the person has wronged you.

would if you had been up-front in the first place. It is very important to communicate with your friends—to tell them that you're upset with something they did or didn't do. In the case of Anthony and Dave, it would have been better for both of them if they had talked with each other regarding their shared plans to ask Lindsey to the dance. Having a simple conversation could have reduced the tension—and stress—that Dave was feeling.

Making friends and fitting in. Another stressor for many kids is the search for friends. Most kids in their early teens seek acceptance from their peer group—other kids who share their interests, hobbies, or activities. The stress of trying to make friends can make life extremely difficult, especially if one person feels rejected or left out of group activities. Kids without friends may often be teased or feel like outcasts.

Sometimes kids develop friendships that create stress. They may hang out with people who really aren't their friends. These

Peer pressure can be a major stressor when it involves friends encouraging you to do things you don't think are right.

so-called friends pick on the other members of their group or constantly put them down.

Stressful friendships can also result when teens experience a lot of peer pressure. Teenagers trying to fit in with the rest of the group or trying to look cool may do things they don't feel comfortable about, such as drinking alcohol or using tobacco products.

The best way to avoid this kind of stress is to choose your friends wisely. Don't settle in with a group of friends who are always mocking you or teasing you. It may be hard to do, but you need to end that kind of "friendship." If a friend is causing you stress by trying to pressure you into doing something you don't want to do, or is simply picking on you, it might be a good idea to spend less time with that person.

While some of your best memories will be of the times spent with good friends, things will not always be perfect. Even with the best of friends there will be occasional bumps in the road. If you find yourself feeling stressed because of friends, try to find a solution to what's bothering you. Be willing to compromise if necessary—but don't stick around with people who cause you more stress then you can take.

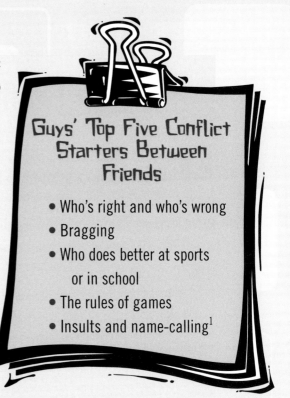

Guys' Top Five Conflict Starters Between Friends

- Who's right and who's wrong
- Bragging
- Who does better at sports or in school
- The rules of games
- Insults and name-calling[1]

CHAPTER EIGHT

School Daze

Day-to-day life at school can get pretty stressful. You may be putting pressure on yourself to earn a spot on the school sports team or in a competitive club. Or you may be feeling stressed out by others. For example, a teacher may have told you that you're not "working to your potential," or you may feel like she's picking on you in class. If you attend a school where you don't feel safe because of the bullying and violent behavior of fellow students, you are being forced to deal with a major stressor.

Dealing with bullies. Bullying can be physical assaults and verbal abuse—or both. You can be pushed, shoved, and threatened. Or you may be called names, or have your belongings taken. Someone might be spreading rumors or gossiping about you at school or on the Internet. Regardless of how you are being bullied, the result is the same: you have fear, anxiety, and lots of stress.

If you are a victim of bullying, you first need to recognize that you are not at fault. It is the other

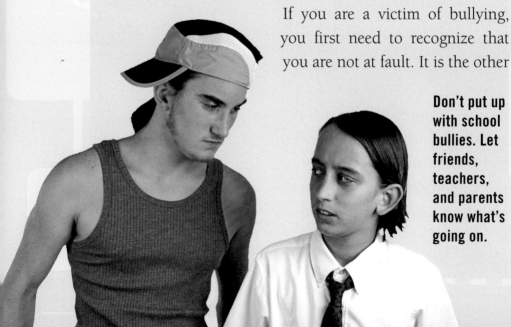

Don't put up with school bullies. Let friends, teachers, and parents know what's going on.

Is Bullying Stressing You Out?

Here are some suggestions to use when faced with a bully:

Take action. Simply ignoring the bully won't make him or her go away.

Go to someone you can trust: a parent, teacher, or friend. Make sure that person is someone you also feel comfortable talking with.

Don't blame yourself for the situation. It's not your fault that you are being picked on. Act confident in situations where you feel bullied—even if you really don't feel confident.

Ask your friends for support. Traveling in a group may help you avoid being confronted by the person who is bullying you.

Find out what your school policy is on bullying. Don't be afraid to report the situation to a teacher.

person who is behaving in an unacceptable way. No one deserves to be bullied.

Next, you need to figure out some course of action. In some cases, the best way to stop a bully is to confront the person. Don't be afraid to speak out against him and do not put up with what he is putting you through. The best thing to do is to simply tell the bully to stop. Then calmly walk away. However, if you believe there is a danger of violence from the bully, then you need to tell a teacher, parent, or other trusted adult.

Academic stresses. You may find another major stress at school is the pressure to do well in everything. You may be pressuring yourself to do well on all your tests, or perhaps you're worried about low grades. You may be stressed out with trying to balance outside activities with piles of homework. Or your parents may be placing a lot of pressure on you to get top

Don't let pressure to do well in everything overwhelm you. Make a list, prioritize your obligations, and concentrate on completing the most important ones first.

Test-Taking Tips

As a student, you may find your greatest stressors are tests. Give yourself an extra edge by following these tips:

1. Take careful notes during class.

2. Begin studying early—perhaps a week before.

3. Think up creative ways to quiz yourself, such as flash cards or a jeopardy-type game.

4. Ask your mother, father, or sibling to help you review.

5. Get together with a group of friends to review the material—great minds think alike.

6. Go in and talk to the teacher. He or she might be willing to give you more time for the test—or at least help you understand the information.

grades. Bringing home mediocre or even above-average grades can often become a source of conflict in families.

According to researchers at the University of Michigan, one third of U.S. teenagers say that stress is a daily problem for them. Nearly two thirds of respondents to a survey reported feeling stressed out at least once a week.[1] Experts suggest that stressed-out teens try to simplify their lives by identifying the obligations or goals that are most important to them. Then, they should concentrate on accomplishing the priorities. Not only will they do a more effective job, but they will also feel less stressed out.

CHAPTER NiNE

The Stress of Change

> *Pete had gotten used to his parents' constant fighting, although it still upset him a lot. But he never thought his mom and dad would divorce. Soon after his parents separated, Pete found himself becoming more and more stressed out by his relationship with each parent. Because of the joint custody arrangement, he spent two nights a week at his dad's and the rest at his mom's. Pete began to lose track of where he left his schoolwork and where he was supposed to be. Things were spiraling out of control.*

Pete's story is just one example of how family problems can be stressful. While his situation is extreme, it is not unusual. Divorce is quite prevalent today. The divorce rate in the United States is 49 percent, and 45 percent of children live in families affected by divorce.[1] It is also common for the mother or father to begin dating again, and the introduction of another adult figure can also cause problems and stress.

If your mom and dad have split up and started to

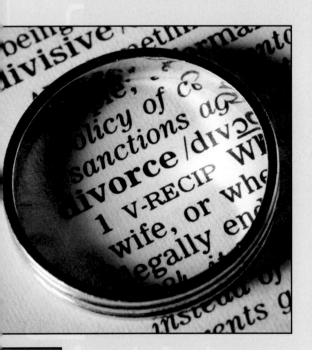

Divorce means many stressful changes are in store for a family.

Tips for Dealing with Divorce

1. Be honest and up-front with your parents about how you feel about the situation.

2. It's their decision, not yours. Be aware that you will experience feelings of powerlessness and lack of control.

3. Ask your parents to be honest with you throughout the situation.

4. To distract yourself when you're feeling upset, try some healthy stress-relief methods. Exercise, read a book, or phone a friend to talk. Having someone to lean on when times get tough can be a big help. Talking things out are better than stressing out about them.

date other people, you have already experienced having to deal with new relationships in your life. Your parent may ask you to approve of the new person or, if he or she remarries, to accept that person as a stepparent. However, you may want to have nothing to do with that person.

The many issues that come with divorce can be hard to deal with. However, by facing them directly, you have a better chance of improving the situation. And you are likely to feel better about yourself as well as toward your family members.

Other family changes. There are many other kinds of events within families that can cause stress. Such family stressors

can include the death of a relative, the birth of a new brother or sister, loss of family income when a parent loses a job, or the remarriage of a divorced mother or father. The chronic disease of a family member or friend can also be difficult to deal with.

You may be familiar with the stress of moving to a new community. Moving can be hard, especially if accompanied by simultaneous family changes such as a divorce or lost job. Not only do you lose the friends from your old community, but you are also faced with having to make new friends in a new school.

To deal with the stress of moving, try to think of the positive aspects of your move.

What can you do? While you can't change the bad things that have happened in your life, your attitude can have a positive effect on what happens next. For example, if your family just moved to a new city, try to think positively about what will happen as a result of the move. Will you live closer to relatives, whom you'll now be able to see more often? Will you be living closer to stores, museums, sports stadiums, or places you'd like to visit more often?

It may be hard, but recognize that with time you'll probably start to feel better about the situation. Give yourself a few

Making New Friends After a Move

1. Begin a conversation by complimenting a classmate. You might say, "I liked the report you gave today in class," or "That was a great game you played."

2. Ask new acquaintances to tell you about themselves.

3. Share some information about your old school or city, but don't overdo it.

4. Ask about what's going on in your new school and community.

weeks to get used to the change, then re-evaluate how you are feeling.

However, don't go it alone. If you're still feeling unhappy and stressed out weeks after a move, talk to somebody. Share your problems with your brother or sister, your parents, or another adult with whom you can easily talk. Sometimes just telling your problems and concerns to someone else can make you feel better. And that person may have some advice that you can try.

As difficult as change can be, it is a normal part of life. You may find that you just need a little time, and your bad situation will turn into a good one.

Whether change is positive or negative, it can cause stress.

CHAPTER TEN

Are You In Over Your Head?

Do you think that you're too stressed out? The amount of stress that you can handle depends on different factors.

One of these factors is your genes. That is, the genes you inherited from your parents affect the amount of stress you can handle. If your mom and dad can naturally deal with large amounts of stress, it is likely that you can, too.

Another factor is how much stress you have had to handle in the past. People who have been exposed to some stress when young can deal with it easier later in life because they've learned some coping skills. However, being exposed to *extreme* stress when young may also increase their sensitivity to it and decrease the amount they can manage.

To get an idea of how well you are handling stress in your life, take the quiz on the next page. A high score may indicate you are feeling the effects of long-term, or chronic, stress that is having a harmful effect on your health.

Do you feel in over your head because of long-term stress?

Stress Quiz

Take this quiz to estimate how high your stress level is. For every answer that describes you, add the point value indicated:

1. Are you angry or short-tempered with people?—1

2. Do you experience dramatic changes in mood?—1

3. Do you feel overwhelmed by schoolwork?—1

4. Do you experience frequent muscle twitches?—1

5. Are you frequently nauseous or do you have an unusual amount of stomach pain?—1

6. Do you feel compelled to do the same routines day in and day out?—1

7. Do you constantly feel tired?—1

8. Do you feel like you never have time to sit down and relax?—1

9. Has a friend or family member passed away in the past year?—4

10. Have you started at a new school or job in the past year?—1

11. Have your parents been separated or divorced within the past year?—3

12. Do you suffer from nagging feelings of guilt?—1

13. Have you had a fight with a friend in the past month?—1

14. Have you failed a test in the past three months?—2

If your score ranges from 1 to 6, then you are feeling a low level of stress. A score of 7 to 13 indicates that you are dealing with a moderate amount of stress. If your score is 14 to 20, you may be dealing with an unhealthy amount of stress.

Confusion, poor concentration, poor memory, depression, anxiety, and anger are often linked to long-term stress.

Your psychological health. Stress can be a quiet danger in your life, especially when stressors are not quickly resolved. Long-term stress can lead to mental illnesses such as clinical depression or anxiety disorders.

Depression is an emotional problem characterized by strong feelings of sadness and helplessness. Everyone feels sad or depressed from time to time. However, clinical depression is a serious mental health illness characterized by deep unhappiness and feelings of despair. This extreme depression can last for weeks at a time and typically interferes with a person's ability to function in school and at home.

If you think a friend may be depressed, talk to him.

Anxiety is uncertainty towards a future event. It's perfectly normal to feel anxious about day-to-day stressors, such an upcoming big test, playoff game, or musical performance. However, when feelings of anxiety are excessive, they can be dangerous. In extreme cases of clinical depression and anxiety disorders, people may even come to believe that suicide is the answer to their problems.

If you're feeling troubled by feelings of depression and anxiety, don't ignore them. Get help by talking to a friend,

Signs and Symptoms of Depression

1. Sadness that won't go away
2. Feelings of hopelessness and boredom
3. Feelings of guilt, worthlessness, and helplessness
4. Loss of interest in usual activities
5. Decreased energy and feelings of fatigue
6. Difficulty concentrating and making decisions
7. Changes in eating or sleeping habits
8. Restlessness and irritability
9. Aches and pains that don't get better with treatment
10. Social isolation, poor communication
11. Thoughts about death or suicide[1]

Top Ten Characteristics of a Highly Stressed Person

If you see any of these characteristics within yourself you may have a high-stress personality.

1. You overplan each day with a schedule that you must follow.

2. You are always multi-tasking (trying to do several things at once).

3. Your desire to win is extreme.

4. You want nothing more than to advance in whatever position you are in.

5. You can't relax without feeling guilty.

6. When you're delayed, you get very impatient quickly.

7. You commit yourself to too many different activities.

8. You are always hurrying others or yourself.

9. You've forgotten what it's like to have fun for the sake of fun.

10. You are always working, constantly doing schoolwork or your job.

If you see a lot of these characteristics within yourself, you probably have a high-stress personality.

your parents, a school counselor, or another trusted adult. And if you have a friend who seems depressed, be sure to suggest he or she gets support. Suicide is the third leading cause of death among fifteen- to twenty-five-year-olds. And 86 percent of all teenage suicides are boys.[2]

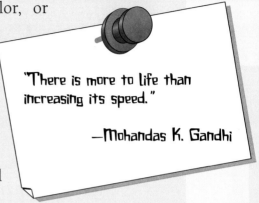

"There is more to life than increasing its speed."

—Mohandas K. Gandhi

Your physical health. Stress has the ability to suck the energy right out of you, making you feel trapped and unable to function properly. The lack of energy and fatigue caused by stress will in turn affect your performance on any athletic teams or in school.

Long-term stress can also lead to health problems that could hurt you both now and in the future. Heart disease and high blood pressure are among the many health issues that have been linked to long-term stress.

Your social relationships. If you let it, feeling overstressed can make your life miserable. Because stress can distract you and keep you from concentrating, it can make learning in school more difficult. When under stress, you are also more likely to become short-tempered with friends, family, teachers, or classmates.

If you are feeling overwhelmed by stress, it is important to take steps to do something about it. Understanding your stress level and limitations will help you figure out when you can handle problems on your own and when you need to turn to others for help.

CHAPTER ELEVEN

When Stress Helps

> *The night before he was to pitch his first baseball game of the season, Bobby couldn't fall asleep. He was really worried about the next day. To try to prepare, he decided to mentally run through how he would approach each batter.*
>
> *At game time, Bobby was ready. He went out and pitched the game of his life, ultimately leading his team to a 9-1 victory. He knew that all his mental preparation had helped him achieve such spectacular results.*

Sometimes stress can be a positive force. If Bobby hadn't been so worried about his game, he might not have been as prepared in dealing with its challenges. In such situations, stress has the potential to be a good thing.

Stress promotes healthy competition and helps people discover new and improved ways for living life. When they get through a difficult situation or impossible challenge, they achieve a sense of pride and accomplishment. In other words, stress can push people to perform beyond their normal expectations.

If there were no such thing as stress, the world would be a much different place. Without deadlines, would people feel

Even the stress that people typically think of as "negative" can have an upside. For example, controlled or directed anger can help you be assertive—to stand up for something you believe in or that you think is right.

Turning Stress into Sport Success!

Ever get that *stressed-out* feeling the night before a big game? Worrying about the game too much will only lead to a poor performance. Here are some tips to reduce and help turn stress into victory.

- Put it all in perspective. It's a game. It's something that you love to play and want to enjoy.

- Concentrate on what you have to do to succeed. Think about throwing the right pitch, making the right shot, or whatever you need to do.

- Keep in mind that you have practiced in preparation for the game. You aren't just going out there having never played the game before.

- Go out and have fun!

pressed to accomplish their tasks at work? If the outcome of a sporting event didn't matter, would anyone compete? Stress often helps provide the motivation that leads people to accomplish difficult tasks and achieve success.

Managing Your Stress

Your science project is due today. You want to try out for the basketball team. You just had an argument with your best friend. Your girlfriend is mad at you for forgetting her birthday. Your parents are threatening to ground you for slacking off on schoolwork.

There are countless situations and events—some good and some bad—that can cause stress in your day-to-day life. The way that you manage that stress starts with you. No one else will be able to tell why you are stressing out. Your family and friends may see the outward signs of your stress, such as angry outbursts, occasional stomachaches and headaches, or a lack of ability to concentrate. Although they may be able to guess that you are stressed out about something, they will have no idea about what is bothering you—unless you tell them.

To manage your stress, you need to recognize what is causing it and understand its effect on you. Then take action to deal with whatever is causing your stress—confront and resolve a conflict or lighten your schedule. If you believe you can't handle a stressful situation

Remember to make time for yourself and to do the things that you enjoy in between work, school, and other obligations.

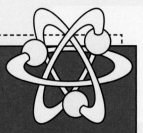

Science Says...

According to a 2006 article in *Men's Health Magazine*, talking to yourself could help you feel less stress. The magazine cites a study by University of California researchers in which people lowered stress levels by repeating a key word or phrase. In the study, sixty-six people were trained to associate an expression (for example, the phrase "Take it easy") with relaxing. Then, whenever they felt they were in tense situations, they silently repeated the phrase to themselves. Later, 83 percent of them reported feeling less stressed when using the phrase than when they didn't use the technique.[1]

on your own, you can decide whether or not you want the help of others. Don't be afraid about asking for help if you feel overwhelmed.

Remember, your peers around you will most likely be dealing with similar experiences and the same stressors. By sharing your concerns and problems with them, and learning how they cope with the stresses in their life, you may get the advice you need.

If that doesn't work, or you aren't comfortable talking about a particular situation with a friend, try talking to one of your parents or another adult you trust. Rather than keeping your problems to

Where to Go When You Need Help

- Home
- Parent's work
- School (teacher, principal, counselor)
- Minister/Clergy
- Mental Health Helpline
- County Social Services
- Hotline (See page 61)
- Emergency Services

Coping with Stress for Life

Although you will never be able to completely avoid stress, here are some tips that you can use to equip yourself in dealing with stressful situations:

Identify your stressor. If you don't know what is stressing you out, you won't be able to fix it.

Practice the art of patience. Sometimes your stressors will not have quick-fix scenarios. Things will work out if you wait for them.

Prepare for potential problems. When possible, take steps to prevent stressors from occurring. For example, if you are worried about doing poorly in school, talk to your teacher, ask for tutoring, and establish study habits that will help you.

Work hard toward your goals, but be realistic. Keep in mind how much time and effort your goals require, and recognize when you can't accomplish them all. If necessary, cut back on your schedule in order to lighten the amount of stress in your life.

yourself, share your feelings with someone else. A parent, school counselor, or other adult may have a different perspective about the situation or have helpful advice. But remember, no one else can know what is going on in your head unless you tell them.

Stress will always be a part of your life in one way or another. And as you grow older there will be many obstacles, problems, challenges, and issues that will be put in your path. Some stressors, such as making new friends, will be the same. Future stressors may include having college or job interviews, paying bills when money is tight, or living with roommates.

"Nothing can be more useful . . . than a determination not to be hurried."

—Henry David Thoreau

The habits that you form now to deal with stress you have today will help you deal with stress you encounter tomorrow—and throughout your life. It's up to you to determine the best way to handle your stress and stressors.

Learning how to handle stress properly can help you become a happier, healthier person.

Chapter 3. Messed with Stress

1. David Elkind, *The Hurried Child: Growing Up Too Fast Too Soon*, Third Edition (Cambridge, Mass.: Perseus Publishing, 2001), p. 151.

2. Adapted from Boys and Girls Clubs of America, "Youth Report to America: 2005 National TEENSupreme Keystone Project Report," 2006, <http://www.bgca.org/news/YouthReport.asp> (March 20, 2007).

Chapter 4. Learning to Cope

1. Mayo Clinic Staff, "Positive Thinking: Practice This Stress Management Skill," *MayoClinic.com*, May 31, 2007, <http://www.mayoclinic.com/health/positive-thinking/SR00009> (July 13, 2007).

2. Adapted from U.S. Department of Agriculture, "Steps to a Healthier You," n.d., <http://www.mypyramid.gov/> (July 13, 2007).

Chapter 5. Unhealthy Ways to Cope

1. Earl Hipp, *Fighting Invisible Tigers: A Stress Management Guide for Teens* (Minneapolis, Minn.: Free Spirit Publications, 1995), p. 26.

2. The National Institute on Drug Abuse, "NIDA InfoFacts: High School and Youth Trends," December 2006, <http://www.nida.nih.gov/Infofacts/HSYouthtrends.html> (July 13, 2007).

3. The National Institute on Drug Abuse, "NIDA InfoFacts: High School and Youth Trends," December 2006, <http://www.nida.nih.gov/Infofacts/HSYouthtrends.html> (July 13, 2007).

Chapter 7. Peer Pressures

1. Naomi Drew, *The Kids Guide to Working Out Conflicts: How to Keep Cool, Stay Safe, and Get Along* (Minneapolis, Minn.: Free Spirit Publishing, 2004), p. 7.

Chapter 8. School Daze

1. "Teens and Stress," *Current Health 2*, February 2000, p. 2.

Chapter 9. The Stress of Change

1. Richard O'Connor, *Undoing Perpetual Stress: The Missing Connection Between Depression, Anxiety, and 21st Century Illness* (New York: Berkley Books, 2005), p. 34.

Chapter 10. Are You In Over Your Head?

1. U.S. Centers for Disease Control and Prevention, "Suicide: Facts at a Glance," Summer 2007, <http://www.cdc.gov/ncipc/dvp/suicide/SuicideDataSheet.pdf> (July 13, 2007).

2. Adapted from National Institute of Mental Health, "Signs and Symptoms," n.d., <http://menanddepression.nimh.nih.gov/symptomslist.html> (July 13, 2007).

Chapter 12. Managing Your Stress

1. "Just Say the Word," *Men's Health*, July/August 2006, p. 46.

acute stress—A short amount of stress that triggers an immediate physical response.

adrenaline—A stress hormone produced by the adrenal glands, located on top of the kidneys.

anxiety—A feeling of nervousness or uneasiness, usually over something that is about to happen.

chronic stress—Stress that builds up over a long period of time.

cortisol—A hormone produced by the adrenal glands that is activated by stress.

depression—Long-lasting feelings of sadness and hopelessness and a loss of interest in life.

de-stress—To release bodily or mental tension.

endorphins—Mood-boosting chemicals released by the brain during exercise.

fight-or-flight response—The initial reaction of the body when exposed to stress.

gene—Basic unit of heredity that transmits characteristics from a parent to a child.

hormone—Special chemical substance that circulates in the body fluids and signals other body cells to action.

hypothalamus—Part of the brain that controls the release of hormones.

overstress—To be subjected to excessive physical or emotional stress.

peer pressure—Pressure from one's friends or peers to behave in a manner similar or acceptable to them.

pituitary gland—A small organ in the human brain that affects most basic bodily functions.

puberty—The developmental stage in which the human body matures to adulthood.

stress—The body's reaction to an external force, situation, or change.

stressor—External force, situation, or change that causes stress.

FURTHER READING

Adams, Mark. *Stress Relief: The Ultimate Teen Guide.* Lanham, Md.: Scarecrow Press, Inc., 2003.

Canfield, Jack. *Chicken Soup for the Teenage Soul: The Real Deal Challenges: Stories about Disses, Losses, Messes, Stresses & More.* Deerfield Beach, Fla.: Health Communications, Inc., 2006.

Seaward, Brian. *Hot Stones and Funny Bones: Teens Helping Teens Cope with Stress and Anger.* Deerfield Beach, Fla.: Health Communications, Inc., 2002.

Sluke, Sara Jane. *The Complete Idiot's Guide to Dealing with Stress for Teens.* Indianapolis, Ind.: Alpha Books, 2001.

INTERNET ADDRESSES

**American Academy of Family Physicians:
Teens and Stress: Who Has Time For It?**

http://familydoctor.org/278.xml

**American Academy of Pediatrics:
Create a Personal Stress Management Guide**

http://www.aap.org/stress/buildresstress-teen.htm

TeensHealth: Stress

http://www.kidshealth.org/teen/your_mind/emotions/stress.html

HOTLINE TELEPHONE NUMBERS

**National Alcohol and Substance Abuse
Information Center Hotline**

1-800-784-6776

National Domestic Violence Hotline

1-800-799-SAFE (1-800-799-7233)

National Suicide Prevention Lifeline

1-800-273-TALK (1-800-273-8255)

CONTRIBUTORS

Author **Travis Clark** is a freelance writer based in Australia, where he is studying for a master's degree at the University of Sydney. He has written numerous columns and articles for local newspapers and is the author of a young adult biography on the comedian Will Ferrell.

Series advisor **Dr. Carroll Izard** is the Trustees Distinguished Professor of Psychology at the University of Delaware. His research and writing focuses on the development of emotion knowledge and emotion regulation and their contributions to social and emotional competence. He is author or editor of seventeen books (one of which won a national award) and more than one hundred articles in scientific journals. Dr. Izard is a fellow of both national psychological associations and the American Association for the Advancement of Science. He is the winner of the American Psychological Association's G. Stanley Hall Award and an international exchange fellowship from the National Academy of Sciences.

FLiP-iT-OVER
GUIDES TO TEEN EMOTIONS

A Guys' Guide to Anger; A Girls' Guide to Anger
ISBN-13: 978-0-7660-2853-1   ISBN-10: 0-7660-2853-4

A Guys' Guide to Conflict; A Girls' Guide to Conflict
ISBN-13: 978-0-7660-2852-4   ISBN-10: 0-7660-2852-6

A Guys' Guide to Jealousy; A Girls' Guide to Jealousy
ISBN-13: 978-0-7660-2854-8   ISBN-10: 0-7660-2854-2

A Guys' Guide to Loneliness; A Girls' Guide to Loneliness
ISBN-13: 978-0-7660-2856-2   ISBN-10: 0-7660-2856-9

A Guys' Guide to Love; A Girls' Guide to Love
ISBN-13: 978-0-7660-2855-5   ISBN-10: 0-7660-2855-0

A Guys' Guide to Stress; A Girls' Guide to Stress
ISBN-13: 978-0-7660-2857-9   ISBN-10: 0-7660-2857-7

GIRLS!

STOP

Boring Guys' Stuff From This Point On!

3 9082 11064 4997

NOV 0 5 2008

J155.4
C

{FLIP-iT-OVER}
GUIDES TO TEEN EMOTIONS

A Girls' Guide to

Stress

Annie Belfield

 Enslow Publishers, Inc.
40 Industrial Road
Box 398
Berkeley Heights, NJ 07922
USA

http://www.enslow.com

Library of Congress Cataloging-in-Publication Data

Clark, Travis, 1985-
 A guys' guide to stress ; A girls' guide to stress / Travis Clark and Annie Belfield.
  p. cm. — (Flip-it-over guides to teen emotions)
 Includes bibliographical references and index.
 ISBN-13: 978-0-7660-2857-9
 ISBN-10: 0-7660-2857-7
 1. Stress (Psychology)—Juvenile literature. 2. Boys—Life skills guides—Juvenile literature. 3. Girls—Life skills guides—Juvenile literature. I. Belfield, Annie. II. Title. III. Title: Guys' guide to stress ; A girls' guide to stress. IV. Title: Girls' guide to stress.

 BF575.S75C545 2008
 155.4'18—dc22
                          2007026458

Printed in the United States of America.

10 9 8 7 6 5 4 3 2 1

3 9082 11064 4997

Produced by OTTN Publishing, Stockton, N.J.

To Our Readers: We have done our best to make sure all Internet Addresses in this book were active and appropriate when we went to press. However, the author and the publisher have no control over and assume no liability for the material available on those Internet sites or on other Web sites they may link to. Any comments or suggestions can be sent by e-mail to comments@enslow.com or to the address on the title page.

Photo Credits: © 2008 Jupiterimages Corporation, 30, 35; © iStockphoto.com/Aldo Murillo, 33; © iStockphoto.com/Quavondo, 10; © PhotoDisc, Inc., 27; Used under license from Shutterstock, Inc., 1, 3, 4, 8, 12, 13, 19, 20, 25, 26, 37, 38, 39, 42, 44, 45, 46, 48, 50, 52, 54, 57.

Cover Photo: Used under license from Shutterstock, Inc.

CONTENTS

What Is Stress?

Zoe sat nervously at her desk, tapping her pencil and chewing on her hair. The math final was today, and even though she had studied really hard, she just didn't get it. If she didn't do well, her parents said she was going to be grounded for a month. It wasn't fair.

On the day of a major exam in just about any class, you're likely to see signs of nervousness. Kids are frantically looking over their notes, biting their nails, chewing their pencil erasers, cracking their knuckles, or taking deep breaths.

In fact, you may be doing the same thing. That nervous, jittery feeling you are having is called stress. Its source—the test—is your stressor. Even if you usually feel confident during tests, odds are you've experienced stress in other situations.

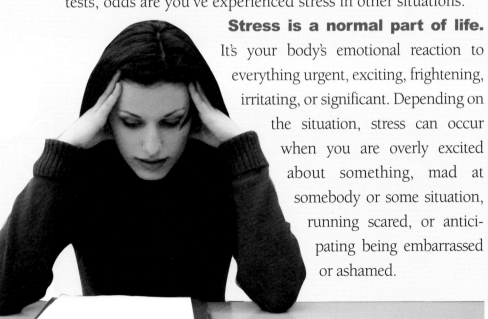

Stress is a normal part of life. It's your body's emotional reaction to everything urgent, exciting, frightening, irritating, or significant. Depending on the situation, stress can occur when you are overly excited about something, mad at somebody or some situation, running scared, or anticipating being embarrassed or ashamed.

You and Your Emotions

A part of everyone's personality, emotions are a powerful driving force in life. They are hard to define and understand. But what is known is that emotions—which include anger, fear, love, joy, jealousy, and hate—are a normal part of the human system. They are responses to situations and events that trigger bodily changes, motivating you to take some kind of action.

Some studies show that the brain relies more on emotions than on intellect in learning and in making decisions. Being able to identify and understand the emotions in yourself and in others can help you in your relationships with family, friends, and others throughout your life.

Stress can be positive when it pushes you to do your best at a task. For example, it can give you the mental alertness you need to do well in a major test. Or it can give you that extra physical energy in a race that propels you first across the finish line. However, stress can also be bad for you. When you have too much stress—and it lasts over a long period of time—you can feel overwhelmed and helpless. People often describe such feelings as being "stressed out."

Has someone ever implied that your stress isn't important because of your age? Well-meaning adults don't always get it. You probably don't work full-time, pay taxes, or have anyone

Stress helps by challenging and motivating us to act.

The Surveys Say...

A 2001 poll found that almost 75 percent of teens say they have felt nervous or stressed out "some of the time." About 50 percent reported feeling that way "often."[1]

who depends on you for everything. Some adults may think this means you have no real problems. They only remember the fun times of when they were young, and have forgotten the miserable moments. At this stage of life you may be faced with difficult situations that would overwhelm anybody.

Stress isn't the most enjoyable emotion, but it's not necessarily a cause for panic. The key is learning to handle your stress in a healthy way so you can control it, live with it, and maybe even benefit from it occasionally. Knowing what to expect and how to cope will help you deal with common stressors.

Signs of Teen Stress

1. Feeling down, on edge, guilty, or tired
2. Having headaches, stomachaches, or trouble sleeping
3. Wanting to be alone all the time
4. Not enjoying activities you used to enjoy
5. Feeling resentful of others
6. Feeling like you have too many things you have to do[2]

Common Stressors

Family trouble: divorced, separated, or remarrying parents; pushy parents who expect too much; different priorities from family members; competition with siblings.

Issues with friends: arguments; mean and catty behavior during difficult times; getting trapped in the middle of group fights; friends who need urgent help.

Academic and social aspects of school: making friends, especially when new to the neighborhood; pressure to get top grades; increasingly difficult tests and projects; too much homework; bullies.

Insecurity with self: the urge to be the best at everything; negative body image.

Change in general: new settings; loss or illness of loved ones; growing apart from friends.

This book gives specific strategies and solutions to help you understand and manage your own stress. It includes information on how people respond—in good ways and unhealthy ways—to stressful situations. It also describes common stressors—family, friends, school, and life in general—and suggests ways to manage them.

Different **stressors** can cause you to feel a variety of emotions, including anger, fear, and humiliation.

How Your Body Reacts

Did you know that the emotions associated with stress actually cause physical changes in your body? A Hungarian scientist and physician named Hans Selye identified this response in 1936 while experimenting on mice. Although he injected the animals with various kinds of fluids, they all developed ulcers, swelling glands, and depleted immune systems. (The body's immune system helps fight infection.) The mice's bodies changed, or adapted, in the same way.

Selye called this response general adaptation syndrome. Later, as he expanded his work on general adaptation syndrome, he began referring to it as stress. At the time, physicists used the term, which comes from a Latin word meaning "to pull apart," to describe elasticity.

According to a colleague of Selye's, the word *strain* was closer to the idea of what the researcher was trying to describe. (*Strain* refers to an injury to the body caused by extreme physical tension.) If Selye had been more proficient in English, people today

Stress can cause many changes in the body.

might be talking about "strain relief" instead of "stress relief"![1] But the name stress stuck, and others began researching the subject as well.

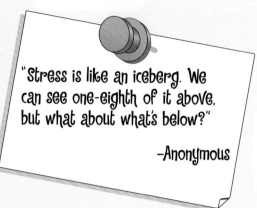

So exactly how does stress affect people? Actually, it's all in your head—more specifically, in your brain. The physical reaction to stress is triggered by a part of your brain called the hypothalamus. Although the hypothalamus is only about the size of a marble, it affects your entire body. This tiny region of the brain is a control center that sparks many complex chemical reactions. Among them is the release of hormones—special chemical substances that signal other body cells to action. In emergency situations, the hypothalamus sets off an alarm resulting in the release of two important hormones—adrenaline

Adrenaline and Cortisol

Adrenaline and cortisol are produced by the adrenal glands—two boomerang-shaped glands located near your kidneys. Adrenaline increases the heart rate and raises your blood pressure. Cortisol regulates metabolism, which is the process in which the body breaks down substances so the cells can use them. Both adrenaline and cortisol increase the amount of sugar in the bloodstream, which results in feeling a rush of energy.

and cortisol—into the bloodstream. They cause changes to quickly occur in the body: the muscles tense and breathing becomes rapid.

This stress reaction is called the "fight-or-flight" response—your body is prepared to fight the perceived danger or flee from it. The fight-or-flight instinct is a natural response that dates to prehistoric times, when humans had to struggle for survival.

Stress can be overwhelming, and cause you to cry easily or feel upset.

Stress

The Power of Adrenaline

You may have been surprised by your own strength or speed in an emergency situation. Chalk it up to the adrenaline rush of your body's stress response. For example, when you stumble on a steep flight of stairs, you don't have to think about reaching out to grab the railing. It just happens in a split second. Stress-induced adrenaline can also sharpen your reflexes and give you a "second wind," delivering a burst of renewed energy that allows you to keep working even when you're tired.

Although you probably don't have to face mortal danger on a regular basis today, you still experience fight-or-flight moments. The stress response can occur when your emotions cause your body to react as it would in an actual emergency, even when there is no physical danger.

Once the stressful event or threat that set off your hypothalamus alarm has passed, the levels of adrenaline and cortisol decrease in the bloodstream. Your body returns to normal.

Everyone Reacts Differently

What stresses you out may have no effect on someone else, and vice versa. For example, some people are terrified of public speaking. Others may thoroughly enjoy talking in front of a large group. Some people may not care either way. What would be major stressors for some people are just part of everyday life for others.

How Stress Makes You Feel

Kayla was nervous. She had practiced her speech for the school assembly over and over again. But as she walked over to the podium, she forgot everything she was going to say. Her heart was pounding, her stomach hurt, and her hands were shaking so much that she couldn't see the words on her note cards.

You probably are familiar with many of the symptoms of stress. It can cause a number of unpleasant side effects in your body, in your mind, and in the way you behave. There's no reason to be anxious about the symptoms of stress. However, it's important to know what they are. When you have an idea of what to expect, you can recognize when you need to figure out ways to cope.

Physical reactions. Like Kayla, you might exhibit a variety of symptoms when under stress. Your heart beats fast, your breathing becomes heavier, and you sweat. You might feel various aches and pains as your muscles clench up or get tense. If they remain that way for a long time, they may cause pain, especially in the neck, back, and shoulders.

Headaches are often a common response to stress—a result of the increased amount of blood rushing to the brain. At the same time, the digestive system is receiving less blood, so your stomach typically feels queasy. Whenever you're nervous, the stress response can produce a sensation often referred to as "butterflies" in the stomach.

There are two specific types of stress—acute and chronic. Acute stress occurs when the fight-or-flight response is triggered

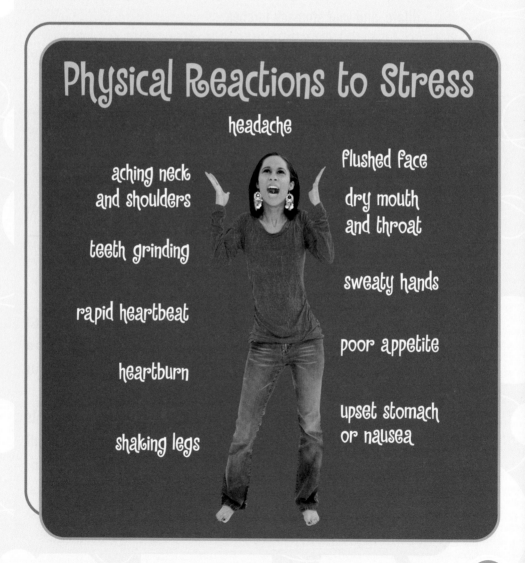

Physical Reactions to Stress

headache

aching neck and shoulders

flushed face

dry mouth and throat

teeth grinding

sweaty hands

rapid heartbeat

poor appetite

heartburn

upset stomach or nausea

shaking legs

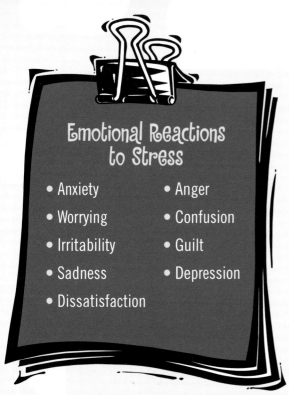

Emotional Reactions to Stress

- Anxiety
- Worrying
- Irritability
- Sadness
- Dissatisfaction
- Anger
- Confusion
- Guilt
- Depression

prolonged stress can make that cycle irregular. After stress levels are lowered, it will return to normal.

Emotional and behavioral reactions. Chronic stress typically affects emotions and behavior. For example, if you're struggling for several months to deal with a bully or your parents' divorce, your low feelings and mood swings will affect your behavior. You may react to situations without thinking and have a low threshold for tolerating or dealing with challenges. If you are dealing with long-term stress:

- You may be tense, panicky, on edge, and easily startled.

- You may feel like you'll go crazy if one more thing happens.

Anxiety vs. Depression

Anxiety refers to a deep uncertainty and nervousness about an upcoming event or situation. It involves a number of different emotions, including fear and shame, and sometimes guilt.

Depression involves strong feelings of sadness, fatigue, and hopelessness.

- Your mind may wander so often you can't concentrate, keep track of time, or make decisions.

- You may find yourself crying for no reason, or getting furious over something that's no big deal.

- Depending on the stressor, you're also likely to feel angry, afraid, or humiliated.

- You may also not feel like doing anything. In fact, you probably wish people would just leave you alone.

Be aware that your low emotions and moods not only affect your actions but also how others react to you. People undergoing long-term stress often reach a point where they simply don't care what others think of their behavior.

If you're dealing with a long-term stressful situation, you're likely to become preoccupied and distracted. Your parents think you're being rude. Your friends start to wonder why you're giving them the silent treatment. Because you are having so much difficulty concentrating, you can't focus in class. Your teachers think you're not paying attention, and so your grades suffer. Stress can make your relationships with others become more difficult.

It's important that you recognize when you're stressed

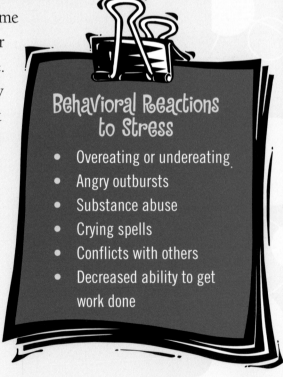

Behavioral Reactions to Stress

- Overeating or undereating
- Angry outbursts
- Substance abuse
- Crying spells
- Conflicts with others
- Decreased ability to get work done

Quiz: How Stressed Are You?

Determine how you react to stress. Count up the number of sentences you agree with. Then evaluate how stressed out you are by using the following score: 6 or more = stress level is high; 2 to 5 = stress level is average; 1 or 0 = stress level is below average.

1. I often feel tense or anxious.

2. I frequently have stomachaches.

3. My family often makes me feel upset.

4. I get nervous around people at school.

5. I often get headaches.

6. I have trouble falling asleep at night.

7. I worry about school.

8. When I get nervous, I tend to snack.

9. I have trouble concentrating on one thing because I'm worrying about something else.

10. I have considered using drugs or drinking to relax.

11. I have a full schedule of responsibilities at school and at home.

12. I have trouble finding time to relax.

13. I often feel guilty that I'm not doing my homework or other chores.

out. Then it will be easier to see how your behavior is affecting others. Try to be considerate of others as you attempt to function as normally as possible. For instance, no matter how irritable you're feeling, try not to snap at anyone who shows concern.

Similarly, try to be patient when somebody else's stress is driving you crazy. Keep a low profile when it seems like all your friends are stressed out. In fact, you might want to stay out of everybody's way until things calm down.

Try to keep your cool when you're stressed—don't overreact!

What to Do When You're Stressed

Hurry up—you need to finish this by noon. Is your homework done? Did you practice your music today? I'm mad at you. Did you make the team? Do you know if you got the part? We don't like your friends. Don't you think you should lose some weight? Can't you get better grades? Why didn't you play a better game?

Messages like these can certainly stress you out. This is especially true if you feel that countless demands and pressures are coming at you from all directions: from parents, friends, teachers, coaches, and even yourself. If you are feeling overwhelmed, you can use the following suggestions to cope:

Learn to recognize when stress is affecting you. When you first feel the physical stress response coming on—stiffened muscles or flushed face—recognize you are having a fight-or-flight response. Identify your stressors as well as the emotion or combination of emotions you are feeling.

Put your stressors in perspective. Perspective refers to viewing things according to their importance. Remember, the fight-or-flight response can kick in whenever your emotions make your brain think there is an emergency.

When you're stressed, take some time to prioritize your obligations. Start by making a list, and cross things off as you complete them.

When you recognize you are feeling stressed, think to yourself, "How serious is the danger? How likely is the threat?"[1] Learn to recognize the difference between true emergencies and events that are important, but not life threatening. As author Natalie Goldberg has explained, "Stress is an ignorant state. It believes that everything is an emergency."[2]

"Tension is who you think you should be. Relaxation is who you are."

–Chinese Proverb

You may find that you can calm yourself down (or reduce your stress response) simply by putting the situation in perspective. Say, for example, you failed a history test because you studied the wrong chapter. Find out how much of that grade will affect your overall standing. You may learn it will be only a small part, or may not count at all. You could also try talking to your teacher to see if you could take the test again. Rather than get upset, take positive steps to deal with a potential stressor.

Prioritize your obligations. Similarly, if you feel overwhelmed because you have a busy schedule, be willing to make some changes. Evaluate your current schedule. Decide what needs to get done sooner, and what can be finished at a later time. You may find that you have to drop some things, and be willing to do so. Recognize your limitations and set specific goals.

Make large tasks manageable. If you have a large assignment to do, can you find a way to break it down into smaller, more easily achievable tasks? For example, if you have an hour to finish twenty math problems, break down your work in a way that will let you stay on track. One way might be to plan to finish five problems every fifteen minutes.

1. Spend some time by yourself.
2. Go for a run.
3. Work on your favorite hobby or start a new one.
4. Sing with a group of people.
5. Bake or cook something special.
6. Play a musical instrument or listen to music.
7. Play a sport that you enjoy.
8. Talk to someone who is a good listener.

Be assertive in standing up for yourself. Being assertive means being able to express your feelings, opinions, or beliefs clearly, while respecting the needs and rights of others. You can often bring a stressful situation—with parents, friends, or siblings—to a close when you are assertive. But when dealing with a stressful conflict, be sure to state your feelings calmly and politely.

Take care of yourself emotionally. Take a break when you find yourself in a stressful situation. Walk away when someone is upsetting you, or leave the room to give yourself the chance to "talk yourself down" from your own anger.

Do something to take your mind off your stress. Play your favorite songs—whether they're relaxing, angry, or somewhere in between. Take a shower. Play with your pet. Make faces at yourself in the mirror. Make yourself laugh by thinking about some joke that never gets old. Some people find that prayer, meditation, yoga, and sleep help them if they are feeling stressed out. Others may use breathing or muscle relaxation techniques such as the ones that appear on pages 24 and 25.

Writing your feelings down in a journal can be a great outlet when you're stressed. Like any negative feeling, stress can seem like less of a big deal once you write about it. A lot of people like to record their actions and verbalize their daily feelings through prose or poetry. Journaling is ideal for when you want to blow off steam but don't feel like talking about what's bothering you to anyone else.

However, sharing your problems with a trusted friend or adult can help. You might also find relief by joining and participating in a support group whose members are dealing with the same stressful issues you have.

Take care of yourself physically. You will be better able to minimize the negative effects of stress if your body is healthy. Three important ways to maintain good health are to eat well, exercise regularly, and get plenty of sleep.

When you're stressed, some foods are more helpful than others. Foods rich in carbohydrates such as rice, potatoes, pasta, cereal, and bread can boost energy. The fiber in grains, fruits, and vegetables helps keep the digestive system moving.

Science Says....

Playing with your pet can reduce stress. Many nursing homes, psychiatric wards, and rehabilitation clinics bring rabbits, cats, or dogs into their facilities so the animals can provide therapy for patients. People who have the opportunity to interact with the animals have reduced blood pressure and feel more positive.

Breathing Relaxation

1. Sit in a comfortable chair, feet flat on the floor.

2. Close your eyes or focus on something in the room.

3. Paying attention to your breathing, inhale slowly through your nose.

4. Let your lower abdomen relax and expand as your lungs expand and fill with air.

5. When your lungs and abdomen are full, slowly exhale, letting air out through your mouth.

6. Repeat. If your mind wanders, return your attention to your breathing.[3]

Such foods can also settle your stomach if stress is making you nauseous. Fried food, on the other hand, can worsen your stomachache.

Regular exercise decreases the production of stress hormones in the body. And physical activity also causes the body to release mood-boosting brain chemicals called endorphins. As a result, exercise will reduce your stressful feelings and make you feel good, too. If it's not possible for you to maintain a regular exercise schedule, try to get moderately strenuous exercise at least twice a week. This could include a short walk, bike ride, or jog.

Muscle Relaxation

1. Work on slowly tensing and then relaxing each muscle group in your body.

2. Begin by tensing and relaxing the muscles in your toes. Then work your way up various muscles in the body until you reach the ones in your neck and head.

3. For each set of muscles, hold the tension for at least five seconds. Then relax for thirty seconds.

4. Repeat until you feel less stressed out.[4]

Get enough sleep whenever you can. Most teenagers need between 8.5 and 9.5 hours per night, researchers say. However, a large number of teens don't get nearly that much. In a 1997 study, professors from Brown University and College of the Holy Cross found that only 26 percent of surveyed teens regularly slept for 8.5 hours.[5] In other words, almost three quarters of all teens are sleep-deprived. Exhaustion saps concentration, weakens the immune system, and makes existing stress worse.

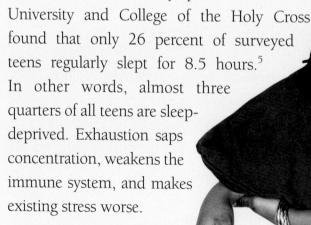

Harmful Ways of Coping

As she stomped home from school, Maya grew more and more worried. Her best friend had picked a fight with her for no apparent reason. She wouldn't have much time to study for tomorrow's history test because she had a dentist appointment that afternoon. When she arrived at home, Maya slammed her backpack down and collapsed on the floor.

"How come you're so grumpy?" her little sister asked curiously.

"Why do you care? Mind your own business!" Maya snapped.

If you're stressed, there are many ways you can relieve your tension and anger. But a few approaches to dealing with stress are never helpful, especially if they involve being inconsiderate of others or mistreating your body. Unfortunately, these counterproductive actions can be hard to recognize.

Lashing out, overreacting, or venting. Maya's problem wasn't really with her sister. What she was doing was taking her anger out on someone else who actually had nothing to do with her stressors: her angry friend, her upcoming test, and her tight schedule. It's unfair to lash out at people or other living things. And if your target strikes back, you could find yourself with an even more stressful situation.

Before you snap in anger at someone who has had nothing to do with your problems, try counting to ten. During this time,

remind yourself that venting will do nothing to solve your difficulty. It most likely will only create additional problems. If you find that you can't stop from lashing out at others, you may be having issues that would be helped by counseling.

Suppressing, avoiding, or ignoring. Suppressing or ignoring your stressor and hoping it will go away on its own may keep you from panicking. However, the longer you ignore a stressful situation, the more urgent it may become. By not dealing with your stress, you run the risk of having it negatively affect your health over the long term as chronic stress.

Eating too much—or too little. Many people drastically change how they eat when they're stressed out. Some overeat, or binge, on "comfort foods" while others go hungry. Both overeating and undereating can do real harm to your health.

While eating cookies might improve your mood because of the short-term effect of additional sugar in your bloodstream, the "sugar rush" won't last long. Be aware that eating in response to your emotions—rather than simply in response to the hunger drive—can lead to serious eating disorders. Overeating can also cause health problems such as being overweight or obese.

And don't skip meals because you're stressed out. Make sure you eat three balanced meals a day of nutritious foods. Even if you lose your appetite or feel queasy because you're anxious, keep yourself healthy by eating properly—even if you can't eat very much.

Carbohydrates in foods such as sweets, potato chips, and bread cause a temporary increase in serotonin, a brain chemical that affects emotions, memory, and other things. Increased amounts of serotonin in the brain make people feel good, so they think they can better handle stress. Because of this, some people will respond to stressful situations by overeating foods that are rich in carbohydrates.[1]

Using alcohol and illegal substances. In some cases, people try to escape from their problems by using alcohol, nicotine, and drugs, including illegal substances. Using artificial means to deal with stressful situations won't help solve problems. They often tend to create new ones. Substance abuse is habit-forming, and it is easy to become addicted to alcohol and drugs.

You may have heard that people are more cheerful and playful while drinking, but appearing cheerful and actually being happy can be two different things. Alcohol is actually a depressant, which is a kind of drug that calms nerves and relaxes the muscles. However, in large amounts depressants can cause confusion, lack of coordination, slurred speech, and shaking. Mood swings are common with heavy drinkers, who are just as likely to feel gloomy or aggressive as a stressed out person who isn't drinking. Because the use of alcohol is illegal for anyone under the age of twenty-one, getting caught using it can also lead to problems with the law. You definitely don't want that kind of stress.

You're also likely to have heard that smoking cigarettes calms the nerves. But the exact opposite is true: when a smoker lights up, adrenaline is released into his or her system. Even if nicotine really did have a calming effect, this benefit still wouldn't be worth the risks. Not only is nicotine use addictive, but its long-term use has been linked to serious lung diseases such as emphysema and lung cancer.

Another unhealthy way of dealing with stress is using illegal substances such as marijuana. Its active ingredient, THC (delta-9-tetrahydrocannabinol), induces relaxation when it reacts with substances in the brain. But marijuana is an illegal drug whose use has been linked to numerous adverse effects, including short-term memory loss.

There are many healthy ways to deal with stress. Using alcohol, tobacco, or other drugs to cope is not one of them.

Problems with Caffeine

The world's most commonly used drug, caffeine is a stimulant found in foods like coffee, tea, chocolate, and sodas. Millions of people start their day each morning by drinking caffeine. It affects the nervous system (the brain, spinal cord, and nerves) and energizes the body. However, caffeine is a drug and it is possible to have too much at once or to become dependent on it. Consuming even a moderate amount of caffeine can affect your sleeping patterns and cause headaches and muscle pains.

Stressed Out by Family

Most parents love their kids and want the best for them. But without meaning to, they can pile on unreasonable amounts of pressure to get top grades, win an athletic scholarship, or be one of the popular kids. It is easy for teens to feel stress when parents make them feel like their best just isn't good enough.

Just remember, your parents really do have your best interests in mind. But if you are upset by their expectations, you need to tell them what you're feeling and what it is that you want. Similarly, if you think they don't treat you fairly in other ways, you need to talk to them.

In any conversation you have with adults, make your case quietly and calmly. Then, listen to and honestly consider their

Fighting with parents can be a source of stress for everyone involved.

Tips for Talking with Your Parents

1. When your parents say something that makes you angry or tense, don't confront them while emotions are running high. Excuse yourself and take some time to cool off.

2. Give yourself a little while to gather and organize your thoughts. What exactly do you want them to know? You might want to write your arguments down in a list.

3. After figuring out what you'd like to say, ask to speak with your parents.

4. Be levelheaded and avoid exaggeration; they should be more likely to consider your points if you present them calmly.

response. Don't sigh or roll your eyes, no matter what they say. Your parents may not agree with you or change their minds, but they'll probably be impressed by your maturity. As a result, you may be able to reach a compromise.

If it seems like your parents expect you to be perfect or don't respect your uniqueness, you shouldn't accept this kind of pressure. Let them know you need them to change their way of thinking because it is hurting you.

In the same way, don't get stressed out by conflicts with brothers and sisters. When siblings tease or misbehave, keep your cool. Talk out your issues calmly, following the same suggestions given above for talking with parents.

Stressed Out by Friends

Your good friend Nicole just came crying to you. She says that Shannon had asked out Ben, Nicole's ex-boyfriend, just to be mean. An hour later, Shannon furiously tells you that Ben had asked her out—not the other way around. She says that Nicole's spreading lies because she's jealous.

You really don't want to get involved, but you realize that both your friends expect you to pick a side. If you defend one, the other will get mad at you, and if you ignore the whole thing, they'll both get mad at you! Suddenly, you're stressing out over an issue that otherwise wouldn't affect your life at all.

Friends. You'd trust them with your life, and they've heard stuff you'd never consider telling anyone else. When something terrible happens, your first instinct is to call them. But when friends know all each other's secrets and quirks, they're able to hurt each other like no one else can. Your friends can be great at helping you deal with stress. Other times, friends are the stressors.

When friends involve you in their conflicts. It's hard to know how to react when other people impose their problems on you. Sure, it's not fair when others expect you to get involved in a conflict you're not part of. And it can be difficult to know what to do when you constantly have to hear about someone else's personal issues.

It may be tempting to yell "Will you just shut up already about Nicole and your stupid boyfriend? Why do you think I

Relationships with boys can be a common cause of conflict between friends.

care?" Needless to say, venting like that will only make every-one involved even angrier.

However, you could take a more tactful approach by being assertive and calmly stating your point of view. "Shannon," you

Science Says....

A University of Pittsburgh study found that among people subjected to stressful laboratory experiments, those who were accompanied by friends had lower heart rates and lower blood pressure than those who came alone. In other words, supportive friends reduce stress.[1]

could say, "I'm sorry about this fight, but it's between you and Nicole, and nobody else. I can't judge whose fault it is—and frankly, I don't really want to. Let me know if I can help, but otherwise, can we just not talk about it?" Even if such a response annoys your friends at first, it lets them know where they stand. They'll probably work out their conflict on their own. And in the meantime you won't be stressed out by it.

When you have conflicts with friends. All friends fight. And conflict can be stressful. You may wonder, "Will we ever be friends again? Will she tell the whole school my secrets? What if everybody else sides with her and I lose all my other friends?" In addition to those worries, you may be flooded by emotions of anger, betrayal, and humiliation. It may seem like your whole world is collapsing.

Sometimes you just can't avoid getting into an argument. However, you can learn ways to deal with conflicts so they end quickly and are less stressful for all involved. Remember, when fighting breaks out, keep your comments fair and civil. More tips for resolving conflict appear on page 36. These tips apply to fights with family members, too.

Dealing with peer pressure. Friends can be a stressor in another way—when they push you to behave in

Talking to Friends

One of the best ways to deal with a stressful time in your life is by sharing your concerns with a friend. However, there's a difference between talking about your problems with friends and dumping on them. Talking about your problems with someone who is willing to listen can let you get rid of some bad feelings. However, if you're simply complaining and dwelling on the problem without considering solutions, then you are dumping on a friend.

Talking with a friend about your stress can help you feel better and allow you to gain another perspective.

When a friend's dumping on you, excuse yourself from her rant. But don't criticize or dismiss her stress as unimportant. Asking something like "Is this really worth freaking out over?" isn't very helpful. Instead, you could ask, "Is there any way I can help?" If she says no, then simply say, "So, if we can't do anything about this, maybe you'll feel better if we talk about something else."

Tips for Resolving Conflicts

Do: Explain your reasons carefully. Saying "I was upset when . . ." is friendlier than accusing with a statement like "You upset me when . . ."

Do: Listen quietly while the other person is speaking. Instead of interrupting, shouting down, or deliberately ignoring the other person, wait your turn.

Do: Accept responsibility for your role in the argument, even if you've been treated poorly. Fights are rarely just one person's fault.

Do: Remember that one argument doesn't doom a friendship. If you spend a lot of time with someone, it is natural that you'll disagree on occasion.

Don't: Spread gossip. Not only is it unkind, it often just makes things worse.

Don't: Use blanket statements like "You're always late," or "You've never cared about anyone but yourself!" Words like *always*, *whenever*, and *never* are dangerous when used in statements accusing others.

Don't: Complicate things and make the conflict worse by bringing up old arguments, making personal attacks, or attempting revenge.

Don't: Be afraid to apologize first. Even if the argument wasn't your fault, that doesn't matter. What really matters is ending the conflict.

a way that you're not comfortable. It can be particularly stressful when your peers—the people who are your age—pressure you into making bad choices. Peer pressure can lead to bad decision-making, especially when it comes to the use of drugs, alcohol, or tobacco.

It can be stressful when you find yourself going against the wishes of the group, especially if you want to be liked or to fit in. However, when you know something is wrong for you, let the group know. You might try talking to just one member of the crowd. Perhaps you can get her to agree with your way of thinking. Having the support of one other person can make it easier for you to resist the pressure to do something you believe is wrong.

Fighting with friends is never easy. However, if you avoid a screaming match, you'll have a better chance of resolving your conflict and reducing your stress.

Surviving School

No matter how hard Carmen studied, she just didn't understand her algebra homework. But she worked hard and managed to earn a B in the class. Carmen was relieved when she saw her grade, but when her parents looked at her report card, their faces grew stern. "A B-average in math?" her mother asked. "We expected better from you. This is unacceptable."

Some parents place a lot of pressure on their kids to get top grades in school. You may even be putting that same pressure on yourself. It can reach the

point where you start to think "If I mess up on this test, my future is ruined." Of course, no one test will make or break your future plans—there will be opportunities to make things better if you fail to do well on one test or report. What can cause harm is when you have to deal with the stress that accompanies unrealistic expectations.

You need to be up-front with your parents if you think they are making unreasonable demands. Let them know you are doing your best and that they need to learn to accept you as you are.

However, if you are not working as hard as you could be, and are bothered by your grades, then you can take steps to improve them. Talk to your teachers about getting some extra help, look into tutoring possibilities, be sure you do your homework and turn it in on time, and try to improve your study habits.

Determine the study schedule that works best for you. You might find you're more productive if you do the easiest assignments first to get them out of the way, or you might prefer to save the easy stuff for later. Maybe you work well with

Try not to get overwhelmed with your schoolwork by leaving it all to get done at the last minute.

partners, or maybe you're better off on your own. Only experience can determine what study routine works best for you. However, once you've hit on an effective formula, stick to it.

Dealing with bullies and fake friends. Another major school stressor can be bullies. The word *bully* doesn't refer only to the tough guy who beats up someone smaller than him. It can also be the girl who targets members of her own group. She mocks and insults those she claims to like, often convincing mutual friends to join in. If anyone calls her on that behavior, she insists she is not really serious. She's just joking.

Tips for Improving Study Habits

- Do your best to find a quiet, well-lit place with as few potential distractions as possible (no TV, no phone).
- Ask your family not to disturb you unless there's an emergency.
- If you study in your room, don't risk falling asleep by sprawling on your bed.
- Make sure you have everything you need before you start to work.
- Take a break occasionally to collect your thoughts and to avoid fatigue—but keep it quick. Don't lengthen your break by getting involved in other activities, like watching TV or making a phone call.
- Avoid going online when working at the computer. It's easy to lose track of time or become involved in instant messaging with friends.

This form of bullying is often called relational aggression. Its purpose is to hurt another person by damaging her ability to have friendships with others. Relational aggression typically involves isolating the person, spreading false rumors about her, and name-calling.

Being put down or insulted is stressful. If you believe a friend honestly doesn't realize she's being mean, you need to let her know how you feel. If she laughs or insists you're lying, you're better off without her. A real friend would be shocked and upset to learn about your issue, and willing to apologize. If she really seems sincere, then consider giving her the benefit of the doubt and accepting her apology.

If someone is bullying you, there are different ways to respond. Ignoring a bully can work, but sometimes that route is not always enough. A direct confrontation might be the best

way to go. Try saying something like, "Look, I don't know what your problem is with me, but this isn't cool or funny and I think you'd better stop." Make eye contact and keep your voice level—don't whisper or shout. The bully might insult or dismiss what you've said at first, but at least you've proven you're not an easy target.

If you can't bring yourself to confront the bully—or you tried and it didn't work—you can tell your parents, a teacher, or guidance counselor what's happening. That solution is also the best plan if you fear for your physical safety. What's most important is that you take steps to stop the bullying behavior.

What to Do if You Are Being Bullied

1. Tell an adult.

2. Tell the bully to stop; then calmly walk away.

3. Do not fight back because you could also end up in trouble.

4. Lighten the mood and distract people by making a joke.

5. Make new friends and get involved in activities that interest you.

6. Don't blame yourself.

7. Be strong and believe in yourself—it's the bully who has a problem, not you.[1]

Putting Pressure on Yourself

Veronica has a 4.0 GPA, is editor of the yearbook, plays varsity lacrosse, and serves on student council. After school, she takes piano lessons and volunteers with her youth group—after she's done her homework, of course. She goes out of her way to be friends with everyone. Veronica's teachers admire her and her parents are proud. No one would ever guess that she averages four hours of sleep a night, plagiarizes to keep those grades up, and cries whenever she's alone.

Nobody's amazing at everything. But some girls, like Veronica, have a hard time accepting their own limitations. They are perfectionists, who stress over every mistake they make. Perfectionists obsess about or overemphasize doing everything correctly. Psychologist Roni Cohen-Sandler writes that perfectionists "equate being successful with being extraordinary . . . [and] consider weakness in any area unacceptable."[1] Too often such goals are unrealistic.

Ambition and drive are normally good things. But they can be very bad if taken too far. You've heard of athletes abusing steroids, students cheating on exams, and politicians lying—all of them jeopardizing their careers—in the name of achievement. If unchecked, perfectionism can lead to misery. Perfectionists have a hard time accepting when

they have done a competent job. Too often they aim for the unattainable, extraordinary effort.

Negative thoughts. When you're your own harshest critic, you are also your own stressor. If you don't think the job you've done is good enough or you're always comparing yourself to everyone else in your class, it is hard to be happy. And it's easy to feel stressed out.

If you keep telling yourself that you'll never be smart or athletic or talented enough, or that a situation is completely hopeless, you are piling on stress from within. Recognize that when you change your attitude, you will find relief from some of that stress. Try to take a more positive look at yourself. Make a list of your positive characteristics and of what you've done. Give yourself some credit, and don't let feelings of failure keep you down.

Problems with self-image. Most girls have no problem coming up with a negative comment about some aspect of their appearance. Something is wrong with their height, weight, nose, complexion, or hair—you name it.

During the teen years, when the body is undergoing the rapid changes of puberty, you may be especially sensitive about your looks. At the same time, you are being targeted

Are You a Perfectionist?

If you feel the burning need to excel, ask yourself the following questions—and do your best to be honest:

- Why do I want to improve or do well?

- When will I be satisfied with what I've accomplished?

- How will I react if I fall short of my expectations for myself?

- Can I handle coming in second or worse in a competition?

Self-Image Stressors

- I don't think I look very attractive.

- I'm not very good at sports or music or dance even though I practice a lot.

- I need to lose weight.

in advertisements that say you have to be like impossibly pretty people. It's hard to have a positive self-image.

Just remember, the unpredictable changes your body is going through during puberty are completely normal. You're supposed to get taller, grow body hair, and gain weight while growing up. (And if you haven't yet, don't worry. It'll happen.)

The Surveys Say...

If your appearance stresses you out, you're not alone. In 2004, a British youth magazine named *Bliss* surveyed two thousand girls ages ten through nineteen. Nine out of ten of respondents said they were unsatisfied with their bodies.[2]

Remember, your peers are going through many of the same feelings that you are experiencing.

Try to keep in mind that your physical appearance isn't what should count in any relationship. Your real friends like you for who you are, not for how you look.

However, you may be finding faults with yourself that you really do want to change. If so, talk about your concerns with your parents or friends to see what they think. If they agree that you should lose some weight, for example, then do something about that goal. Contact your doctor to set up a weight-loss diet and exercise program, and then do your best to follow it. On the other hand, if your friends and family assure you that you don't need to make changes, listen to them.

Death, Loss, and Change

Jill's grandfather had been sick for many years. When he passed away last week, Jill was relieved that he was no longer in pain. But she also felt terribly guilty. What is wrong with me? she asked herself. How could I be happy that my grandfather is gone?

Most changes and transitions cause a great deal of stress. One of the hardest—and most stressful—changes to deal with is the death of a close friend or family member.

Dealing with grief. When someone you really care about dies, you can experience agonizing emotions, including anger, shock, sorrow, and depression. Grief is one of the most difficult emotions to face, and the grieving process is grueling. One way to cope with your loss is to pay tribute to your loved one. Work through your grieving process by helping with a memorial service, putting together an album of favorite photographs, or creating a Web page that honors the deceased. The process of creating such remembrances can help you deal with your grief and stress. However, it will take time to work through your stages of grieving.

Five Stages of Grieving

First identified by psychiatrist Elisabeth Kübler-Ross in 1969, the five stages of grieving can apply to situations involving traumatic change (such as diagnosis of terminal illness), as well as the death of loved ones.

Denial—refusal or inability to understand the bad news; pretending that nothing has happened.

Anger—outpouring of feelings of anger, blaming self or others.

Bargaining—hoping that bad news isn't true or negotiating with others to prevent change.

Depression—sadness, regret, fear, uncertainty combined with beginnings of acceptance of what has happened.

Acceptance—ready to become actively involved in taking steps to move on.

When friends grow apart. Yet another difficult change in life can be losing a friendship. Are you still as close to your favorite people as you always were? Maybe you've noticed a distance that wasn't there before. Sometimes, there isn't really any reason for friends to drift apart. It just happens during the process of growing up. As people learn more about who they are, they want new friends to reflect what interests them. And those interests can change as the years go by.

If it seems like one of your best friends is hanging out a lot with someone else, it is natural to feel jealous. But try not to stress over the situation. Give the new person a chance, and maybe you'll end up liking him or her, too.

Moving. Sometimes you lose friendships because of something over which you have no control. It can be a major stressor when your family moves—you've lost familiar friends and surroundings. You have to make new friends and attend a new school. Feeling stress in this kind of situation is to be expected.

Whether you're dealing with having moved from one place to another or simply changed schools, be patient and try to stay positive. If you're not happy with your new school right away, don't worry. Just give yourself time to settle in. It will get easier if you take advantage of the new opportunities your school offers. Go out of your way to talk to people in your classes. Join clubs that interest you. Just be true to yourself. That's the most effective way to make good friends who will be there for you.

Dealing with divorce. Life can also be stressful when parents don't get along or argue a lot. When their inability to get along ends in their breakup,

Moving is chaotic for everyone, but it's important to remember that things will eventually settle down.

Situation Stressors

- A close relative or family member has died.
- Someone in my family has been diagnosed with a serious disease.
- Money is tight since one of my parents was laid off.
- My family is moving.
- My parents are getting a divorce.

you will find yourself dealing with a major family change—and a major stressor.

In 2005, out of every one thousand marriages in the United States, about seventeen ended in divorce.[1] Many divorced couples have children who may have to move to new homes or choose between which parent to live with. Whether these kids are toddlers, teenagers, or adults, the changes resulting from divorce can be difficult to handle.

If you are one of these kids, it is natural for you to feel angry with one or both parents. Let them know if it bothers you when they say negative things about each other in front of you. If their behavior is stressful, you need to make it clear that you expect them to be civil with one another—for your sake.

Whenever you are dealing with change, it can help to share your feelings with friends and with others. Remind yourself that you're not alone, that you'll get through this, and that it's natural to feel stress and fear. But once you can recognize that things aren't going to go back to the way they used to be, you can begin to make plans to move on.

When Stress Is Dangerous

"My parents hate me."

"I wish I was skinny like you; I'm such a pig."

"This class makes me want to kill myself."

When people make negative comments about themselves they usually don't mean what they are saying. Most likely they are simply exaggerating a situation or even searching for a compliment by putting themselves down.

But sometimes when a person makes comments like these, they are signs that he or she is feeling overwhelmed and possibly

You can help yourself and your friends by learning to read the danger signs of stress.

Warning Signs of Depression or Suicide

- Loss of interest in life
- Long-term feelings of sadness
- Weeks of constant anger and bad moods
- Severe changes in eating habits
- Unexplained injuries
- Negative comments about self-worth
- Giving away belongings

spiraling out of control. If a friend has been suffering from chronic stress, he or she is at increased risk of developing serious emotional illnesses such as clinical depression and anxiety disorders.

Clinical depression is usually diagnosed when a person's strong feelings of sadness and helplessness last for more than two weeks. He or she will have difficulty in thinking and concentrating and may have significant changes in appetite and sleep needs. Clinical depresssion interferes with the person's ability to connect with others and function in any environment—at work, at school, or at home.

Some anxiety in life is perfectly normal—who hasn't suffered from a bit of stage fright before giving a speech? However, when anxiety is excessive, it can be harmful. Anxiety disorders make the tasks of everyday life seem overwhelming and impossible. In many cases, it's hard for sufferers to function in social settings. Physical symptoms typically include heart palpitations, migraines, and panic attacks.

If you think a friend has a problem with drug abuse, talk to her about it, and ask an adult for help.

Clinical depression and anxiety disorders are linked to self-injury (such as cutting) and suicide. Yet, both mental health disorders are treatable with the proper medication and professional counseling. A friend with issues may not want others to know there is a problem. But remember, by getting help for your friend, you're doing the right thing.

Did You Know?

Facts About Self-Injury

Self-injury (purposely inflicting wounds on one's own body, frequently by cutting or burning the skin) is an extremely dangerous, unhealthy way to cope with stress. Those who self-injure may think it's a normal stress reliever, but it indicates a serious mental health problem. If you have this habit or suspect a friend does, tell a trusted adult immediately.

When You Should Ask for Help

- You have been feeling sad for more than two weeks.
- Your grades are dropping.
- You worry a lot.
- You easily get moody or angry.
- You feel tired all the time.
- You get a lot of headaches, dizziness, chest pain, or stomach pain.
- You feel bored all the time and are less interested in being with friends.
- You are thinking about using alcohol or drugs to try to feel better.
- You are thinking about hurting yourself.[1]

People suffering from depression and anxiety disorders are at risk of causing harm to themselves. Suicide is the third leading cause of death among fifteen- to twenty-five year-olds.[2]

When a Friend Needs Help

If you think your friend may be exhibiting signs of depression, an eating disorder, drug use, or self-injury, or is having suicidal thoughts, you need to get help. Tell a trusted adult (a parent, school counselor, your family doctor, or religious leader) about your concerns. Or call one of the hotline numbers listed on page 61.

Managing Your Stress

Would you want to live in a world without **stress?** For most people, the answer is no. What would motivate people to get anything done in a completely stress-free world? The shock to the system that stress provides often gives momentum needed at the right moment.

Stress can result from good things, too. Not all stressors are unhappy or frustrating situations. Stress can result from emotions like extreme excitement and anticipation, as well as from anger and humiliation. The intensity of your emotions can directly affect the amount of stress you feel.

Have you ever spent all evening getting ready for a dance you'd looked forward to for weeks? Did your face break out the day before? Did a run in your stocking make you panic? Did your stomach churn every time you looked at the clock? Maybe so, but more likely than not, it was all worth it once you got there and started having fun.

Many experts refer to stress from negative sources as distress and stress from

Managing your stressors takes practice, so don't expect to get it all perfect right away.

positive sources as eustress (literally "good stress"). Other moments of eustress that you may have experienced include performing in a play or concert, planning a party, going on a date, getting ready for a vacation, or playing a competitive sport. Eustress can give you the focus that that allows you to perform at your very best.

Still, you need to recognize that too much stress—whether from positive stressors or negative ones—can be bad for you. If you let it, eustress may keep you working too long on something that interests you and keep you awake so late at night that you don't get needed sleep. And any stress that lasts a long time can lead to health problems.

Whether your stress is part of positive emotions (interest or excitement) or negative ones (anger, humiliation, or sadness), it is important to stay on top of it when you can. Just remember that *perspective* is the magic word in stress management. Almost no mistake will ruin your life. You can gain control of the situation. When you find yourself feeling stressed out about something, remind yourself, as many times as necessary, that it's not the end of the world. Life will go on.

Recognize your limitations and set reasonable goals. Be ready to prioritize: What needs to get done sooner? What will take longer? Do you need more resources? Can you break something into smaller steps? Everything can't always get done perfectly, and it isn't fair to expect perfection from yourself or anyone else.

You can't always change the way other people think and act, but you do have the power to change the way you react to them.

Tips for Reducing Stress

- Keep a positive attitude.

- Accept that there are events that you cannot control.

- Be assertive instead of aggressive. "Assert" your feelings, opinions, or beliefs instead of becoming angry, defensive, or passive.

- Learn and practice relaxation techniques.

- Exercise regularly. Your body can fight stress better when it is fit.

- Eat healthy, well-balanced meals.

- Get enough rest and sleep. Your body needs time to recover from stressful events.

- Don't rely on alcohol or drugs to reduce stress.

- Seek out social support.

- Learn to manage your time more effectively.[1]

Learn from the past. After a period of stress is over and the stressor is taken care of, see if there's anything you can learn from the experience. Staying up late at night to finish a report might teach you not to put off large projects until the last minute. There might even be a bright side that will become clear later—for instance, a fight with your friends in which you fear losing their friendship can help you realize how important they are to you.

Know when to ask for help. There's no shame in asking for help from others when you feel stressed out. At the

same time, being private about your stress is fine, too. Everyone has different needs and preferences. Try to figure out what yours are.

Throughout your life you will have to deal with stress. There will be bullies or difficult people. There will be disappointments, changes, and losses. Brooding over your problems, your failures, or other issues won't really accomplish anything. In fact, your negative emotions will only make things worse.

But when you take positive steps to deal with the stress in your life, you can make a difference. Look to support from family and friends. They can help you take the steps needed to solve stressful conflicts or deal with change. At the same time, be positive about yourself and what you can accomplish. That positive attitude will ensure that you stay on top of your stressors and reduce your stress.

Effectively managing your stressors can help you live a happier life.

Chapter 1. What Is Stress?

1. Laura Sessions Stepp, "Perfect Problems: These Teens Are at the Top in Everything. Including Stress," *Washington Post*, May 5, 2002, p. F01.

2. Family First Aid: Help for Troubled Teens, "Teen Stress" n.d., <http://www.familyfirstaid.org/teen-stress.html> (May 8, 2007).

Chapter 2. How Your Body Reacts

1. Paul J. Rosch, "Reminiscences of Hans Selye, and the Birth of Stress," *The American Institute of Stress*, n.d., <http://www.stress.org/hans.htm> (July 15, 2007).

Chapter 3. How Stress Makes You Feel

1. "Link Found Between Teens' Stress Levels and Acne Severity," *Science Daily*, March 6, 2007, <http://www.sciencedaily.com/releases/2007/03/070305141029.htm> (May 8, 2007).

Chapter 4. What to Do When You're Stressed

1. Jeanie Lerche Davis, "Anxiety/Panic Guide: Coping with Anxiety," *WebMD*, n.d., <http://www.webmd.com/anxiety-panic/guide/coping-with-anxiety> (May 8, 2007).

2. Natalie Goldberg. *Wild Mind: Living the Writer's Life* (New York: Random House, 1990), p. 229.

3. Adapted from eMaxHealth, "Breathe Deeply to Manage Stress," March 18, 2006, <http://www.emaxhealth.com/32/5020.html> (July 13, 2007).

4. Mayo Clinic, "Relaxation Techniques: Learn Ways to Calm Your Stress," March 7, 2007, <http://www.mayoclinic.com/health/relaxation-technique/SR00007> (May 8, 2007).

5. Siri Carpenter, "Sleep Deprivation May Be Undermining Teen Health," *Monitor on Psychology*, October 2001, <http://www.apa.org/monitor/oct01/sleepteen.html> (May 8, 2007).

Chapter 5. Harmful Ways of Coping

1. Doris Pastore "Ask Us Anything," *Teen People*, October 2005, p. 7.

Chapter 7. Stressed Out by Friends

1. Florence Isaacs, *Toxic Friends, True Friends: How Your Friends Can Make or Break Your Health, Happiness, Family, and Career* (New York: William Morrow & Company, 1999), p. 178.

2. Barbara Crawford, Ellen Beth Levitt, and Gwen Fariss Newman, "Laughter Is Good for Your Heart, According to a New University of Maryland Medical Center Study," *University of Maryland Medical Center*, November 15, 2000, <http://www.umm.edu/news/releases/laughter.html> (July 13, 2007).

Chapter 8. Surviving School

1. From "Bring Bullying to an End," *girlshealth.gov*, n.d., <http://www.4girls.gov/factsheets/bullying.pdf> (March 27, 2007).

Chapter 9. Putting Pressure on Yourself

1. Roni Cohen-Sandler, *Stressed-Out Girls: Helping Them Thrive in the Age of Pressure* (New York: Penguin Group, 2005), p. 4.

2. James Meikle, "Teen Girls Just Wanna Look Thin," *The Guardian*, January 6, 2004, <http://www.guardian.co.uk/uk_news/story/0,3604,1116679,00.html> (July 13, 2007).

Chapter 10. Death, Loss, and Change

1. Tyler Cowen, "Matrimony Has Its Benefits, and Divorce Has a Lot to Do with That," *New York Times*, April 19, 2007, p. 3.

Chapter 11. When Stress Is Dangerous

1. Adapted from American Academy of Pediatrics, "A Teen's Personalized Guide for Managing Stress: When To Turn for Help," <http://www.aap.org/stress/buildreshelp-teen.htm> (May 8, 2007).

2. U.S. Centers for Disease Control and Prevention, "Suicide: Facts at a Glance," Summer 2007, <http://www.cdc.gov/ncipc/dvp/suicide/SuicideDataSheet.pdf> (July 13, 2007).

Chapter 12. Managing Your Stress

1. WebMD, "Tips for Reducing Stress," December 2006, <http://www.webmd.com/content/pages/7/1674_52148.htm> (July 13, 2007).

acute stress—A short, quick amount of stress that triggers an immediate physical response.

anxiety—A feeling of fear, apprehension, or worry, usually over a future event.

binge—To eat large quantities of food.

chronic stress—Stress that lasts over a long period of time, causing damage to the body.

conflict—A disagreement or argument resulting from differences in needs, wishes, or opinions.

depressant—A drug that reduces body function and activity.

depression—Feelings of sadness and hopelessness and a loss of interest in life.

endorphins—Mood-boosting chemicals released by the brain during exercise.

fight-or-flight response—The initial reaction of the body when first exposed to stress.

hormone—A chemical substance that signals other body cells to action.

hypothalamus—A part of the brain that controls chemical activity in the body.

puberty—The developmental stage in which the human body matures to adulthood.

relational aggression—A form of bullying in which a victim's ability to form relationships is damaged; it often includes isolating the person and spreading false rumors about him or her.

self-image—The way you view your appearance, abilities, and personality.

stress—The physical and mental response to an outside force or some kind of change.

stressor—A stimulus that causes stress.

FURTHER READING

Carlson, Richard. *Don't Sweat the Small Stuff for Teens: Simple Ways to Keep Your Cool in Stressful Times.* New York: Hyperion, 2000.

Fox, Annie, and Ruth Kirschner. *Too Stressed to Think? A Teen Guide to Staying Sane When Life Makes You Crazy.* Minneapolis, Minn.: Free Spirit Publishing, 2005.

Normandi, Carol Emery, and Lauralee Roark. *Over It: Getting Beyond Obsessions with Food and Weight.* Novato, Calif.: New World Library, 2001.

Rutledge, Jill Zimmerman. *Dealing with Stuff That Makes Life Tough: The 10 Things That Stress Teen Girls Out and How to Cope with Them.* New York: McGraw-Hill, 2003.

INTERNET ADDRESSES

American Academy of Pediatrics:
A Teen's Personalized Guide to Managing Stress
  http://www.aap.org/stress/buildresstress-teen.htm

Mind–Emotion Commotion: Handling Stress
  http://www.girlshealth.gov/mind/stress.htm

National Institute of Mental Health: Depression
  http://www.nimh.nih.gov/health/topics/depression/index.shtml

HOTLINE TELEPHONE NUMBERS

National Alcohol and Substance Abuse Information Center Hotline
  1-800-784-6776

National Domestic Violence Hotline
  1-800-799-SAFE (1-800-799-7233)

National Suicide Prevention Lifeline
  1-800-273-TALK (1-800-273-8255)

CONTRiBUTORS

Author **Annie Belfield** was born in Charlottetown, Prince Edward Island, in Canada, and currently lives near Boston with her cat, Stevens, and dog, Snoop. She is an English tutor for young people, and this is her first book.

Series advisor **Dr. Carroll Izard** is the Trustees Distinguished Professor of Psychology at the University of Delaware. His research and writing focuses on the development of emotion knowledge and emotion regulation and their contributions to social and emotional competence. He is author or editor of seventeen books (one of which won a national award) and more than one hundred articles in scientific journals. Dr. Izard is a fellow of both national psychological associations and the American Association for the Advancement of Science. He is the winner of the American Psychological Association's G. Stanley Hall Award and an international exchange fellowship from the National Academy of Sciences.

A Guys' Guide to Anger; A Girls' Guide to Anger
ISBN-13: 978-0-7660-2853-1   ISBN-10: 0-7660-2853-4

A Guys' Guide to Conflict; A Girls' Guide to Conflict
ISBN-13: 978-0-7660-2852-4   ISBN-10: 0-7660-2852-6

A Guys' Guide to Jealousy; A Girls' Guide to Jealousy
ISBN-13: 978-0-7660-2854-8   ISBN-10: 0-7660-2854-2

A Guys' Guide to Loneliness; A Girls' Guide to Loneliness
ISBN-13: 978-0-7660-2856-2   ISBN-10: 0-7660-2856-9

A Guys' Guide to Love; A Girls' Guide to Love
ISBN-13: 978-0-7660-2855-5   ISBN-10: 0-7660-2855-0

A Guys' Guide to Stress; A Girls' Guide to Stress
ISBN-13: 978-0-7660-2857-9   ISBN-10: 0-7660-2857-7

GUYS!

KEEP OUT

Nothing But
Girl Talk Ahead–
You've Been Warned!